MW01127014

MIDNIGHT
IN SOAP LAKE

Also by Matthew Sullivan

Midnight at the Bright Ideas Bookstore

MIDNIGHT
IN SOAP LAKE

a novel

MATTHEW SULLIVAN

HANOVER
SQUARE
PRESS

HANOVER
SQUARE
PRESS™

Recycling programs
for this product may
not exist in your area.

ISBN-13: 978-1-335-04179-1

Midnight in Soap Lake

Hanover Square Press
22 Adelaide St. West, 41st Floor
Toronto, Ontario M5H 4E3, Canada
HanoverSqPress.com

Printed in U.S.A.

For Rachel and Lulu, who were babies in Soap Lake

In a field
I am the absence
of field...
Wherever I am
I am what is missing.

—Mark Strand, "Keeping Things Whole"

Alone, alone, alone.
I bed in with many graves.

—Author unknown, "Hut Talk," Irish, eighth- or ninth-century.
Version by Martin Shaw and Tony Hoagland.

PART 1:

THE BOY

CHAPTER 1

ABIGAIL

Something was there.

An animal, Abigail was certain, loping in the sagebrush: a twist of fuzz moving through the desert at the edge of her sight. The morning had already broken a hundred. Her glasses steamed and sunscreen stung her eyes—

Or maybe she hadn't seen anything.

Yesterday, while walking along this desolate irrigation road, she'd spotted a cow skull between tumbleweeds, straight out of a tattoo parlor, but when she ran toward it, bracing to take a picture to send to Eli across the planet—proof, perhaps, that she ever left the house—she discovered it was just a white plastic grocery bag snagged on a curl of sage bark.

Somehow. Way out here.

The desert was scabby with dark basalt, bristled with the husks of flowers, and nothing was ever there.

When Eli first told her he'd landed a grant to research a rare lake in the Pacific Northwest, Abigail thought *ferns* and *rain, ale* and *slugs, Sasquatch* and *wool.*

And then they got here, to this desert where no one lived. Not a fern or slug in sight.

This had been the most turbulent year of her life.

Eleven months ago, they met.

Seven months ago, they married.

Six months ago, they moved from her carpeted condo in Denver to this sunbaked town on the shores of Soap Lake, a place where neither knew a soul.

Their honeymoon had lasted almost three months—Eli whistling in his downstairs lab, Abigail unpacking and painting upstairs—and then he kissed her at the airport, piled onto a plane, and moved across the world to work in a different lab, on a different project, at a different lake.

In Poland.

When she remembered him lately, she remembered photographs of him.

The plan had been to text all the time, daily calls, romantic flights to Warsaw, but the reality was that Eli had become too busy to chat and seemed more frazzled than ever. This week had been particularly bad because he'd been off the grid on a research trip, so every call went to voicemail, every text into the Polish abyss. And then at five o'clock this morning, her phone pinged and Abigail shot right out of a drowning sleep to grab it, as if he'd tossed her a life preserver from six thousand miles away.

And this is what he'd had to say:

sorry missed you. so much work & my research all fd up. i'll call this weekend. xo e

As she was composing a response—her phone the only glow in their dark, empty home—he added a postscript that stabbed her in the heart like an icicle.

P.S. maybe it time since remember using time to figure out self life?

What kind of a sentence was that? And what was a "self life" anyway?

Abigail had called him right away. When he didn't pick up she went down to the lab he'd set up in their daylight basement. She opened a few of his binders with their charts of Soap Lake, their colorful DNA diagrams, their photos of phosphorescent microbes, as cosmic as images from deep space. She breathed the papery dust of his absence and tried to imagine he'd just stepped out for a minute and would be back in a flash, her clueless brilliant husband, pen between his teeth, hair a smoky eruption, mustard stains on the plaid flannel bathrobe he wore in place of a lab coat.

From one of his gleaming refrigerators, Abigail retrieved a rack of capped glass tubes that contained the *Miracle Water* and the *Miracle Microbes* collected from the mineral lake down the hill— she sometimes wondered if her limnologist husband would be more at home on the shores of Loch Ness—and held one until a memory arose, like a visit from a friend: Eli, lifting a water sample up to the window as if he were gazing through a telescope, shaking it so it fizzed and foamed. And then he was gone again.

She hated that she did this. Came down here and *caressed* his equipment like a creep. Next she'd be smelling his bathrobe, collecting hairs from his brush. It was as if she felt compelled to remind herself that Eli was doing important work and, as the months of distance piled up, that he was even real.

Back when they'd first started dating, Abigail had been the busy one, the one who said yes to her boss too much and had to skim her calendar each time Eli wanted to go to dinner or a movie. Of course her job as an administrative assistant in a title insurance office had never felt like *enough*, but when she mentioned this restlessness to Eli, finding her path—*figure out self life*—had suddenly become a centerpiece of their move to Soap

Lake. But they got here and nothing had happened. It wasn't just a switch you flipped.

Abigail slid the tall tube of lake water back into its rack. Only when she let go, the tube somehow missed its slot and plunged to the floor like a bomb.

Kapow!

On the tile between her feet, a blossom of cloudy water and shattered glass.

She stood over the mess, clicking her fingernails against her teeth and imagining microbes squealing on the floor, flopping in the air like minuscule goldfish. She told herself, without conviction, it had been an accident.

And then she stepped over the spill, put the rack back in the fridge and, surprised at the immediacy of her shame, went for a walk in this gorgeous, scorching desert.

Loneliness: it felt sometimes like it possessed you.

She hadn't spoken to anyone in over a month, outside of a few people in the Soap Lake service industry. There was the guy who made her a watery latte at the gas station the other morning, then penised the back of her hand with his finger when he passed it over. And the newspaper carrier, an old woman with white braids and a pink cowgirl hat, who raced through town in a windowless minivan. She told Abigail she was one DUI away from unemployment, but the weekly paper was never late. And the cute pizza delivery dude who was so high he sat in her driveway on his phone for half an hour before coming to the door with her cold cheese pizza, saying, *Yes, ma'am. Thanks, ma'am*, which was sweet but totally freaked her out. And the lady with the painted boomerang eyebrows in the tampon aisle at the grocery store who gave her unwanted advice on the *best lube around for spicing up menopause*, to which Abigail guffawed and responded too loudly, "Thanks, but I'm not even goddamned forty!"

At least she'd discovered these maintenance roads: miles and miles of gravel and dirt, no vehicles allowed, running alongside the massive irrigation canals that brought Canadian snowmelt from the Columbia River through the Grand Coulee Dam to the farms spread all over this desert. The water gushed through the main canals, thirty feet wide and twenty feet deep, and soon branched off to other, smaller canals that branched off to orchards and fields and ranches and dairies and soil and seeds and sprouts and leaves and, eventually, yummy vital food: grocery store shelves brimming with apples and milk and pizza-flavored Pringles.

Good soil. Blazing sun. Just add water and food was born.

Almost a trillion gallons a year moved through these canals. T: *trillion*.

All that water way out here, pouring through land so dry it crackled underfoot.

She halted on the road. Pressed her lank, brown hair behind her ear. Definitely heard something, a faint *yip* or *caw*.

She scanned the horizon for the source of the sound and there it was again, a smudge of movement in the wavering heat. Something running away.

A few times out here she'd seen coyote. Lots of quail, the occasional pheasant. Once, in a fallow field close to town, a buck with a missing antler that looked from a distance like a unicorn.

Not running *away*, the smudge out there. Running *toward*.

She was nowhere near a signal yet her instinct was to touch her phone. She craned around to glimpse the vanishing point of the road behind, gauging how far she'd walked and, if things got bad, how far she'd have to run.

Three miles, minimum. Six miles, tops.

Definitely approaching.

Not some*thing*. Some*one*.

A human. Alone.

Running. A boy.

A *little* boy. Sprinting.

Abigail froze as their eyes met, and suddenly the boy exploded out of the desert, slamming into her thighs with an *oof!* He wore yellow pajamas and Cookie Monster slippers covered in prickly burrs.

He clung to her legs so tightly that she almost tipped over.

When she registered the crusty blood on his chin and cheeks and encasing his hands like gloves, she felt herself begin to cry, scared-to-sobbing in one second flat.

Deep breath. Shirt wipe.

"Hey! Are you hurt? Look at me. Are you *hurt?*"

The boy wasn't crying, but his skin was damp and he was panting hot and wouldn't let go of her legs. She felt a humming-bird inside of his chest.

She knelt in the gravel and unfolded his arms, turning them over at the wrist. She lifted his shirt and spun him around as best she could. He had some welts and scratches from running through the brush, and the knees of his pj's were badly scuffed, but he wasn't cut, not anywhere serious, which meant—

The blood belonged to someone else.

CHAPTER 2

ABIGAIL

"Is there someone else? Sweetie? Can you tell me where you were?"

The boy was three, maybe four. Of course there was someone else.

Abigail scanned the desert but saw no one.

He rubbed his eyes. She circled her palm on his sweltering back.

"What's your name?"

The boy had a mop of black hair with bits of ryegrass in it, light brown skin, and small brown eyes set close together. He wouldn't look at her. He itched a finger into his slippers and dug at his heel, picking for a burr.

"Drink this," she said.

She unscrewed her stainless bottle and he raised it to his mouth. Water trickled down the sides of his chin but he kept drinking, breathing through his nose, until the bottle was empty. He left rust-colored prints on its sides.

There was nowhere to find help this far out, and no bars ever on her phone. The only signs of civilization were the occasional piles of debris that people hauled out here to avoid paying ten bucks at the dump: a springy shredded mattress, a gutted dishwasher, a dead hound in a buzzing black garbage bag.

"Should we go?"

He began jogging straight back into the desert, retracing the path he'd already run.

Abigail stood still for a moment, wishing for a choice, then hustled behind him.

When she caught up, he reached for her hand without slowing down.

They found a dented maroon Cutlass with California plates parked on a rise a mile or so away. At first she wondered if it had wrecked, but its windshield was intact, and the way its tires had flattened the cheatgrass and veered around the piles of rock showed that it had been parked, not crashed. A faint two-track path was visible in the distance.

As they neared the rear of the car, the boy sat cross-legged on the ground, fingering circles in the dirt. He wouldn't look at the car and wasn't going closer.

"Is that yours?" Abigail said. She noticed a smiley face dotted on the dusty trunk. She stepped toward it, her stomach knotting. "Hello?"

As she walked around the rear fender she could see that the two doors on the driver's side were open and that someone was sitting behind the wheel.

"Is this your boy?"

A woman with black, shoulder-length hair was there, sitting with her hands in her lap and her head bent forward as if reading a map. There was a slight breeze yet her hair barely twitched.

"Miss?"

The seat behind her was crowded with trash. Fast-food wrappers and stained paper plates. Plastic soda bottles and crumpled bags of chips. Coffee cups and a yogurt container. A tote bag was tipped on the seat, spilling clothes and coloring books and crayons with wrappers peeled halfway down.

"Do you know this boy?"

Abigail knew the woman was dead even before coming around the door and seeing the blood across her chest, as sticky as tar and nearly as dark. Before seeing the fleecy SpongeBob blanket, also smudged with blood, draped from her legs to the dirt outside. Before seeing her half-lidded eyes and her waxy skin, and before smelling the sour heat inside the car. Before the buzzing flies.

The dead woman had a large screwdriver dangling from her abdomen, just below her sternum. Its handle rested in her lap, and was striped black and orange and stained with dried white paint. The woman's gray T-shirt seemed to spiral around it.

Abigail clutched her mouth but managed not to scream.

At her feet, a single Cheeto clung to the bloody blanket, like a cocoon on a rotting log.

And just over there, the boy stared at the dirt, scraping at his palms.

CHAPTER 3

ABIGAIL

"Flathead or Phillips?"

Abigail was in the passenger seat of an air-conditioned cruiser, being driven on a dirt road through the desert by a youngish cop with a name tag that said *Krunk*. He'd been first to arrive at the scene, not long after she'd found a signal and called 9-1-1.

"What are you asking me?" she said.

"Flathead or Phillips, the screwdriver. Which do you think?"

Abigail stared at him. Krunk was quiet and lanky and oddly polite. He was wearing a dark SLPD baseball cap, black Wayfarers and ankle-high Docs. And he was the best-looking man she'd seen in months, ever since Eli had deserted her in this place-outside-of-time.

"I'm not trying to wager or anything," he said. "I'm just wondering what kind of monster could shove a screwdriver into her gut like that. In a car, in that cramped space, that angle would take some force. Even more if it's a Phillips head, I think. Maybe not." He sighed. "I don't need this shit in my life."

Krunk dropped his cap into his lap, and Abigail saw that his black hair was thinning, and a damp little island of curls stuck to his forehead. She wondered too about his life, and why he seemed so upset given that he was a cop and therefore used to seeing the shittier sides of the human condition.

A few hours ago on the canal road, she'd sat mutely with the boy as paramedics examined him, and Krunk headed into the desert to secure the crime scene. The boy was squeezing Abigail's hand and experiencing mild shock but the medic said he'd be okay. Just as she was about to accompany him to the hospital in Wenatchee, a social worker showed up, driving a county van and wearing a churchy dress that reached her ankles. She surveyed the smudge of blood on Abigail's shorts and proclaimed she'd take it from here. Once the doctors had cleared him, she would take the boy to Spokane, two hours east, or Seattle, three hours west, because it was a Sunday and every child resource in the county was closed.

When the woman pried the boy out of Abigail's lap, he was sobbing and reaching, and she had to turn around so he wouldn't see how upset she was. The boy had been holding her hand for so long that both of their fingers were pruned.

In the cruiser, Abigail realized that no one had touched her in months, which was maybe why she could still feel the boy's fingernails on her palms.

Krunk glanced at her as he drove. "You sure you don't want a doctor?"

"I'm sure."

She stared out the window, scanning the basalt cliffs and rabbit brush, wondering who was out there.

It felt weird to be going home. She was glad for Krunk's slow driving.

"You really go by Krunk?" she said. "What's your actual name?"

"Abe, I guess. Why?"

"I like *Abe*," she said, nodding. "More honest."

He barely smirked. "I happen to like *Krunk*. Gives me some street cred."

"Are there streets around here?"

Abe Krunk took off his shades and pinched the bridge of his nose. He seemed unexpectedly fragile for a cop.

Something occurred to Abigail.

"Did you know her? The woman in the car."

"It's hard to say for sure. But if she is who I think she is, I went to high school with her. She skipped town without telling anyone, the night of graduation."

"Really?"

"If she's her. She looks different. But it's been maybe eight years."

"Does she have a name?" Abigail said.

"Not until she's identified by next of kin she doesn't," he said in an official tone. "But if it's her, she was pretty great. Unusual. Unappreciated. In retrospect, you know? The person you never noticed in the cafeteria but can't stop looking at, at the reunion. Not that we had a reunion. I just mean she always did her own thing. That's rare around here. Sucks if it's her."

"Why'd she leave town like that?"

"Just another American horror show, I guess. Everything was going wrong so she took off. Pretty cool of her. Never occurred to a lot of us that we could just leave like that." He shook his head. "No one should do that to anyone, but especially not to her."

In front of her little boy, Abigail thought.

Krunk squinted at the horizon and blinked sweat from his eyes.

"Why'd you say you moved here?" he said.

Abigail shrugged.

"Sounds about right," he added.

After a moment, she looked over at him. "You were about to tell me her name?"

"*If* she's the woman I'm thinking of," he said, lowering his voice, "her name was Esme."

CHAPTER 4

ESME

Esme's trailer sat in the back of the Desert Garden Mobile Home Community, which everyone in town called the *Falling Fence Trailer Park* because its front fence toppled into the juniper shrubs where the entrance met the road. It never made sense to Esme why they called it a *park*: there was no playground or trees to climb, no basketball court or soccer goal, and not a single other seven-year-old. Some of the trailers had wooden stoops with flowerpots and American flags out front, but others had broken satellite dishes hanging down like loose teeth and tires on the roof and didn't pretend to be anything but what they were: cheap, cheap, and goddamned cheap.

Inside of Esme's trailer, the sunrise through the curtains glowed a pumpkin pink. Her knees bounced in her chair as she ate a bowl of oatmeal with powdered sugar and a splash of root beer to give it a little *zing*. Between bites she eyed her mother's cracked bedroom door, hoping she'd stay asleep in there. Her mom was happier asleep than any other time.

Esme's mom stared a lot. Sat in her chair with a hairbrush in her lap and a glass on the card table as she stared at the television. She also stared at the holes in her slippers, at the scratches on the armrest, and into the drain of the bathroom sink. But more than anything she stared at Esme: Esme eating Trix out of her mermaid bowl. Esme pouring Pepsi into her mermaid cup. Esme coloring in her coloring book or untangling her bag of yarn or clenching her crusty Play-Doh. It didn't matter what Esme was doing, her mom was usually staring.

Her brother, Daniel, was also still asleep, not that it mattered. When he woke up he was like an animal emerging from a cave. He'd shuffle around with his head down and play his Game Boy while putting a frozen hot dog in the microwave, and continue to play it as the hot dog overheated and burst open and made the trailer reek of salty meat for days.

The couch this morning was empty. Dad wasn't on it, which meant Dad hadn't come home last night.

From the other room, a shifting of the mattress. Mom awake.

Esme left her breakfast bowl on the carpet. She grabbed her coat and crammed her feet into her boots and just as she was slipping out the door, she turned and saw her mom emerging from her bedroom, wearing her threadbare nightgown, staring across the trailer.

"Going outside!" Esme yelled, and leaped off the porch.

Esme's father had made it clear that she was not allowed to leave the trailer park under any circumstances, and she was not allowed to wander the streets of Soap Lake alone, and she was especially not allowed to play in the apple orchards that stretched into the desert from the edges of town. But her father wasn't around to stop her, so Esme walked out of the park on the shoulder of a cracky road. She passed the rusty playground by the lake where she and Daniel played a game called Tetanus Island, in which they tried to climb from the slide to the swings without getting scraped by old bolts and chains. She cut between houses and through fields and looked behind her as she walked, half expecting someone in her family to come running after her.

But no one was coming. Which was the point.

When she got to the orchards, she tucked her pants into the green rubber boots, three sizes too big, that her dad had *liberated* from the dairy where he worked.

Stepping into the orchard was like disappearing into a forest.

Before her dad got a job bulldozing cow shit into giant piles at the dairy, he used to run a bunch of orchard crews. He spoke Spanish okay enough and had been a wrestler in high school, but mainly, he said, he knew *a thing or two about how to motivate people.* He also said in the orchards you could eat the apples until your belly hurt as long as you washed them well, but if you breathed the air in there you'd die of cancer and your balls would shrivel up, but *not in that order, and not just your balls.* Plus, he said *bad things happened* in those orchards—but he always said it in a ghost story voice between slugs of beer, so she couldn't always tell how serious he was.

This orchard was the spookiest one around, too. Half of it was dead, with gray skeleton trees that burst out of the ground like giant claws. And the half that was alive stretched to the landfill, where people dumped their old sinks and dead pets. When the orchard owner donated a bunch of apples to the grade school one year, all the kids in the cafeteria bit into them and made faces and swore they *smacked of trash.*

The sunlight peeked between the apple trees, turning the cold ground misty. Esme liked how the crabgrass and fallen leaves blanketed the rows like a carpet, and how she couldn't see the desert in any direction, and how the rotting fruit waited on the ground for birds.

Plus she was alone, which was the best thing ever.

And then she wasn't alone because somehow a sound had found her.

She pushed back her jacket hood. The sound was high-pitched and pulsing.

A crying kitten. Or a hungry bird.

Esme prowled in its direction, slipping between trees, and soon she was deep inside the orchard and not sure which way was out. She stood tall and could hear a tractor starting far away but the squeaky sound had stopped.

When it started again it was just a row of trees away.

Not a kitten or a bird. A *wheel.*

She crouched under a tree and pressed her back into its trunk.

no

Her eyes shut and she didn't move. She felt an earwig on the back of her hand.

no

The squeaks came closer. She should've listened to her dad.

TreeTop.

She'd never seen TreeTop in person but she'd heard stories about him so many times from Daniel and kids at recess and grown-ups at the parade and teachers at school that he'd folded himself into a special cupboard in the back of her brain, one with rusty hinges and cobwebs.

TreeTop killed children and chopped up their bodies to fertilize the town's apple trees.

Fee Fi Fo Fum
I smell the blood of an Americun
Be she alive or be she dead
I'll grind her bones to grow my—

Apples.

TreeTop pushed his wheelbarrow full of bones around the orchards all night, its axle screaming in the dark.

TreeTop climbed into the thin branches at the tops of the trees every morning and stretched out to sleep like a spider perched on his web.

Without TreeTop, there would be no orchards, and without orchards, there would be no town.

Everything would be the desert.

The sun was out now, and TreeTop was probably sloshing his last scoops of ground-up child around the trees before climbing into his branchy bed.

How else, Daniel once said, *do you think all this fruit grows in the desert?*

He was right. It was like magic, watching fruit trees blossom and burst from this hot, rocky land.

She could feel her heart pounding as TreeTop's wheelbarrow rolled closer. She thought she should run, but her dad had told her plenty of times to *never* run from the frothy dogs that roamed the roads outside of town and TreeTop was way worse than dogs, so she pressed into the tree and shut her eyes and only opened them when the squeak of his wheel went silent just a foot or so away.

He was far bigger than she'd imagined, wearing a white hooded jumpsuit and a white mask and blue rubber gloves. It was the same uniform she sometimes saw the orchard guys wearing, driving between trees on their ATVs, spraying bright clouds of pesticide behind them to kill the cutter worms and sucker moths. His eyes were covered with protective goggles, and as he breathed they steamed a little, and his mask clicked in and out.

His wheelbarrow basin was covered with a blue tarp. In its gaps she could see gnarled applewood cuttings, crosshatched over pockets of air—

And a man's boot.

She clung to the tree but shifted to get a better look. Inside the wheelbarrow, she could see the boot's black sole and knotted laces and part of its dusty leather tongue. Its sole had a tread of three small clovers near the toes, and Esme couldn't help but spread out her three little fingers as if she were going to step forward and press the clovers all at once, like they were buttons. But just then TreeTop reached out and sharply tugged the tarp, covering the branches and the boot.

Esme knew she shouldn't look TreeTop in the goggle, so she dropped her gaze to his stained knees. Everything he wore was spattered brownish, blackish, darkish red.

TreeTop paused for a moment. Then he lifted the wheel-barrow handles, and a rhythmic squeaking filled the air as he disappeared between trees.

Back at home Esme dumped her coat and stood by the door, catching her breath. Daniel was stretched out on the couch, play-ing Game Boy, with his hot dog plate on the floor. Her mom was sitting in her saggy chair and watching a game show on TV.

Her dad's sneakers were next to the kitchen table, right where he'd left them a few mornings ago, but he was nowhere in sight.

Esme realized why she'd been so scared. It wasn't because of TreeTop, exactly. Sure, he was as freaky in person as he was in the stories, but he was also strangely calm in the way he just *loomed* there, as if he'd been expecting her. Plus he hadn't chopped her to pieces, which was highly comforting. What wasn't comforting—what was in fact terrifying to consider—was the boot she'd seen in his wheelbarrow, covered with the tarp.

Because question: Why had its laces been knotted?

Because answer: it was still on someone's foot.

"Mom?"

Her mom looked up and seemed pleasantly surprised to see her. "Don't leave your breakfast bowl on the floor," she said. "I stepped in it."

"Sorry."

A colorful ceramic cross hung on the wall behind the TV, next to the portraits of Daniel and Esme that they both hated because they'd shown up to school in old T-shirts and uncombed

hair with no idea it was Picture Day. The cross was a souvenir from Mom's childhood in Yakima, and it was her favorite
decoration, which was weird because it seemed like a constant
reminder that her family had stopped talking to her when she
married Dad and quit going to church. For whatever reason,
though, it made Mom happy.

"Maybe you should go play," Mom said.

Esme sighed and grabbed a two-liter bottle of Dr Pepper from
the collection atop of the fridge and took it into the bedroom she
shared with Daniel. She got into bed and pressed her feet into
the slatted bottom of the top bunk and sipped from the bottle.

Soon Esme grew bored and began paging through her favorite
book, the single blue encyclopedia, *Volume J*, which her dad had
given her one day last year. It was the only volume she had, but
there were definitely worse letters than *J*. She had a particular
fondness for *Joplin, Janis; judo; jellyfish;* and *Jews (see Judaism)*, but
felt incomprehensibly hostile about *Jackson, Andrew (US presi-
dent); Jupiter;* and *jury duty*.

She fell asleep with the book on her stomach. At one point
Daniel came in and said it was time for dinner.

When she saw her dad's spot on the couch still empty, she
felt something shift.

"Is he not home?" she said.

Daniel shrugged. "Is he ever home?"

As the microwave carousel spun around, catching and clang-
ing with every revolution, Esme parted the living room curtains.
Their trailer was tucked near the dumpsters in the back of the
park and therefore twenty bucks cheaper per month because it
smelled sour right outside their door all summer long, but being
so close to the dumpster had its benefits, too.

For one, easy trash-taking-out. For two, free stray-cat-
watching. For three, it gave her dad a place to chaw.

Dad was often loitering out there this time of day, leaning
against the wooden fence that bracketed the dumpster, taking

a dip from his Skoal can. The moondust beneath the fence was always stained with his tobacco spit.

A harelipped cat prowled past. Esme's stomach felt gassy and sore.

"You're awful quiet," her mom said at the dinner table.

Mom had made hot liverwurst sandwiches and Daniel was sullen when he saw her squeezing the pink-gray meat out of its plastic casing.

"I don't eat meat that comes in a tube," he said firmly, arms crossed.

"You eat hot dogs every morning," Esme said.

He thought about it. "I don't eat meat that *squirts* from a tube."

In other moments she and Daniel might have high-fived—a moment of agreement that would've made their mom blink instead of stare—but tonight Esme could only muster the energy to nod.

She kept looking at the door.

"Where's Dad?"

"Probably leading a revolution," her mom grumbled.

Her mom was always saying things like that to Esme, making her feel bad for liking him.

"I'm going to bed."

"You just got up."

It didn't matter one bit: Esme didn't even crack her J encyclopedia and fell asleep the second her head hit the pillow.

es ge up

Glass was breaking inside of her ears.

es me ge up

Lava pooled inside of her lungs.

Esme! Get up!

When Esme opened her eyes, Daniel was standing over her in his tighty-whities, no shirt, slapping her head and yelling: "Fire! Fire! Fire!"

Smoke shimmered and curled around his face. The wall next to her trembled and glowed, and her Dr Pepper bottle folded itself in half. Her cheeks were roasting and she couldn't breathe.

Daniel gripped her shoulders and ripped her out of her bed.

"We gotta get out!" he screamed, slamming her into his dresser so that a cough shocked through her. "Out! Out!"

The door was blocked by fire, and the window above the dresser was jammed. Daniel smacked the glass with his palms and it rattled but didn't break. So he groped among the dirty clothes for the first heavy thing he could find, and suddenly he was bashing the glass with Esme's *J* encyclopedia. Shards crashed out and thick smoke coiled through the hole like an escaping dragon.

Someone out there was shrieking. Possibly their mother.

Daniel hefted Esme onto the dresser and pushed her straight through the window. She landed atop the rusted barbecue her dad had wheeled home from a yard sale but had never once fired up. Seconds later Daniel thudded on top of her and cut his chin when he hit the dirt.

Their mom was already out, running back and forth near the porch, hair singed, screaming for their father.

"Wake him up! Wake him up!"

When she saw the kids she ran over to them, sobbing, and said their dad needed help, that he wasn't moving in there—

"It's okay, Mom!" Esme shouted. "He's not home!"

"But he is!" her mom said. "I saw him!"

Daniel asked where and she said on the couch, and he made like he was going to charge through the front door to save him, but as soon as he neared the wall of flames he turned around and started crying. Esme hugged her mom to stop her from plunging back into the fire, but she just kept pacing and saying, "He's in there. He's in there. He's in there."

The flames rolled out the windows and boiled the tires on the trailer's roof. In the distance, the casual wail of a siren.

★ ★ ★

The following afternoon, Esme and Daniel leaned against the tailgate of their dad's old green truck, picking at his faded bumper sticker—*Unions: The Folks that Brought You the Weekend!*—as they waited for the fire inspector to allow them to salvage what they could from the trailer's soggy ruins. A few neighbors came out to lean against the truck with them but hardly anyone spoke, just nodded somberly and someone said he was a brave son of a bitch, their dad.

That guy could fix anything, someone said.

He could hit, too, said someone else. *Knock out yer teeth with one blow.*

No one said he was nice or smart or funny.

No one mentioned how good he was at doing The Worm.

Her mom's eyes were red and weepy and she was wearing a knit Seahawks hat that someone had given her to help cover up the singed sections of her hair. The fire chief was a young guy with an unruly beard and he lowered his voice as he spoke to her, whispering that her husband must have passed out with a candle burning too close to the curtains.

"Probably related to the drinking. It happens."

Her mom was sobbing again and pressing her palms into her face, and Daniel kept crying, too, then getting mad at himself for crying, then crying some more. The bandage on his chin was already gray with dirt.

Esme's lungs hurt and seeing her home turned into a soggy black crumple made it even harder to breathe. More than anything it felt like a dream, her dad being dead. Her mom had gone with the police and lowered the sheet and identified the scorched horse tattoo on his shoulder, so Esme knew he was gone. And she was definitely sad. But she could also feel something secret happening, like her heart loosening up, getting lighter. But she was definitely sad.

Daniel walked circles through the ash. "What a waste," he said. "What a waste."

Esme tried following him through the wreckage, but she couldn't shake the feeling that something mysterious had happened here last night. The cops said it was a candle and a curtain, and Mom lit her *veladoras* a few times a year, St. Jude and Our Lady of Guadalupe, so they were right there on the shelf. It's just that her dad would never light one. Like what, he came home all drunk and decided to say some candlelit prayers for the first time in his life? She didn't buy it.

Plus there was the matter of the boot.

The powdery dirt along the dumpster fence was speckled with her dad's spit and tracked with his old boot prints. She imagined him standing here (*spit*), then him standing there (*spit*), then him turning around (*spit*), then him turning back (*spit*), until it felt like he was still alive.

She inspected the ground and found a whole footprint, one of the last traces of him on the planet. She studied the patterns left by his boot sole and there, just under the ball of his foot, she found them: the imprint of three small clovers, stamped into the dirt.

"Where's his body?" she said to her mom a minute later.

"Your father?" her mom said. "The police people have him. We'll get him back once they're through." She placed her hand on Esme's shoulder and with her other hand dabbed at her nose with a bandana. "You doing okay?"

"I heard he melted through the cushions," Daniel said, wiping his eyes.

"Sounds like something he'd do," their mother said.

"Was he wearing his boots?" Esme said.

"What are you asking me?"

"Were his boots still on his feet when he burned all up?"

Her mom looked at her with concern. "Don't think about that, sweetheart."

Daniel came around the truck and stood next to Esme. His eyes were bloodshot and his hair stuck out like half a hedgehog.

"Why do you want to know what he was wearing?" he said.

"Why do you think?"

Daniel had that twitchy look he got when he was about to punch her in the stomach, so she didn't say anything about seeing TreeTop, or about his tarp-covered wheelbarrow, or about seeing Dad's boot with knotted laces covered by the branches inside.

Esme flinched when Daniel moved toward her, but then he just pulled her into a sideways hug. When he wasn't ignoring her or punching her, Daniel was protective of his little sister.

"I saved your life last night," he said. "You know what that means, right?"

"It means I get to blame you for everything that goes wrong. *Forever.*"

"It means you're my servant," he said. *"Forever."*

A few feet away, their mom snickered. Daniel nodded toward her flannel back and leaned into Esme's ear. "Just shut up about Dad. She doesn't need it."

Then he led her over to the ground outside of their bedroom window, where he picked up the one blue encyclopedia, *Volume J,* and handed it to her. It was soaking wet and charred in spots, but its pages seemed mostly intact.

When she opened it up—*jazz*—a piece of broken glass fell out.

CHAPTER 5

ABIGAIL

The week that Abigail dropped out of the University of Northern Colorado, two years shy of completing her degree in psychology, her part-time job licking envelopes at a title insurance company in Greeley became a permanent job as a receptionist, and whatever hopes she had of following her heart into a fulfilling career disintegrated under the steady glow of paychecks and health insurance. She thought the job would be short-lived, but soon she'd been there long enough to grow weary of coworker happy hours and the annual rafting trip down the Arkansas River. When she started wearing headphones in the break room, her boss nicknamed her Sourpuss.

For the next decade, as Abigail grew more competent and confident, she gave up on the idea of finishing her degree and began flitting from branch to branch within the title insurance franchise, moving from Greeley to Lakewood to Denver, and rolled into her early thirties with a two-bedroom condo, a fridge pinned with birth announcements, and few prospects for a long-term relationship or a career she actually wanted. She had drinks with friends from work sometimes, braved dinner parties alone, even dated a few Realtors with flawless hair and corny sports cars who, after sex, spoke about *teaming up*, as if their one-night stand had elevated them to a power couple.

After bombing a few interviews for jobs she really wanted and escaping a few relationships she really didn't, Abigail began to feel not so much a looming crisis as an impending reality check: in terms of work and love, this was kind of *it*. Otherwise, where were the jobs that she both *wanted* and *could get*, and how much would she have to borrow in student loans to land them? And where were the men who'd outgrown video games, who could make it through a meal without checking a score or ordering shots, who didn't brag about something they'd *bought*?

At the local food co-op, apparently...

One evening in her thirty-fourth year, while bagging apples at the organic market near her condo, Abigail pushed up her glasses and asked the produce guy if there was a surefire way to tell if an apple was mealy before she bought it.

"Outside of, you know, taking a bite."

She'd noticed him more than a few times, maybe because it was hard not to. He was a hefty guy who stood over six feet tall, so his name tag—*Eli!*—met her at eye level. With his old-fashioned Arrow shirts worn beneath a green apron, and his curly black hair beginning to gray, he appeared to be a few years older than her, which was fine, but he always whistled and hummed to himself as he worked, which was a tiny red flag.

But *hooo-whee*, the guy knew a thing or two about mealy apples. As he dove into an explanation of the microbial process that caused fruit to decay, as well as a segue into the genetic modification of lunchroom apples that made them appear a shade of red that didn't exist in the *natural apple world*, Abigail took notice of his great green eyes, his liquid voice, his cool leather prairie boots, and had to set her hand on the cart to maintain her composure. She hadn't expected to be so...*charmed*. In the midst of his explanation, Eli bopped a huge Honeycrisp off of his forearm and caught it midair, and her image of him transformed from the whistling sad sack stocking kale on a Friday night to the sweet, bright man who could hardly contain all of his knowledge and joy. He finished by unsheathing the produce knife fastened to his belt and slicing the apple with an expert *pop*, then offering her a wedge from the tip of its blade.

On their first date, Eli dazzled Abigail by leading her down the 16th Street Mall until they reached the nook-filled bookstore by the train station. He talked a lot as they walked, which made her feel even quieter than usual, and she worried he would soon become exhausting—but the second they stepped inside the store, she couldn't get over how quiet he became and, more important, how comfortable she felt in his silence. Together they circled the tables and roamed the shelves, and when she caught him staring at her over the top of a Michael Crichton book, he didn't pretend to be daydreaming, but rather lowered it even more, wagging his eyebrows and owning that his focus was on her. Everything about Eli was different.

In addition to being an expert at stacking produce, she learned that he held a PhD in limnology, the study of lakes, and that he was quite the cook and conversationalist. At the end of each shift he'd load up on castoff fruits and veggies and cook her abundant stir-fries and cobblers, and he got her talking about everything: about her air force dad getting stationed in Okinawa when she was seven, and how he'd gone there all alone and never come home; about how her mom didn't say anything about the split-up until Abigail was ten and saw a checkmark in the box that said *Divorced* on an insurance form for a school band trip; about how in fifth grade, she had a series of crippling panic attacks at school and confessed to her teacher that her mom blatantly favored her big sister, Meghan, and how when the teacher told her mom, her mom rolled her eyes and said, *I wonder why*; about how these days her mom and Meghan lived side by side in a duplex in Florida, literally leaving no room for her; about how she'd always believed she was pretty different, pretty unique, but was in fact not that remarkable, the kind of person who only ever read the *big* books and watched the *big* shows that everyone else was also reading and watching; and about how she was learning to embrace the reality that she might never figure out what she was actually *into*.

"Maybe you're *into* not being *into* things?" Eli said with a shrug.

Before he could say another word, she dove into a kiss. He tasted like oranges.

On Halloween, just when Abigail couldn't imagine their relationship going any better, Eli showed up at her condo with a cold bottle of rosé, a variety bag of bite-size candy bars, and some of the biggest news of her life.

"You know how you asked me why a limnologist was working in a grocery store?" he said, adding the candy to her bowl and pouring wine into a pair of jam jars. "Well, I finally got the job offer I've been holding out for. The perfect job, actually. I'm kind of stunned."

"Wow. Okay? Go on."

"There's this lake," he said, and she, too, grew stunned as he explained, in his calm, impassioned way, about a mineral lake in the shrub-steppe, the rarest of the rare, with a microbiome in its depths that had never fully been studied. "I can't believe no one has gotten to it. Kind of a legendary lake. At least in some circles."

"That's a little spooky. Why legendary?"

"Good question," he said, and swallowed some wine. "It just... I can explain more later."

"Okay," she said, wary. "So, what's the problem?"

"Problem is it's far. Desolate. And I have to move there by the New Year if I take it." He stared into the colorful candy. "I thought we might work something out, but there's absolutely *nothing* for you there."

"Except *you*," she said, stifling a spike of panic. "How far is it? How desolate?"

"Soap Lake, Washington. Population fifteen hundred. And withering," he mumbled.

"Washington *state?*" she said, and a soothing wave of associations rolled through her: Flannel. *Twin Peaks*. Beer. "You have to take it, Eli."

"I want to, more than anything. Believe me. But I want *us*, too."

Some amped-up trick-or-treaters chose that moment to bang on the door, and Abigail jumped up, dished out some candy, shut off the porch light, and was crossing her legs on the couch in no time.

"I can see the dilemma," she said, pure gloom.

"Unless, you were ready to…you know. I would, Abigail. Without a doubt. If."

She took a deep breath. "You would what, Eli?"

"Go further. There are different levels, of course. Degrees. Gradations—"

"Gradations?"

He looked into her eyes and grinned. "I would propose. Marriage. If you were ready."

Abigail's first thought was how *extreme* that seemed.

Then again, just last night, with Eli snoring beside her, her knee over his thighs, she felt like the least lonely person on earth.

"If you did? I think I'd say yes."

Eli stared at her for an eternity, then fell to his knees, squeezed her hands between his and proposed. Just as Abigail was grinning widely and saying, *"Yes!"*, the trick-or-treaters knocked again, harder this time, and Eli hopped to the door and dumped the whole bowl of candy into their pillowcases.

"Jackpot!" he yelled, then slammed the door and locked it.

"Where is this place?" she said, laughing, once he was back on his knees.

"Soap Lake? You're gonna love it, Abigail. Wait until you hear about the Lava Lamp!"

CHAPTER 6

ABIGAIL

The Lava Lamp was coming.

Abigail woke up with her forehead clattering against the U-Haul's passenger window. The glass was cold and her eyeballs were tight and dry. Beige treeless hills flowed into the horizon.

"You're awake," Eli said from behind the wheel, grinning as he pointed to a green highway sign: *Soap Lake 18 miles.*

"The Lava Lamp is coming," she said, perking up.

After Eli's proposal, Abigail had immediately googled *Soap Lake* and the first result referenced the World's Largest Lava Lamp. It was over sixty feet tall, perched on the shore, and wax globules the size of boulders bubbled in slow-motion through its colorful liquid. The roadside attraction encapsulated the vibe and geology of the area which, fifteen million years ago, was the site of cataclysmic lava flows that hardened into basalt, several miles deep. The images she'd seen showed the World's Largest Lava Lamp beaming colorful light into the night sky, surrounded by people wading in the lake.

Abigail slid forward on the U-Haul's front seat. An orb of sun was dropping behind the gray horizon, giving off a metallic light. Their timing was perfect.

"Just look for the glow above the lake," she said. "I'm imagining one of those UFO tractor beams coming out of its top."

"Like our own little Chernobyl," Eli said. "You know, not to be...but it might not be that great."

She turned toward him and stared.

"I'm just saying that every circus I've ever been to was depressing," he added.

"Noted," she said through narrow eyes.

Soon they were on the outskirts of town, where the only businesses seemed to be storage units and repair shops.

"There's really not a single fast-food place?" she said.

"Not a franchise in sight. It's like the opposite of America."

"Really no Target?"

"Not for sixty miles."

"As long as I can get a hayfork," she mumbled, casting off the approaching cloud.

Soon they were on the side streets of their new town. Peppered between some of the smaller, derelict homes were bright, fairy-tale cottages, with frilly curtained windows and birdhouses hanging from trees. They drove down Main Street with its gas station, diner, taco truck, dive bar, and hotel, but saw only one person: a bearded guy in a hooded red coat, standing on a corner, talking to himself while trying to fold up a huge paper map. Eli pretended not to see him.

Finally the long gray disk of the lake floated into view. It was fairly narrow and two miles long, framed by rocky hills and steep cliffs carved out of the emptiest emptiness she'd ever seen.

Eli parked the U-Haul in a gravel lot.

"Are you sure this is the right lake?" Abigail said. "Maybe we have to be at the right angle to see the Lava Lamp. Like Stonehenge."

An American flag stood tall and still in front of a cinder block library. That seemed promising, and sure enough its walkway led down a rocky path to the shore.

She saw it in the distance, surrounded by a chain-link fence: a steel structure, fifteen feet high and nearly as wide, bolted to a concrete pad sprinkled with cigarette butts and broken bottles. It resembled a giant cocktail jigger, an association that made Abigail want a drink. Soon she realized she was looking at the base of the World's Largest—

"Where's the lava lamp part?" she said.

"Look at this," Eli said, and lifted a threadbare sign, fastened to the fence, shredded by the wind: *Home of the World's Largest Lava Lamp*™.

"*Base*," she said. "It should say 'Base' at the end. Because there's no actual lamp?"

"Doesn't quite have the same ring, does it?"

The air off the lake was frigid, the concrete slab as cold as an ice rink. This was disappointing.

Eli stretched out the sign and Abigail could see the familiar image it held: a giant red lava lamp with little people looking up into the glowing light. A message was scrawled in thick black marker across the bottom of the banner.

Project Infinitely Postponed

Followed by a frowny face.

"They can't really mean *infinitely*, can they?"

"It's an architectural what have you," Eli said, seeming impressed. "A rendering. Really nicely Photoshopped."

"So it's just not here?"

"I mean, the website did say it was under construction."

"The website hasn't been updated in ages, Eli. I was so looking forward to this. I bragged on social media."

Eli looked surprised. "Are you on social media?"

This was not the time to explain her pattern of posting, losing sleep, deleting, and not logging in again for months. So she cryptically said, "Exactly!"

"We'll be okay," he said.

Abigail caught sight of some graffiti scrawled on the side of the lamp base. Someone had attempted to cover it up with matte-black spray paint, but didn't quite block the whole thing.

"That's really bizarre," she said, taking a step back, holding her own hands.

"It is a bit grim," Eli said, tapping his chin in contemplation, as if the phrase were on a gallery wall. "Makes me miss the halcyon days of cartoon cocks. And cute little Kilroy, goes without saying."

"This *sucks*," Abigail snapped, unable to hide her disappointment. "Sorry, but this was supposed to be the highlight for me. I thought it would be so relaxing to walk down after dinner and bask in the glow of the World's Largest Lava Lamp." She pointed at the giant metal base. "Instead, we come to the middle of nowhere and get the world's biggest, trashy-ass, stupid-fucking egg-cup dumpster spittoon thing?"

"*Trademark,*" Eli said, pointing to the tiny "TM" on the sign.

She stared at him. "Please don't do that."

"Come check out the lake," he said, holding out his hand. "That's the *real* magic."

"This is why the Lava Lamp is even here," Eli said, stooping to his haunches on the water's edge, between dark rocks and mucky sand. He scooped his hand gently through the lake, making silver ripples in the dusky light. "This is why *we're* here."

Abigail stood above him, hands fisted in her fleece for warmth. She felt her disappointment wither and forced herself to release it, a balloon into the sky.

"It's incredible," she said.

"Nothing like it."

The lake spread before them was somehow both transparent and gray, like a lens popped from an old pair of shades. In the dusky winter light, the basalt cliffs and scree along the shoreline resembled a moonscape. Even the water seemed lifeless: no feeding fish, no hatching nymphs, no milfoil or moss swaying beneath the surface. Water lapped lightly, edged with thick foam that quivered as if breathing.

Eli held her hand and told her how indigenous peoples believed these waters were sacred, and gathered here for healing and protection. Centuries later, between the World Wars, these shores used to be packed with visitors staying at spas and hotels. How people came from all over the country to seek healing in these waters. How veterans made up a third of the town's population, men who came for months at a time to cure the diseases they brought home from the battlefield. Gangrene and Buerger's and infected amputations. Arthritis and all manner of skin disease. The federal government was convinced enough of the lake's healing power that they constructed a VA hospital in town where they could treat the afflicted.

"These days it's a nursing home," Eli said, shrugging. "But can you see why I'm so excited to study this place?"

"But there's nothing here," she said, tapping the water with her boot. "Not even any seaweed or plants? What could possibly live in this?"

"That's precisely the question. Here. Feel."

They ran their fingers through the cold water and it felt silky, thick, and alien—closer to dish soap than water.

"Soap Lake," she said. "I get it."

"It gets all sudsy, especially in the wind," he said, gleeful. "I've seen old photos with massive blobs of foam, six feet high, just tumbling through the air. This water isn't water, you see? More like a mineral brew. And *very* rare. Especially down deep."

"What's down deep?"

"Down deep," he said, "there are *miracles*."

Abigail turned toward Eli, surprised by the word. She searched his face for sarcasm but all she saw was awe. There was some times a side to him that seemed more like a cryptozoologist than a limnologist.

"The far end of the lake, way over there, is where the special stuff is. Down in these underwater vents, almost a hundred feet deep. That's the main reason I'm here—to figure out what it's up to down there."

"What it's up to? You talk like it's alive."

"Most lakes move," he said. "They churn as the temperature shifts, so the water on the bottom trades places with the water on the top throughout the year."

"I think I knew that."

"But not this lake. Because of the minerals and the geology and the climate, the water on the bottom of the lake hasn't moved in at least two thousand years. It's very rare for a lake to *never* turn over. Might be the oldest stratified water on the planet."

"So what's in the vents?"

"Trying to figure that out. The pH levels are through the roof. Ammonia. Saline. Arsenic. All occurring naturally. And no oxygen down there at all. The main thing is that the water in those vents is the same water that was there thousands of years ago, when the lake was formed. *Exactly* the same. It's this *goo*, really, that's been sitting deep in the basalt, undisturbed. The vents have become their own little ecosystems with their own species of microbes living in them. Untouched. Like, *ever.*"

"Your miracle microbes?"

"That's them."

"I'm sorry," she said, covering her smile. "Just that word: *miracle.*"

"*Anyway,*" he said, "it's like going back in time. They've been evolving down there all on their own, in this harsh, toxic environment. Who knows even what they ingest or excrete or how they move. It's hard to believe they're even alive."

Abigail felt her balance waver for a second, probably because she'd never seen Eli speak with such intensity. This was Eli at his best, the guy who'd gushed over the beauty of an apple. The only person she knew for a thousand miles. She felt herself melt.

Even in the near dark she could see the lake's gentle undulations, webby white lines of foam floating atop the surface like a net.

"It does look like it's breathing," Abigail said.

Eli pulled her into his soft, warm body. "Whatever is surviving in it, deep down—it's hard to even fathom. The potential. My god. What I can't figure out is why there aren't industry vultures all over this town. Biotech, especially."

Abigail turned to face him. "What do these microbes do, exactly?"

"There's a lot I still don't know," he said, "and I haven't told you everything. But what I do know is pretty scary. Like this place could change...well, the world."

"I admire your humility," she said, tugging on his hand. "Could you be more specific?"

"Too many variables," he said, squinting out at the water. "The researcher who was here before never published her findings. She just left, so I have very little to go on. Just trust me that it could be huge."

Abigail reminded herself that the first time she'd seen Eli, he'd been unboxing bunches of bananas. And according to his best man's drunken wedding toast, he'd worn shoes with Velcro straps all the way through college because tying laces was a waste of brain cells.

"Why'd you wait until now to tell me all this?" she said.

"I guess so you don't talk about it. With anyone here."

"Like my hay dealer?"

Eli didn't smile. He was busy peering past her, looking up the length of the shore as if to ensure they were alone.

They were.

CHAPTER 7

ABIGAIL

After spending two weeks ripping out the carpet, plucking staples from the oak floors beneath, and replacing the garish gold fixtures, the new house had begun to feel like their home. It was a 1950s ranch, remarkably affordable, a few blocks uphill from the lake, with a brick fireplace and wide living room windows. Downstairs, a daylight basement with a separate entrance was built into the hillside, perfect for Eli's new lab. When his equipment arrived from the university, Eli disappeared down there for fourteen hours a day.

Between Eli's well-funded grant and the profits Abigail had made from selling her condo in Denver, they had paid for this house outright. Which meant that Abigail, for the first time in her adult life, could take a pause before finding full-time work and focus instead on figuring out what she wanted to do with the rest of her career. Eli encouraged her to think long-term, maybe finish her psych degree online or look into one of those certification programs she'd mentioned, gerontology or social work. She just wasn't sure what would be a good fit.

Abigail had always been fine working the title company reception desk, but a dozen years of doing so had come with a blunt realization: she would rather deflect attention away from herself, and toward the person customers *really* wanted to see, than step into a leadership role. People must have liked her, though, because, god, they told her everything, switching casually from chatting about Denver's real estate market to sharing the affair they were having with a bike mechanic or how they'd recently buried a brother. She thought it was maybe because she sat so low at the desk and was therefore nonthreatening, or maybe there was something receptive in her face—the little gap between her front teeth, her slightly outdated glasses. Abigail had spent months anticipating this time of discovery, when the job would be behind her, the move would be over, and she could finally begin again. Yet here she was—

Life among the tumbleweeds. Not exactly Jane Goodall.

Suddenly jobless and alone, Abigail found herself peering out the windows at the neighborhood and feeling, she hated to admit, a light dose of regret. There was a lot of mucky open land between the little houses and trailers, mostly filled with prickly cheatgrass and goat head thorns, not unlike a meadow in hell. There were few streetlights and no sidewalks, and the roads just kind of *fell* into the lawns. The area felt more like a settlement than a neighborhood.

Eli called it *libertarian*. She felt like a total snob.

Rather than focus on the old cars and boats in the yards, the toppled swing sets and deflated holiday inflatables, the abandoned exercise equipment and piles of tires—so many tires!—she reminded herself to pay attention instead to the many charms of the place: the cute, brightly painted cottages, the garden gnomes and bottle trees, the old woman she'd spied reading in her garden with a blanket in her lap. A few times she brought a thermos of tea to the picnic table down at the lake, where someone long ago had carved *Be Nice to Your Mother*, which almost made her cry because her own mother was so hard to be nice to.

As winter came to an end, the beige grasses and sodden fields turned a dozen shades of green, and the land began to resemble pastoral Ireland. The sagebrush perked up a bit, and wildflowers sprang to life overnight—balsamroot and phlox, lupine and mariposa—and she began to take long daily walks on the sprawling roads around town. Things only got better when she discovered the gravel maintenance roads that ran alongside the irrigation canals and into the desert for as far as the eye could see.

One afternoon in early spring, when she returned to the house after a walk, she found Eli leaning against the kitchen counter, transfixed by his phone. He still wore his safety glasses and was munching cocktail peanuts from the stash in his bathrobe pocket.

Something was up.

"What is it?" she said.

He handed her his phone then sat on the couch, hugging a pillow. She looked at the screen, expecting a death in the family, but instead saw a formal email composed by Eli *regretting to share that* he was *unable to accept...*

"A job?" she said, softening. "In *Poland*? You had me worried, Eli."

He wrung the pillow between his enormous hands and explained: after spending years applying for limnology grants and jobs, he'd been contacted by one Professor Grazyna Salecki, a limnologist at the University of Łódź, on whose work he'd based most of his graduate research. Years ago, he'd sent her a copy of his dissertation as a professional courtesy. When her assistant recently announced she'd be taking maternity leave, Dr. Salecki reached out to Eli, inquiring if he was interested in temporarily filling her position.

In Poland. Home, he explained, to some of the rarest mineral lakes in the world.

"There's a perfectly rare mineral lake just down the hill," Abigail said, half smiling.

"I know that," he said. "Read what I wrote. That I'm declining the position because of *this* grant, and I'm recently married and bought a house and—you know all the reasons."

"Yeah. I know the reasons, Eli. So why haven't you hit Send?"

"She has *microbes* named after her. *NASA* is using her research on extremophiles in their search for life on other planets. Think *Mars*, Abigail. Think *beyond*." He picked at the pills on their big blue couch. "The pay is miserable, anyway. And I'd be rooming with some guy in the dorms. Probably a soccer hooligan."

"*And* you already have a job."

"That's the thing," he said, raking his hands through his hair. "I figured out a way to do both. Jobs. At once. My first reaction was like, *New job? No way.* But then I was thinking, in terms of what it would do for my career, six months is just a blip—"

"Six months?"

"I know," he said, staring at the floor. "But Salecki knows everyone. She served on the board at Hydrolicon." He lowered his voice. "Abigail, if these microbes pan out, I'm going to need connections. People in industry. I can't scale this up on my own. If it comes to that."

"What do you mean, 'scale this up'?"

"All I know is my work here is ahead of schedule," he said, holding out his hands. "So if I gathered enough data over the next few weeks, technically I could take it with me and work on both lakes at once. I would be insanely busy, but I could be back here by Thanksgiving, latest, in time for the next stages of research."

"You keep saying *I.* As opposed to *we.*"

"Unfortunately it's not a plus-one," he said. "I actually thought it might give you some time to figure things out."

She dropped the phone in his lap and wandered toward the kitchen, caught in the grip of an emotional whiplash: she'd quit her job, sold her condo, and thrown herself into Eli's arms, betting on the shared beauty of their new life. And now their life was hardly shared at all.

She tried to calm down but found herself embracing the hot anger expanding through her.

"I'm not upset you're thinking about this decision," she said, her fingers splaying, as tight as twigs on a branch. "You should be. It's huge."

"Okay."

"I'm upset that you know what you want to do, and the only reason you're *not* doing it is because of me."

"It's not about you, Abigail," he said, and he sat up a bit, like a teen waiting for permission to drive the station wagon. "It's about the work."

"It's *always* about the work, Eli," she said. "I'm going for another walk. Make up your mind before I get back."

Though she could sense that he already had.

Three long, lonely months after Eli left for Poland, the temperature had jumped sixty degrees, and all things green had been scorched from the region. The gravel canal roads crunching under Abigail's feet had become as comforting and familiar as her own empty bed, and even the desert, stark and crispy in the summer sun, brought a meditative stillness that she could sometimes feel inside.

And then one morning, after dropping a glass tube of miraculous water in Eli's dusty lab, she looked up from her walk and saw a boy in the desert, sticky with his mother's blood, sprinting in terror at *her.*

CHAPTER 8

ESME

Within days of the trailer fire, Esme's mom had rented a stone cottage on the west side of the lake, in a little settlement perched on a bluff between orchards. Esme liked their new home right away, especially because it was painted her third favorite color, turquoise, and had a big tree in the yard with a sprawling shadow that spent each morning inching across her bedroom floor. When she ran through the desert toward the lakeshore, high-strung quail burst in all directions, freaking out about nothing, and when she lifted big flat rocks, clueless skinks with purple tails pretended to be invisible. On windy afternoons, blobs of foam leaped from the lake and wobbled through the air like ghosts on a dance floor.

Daniel was the best, always at her side…except when she tried to talk to him about TreeTop. Esme had been thinking about that day in the orchard a lot, and a few times she'd even startled awake in the middle of the night, certain TreeTop was in her room, dragging his metal rake across her bedroom wall. Once

when she woke up screaming, Daniel burst into the room bran-
dishing a soccer trophy, which was the closest thing to a weapon
he could find. When she tried to tell him what happened, he
stormed out, yelling, *I don't want to hear about TreeTop!*

Something had happened to Daniel after Dad died, beyond
him just being sadder. When she was little, Daniel loved scaring himself with stories of TreeTop, and he'd get so worked up
that he wouldn't even peek down the orchard rows when they
were walking home from school. One afternoon back in first
grade, a year before the fire, Esme was kneeling on the kitchen
floor, watching her dad unclog a hairball from the sink, when
she heard Daniel shrieking through the trailer. Her dad scrambled out and dropped his wrench just as Daniel came running
in, flapping around a book like it was on fire.

"What is it?" her dad yelled. "What happened?"

Between sobs Daniel explained that he'd gone to the library
with his third-grade class earlier that day and checked out a
chapter book on Jackie Robinson, only when he got toward
the back of it, in the middle of an illustrated outfield, he found
a scribbled message:

As Daniel dried his tears, her dad sat the two kids at the table,
which only added to the gravity of the situation. He stared at
the page in silence for a long time.

TreeTop Kills. Daniel's reaction totally made sense. Every time
Esme saw those words her heart felt like it might explode. Her
dad had pointed them out many times, scrawled and scratched
in spots around town: behind the cubbies at the roller rink,
above the back door of the Pentecostal church, under the sink
in the grocery store restroom. He always pinched her neck and
pulled her ear to his mouth, and then with hot beery breath and
stubbled chin, told her that ever since he was a boy, that phrase

had been secretly written around town by those trying to put
an end to TreeTop.

Esme sat on her hands while her dad interrogated Daniel about
the book, how exactly he'd found it and whether anyone at the
library had encouraged him to borrow it. Before long, she realized he was trying to decide if the message was left at random
or if it was some kind of a warning that TreeTop was coming
after one of *them* next.

"I just grabbed the first book I saw about baseball!"

"Okay," Dad had said, scratching at his chin, sounding relieved. "We're good. Okay."

He squeezed their shoulders and crawled back under the sink.
Esme thought that was the end of it, but as she and Daniel were
wandering away, feeling scared and excited, their dad yelled out
from the darkness: "Now on, library's off-limits!"

The two kids looked at each other and added it to the growing list of places where they weren't allowed to step foot. Like
the orchards.

Now that their dad was dead and Daniel was, in his words,
the *man of the house*, he was acting all tough about TreeTop. He'd
stopped telling stories and refused to listen and forced Esme to
be scared all alone…which everyone knew was the worst way
to be scared.

In her desperation, Esme came up with a plan.

One Saturday in winter, she lured Daniel outside and convinced
him to play a game called Houdini that involved tying themselves
to a tree so tightly they'd have to cut the rope to get free.

"Got a knife right here," she said, patting her coat pocket.

Daniel took the bait. Esme led him to the ash tree in their
front yard and made him stand with his back to it, then she
looped a strand of rope around until she could barely squeeze in
on the opposite side of the trunk. It wasn't very tight, so when
one of their neighbors down the road was getting into his truck,
Esme called him over and asked if he'd tie the knot for them.

"Make it good and tight," she said, patting her pocket. "I got a knife."

"Nothing would make me happier," he said.

The neighbor was late for work at one of the cold storage plants in Quincy, but he kept looping the rope around the tree as if he were taming it, and talking about knots with complicated names, like the Laredo Lasso and the Tuckered Stowaway.

"Tighter!" Esme yelled.

"That's good," Daniel said.

"I'll be back in twelve hours, just in case!" the guy said, jogging away.

It was just past noon and without being able to move the day was suddenly colder. Then it began to rain. The two siblings couldn't see each other, but she could feel in the ropes when he squirmed, like they were spiders sharing a web.

"This game sucks," Daniel said, then mimicked her. *"Tighter! Tighter!"*

But soon he relaxed. Which meant it was time.

"Daniel, do you ever feel like you're still inside of that burning trailer?"

She could feel the ropes constrict as he took a deep breath. "All the time," he said.

"You know, Dad didn't die that night," she said, feeling her secret break loose, as if it, too, had been tied.

Daniel sighed and she could tell he closed his eyes.

"Dad didn't die in the fire," she repeated.

"Cut us loose, Esme. Houdini was a chump."

Esme told Daniel that she hadn't figured out all the connections just yet, but that morning she'd been prowling around the orchards and saw a man's boot, *Dad's boot*, in a tarp-covered wheelbarrow being pushed by TreeTop—

Daniel cut her off. "We're really back to *TreeTop*? He's a *story*, Esme. He's like Sant—"

"Don't say it!" she said, thrashing her head.

"Think about it, Esme. Everyone who sprays the orchards wears that same outfit."

"I think what happened," she said, ignoring him, "is TreeTop killed Dad then wheeled his body to our trailer and set the couch on fire."

"Listen," Daniel shouted, and she could feel him slamming into the trunk. "Dad was crazy, Esme. So paranoid he barely even let us go to *school.* And then he got drunk and lit a candle and the trailer caught fire. He passed out and went up in *flames.* It's the kind of thing he always did, only this time he almost *killed* us!"

Both kids froze when their mom stepped out to the porch, wearing her pink bathrobe. She peeked into the mailbox but it was empty, as usual, except when it had colorful coupons for Whopper Meal Deals, even though the nearest Burger King was sixty miles away in Wenatchee. She shuffled back inside without noticing her two kids roped to the tree.

Esme's hands were numb, her toes tingly. In the window of the cottage next door, where witches definitely lived, a curtain closed.

"TreeTop is pretend," Daniel said. "I don't blame you for wanting a different answer, or even a different dad. But you don't need that stuff dragging you down, and Mom *definitely* doesn't need it. You're your own person, Esme. Try to think about good things instead, okay?"

In the dirt road out front, the rain gathered in muddy puddles.

"Daniel?"

"Yeah."

"I don't have a knife. I lied."

"I know, Esme."

That night, after a chuckling neighbor cut them loose, and after a dinner of hot dogs and ketchup, Esme's bedroom door wobbled open and Daniel's disembodied hand appeared and flung a coloring book at her.

She picked it up: "TreeTop Activity Book."

"It's all pretend," he said. "That's all I know."

He closed the door, leaving her alone. They'd been handing these out for free at school for as long as she could remember, updating them every few years with new coloring pages and word-search puzzles and dot-to-dots that anyone with a crayon could solve. She could see that when Daniel was in first grade, he'd colored every single page and had even written his name on the inside cover with a backward *a*. It should have been cute, seeing his writing, but the sight of TreeTop's face scribbled out like a black tornado raised goose bumps on her skin.

The activities themselves were pretty lame, with lots of references to local fruit and crops, and an elaborate origin story that connected TreeTop to the region's *glorious agriculture*, and to the *water that brought life to this parched desert*. But the section at the beginning, with black-and-white photos of *TreeTop through the Years*, mesmerized her the most.

In the early years, he wore a black rubber outfit and a gas mask with a floppy cartridge that drooped from his chin like a Slinky. Over time the rubber outfits gave way to coveralls and biohazard jumpsuits with a mask over his mouth and nose and sometimes eyes, so at times TreeTop looked like an old-time surgeon or one of those faceless microchip factory workers on commercials. He always gripped a rake or a shovel, a hatchet or a pruning saw. And he was always pictured wearing black rubber gloves. But when she saw him in the orchard that day his gloves were definitely blue. In the final photo, TreeTop could be seen up close, aiming a fat nozzle directly at the camera, spraying fog at her face—

Like he was right here in her room.

She stomped to the kitchen and shoved the workbook into the trash, then stood staring at it, her knuckles smeared with ketchup, aware that she could throw a million of those away and it wouldn't matter one bit: TreeTop wasn't going anywhere.

CHAPTER 9

ABIGAIL

Sixteen hours after the boy burst out of the desert and into her life, Abigail, sleepless and despondent, returned to Eli's lab and began sweeping up the glass tube she'd dropped early that morning. It was the middle of the night and the precious lake water that had been stored inside of it had evaporated, leaving behind chalky yellow smudges. That made her feel worse.

She'd taken a long shower this afternoon after Officer Krunk had dropped her off, yet somehow there was still blood under her thumbnail. Otherwise she'd spent the day texting Eli and staring at her phone, awaiting his reply. She knew he was visiting some lake in the Tatras on a research trip, but not that he'd be away from a signal for days.

She dragged the broom across the tiles.

Loneliness, she reminded herself, was not being separated from your brilliant lake doctor husband for six months so you could find yourself and take empty walks while he studied microbial life in Poland. Loneliness was having your mother stabbed in the gut with a screwdriver in front of you and having to flee through the desert to get away from the monster who did it.

Abigail thought she heard something on the far side of the lab, near the sink. Just a *click*. But nothing was there. Or a mouse.

This had been happening a lot.

She'd lived alone for years in her condo in Denver, yet she'd never really felt alone, not like this.

These past three months without Eli, she'd been having the strange sense that the house was getting quieter. She found herself soft-stepping from room to room, even whispering to herself, as if her normal volume might shatter something fragile around her.

A few weeks ago, in a moment of desperation, she'd reached out to her mom down in Florida about scheduling a long overdue visit. But her mom, in typical fashion, made her feel worse.

You don't want to come down here with all of us old people, she'd said. *Besides, I got another cat! Aren't you still allergic?*

The previous time Abigail had raised the possibility of a visit, her mom had told her she'd moved all of the exercise equipment into the guest room.

You want me to live a long life, don't you? But you should see me! I'm getting ripped!

She could hear Meghan feeding her kids in the background.

Abigail had grown up in the shadow of her big sister, Meghan—loud, freckled, and platinum blonde, Mom's favorite from day one—and had survived childhood by hanging back, being quiet and unobjectionable, especially after Dad took off. Mom acted more like Meghan's friend than her parent, and the two of them made a pastime of bad-mouthing Dad, planning themed birthday parties, and picking out the cutest boys in the class. So it was little surprise that Abigail settled into place as the family buzzkill—the one who wanted to buy a plastic Snoopy mask for Halloween rather than spend weeks sewing an elaborate costume, and ran off crying at her grandma's birthday party when it was her turn to dance on the coffee table.

Not surprisingly, as an adult, Abigail was moderately insecure (only freaks weren't), but she wasn't antisocial by any means. She just felt most comfortable in the periphery, most dreadful in the center. For years she'd carved out a life that allowed her to follow these internal grooves without really noticing them. But now, in Eli's absence, when she had little to do but think, she began to recognize how deeply these patterns had risen out of her childhood and into her marriage, like the delayed hatch of a horrid insect.

Eli leading the way, Abigail tagging along.

When they went to the grocery store, Eli pushed the cart, chatted up the clerk, and always swiped his card.

When they were deciding between couches, they went with Eli's shade of blue.

Going to the diner with Eli, she clung to his side, stayed for coffee and dessert.

Going there alone, she rushed in and grabbed a Styrofoam vat of spaghetti to go.

No wonder she'd been having such a hard time leaving the house in his absence. When she did venture out, usually for groceries, she tugged on a hat and wore shades like a celebrity in disguise. The few times she'd walked down the hill instead of driving, she snuck past the cottages and trailers, studying her feet as she passed a woman mowing her lawn, a man drinking beer on his porch. She wore headphones but often didn't connect them to anything.

She'd been telling herself for months she was just weary from upending her life and needed some time to recuperate. But now she was beginning to wonder if she wasn't a little depressed.

People needed people, she knew that. And purpose—
Click.
There it was again.

She scanned the lab. Except for a bathroom, and a bedroom in the back that Eli used as an office, the space was wide-open, with a kitchenette on one end, a living room lined with shelves and specimen lockers on the other, and a few workstations in between. The walls held a gridwork of Eli's sticky notes and a topographic map of the lake covered in colorful pins marking the spots where he, or the previous researcher, had extracted water samples. To the left of the door, three wide windows looked out across a yard and up the hillside toward a cluster of cottages and trailers and manufactured homes.

Abigail had hardly spent any time down here, except when Eli enlisted her help. One day last week, he'd texted in a tizzy about the stress of studying two lakes at once, the struggle of not conflating data. He needed her to rush down and confirm the blinds were closed and the thermostat was set at precisely seventy degrees to ensure that sunlight and heat weren't wreaking havoc on his samples or equipment. And even though she was on her way out the door for her afternoon walk, she unlocked the lab and texted him the temperature and explained that all the blinds were now closed, except the tangled one by the door that wouldn't budge. Then she stood there, covered in sunscreen, cradling her water bottle, lamely stretching her hamstrings, dutifully staring at the heart emoji that popped up on her screen, waiting—

Clickety-tick.

There it was. She stopped sweeping. Squinted toward the sink.

Eli had told her there were spiders here so big that you could hear them walking across your floors as you slept.

Click. Click.

Maybe one of Eli's pricey devices. Or possibly her phone, vibrating because he finally had a signal. Only when she reached into the back pocket of her cutoff sweats did she realize she'd left it next to the bed upstairs.

She turned and caught sight of her reflection in the window.

Her hair was a clingy brown mess, and Eli's Tip of My Tungsten T-shirt draped to her thighs. She looked to herself like an overgrown child.

Tik.

One set of blinds remained tangled, its cord looped into a knot near the top, clogging up the works. She reached up and began to loosen it. Her nose bumped the glass, and the double panes cast an aura around her reflection, a blur of motion—

Then she moved, a quick hypnic jerk.

Tik. Tik.

Only she hadn't moved. She *knew* she hadn't moved. Her reflection had. A rush of cold swept up the back of her thighs. She lowered her tiptoes and stared at her wide eyes behind plastic glasses, her rounded chin. She switched off the light, so a shroud of darkness fell through the room—

And she was suddenly looking into the eyes of a giant man, standing outside, watching her. Tapping on the window with a black latex finger.

Tik tik tik.

He wore big goggles and his mouth was shrouded in white fabric. He was tall, towering, and staring down at her. Abigail stumbled back and tripped on a stool and fell straight into the tiles. Her teeth pierced her lips and she tasted blood. Her forehead throbbed but the goggle man was tapping—

Tik tik tik.

—so she kicked through the stool and lurched into the basement bathroom, slamming the door behind her and hitting the lock. She scrambled into the tub and yanked the shower curtain down and around her, never in her life more alone.

CHAPTER 10

ESME

Esme's dad couldn't have been more clear when he banned her from visiting the Soap Lake Public Library, but it was hard to know if rules like that expired after a dad was dead. When she asked Daniel about it, he just clutched his hair, saying, *Lord god above.*

For several years after her dad's death, Esme honored his wishes and stayed away from the library entirely. But that all changed during the dark winter of fifth grade, when low damp clouds dropped from the sky and pressed into the region for weeks. The town was small, the days were cold, and there just weren't many places to go. So she stepped inside the library's swinging glass door, shook the fog out of her hair, and parked at a wooden table in the back.

Esme had simply been seeking a dry place to ride out the gloom, so she was surprised at how cozy the library felt. The carpet was gray, its shelves metal and lights dim, but the windows near her table were bright, even in winter, and the misty hills above the lake looked like a camel leaning in for a drink. She didn't even need to daydream, looking out there.

The first thing Esme did was scribble fake headings on sheets of loose-leaf paper, *Esme Calderon, Language Arts*, and spread them all around her, in case anyone asked why she was sitting there. She couldn't remember how the whole book part worked, so whenever Miss Nellie, the gossipy librarian in loose flower blouses, disappeared into the echo-chamber bathroom to fart, Esme tugged a few titles off the shelves and got lost in them for hours.

She noticed her heart got fluttery anytime she walked past the middle-grade nonfiction section, where the chapter book on Jackie Robinson was shelved—*TreeTop Kills*—so she took a lesson from Daniel and veered around it. Problem solved.

Esme stayed that day for the entire afternoon, and when no one came around to tell her to leave, or bothered her about the books she used to build walls all around her, she began spending all of her free time, year after year, at the table in the back by the window.

One day in seventh grade, while pacing along the reference books outside the bathroom door, she glimpsed a row of blue encyclopedias.

Each spine said *Book of Knowledge* and matched the charred volume her dad had given her when she was little. She didn't look at the encyclopedia that much anymore and it still smelled like smoke, but it was one of the few gifts he'd ever given her, so it earned a special spot in the milk crate next to her bed. She'd been coming to the library for years and had noticed the encyclopedias before—

But never that the volumes skipped a letter.

...*H. I. K. L.*...

J wasn't on the shelf. Which was weird.

Because it was in her milk crate at home.

Because her dad had *stolen* it and given it to her.

She scanned the aisles. A young guy with a backpack was snoring by the printers, and Miss Nellie was at the desk, chatting with her loud brother, Hal, a big old cowboy who stopped by so much that he might as well have worked there.

Esme wedged her finger into the space between *I* and *K*, creating a little slot where the *J* should go. She felt small enough to hide in it.

In the bathroom behind her, someone ratcheted the paper towels.

The bathroom. Now she understood.

As far as she knew her dad had never visited the library in his life, but it was the one place on Main Street with a public restroom, so he could have easily swung by during his lunch hour to use the toilet and swiped the encyclopedia on his way in. Just something to read on the pot. And when he left, he probably tucked it under his shirt and took it home because he wanted to distract Esme with a gift since he'd given Daniel a brand-new Game Boy that year and gave her a shattered candy cane with sharp pieces stabbing through the cellophane.

She felt so overwhelmed by this revelation that she barely reacted when the bathroom door swung open and a middle-aged man came halfway out, holding a can of Strawberry Febreze.

"Whoops!" he said, going back in and setting it on the back of the toilet. "You didn't see that."

It was Pastor Kurt, from the youth group meeting she and Daniel had been suckered into last year because they gave away free pizza. He was wearing white jeans and a short-sleeved Hawaiian shirt, despite the cold.

"Esme, right?" He took her in. "Everything okay?"

Pastor Kurt's hair was sandy and thin, and some of his moustache hairs were white and grew in the wrong direction.

She shrugged.

"I see," he said. "Want to talk about it?"

She shook her head.

"That bad?" After a few seconds, he leaned forward and lowered his voice. "Esme, what's your take on babies?"

"Babies?" she said, expecting him to bust out a pamphlet that explained why half the girls in the high school were prego.

"I mean, you like them, right?"

Like them? Esme freaking *loved* babies. She only ever saw them at the grocery store or playground, but even when they were crying they were hilarious, and they always did whatever they wanted: spat out food they didn't like, screamed at the top of their lungs, gobbled up ants and dirt. It was the easiest thing in the world just to love them.

Pastor Kurt must have recognized the joy in her face because he smiled. "You going to be here a minute? I've got a surprise for you. Might just help turn that frown...you know."

"That's my table," she said, pointing toward the back, as if she were a regular at a bar.

She had a feeling Pastor Kurt was going to grab one of the plastic-smelling, blond-haired, blue-eyed dolls leftover from the Giving Tree at his church, and she'd have to tell him that she'd outgrown those a few years ago. Either that or one of those holy cards with pictures of Jesus on them that all the preachers loved to dish out. She had a collection of them at home that she liked to spread out and compare this Jesus to that Jesus. Sometimes he looked like he camped a lot and just climbed out of his tent to borrow some bug spray or a marshmallow fork. Sometimes he looked like he'd been at the mall in Wenatchee, getting a haircut and a blow-dry. Sometimes he looked like a professional wrestler, drenched in sweat and blood, who'd just been clobbered by a folding chair. Like how an actor could star in different movies.

Across the library, she spotted Pastor Kurt's son, Silas, checking out a stack of DVDs at the desk. Silas was two or three years older than Esme and had already been in rehab for getting drunk last summer and spinning doughnuts around the baseball diamond in his dad's station wagon. His hair was longer than any other boy's in school and he was on track to be the town's youngest dropout.

Pastor Kurt probably thought Silas could use a few Jesus cards as he skimmed through his stack of movies, returning all the R-rated ones to the cart. Silas threw up his arms and they walked out separately, as if they didn't know each other.

A short while later Pastor Kurt returned, joined by a young woman with cowgirl jeans and one wet cuff, as if she'd crossed a creek on the way in. She had a long ponytail and was holding an infant wrapped in a blankie.

"Esme," Pastor Kurt said, "this is my daughter, Grace."

For a second Esme wasn't sure whether Grace was the woman or the baby, but then the woman held out her hand.

"I'm Trudy," she said, "Grace's mom." Trudy leaned down so Esme could see Baby Grace. She looked like half Fisher-Price person, half Charlie Brown. "Guess how old she is."

Esme had no idea. "One?"

"Just ten days old," Pastor Kurt said, "if you can imagine."

Now it was making more sense: Pastor Kurt was the one whose wife got cancer a few years ago and died within months. Trudy must've been her replacement.

Esme still didn't quite know what was going on, but when Trudy rested Grace into the crook of Esme's arm, something stirred within her. As Trudy and Pastor Kurt looked for books, Esme held the infant for a half hour, until the front of her Froot Loops T-shirt held a sweaty blob in the shape of a sleeping baby.

"I knew she'd cheer you up," Pastor Kurt said.

"When Grace gets a little older," Trudy said, "you can babysit."

Esme was so excited by the prospect that the second they left she returned to her table, shoved her face in a book and cried so hard that she forgot all about her dead dad and the stolen *Volume J*.

★ ★ ★

One spring day in seventh grade, not long after holding Pastor Kurt's drooly little caterpillar, Esme came into the library after school and saw the new TreeTop activity books piled on the circulation desk, alongside a tower of crayon boxes. A sign beneath said *Free! Take ONE!!!*

A lot of the coloring pages and puzzles were unchanged, but the books seemed especially polished this year, with a few pages of glossy paper in the back for the vintage photos of TreeTop, and a new Acknowledgments page, with color images of happy white farmers with gleaming white teeth leaning against fancy white trucks. They were so sunny she had to close her eyes.

Esme barely glanced up when Kevin Polk, a kid in her class, came in with his dad, and Miss Nellie emerged to greet them. Kevin waved and Esme gave him a small smile.

Kevin was a nice guy with bushy brown hair and John Lennon glasses too huge for his face. He was a shoo-in to be valedictorian someday, not that there was much competition. As far as Esme could tell, kids like her who didn't have the internet at home got all C's, and kids like Kevin who had the internet got all A's, and the only difference between them was whether they lived in a trailer out in the country with cats running wild, or a home with a fence and a yard and just the right amount of pets. Besides his good grades, Kevin was famous at school for walking out of science class last year when their teacher showed a documentary about how humans used to hunt dinosaurs, and how God secretly planted fossils in the earth to test humanity's faith. Mr. and Mrs. Polk raised hell with the school board and the walkout even made the Wenatchee paper. Then everyone just pretended it didn't happen, prayed on it, and waited for Kevin to be older so they could show the documentary again.

Today Kevin wore blue corduroy shorts and, as always, the handcrafted leather belt stamped with pictograms of his life— cedars, highways, Autobots and seagulls—made famous in show-

and-tell last year. It was the coolest and dorkiest thing Esme had ever seen.

"Help yourself, Esme," Miss Nellie said from down the counter, pointing at the activity books. "Free crayons, too. Thank a farmer, you get a chance." Her smile practically sparkled.

Then she turned her attention to Kevin's dad, a bubbly man with wild gray hair who had a box of *Popular Mechanics* magazines from the 1950s that he wanted to donate, in case anyone needed to repair their icebox or telegraph machine.

"His gloves are *blue*," Esme said, more loudly than she'd intended. She pointed to the comic book illustration of a masked-and-goggled TreeTop on this year's cover, standing in an orchard with a lantern in his hand. "Not black. His gloves are *blue*. In real life."

She didn't mean to be so blunt, and for a long time had managed to avoid the town's TreeTop weirdness. But something about the arrival of this year's activity books made her feel reckless, even angry.

Miss Nellie shook her head. "This one here," she said to Mr. Polk, discreetly pointing at Esme. She placed her hands on his pile of donations. "So. What do we have here? Back issues of *Cosmo*?"

Esme could feel Mr. Polk looking down the counter at her, not in a mean way, but Miss Nellie was so gleeful that Esme couldn't help herself: she swept the pile of activity books to the carpet. The tower of crayons toppled, too.

"Pick those up!" Miss Nellie snapped.

"Someone should burn them," she said, feeling feverish.

"That's not something we do at libraries, Esme*ralda*," Miss Nellie said with her stupid face. "Now put those back. Or you can start doing your homework at *home*."

Esme stared at the kaleidoscope of TreeTops spread around her feet.

"I got it," Kevin said.

He scooped up the pile and stacked them back on the counter.

"Kevin Polk, *please* do not—" Miss Nellie started to say, but Mr. Polk cut her off.

"He's fine," he said, firmly. "They're classmates."

Kevin took a step back to size up his efforts, then shifted the pile so it was perfectly straight. Esme half expected him to bust out his protractor.

"So," Mr. Polk said, "can we talk donations or what?"

Miss Nellie turned her attention back to him, but she was flustered.

Kevin chewed on the inside of his cheek, hands folded politely, as if he were in front of an assembly at school.

"Thanks," Esme whispered, but she felt like crying. As she marched toward the exit, staring at the ground, she could hear Kevin's corduroy shorts swishing right behind her.

"I believe you, Esme," he said, and she paused at the door. "About TreeTop's gloves being blue."

"I don't," she said, faintly, and she could feel him watching her as she left.

CHAPTER 11

ABIGAIL

After what felt like hours, when she was certain that no one was out there, Abigail unlocked the bathroom door. It had to be nearly six in the morning. She took a deep breath and turned on all the lights in the lab, studying Eli's workspace for any sign of an intruder, but all was quiet except for the hum of his equipment.

Her plan had been to run upstairs and grab her phone off the nightstand and call 9-1-1. But when she left the lab and entered the dark, she was startled to see, as she rounded the corner, a yellow light glowing on the porch of the cottage next door.

A camping lantern, perched on a table. And a woman bending into its radiance.

The cottage was so overgrown with weeds and half-dead trees that, back on moving day, Abigail had pegged it as one of those charming collapsed homesteads that show up on calendars of the Pacific Northwest. Upon closer inspection, she'd found an actual house in there, not so charming, with filthy windows draped in mystical tapestries, scabs of crumbling stucco, weathered junk mail and wrappers sprinkled in the overgrowth. A pair of elms planted too close to each other tangled over the walkway. Most unexpected had been the sight of the orange extension cord snaking out of a window and up the utility pole, where it was woven straight into the power lines.

"Don't people get electrocuted doing that?" she'd asked Eli one day early on.

But he just yelled out the window, "Stick it to the man!"

Now Abigail crossed her yard, drawn to the lantern's glow like a moth. She told herself she was doing this to find out whether the woman had heard anything, had seen her Peeping Ghost, but part of her knew that what she really wanted was simply to stand in the waves of another person's voice.

"Hello?"

The woman's back was to her, but her shoulders jumped and she craned sideways with alarm. She lifted the book in her hands like a shield.

"You *startled* me," she blurted.

"Sorry! I saw your light and I live next door and—"

"Was I being too loud? Too bright?"

"Nothing like that. I'm sorry," Abigail said. "You're fine."

The woman lowered the book and she was interesting looking, with big brown eyes spread far apart and pale lips pressed into a pucker. A frizzy, strawberry blond braid draped over one shoulder, and a thin rattail, wrapped in colorful thread, draped the other. She looked to be around forty and wore a black T-shirt above jean shorts, both splattered with paisleys of bleach.

"Everything okay?" she said.

"I don't know," Abigail said.

The woman closed the book and shook the extension cord hooked to the wall behind her. "It came undone or something blew. So no power. No fan. It just gets so hot inside. But if the lantern is bothering you..."

"It's not."

On the tiny table next to the woman sat a few melted candles and a pile of faded paperbacks. Given the state of the place, Abigail expected horror, but from the covers and titles she could tell that they were romance novels—not the steamy ones with six-pack abs that her mom and Meghan always read, but a more naive variety, published decades ago and beaming with optimism.

A Date for Doris. Sixteen Summer. P.S., You're Swell!

The others in the pile were also teen romance, but they were more familiar, with titles in team-pennant font.

"*Sweet Valley High?*" Abigail asked. "I loved those. That series got me through junior high."

"Kind of finding my way back," the woman said, fanning the yellowed pages.

The presence of the books, paired with the way the woman was seated, as if at a desk, sparked recognition.

"Do you work at the library?"

"I'm in this job program," the woman said, waving her off, as if she'd been caught doing something wrong. "But yeah, I'm her. Library helper. Or something."

In the first weeks of living in Soap Lake, in search of things to do, Abigail and Eli had made several visits to the library, a sunny cinder block building with an open view of the lake. In addition to the 1980s home decor books Abigail had checked out for inspiration and a laugh, she'd borrowed some cookbooks and gardening titles, feeling hopeful in this new stage of her life. Later, after those titles were long overdue, she dove headlong into boxed wine and Netflix and hadn't returned to the building again.

"I'm Abigail," she said, grinning. Probably weirdly.

"Sophia." She squinted at the cut on Abigail's lip, the knot on her forehead. "Is that from finding the boy?"

Abigail faltered, as if she'd stepped on a rock.

"This? Why? No. How did you...?"

"Everyone knows everything here," Sophia said, lowering her voice. "It's unfortunate."

Once her bearings returned, Abigail pointed across the dark yard to the lower half of her house. "A few hours ago, some guy was watching me through my window." She touched her lip. "I freaked. Tripped. You didn't see anything, did you?"

Sophia sat up. "A few hours ago? Did you scream?"

"I don't think so? There wasn't anyone around to hear it anyway."

"There was," Sophia said, rubbing her chin. "You okay?"

"Just scared."

"I bet."

"I'm all alone over there."

"I know. Me, too."

Sophia glanced down, fanning the pages of her book, as if ready to return to her reading, but Abigail was still upset. Somewhere a wind chime tinkled.

"He was just standing there, this guy. He tapped on my window."

Sophia nodded, tight-lipped.

"Will you keep an eye out?" she continued. "In case he comes back?"

"Of course. Scream anytime. I'll try to hear it."

Abigail nodded, though her neighbor's advice was far from reassuring.

"You don't think he was looking for the boy?" she said. "Because why else come around, you know? This night of all nights."

"That adds up," Sophia said, but she didn't sound convinced.

"Except the kid's long gone," Abigail said. "He got carted away by CPS, put into foster care until they sort out where he belongs. I think he's in Spokane? Does that sound right?"

"Definitely not," Sophia said, shaking her head. "He's here. In town."

"What?"

"I'm sure of it."

Abigail was miffed. Whoever had killed the boy's mom was probably still around, and the boy might have witnessed something, and—

"That seems really stupid to bring him back to Soap Lake," she said. "Did you know her...his mom?"

"Esme? Not really. She left town years ago and dropped off the map. I guess I spent a lot of the past decade not paying attention to people. Unless they could help me get the next...you know." She scratched her neck. "I'm almost two years clean, though. So you don't need to worry about me pawning your husband's lab equipment."

"What's his is yours," Abigail mumbled, wondering what else this woman had observed.

"Best part about meeting new people," Sophia said. "I haven't stolen money out of your purse while you were in the bathroom. Haven't hocked your grandmother's earrings. Nice to meet you, Abigail. May I never screw you over."

She reached out her hand and Abigail shook it. She noticed that Sophia's cuticles were cracked and raw.

"Clean is good."

"It's easy to forget that," Sophia said, staring into the lantern. "After rehab, my counselor told me it was important that I *rediscover joy*, to find something, you know, that I used to love, before I loved meth and oxy and heroin and cough syrup and grain alcohol and farm chemicals. I started young. Too naive to pick my poison, so I picked them all."

"But you left all that behind."

Sophia nodded toward the dark cottage doorway. "Right after I found my fiancé overdosed on the couch in there." And then, as if to avoid any confusion, she added, "Dead."

"Sorry to hear that. My god."

"It's what it took."

A rig roared past at the bottom of the hill, probably hauling hay out to the coast. Abigail pointed to the Sweet Valley High volume on top of the pile, its cover showing an aghast blonde teenager standing back-to-back with her tawdry brunette sister: *The New Jessica*.

"These help?"

"They make for an easy escape, which is the kind I'm after these days. *One page at a time*, right?"

"I like that."

Abigail looked downhill, in the direction of the lake. In the darkness, the rare porch lights and streetlights looked like buoys bobbing in a black sea.

"Any idea what Esme was doing out there?" Abigail said.

"In the middle of the desert, middle of the night, in a car? Sounds like a meeting. Which means drugs. Maybe the deal went bad, or she was trying to rip off the wrong lowlife. But no one stumbled upon her by accident. Not out there. Out there, it's planned—you *meet*."

"Unless you're me," Abigail said.

Sophia grunted. "Yeah. Well."

Abigail was unexpectedly touched by Sophia's openness and had to remind herself that it was practically dawn and that she should probably make sure there was no one in her house.

"I'm going to go inside. If I scream, will you help?"

"You bet."

Abigail clapped her thighs, a prelude to exit, but before she could leave, Sophia spoke.

"I know where you can find the boy," she said. "Other side of the lake. Quarter mile beyond the shore. One of those tiny homes between the apples."

Abigail had spent enough days staring downhill in the direction of the lake to know that, barely visible up the opposite shore, a small settlement of small homes sat atop a low bluff. Above them, the thin blue vein of an irrigation canal. On either side, acres of apples growing in rows.

"Esme used to live in one of those cottages," Sophia continued. "Her mom still lives there, but don't expect cookies and milk. Or consciousness. Her brother is there, too. Daniel. My bet is he's the one keeping an eye on the kid you saved."

CHAPTER 12

ABIGAIL

In the rising light, Abigail collected her phone from the night-stand and nothing: Eli was still off the grid.

She held a frozen bag of corn to the shrinking knot on her forehead and grabbed Officer Krunk's card off the refrigerator door. She dialed, and off it went to voicemail.

"I don't even know if this is something I should be calling you about," she said, "but are you going to let me know when you catch the guy? You probably already have. Pulled him over for a broken headlight and found a set of screwdrivers on his dash? Also, next time you're on duty, could you drive past my house? Something happened here last night. Okay. You can delete this now. So long!"

Abigail gathered her newspaper from the driveway and sat with her cold corn and coffee at the kitchen table. On the front page: a yearbook photo of a buoyant teenage girl. A younger iteration of the waxen corpse she'd discovered yesterday in the Cutlass.

Esmeralda Bridget Calderon had short black hair, a small silver lip ring, and warm brown eyes with a sly crinkle. According to the paper, she'd grown up in Soap Lake but had left town after high school and had been living near Bakersfield, in California's Central Valley, these past eight years. Authorities speculated that Esme and her young son had driven up from California and arrived in town well after dark. It's possible they parked in the desert to sleep until daylight, when they would head to Esme's family home, perhaps to surprise them. But she hadn't survived the night.

No one in Esme's family had known she was coming to town, the article said. Her older brother, Daniel, a local orchard foreman, was inconsolable:

Esme finally escaped this place, and this is what happened the day she came home.

There was no mention of the boy's father, nor of the boy's current location.

There were no suspects in her murder, no persons of interest.

The area around the crime scene was especially desolate, the article said, with no homes or farms nearby. But there was an old homestead called the Rock Shack a mile or so downhill, a gathering place where local teens sometimes met for bonfires.

The only reference to Abigail came in the last sentence of the article, which said: *Calderon's son was rescued by a walker new to town, whose spouse is researching the lake.*

She was relieved by the anonymity, yet uneasy about what she'd become.

A walker, a wife, living here alone.

Through the window above her sink, she spotted a tricked-out blue Accord zip into her driveway. A guy in his late twenties hopped out.

Her heart was thumping until she realized it was Officer Krunk. He was out of uniform, wearing jeans and a black T-shirt with a red hourglass. Not a superhero reference, as she first thought, but a lava lamp, with the word *BELIEVE* wavering beneath.

As she met him on the porch, she was surprised at the relief she felt, just seeing a familiar, friendly face. The frozen corn had softened in her grip.

"That was fast."

"I used to deliver pizza," he said.

"I guess this means the bad guy is still out there?"

"We're working on it. Or someone is." He pointed to her forehead and lip. "You okay?"

"I'm fine," she said. She leaned inside, tossed the corn onto the entry bench and pulled the door closed. She couldn't quite pinpoint why, but she felt slightly embarrassed about the possibility of Krunk seeing inside her home. At first she thought it was because she didn't want to draw attention to the ways solitude had come to define her life. The dish rack on her kitchen counter had long ago stopped being a place where dishes dried and became instead a permanent cupboard for the only five dishes she ever used. The pile of unfolded clothes atop her dryer had fully replaced the drawers in her bedroom bureau. And it seemed absurd to hide tea, cereal, and cookies in the cupboard when she was just going to fish them out four times a day, so onto the counter they went. But more than even those associations, she realized, was the unfair shame she felt at being both *married* and *alone*, not unlike the self-consciousness she used to feel when people asked if she wanted kids someday, or, she imagined, the embarrassment of the recently divorced.

"You said something happened here last night?" Krunk said.

He was acting both warmly familiar and coldly professional, which she decided was just right, given that her bed was empty and her husband was far, far away. She told him about the pale figure watching her through the window of Eli's lab.

"Any other details?"

"Like I said, just a figure in white. I don't know. *Peeping*. He was dressed sort of like a ghost."

"Why *he*?"

"He was tall? I was looking up."

She led him on a walk around the house and Krunk stood in front of the window downstairs, studying the walkway as if expecting to find dance-class footprints there. He looked up the empty hillside, covered with weeds, and squinted at Sophia's weathered cottage next door.

"You must've been terrified."

"I was. Though today I'm having a hard time deciding whether I'm sad or scared."

He tapped his chest. "Over here, it's sadness all the way."

"Because of Esme?"

"Yeah. That and some really bad timing," he added. "I had to cancel some big plans recently. All kinds of fallout."

"Like life plans?"

"Like wedding plans," he said, cockeyed. "Why are we talking about this?"

"*Sadness all the way.*"

He scratched his neck. "Any other trouble?" he said, then added under his breath, "Unrelated to my crappy love life."

"I guess not."

"I can write up a report so if anything, you know, happens—"

"You mean if I get stabbed with a screwdriver?"

He tilted his head. "You're suggesting this is related to Esme, but we have no way of knowing that."

"And you're suggesting I wasn't in danger?"

Krunk toed a brick on the border of the flower garden.

"If he wanted to hurt you, or get inside this lab, he could have."

"It's the little things," she mumbled, squeezing her elbows.

He wrote something down in his small notebook.

"I'd rather not have this end up in the sheriff's blotter," she said. "You know, broadcast that I live here alone. So maybe no report?"

He clicked shut the pen. "Sure. I'll keep it quiet. Okay, though, if I pass it on to the detectives you spoke to? They can decide whether there's any connection—"

"I haven't spoken to any detectives," she said.

Krunk didn't hide his alarm. "*No one* interviewed you after I dropped you off yesterday?"

"Just the statement I gave you in the road."

"I thought that was, like, an outline. *No one* followed up?"

"Some softy in bright blue sneakers," she said, peering at his feet.

"Did he have a caveman name?"

She laughed out loud. Up the hill, a curtain twitched in a trailer window.

"Believe it or not," he continued, "I like being a softy. Last time I had to taze a DUI I ended up in therapy chat rooms all night."

"Why are you a cop?"

"Just a job, like putting French fries in a basket." He shrugged. "Not sure what I'm doing, to be honest."

"That makes two of us," she said, tucking her hands into her shorts pockets.

"Your message," he said, clearing his throat. "You asked about the screwdriver? Not much to it, unfortunately. Craftsman, 1980s, sold alone and as part of a set."

"Meaning half the garages in the country have one in the old family toolbox?"

"It wasn't engraved, I'm saying, and even the paint spill on the handle isn't likely to help. I mean, who hasn't painted something white in the past four decades?"

"No footprints at the crime scene?"

"They've got a few partials, but all the ground up there is either blanketed in cheatgrass or is rocky and uneven. Plus there was some activity, what with you and the kid and a bit of wind. I'm hearing maybe rubber muck-boots, same kind worn by farmers and hunters and pretty much anyone who works outside. So, yeah. Whole lot of nothing."

"How's the little guy?" she said.

"George?"

"George," she repeated. "Is that his name? I didn't realize anyone knew it."

"It took some digging but yeah. George Calderon. Four years old."

"Has he asked about me?"

"I couldn't tell you even if I knew," he said. "Sorry."

Already the day was getting hotter, the finches going quiet in the poplars along the driveway.

"Should I be worried?" she said. "I mean for real."

"I don't know," he said, hands up. "We're looking into some local calls with Esme. Payphone calls, which makes it a lot harder to—"

"The payphone behind the gas station?"

He nodded.

Abigail knew the phone: Eli had called it *The Last Payphone on Earth* and was thrilled when he'd discovered it back there, bolted to a cinderblock wall, surrounded by cigarette burns and slashes of graffiti. One night on a downtown walk he got all excited listening to the dial tone, but when he stuck his finger into the coin return, instead of coming out with a forgotten quarter, his fingertip emerged with a small brain of gum.

"Not everyone can afford a smartphone," Krunk said, "or wants the world in their pocket, especially out here. A lot of migrant workers prefer calling cards so they don't have to worry about billing or coverage. All of which suggests—"

"Someone local." She blinked a few times. "Aren't there any cameras at the gas station?"

"Out front with the pumps and inside at the register, but

not pointed at the phone. Nothing on Main Street either. Big Brother is not watching."

"Here's to freedom," she said dryly, "and getting away with murder."

He met her eye for a moment before looking at the ground, biting his lip. "Can I show you something? Get your take while your memory is fresh?"

"Sure," she said, wary of how somber he'd become.

"We'll have to use your computer if that's okay," he said, nodding toward the house. "It's Esme."

Sitting next to Krunk on her blue couch, the cool *whoosh* of the ceiling fan breathing against their skin, Abigail wished she had a cat to chaperone the horny space between them. When she tugged the cord on the blinds to dim the glare, her tank top lifted and she felt him glance at her stomach and hip before shooting his eyes at her bookshelf, and maybe at the wedding photo perched in its middle. She killed the dozen open tabs on her laptop, and he fiddled with a small silver flash drive. The tiny letters scrawled on it were an icy reminder of why he was here: *CALDERON, ESME.*

Krunk opened the .mov file and pressed Play.

"What am I looking for?" she said, quietly.

"In case anything you remember from the crime scene makes *this* make *sense.*"

He pointed on-screen, at a surveillance recording with a white time stamp and the words *I-90 RYEGRASS* in the corner. The camera was focused on a rest area, with its row of parking spaces and trash cans, all lit by walkway lights. Esme was nowhere in sight.

"That's the other night?" Abigail said, hesitant.

"A few hours before she was stabbed," Krunk said, quietly. "Up on Ryegrass Pass, an hour west of here. That rest area on I-90."

"The hills with the wind turbines," she said. "Middle of nowhere. Where the forest ends."

She could feel Krunk turn to look at her.

"Where the forest ends," he said, "and the desert begins."

She recalled stopping at that rest area with Eli on a weekend trip to Seattle and standing in the ferocious wind at the edge of the parking area. Wind towers peppered the horizon, propellers sweeping as they generated electricity for distant places. It brought to mind the future.

In the video, a battered Oldsmobile Cutlass pulled into a space and Esme stepped out, wearing the gray T-shirt and jean shorts she'd been wearing when she'd died.

Abigail felt her breathing stop. "Krunk? Is something going to happen to her? I can't watch if—"

"Nothing like that."

Moths and flies and a single bat flickered across the screen. Next to the car, Esme stretched and rubbed her hair. She seemed sure-footed, not endangered. She opened the back door and helped George out, then locked the car. She fixed the elastic on his yellow pajama bottoms and tugged up his Cookie Monster slippers. They held hands and made their way up the walkway and out of the frame.

"Another camera shows them going into a family bathroom together. Nothing else."

Abigail studied the parked Cutlass, half expecting to see a shadowy figure crawl into the back, but none did.

"Is George doing okay?" she said, squeezing her own fingers. "Just tell me."

"I don't really know," he said, sighing. "But no. Of course not."

A few minutes later Esme and the boy arrived on-screen again, and she settled him into his booster, but left the car's back door open and didn't get behind the wheel. Instead she made her way over to the trash cans by the fence.

She lifted the lid off the first one, peered in, leaned back, clearly disgusted, and shut it. Abigail could practically smell the warm trash, the carrion of the modern driver, all those wrappers and cups and butts stewing in the day's trapped heat. Esme leaned into the next can and pulled out a fast-food bag. Then she shook the drips out of a few soda cans and tucked them under her arm. She considered but rejected a floppy banana peel. She grabbed an empty potato chip bag, a small stack of napkins, a personal pizza box, a few plastic bottles, a long crumpled receipt, some empty Styrofoam cups, and a yogurt container. Then she moved on to the next can. The pile of trash she'd extracted was more than she could hold in her arms, and scraps of it fell behind her as she jogged to the car and leaned into the back door, where George was sitting.

She threw the trash inside at his feet. She picked up the scraps that had fallen and threw those into the car as well, spreading them out along the floorboards in back.

She made one more trip to the trash cans and soon walked to the car holding two small, cubed containers.

"Juice boxes," Krunk said.

Esme squeezed the juice boxes until they were empty, and Abigail could imagine their wet wheeze. These she put up front.

On-screen, Esme shut the boy's door, then trotted over to a sprinkler to rinse off her hands.

A minute later she drove away. No one followed her. Krunk paused the clip.

"That's it."

"What was the trash all about?" Abigail said.

Krunk hesitated a moment, elbows on knees, staring into the soft pyramid of his hands. "You really can't talk about this, okay? But the current line of inquiry is drugs. Meeting someone in the desert like that? If so, this may be part of the handoff. Could've been a stash of drugs mixed in with the garbage, waiting for her to pick up. Not much else makes sense. But going back through the day's footage it all looks exactly as you'd expect—drivers chucking out their trash in the most predictable ways. A pink Mary Kay Cadillac dumping out her ashtray."

"A minivan dumping juice boxes," she said.

"Which is why I'm showing you this," he said. "Nothing stands out?"

Abigail shrugged. "With the trash, maybe they were just hungry? People forage when they're desperate."

"Yeah, but there was food in the car. Plus she had cash in her bag when she died. I want to say like sixty bucks, folded into a sock. And over a hundred bucks in her account."

"So she was really collecting trash."

"Looks that way," he said. "And she didn't appear to meet anyone there, or use the phone, unless she borrowed some trucker's phone somewhere away from the camera."

"She definitely didn't seem threatened," Abigail said, squinting, "the way she stuffs her keys into her back pocket before going to pee. If she was scared, she would've had her keys out. In case she needed to get back into the car or to use as a weapon. If that were me, rest area in the middle of nowhere, all alone at midnight, mine would be out."

"Remember that she grew up here," Krunk said. "Being alone in the desert, an hour from home, isn't all that scary if it's your world. It's not like—"

"Not like me?"

Krunk didn't say anything, and she knew that he was at least partially right.

"Still," she said, voice low, "if she was on her way to meet someone she was scared of, she'd be anxious, not stretching and looking at the wind turbines. I mean, she seems pretty carefree. And she wouldn't have brought George with her if she thought she was in danger."

"Unless she didn't have an option."

"Except she did, right? Newspaper said her family was right here in town the whole time."

"They didn't even know about George," he said, "so maybe she just didn't want to have that conversation. Or didn't trust them."

Krunk unplugged the flash drive and looked around the room, as if he were reluctant to leave its cool air and step into the cauldron outside.

"I'll encourage the detectives to come by and talk to you," he said, standing from the couch, "but if you could keep this between us? I don't need to tell you what it means to be unemployed around here, not to mention if I ever get my shit together and try to land a job somewhere else."

"Is that happening?"

"Maybe? I don't remember the last time I slept through the night. Thank god for mandatory drug tests."

"Your secret is safe with me."

"Fabulous," he said, then blinked too much in a way that was cartoonish and sweet. He became more professional as he walked out to the porch. "In the meantime, I'll keep an eye on your place. As for your peeper downstairs, drop the blinds, keep your phone with you. Don't hesitate to call."

When he reached the driveway he gazed downhill at the sunlight hitting the lake. She noticed again how the water seemed to change colors all the time, like a mood ring.

"Nice view. It's peaceful up here."

"Yeah."

"Just lock up and go easy for a few days," he said. "Read a book or do a jigsaw puzzle or something. Call if I can help."

"With a jigsaw puzzle?"

He shrugged and smiled, and as she reentered her cool, dim home, her cheeks were blooming pink.

CHAPTER 13

ESME

The house was so *dark*: that was the first thing Esme noticed when she stepped inside Pastor Kurt's home to babysit, her owl-shaped pocket purse slung over her shoulder. She was nervous to be there, especially at 7:30 on a Saturday morning, when she was usually either sound asleep or trying to cram in some TV before her mom woke up.

It had been over a year since she'd held Baby Grace in the library, so she'd been more than a little surprised when Mrs. Trudy called her home phone the other day and asked if she was free. Esme kept waiting for her to ask whether she'd finished the BabySmart: First Aid for Babysitters class in Wenatchee that all the church girls took on a Saturday in sixth grade while their moms had muffins at Starbies. Esme was probably scooping her mom up off the bathroom floor while they were giving CPR to plastic dolls.

This was her first babysitting job ever.

Pastor Kurt hardly said a word when he answered the door,

just that Mrs. Trudy and Baby Grace would be down soon and she should make herself at home. Then he proceeded to run barefooted through the house, head wet from the shower, yelling something about finding his notes and getting there on time.

He was speaking at a church in Spokane later, and Mrs. Trudy needed a break so she was going, too, but Silas couldn't be trusted to watch his new baby sister—half sister, whatever.

Mrs. Trudy was way younger than Silas's real mom, whom everyone called a *stuck-up bitch* until the cancer, and then a *real fighter*, and then an *angel in Heaven*. A few months after the funeral, Mrs. Trudy had come over from Montana with her father to drop off a load of hogs, stopped into Pastor Kurt's church for Sunday service, and never left. The joke in town was that she came to sell her pork but got porked by the pastor instead.

Esme roamed the small entryway and living room. It was a sunny morning yet every curtain was pinched closed. The walls were dark wood paneling, the carpet brown. A needlework sign saying *Father Forgive Them (Luke 23:34)* hung in the hall next to a simple brass cross and a painting of Camping Jesus, minus the marshmallow fork.

It felt like the kind of house where kids got whipped, even if they weren't that bad. Maybe that explained Silas being a little wacko.

Mrs. Trudy came down wearing a floral dress that was so long Esme thought she might tumble down the stairs.

"Hola!" she said, for some reason. "This girl is driving me bozo! We were up half the night again so she should be ready for a nap. Though you never know with this one!"

Esme's legs were shaking as Mrs. Trudy pressed Baby Grace into her arms.

"You sure you want me?"

"You are too much," Mrs. Trudy said, staring so deeply into Esme's eyes that she felt like she was hypnotizing her.

"Are there any...instructions?"

"Silas can tell you what to feed her and show you where ev-erything is," she said, then lowered her voice and got serious. "Just remember we're paying *you*, not him. You're in charge of Baby Grace." Then a giant smile overtook her face and she was on the move. "Help yourself to breakfast!" she said as she raced into the kitchen and began tossing string cheese and elk jerky into a tote bag. A tiny staticky sock, barely bigger than a thumb, was stuck to the back of her dress.

Silas was at the kitchen table, staring at the back of a cereal box, shoveling cereal into his mouth. His brown hair was long enough to cover his eyes, and acne spread over his cheeks and chin. He barely looked up when Esme entered, but when he saw the sock on his stepmother's back, he pointed at it and ges-tured *shhh*. Esme smirked.

"Time to go!" Mrs. Trudy shouted as they left. "Adios!"

Baby Grace squirmed on Esme's chest. It was hard to believe this was the same little larva she'd held in the library last year. Esme wanted to park her on her hip but her hands were sweaty and she was worried she'd slip out like a jellyfish.

Silas stared at her without offering to help. This was going to be a long day.

Silas was in ninth, the grade above her, but had been held back at least once, maybe twice, so he was two or three years older, and lately he was starting to look it. Since she'd last seen him he'd grown a little smudge of moustache and his Adam's apple had sharpened to a point. He'd always had bucked front teeth, but kids stopped teasing him about them back in fourth grade, at the Halloween Carnival, when he dominated the apple-bobbing contest by latching on to a Fuji every time he plunged his head into the tub of water. He still got teased, but now it was for different stuff, like being a pothead, failing art class, and staring at girls' chests in a way that was universally considered creepy. Esme didn't mind him, but she was also never happy to see him, which was how she felt about most kids in Soap Lake.

As soon as Pastor Kurt's car left the driveway, Silas jumped onto the counter and grabbed a handful of chocolate chips from a Tupperware tub in the cupboard. His Joker T-shirt was so huge it reached his thighs. He hopped down and sat across from Esme, chewing.

Esme perched Baby Grace on the table. Her wispy blond hair smelled fresh.

"Your sister's cute," Esme said.

"For being the spawn of Satan." He stood and pushed his chair back. "Check it out," he said, and scooped Grace off the table, spun her into the cradle of his arm and blew a spitty fart into her cheek. She squirmed and smiled, and when he did it again she began laughing. Esme stood behind him with her hands out like she was guarding him in basketball. He did it three more times and then Grace went from smiling to disturbed and spat up some white curdled drool. Esme wiped her chin and Grace started laughing.

"It's like she's baked," Silas said.

"Don't say that!"

"What if we sparked one and blew the smoke into her ear, the way you do with a dog?"

Esme took Grace out of Silas's clutch. He was making her nervous, but there was something mesmerizing about how little he seemed to care.

"C'mere, baby girl," she said. "Your big brother would never do something like that. He loves you too much. Yes he does!"

"Just don't tell my parents," he said, then he spoke in a musical baby voice that may have been mocking her. "'Cause they're assholes! Yes they are!"

"Don't," Esme said, but she was smiling. She could smell Silas's milky breath and see flakes of skin inside of his ear.

"Idea!" he said. He rummaged in a drawer by the sink and

came back holding a bunch of random stuff: a potato peeler, a purple candle, a Zippo lighter, a pizza cutter, a screwdriver, some rubber bands, a corkscrew, and a buck knife, which was probably the same one he'd used to carve his name into the wooden *Soap Lake History* sign down at the lake:

SILAS

"Silas, don't," she said, holding Baby Grace from behind.

He ignored her. Starting with the buck knife he spread open Grace's little fingers and pressed the handle against her palm. She tightened it in her fist and jerked it around as if it were a rattle. Esme held Grace's wrist away from her body just in case.

"Don't do that!" she said, but she couldn't help but laugh.

"Camera! Quick! Gimme your phone."

"I don't have a phone."

"Cough it up, liar."

Esme did: from the pocket of her owl purse she pulled out the crappy blue flip phone that she'd inherited from Daniel, who'd bought it cheap from some kid at school. It wasn't connected to an account so she couldn't call anyone and the photos always came out foggy. Silas looked at it and laughed, then aimed the phone at Esme holding Grace, and Grace holding the knife. The camera clicked.

"Oh my god! Perfect! *I'll cut ya! I'll cut ya!*"

Esme unpeeled Grace's fingers from the knife and placed it in the sink. But Silas wasn't through. She felt kind of woozy but couldn't stop staring at him, eager to see what he'd do next. He was really pretty funny if you ignored all the bad stuff. One by one he moved on to the other tools, snapping photos of Baby Grace waving each one as Esme, growing braver with each pose, leaned her cheek into her hand and smiled like a '50s housewife, which made Silas slap his hand on the table.

"Yes!"

When Silas lit the taper candle and snugged it into Grace's fist, Esme blew it out and tried to grab it but grabbed his hand as well. They looked at each other and both quickly let go.

The photo shoot was over. Silas called her a worrywart and sat across from her.

"Well, that was fun," he said, but his voice was flat and he didn't mean it. "Want to drink cough syrup?"

"What? No."

"Want to pop a snoozle and run around the block?"

"What?"

"One of Trudy's sleeping pills. It's hilarious."

"I'm babysitting, Silas."

"I'm babeeesiitting, Siwasss," he repeated in a whiny toddler voice. Grace giggled and palmed Esme's face. "Too bad we can't get into my holy father's gun safe. No combo." He tapped the table and looked around. "Forget it. Let's just watch cable."

The basement was even darker than the rest of the house. An exercise bike piled with unfolded laundry sat in the corner. Esme could feel the cool concrete beneath the tan carpet and was tingly at the notion of getting paid to watch TV all day with a baby in her lap. She told herself she and Grace would go back up to the kitchen at the first sign of Silas trying to play truth-or-dare or doing anything weird. She'd successfully fended off an older boy once before, so wasn't that worried, and Daniel loved to brag about how he'd *destroy* anyone who messed with her like that. She believed him.

"We have a shitload of channels," Silas said, standing in front of Pastor Kurt's TV. It was huge and gray and blocky—a rich people's TV from fifteen years ago, which was a poor people's TV today.

Esme stared at the dusty screen, but nothing happened when Silas pressed the buttons on the remote: his dad had disconnected the cable.

"He is *such* a prick. He unplugs the box when he leaves because he doesn't want me watching anything violent or sexy."

Somehow between the kitchen and the basement Baby Grace had fallen asleep against Esme's neck.

"You have any board games?" she said.

"Noah's Ark Monopoly? Nah. I'll figure it out."

Silas plugged in the TV, but the screen just glowed blue and she smelled hot dust. As if to test the laws of physics, the monstrous TV sat atop a waist-high entertainment stand made of flimsy particle board with peeling veneer grain. It rocked a bit as Silas squeezed in behind it. Esme didn't know how he fit back there, though he was pretty scrawny. He held up a black coaxial cord.

"Aha!"

He tried to screw the cable into the TV.

"I can't see where it goes," he said between grunts. "Grab the flashlight on top the fridge."

Esme could feel the warm weight of Grace sleeping in her arms, and she tried to imagine carrying her back upstairs and climbing on a chair and reaching the top of the fridge for the flashlight. She thought about leaving her on the couch but then worried she might roll off. A fringed Seahawks blanket was draped over the back of a chair, so she spread it over the carpet between the coffee table and the television, and laid Grace there.

"On top the fridge," Silas said loudly. "Flashlight."

"She can't crawl, can she?"

"Dude. She's not going anywhere."

She found the flashlight above the fridge, then found the Tupperware in the cupboard and treated herself to some chocolate chips. She could hear Silas in the basement, grumbling. Halfway down the steps, still chewing, she heard him utter, *"Fuck!"*

"Wha?" she said, her mouth gloppy with chocolate.

"Fuck!"

She stopped and her palm pressed the wall. Behind the television, Silas squirmed.

"Esme, hey come help!"

She hopped down another step and could hear the creak of particle board as Silas struggled behind the TV stand, bent in half, bumping into it—

"Esme!"

A flash of panic immediately became blame. She had *asked* him.

"Come help!"

She had *asked* if Grace could crawl.

"Esme, fucking help!"

But that wasn't the point. The point was the blunt weight of the television—

"Get Baby Grace!"

And the direction it would fall—

"Esme, help her!"

The point was a sleeping baby.

Yet Esme stood at the base of the stairs, watching the room as if behind glass. Silas was so red he was nearly purple, struggling to hold the TV cord with one hand, the top of the TV with the other. The stand beneath was tipping.

"Get her get her get her!"

The television sliding—

"Esme, grab!"

The fake wood buckled until the nails and staples popped, the sides of the shelf shot out, and it all finally collapsed. For a fraction of a second, Esme and Silas locked eyes across the room as the television slid, toppled, dropped—

please get her esme please for me

But Esme turned, unable to look, unable to even be there, and stormed up the stairs and down the hall, past the brass cross and the *Father Forgive Them* needlework, and out the front door just in time to hear the sounds of her life changing forever.

CHAPTER 14

ABIGAIL

"Like a *body*?"

"Yes, Eli," Abigail said into her phone, absently opening and closing his empty dresser drawers. "A woman named Esme. Twenty-six. She's dead."

It had been three days since little George had burst from the sagebrush, but Eli—fresh from his research trip—had only this morning returned to the grid and received the onslaught of her distressing messages.

"Abigail, that's *awful*!" he said, and she could picture him rubbing his hair as he paced his Polish dorm room, overcome with resolve. "I'll catch the next flight home. I just need to talk to Dr. Salecki and find someone to—"

"No need," she said, "I'm fine." Though she wasn't. She was pretty sure Eli really would abandon his project and jump on a plane, arrive with flowers and a pair of amber earrings bought at the Warsaw airport. But as much as she wanted him here, she wanted him *there* even more, overseas, pursuing his work in the way that made him happy, maybe because she knew that a trip home would be more performative than practical, and might sow quiet seeds of resentment between them. So as she spoke she filtered what she shared, omitting her visit from the Peeping Ghost, but telling Eli that the local cops had been surprisingly supportive. She didn't mention Krunk by name, nor did she discuss the video they'd watched of Esme gathering trash at the rest area, but she did tell Eli about meeting Sophia, and explained how knowing someone so close made her feel safer. She left out Sophia's history as an addict.

"Not the place with the extension cord?" Eli said.

"She's a *librarian*, Eli. She's nice."

"I'm sure she's awesome. Can't wait to meet her. Just don't let her into my lab, okay?"

They tried steering the conversation away from Eli's research and into shared territory, food and bills, and whether she'd received his postcards and packages (pictures of Polish lakes, a painted wooden horse, a bag of buttery toffee she'd devoured in a sitting), but inevitably they meandered back to his work.

Eli was desperate for data again: he had another lab task for her.

"This could be bad," he said with concern. He told her exactly which binder she needed to find. "You'll see long lists of elements and chemicals saying 'ppm,' parts per million? Scan it all. Any chance you can do it soon?"

Out her bedroom window, the bearded guy in a puffy red coat walked past in the street again, still clutching his paper map as if lost. She'd seen him wandering by every few days, sweltering inside of his coat, hood up, even when the temperature broke one hundred. And he always seemed intent on *not* looking in her window, which made her feel like he was looking in her window.

This town with its wandering dudes. She locked the front door.

"I'll send it in a little while," she said, but didn't add, *once the coast is clear.*

★ ★ ★

Once the coast was clear, Abigail scanned and sent Eli's paperwork, then drove across town to the settlement of *tiny homes between the apples* on the far side of the lake, with only a vague idea of where to find Esme's mom and brother. She took Medusa, her twenty-year-old gorgon-green Subaru that she'd towed out behind the U-Haul. Abigail loved Medusa, but she had a tendency to break down in tunnels and drive-throughs, and her muffler was missing, so it sounded like a lawn mower was throttling in the back seat.

She drove up one dirt lane and down the next, careful not to hit a literal chicken literally crossing the road. Soon she came upon a turquoise cottage with a patchy yard and a large ash tree out front. Then she saw George. He was standing inside of a plastic wading pool, using it as a sandbox. When he spotted her climbing out of Medusa he ran across the yard to her.

"Hi, George! Remember me?"

Abigail tried not to act surprised when he pulled her into a hug. She brushed his dusty hair to the side. He was wearing jean shorts, cowboy boots with hollow teardrops, and a gray *Incredibles* T-shirt, a size too small. He smelled like maple syrup.

It had been days since she'd seen him in the desert. She'd decided to wait until after the memorial service, a tiny, private affair, hoping to grant Esme's family more room to grieve. Now she regretted not coming sooner.

As she held him, feeling his hummingbird heart again, a voice spoke behind her:

"*J.Jill* to the rescue. I've seen *this* movie before."

Abigail looked up. A man with thick black hair and light brown skin was standing in a pink button-down, gray jeans, sandals. He was around thirty and the sides of his hair were cut close and clean, the top swooshed back.

"Let me guess," he continued. "You want to enroll him in Montessori? Teach him to play the cello?"

"Did you just call me *J.Jill?*" she said, still processing that one.

"Maybe?" he said, tilting his head, amused.

She whispered over the boy's head. "*He* found *me.*"

The man smiled and her defensiveness softened. A duct-taped boxing bag hung from the ash tree behind him. He caught her looking at it.

"Don't worry," he said, studying his knuckles, "it's mostly for show. Like those yard signs for home security."

"Maybe I should get one," she mumbled, and he glanced up and met her eye.

"Everything okay?"

"I just came to extend my condolences. And to check on George. You're Daniel?"

He nodded. "And you're Abigail, right? The *walker.*"

She liked him right away, even with the Montessori comment, maybe because he smelled good when he shook her hand, like soil and soap, or because of the raw grief beneath his every word. He tried to cover it up, but not very hard.

"Do you want to sit?"

"Only if you don't call me J.Jill."

"I'm a little irritable right now. As you can imagine."

Daniel led her to a pair of sagging chairs in the shade of the tree, next to a stone ring of midsummer flowers, echinacea and peonies.

"Hey guy," he said when the boy followed them over. "Go dig."

The boy strutted across the lawn, back to the wading pool full of dirt.

"How's he doing?"

Daniel rubbed a thin white scar on his chin. "It was a full day before we even knew his *name*, not that he responds to much. It's like he's encased in ice. Him hugging you back there is about as peppy as he's been. It's good to see."

"I'm sure he'll come around."

"It might help if I knew a single thing about him. The day I learned my sister was murdered was the same day I learned she had a kid, so it's all new to me. But he's seeing some woman from Wenatchee, a shrink with a box of art supplies. You'd probably like her. She drives a Prius."

"Do you call her J.Jill, too?"

"I saved that one just for you," he said, smiling. "She's been here twice already, sits next to him on the couch and shows him old photos of me and Esme together, apparently so he knows I'm his uncle. She thinks there must have been a picture of me on his fridge back at home, in Bakersfield or wherever, which is why he's pretty loose around me. My mom, too. He was expecting to meet us, I guess."

"Your mom's here now?"

"Depends on what you mean by *here*," he said, glancing up at the house. "This is hard on her. Obviously."

"And he's not speaking?"

"Yesterday he asked for juice, but shoved it away when I got him some. At least he's showing emotion. His shrink told me the not-talking might have to do with him hiding from his mom's killer that night, being forced to stay quiet so he wouldn't be found? And last night I found out the hard way that he breaks into a panic when he has to sit in the back seat of a car, but apparently only when it's dark. I think he's okay up front. Cops say there's a dad in California, but he's been out of the picture since Esme got pregnant. She had full custody. He's never even met George, so it's looking like he's ours now."

"Is the dad—?"

"A suspect? The cops say it wasn't him. He was working the electronics counter at a Walmart in Bakersfield at the time. Long out of the picture. Apparently Esme raised George alone. Came here alone. Didn't even call. Not the night she arrived, not in all the years since she left. No social media, no birthday cards, nothing. I had no idea where she was, but I always knew she'd be okay as long as she didn't come back *here*. So why did she? And why *now*?"

Abigail settled into the silence that followed, watching black birds murmur over the distant orchards. She'd been hoping to ask Daniel whether Esme was into drugs, and if that might explain her meeting in the desert, the way Sophia and the task force thought it had, but he was staring at the boy with such pain that she couldn't.

The screen door opened and a woman with stringy white hair in a pink bathrobe came out to the porch and peered into the mailbox. She flipped through a small pile of mail and, without looking in their direction, dropped a purple magazine onto the porch's top step.

"Yours," she announced without a glance.

George looked up, worried, then returned to his digging.

"Hey, Mom," Daniel said, "this is Abigail."

Esme's mom turned to go back inside, but might have raised her hand into a half-hearted wave. Either that or flicked something off the screen. Her bathrobe dragged over the threshold.

"I can tell she likes you," Daniel said out of the corner of his mouth.

Abigail couldn't really blame Esme's mom for her bitterness: her daughter's ashes had barely cooled and already she was expected to be sipping her drinks from a *World's Best Grandma* mug and stocking the freezer with Otter Pops. She hadn't even known she was a grandma. That had to wreak havoc on the psyche.

"Maybe that's why Esme came back here," Abigail said. "So George could meet his grandma and Uncle Daniel."

"But we could've saved up and met at Disney or something. She knew it would only take a single call. I just can't believe she came back."

"What happened that was so awful back then? When she was in high school."

"Why'd she *leave*?" he said. "Wow. You really aren't from

here. Simple answer is the love of her life got shot right in front of her. Eighteen years old. They got caught up in some drama and her boyfriend ended up dead. She blamed herself. I blame this country. And this fucking town."

"So she just left?"

"After graduation. Middle of the night. I thought she'd be back. Should've followed her."

"You think George understands what happened?"

"He was with her when she died," he said, lowering his voice. "Cops said *as* she died. Something about the blood pattern on his pajamas."

Abigail could picture Esme's blood, sticky on his skin and creating crispy curls in his hair. She'd been smelling it for days, awake and asleep.

"Yeah," she said, barely above a whisper, "he was pretty—"

"Covered," he said. "They said she must've been sitting there with the screwdriver stuck in her for a long time. Up under her ribs, I guess. Does that make sense?"

"From what I saw."

"And the kid was with her. His prints were the only ones on the handle."

The shade cast by the ash tree seemed to thicken, and Abigail could feel the shadow sliding into her lungs, making it hard to breathe.

"You alright?" Daniel asked.

She thought about the blood on the boy and realized what it meant: he'd tried to take it out. The screwdriver. Of course he had.

"What is it?" he said.

She thought about those gruesome stories of construction workers being carted to the emergency room with a piece of rebar sticking out of their chest, taped into place by the paramedics; or the wounded soldiers on *M*A*S*H* with a piece of shrapnel damming up an artery, the only reason they were still alive. The lesson was always the same: *don't yank out the arrow.* Without it, their life would pump right out.

The screwdriver had dangled out of Esme at an angle because the boy had unplugged it, then pressed his palms over her abdomen like a medic. And maybe dragged the blanket into her lap to cover the blood. Esme would have died anyway, but more slowly, with a chance of being saved.

"Seriously—what is it?"

"Just thinking about finding her," she said.

Daniel might not yet have realized the boy's role in his sister's death, and Abigail swore to herself she'd never mention it to him or anyone else.

"Do you want a drink or something?" he said. "You look kind of..."

"I'll just hit this," she said, and lifted a dribbling garden hose out of the flower bed.

As soon as she raised it to her lips, Daniel touched her shoulder.

"Yeah, don't drink from that," he said, setting it back in the flowers. "Irrigation water. Great for washing tractors and watering fields, but not so great for the gut. That water traveled all the way here from Canada, collecting grody little souvenirs the whole way. We have a separate water line to the house. One of the benefits of all these orchards. That and the free insecticides blowing through our screen doors. Not a bug in sight." He stepped up the porch. "Sit tight and I'll grab some Kool-Aid."

He disappeared inside, and Abigail wandered along the flower bed to play with George, but paused as she passed the porch steps. The purple magazine Daniel's mom had left there wasn't a magazine at all, but rather a course catalog for University of Washington's Cinema Studies Program. Abigail picked it up for long enough to see it was addressed to Daniel.

It was clear that he was conflicted about being stuck in this house with his mom, but the arrival of the catalog suggested he'd been making concrete plans to get out when Esme had been murdered. Film school in Seattle. With George now living here, she imagined he'd be putting his plans on hold.

When Daniel came out with cups of punch, Abigail was kneeling in the dirt next to George. Daniel dragged a chair over.

She chugged her punch and the boy did the same. Then she helped him tug the hose over and began filling up the hole he'd dug. He grabbed the coffee can he'd been using as a scoop and turned it upside down next to the little lake he'd made.

"Are you seeing this?" she said, sitting up. "If that's the lake…"

"What?" Daniel said.

"Is he making a lava lamp? On the shore."

"What?"

"The coffee can. If that hole is the lake, then the can is like a giant—"

Just then George grabbed the can and filled it with dirt and tossed it to the side.

Daniel stared at her.

"Mind's playing tricks," she said.

"Is it?"

"Okay," she said, lowering her voice, "this is kind of wacky, but maybe Esme wanted him to see the World's Largest Lava Lamp? Maybe it gave her an excuse to come back here. A destination. Mommy-son road trip."

"Except it's not a lava lamp," Daniel said. "It's a slab of concrete. Holding a giant metal bucket. Permanently on hold because some archaeologist found old flint knapping, or some engineer didn't like the specs."

"Yeah, but Esme may have seen the pictures online and thought it was up and running."

Daniel shook his head. "No chance. Only a bonehead."

"Yeah," Abigail said, thumbing at herself. "Only a bonehead."

"Wait. You thought?"

She kept nodding, eyes closed, feeling embarrassed.

"For real? Like when you moved here?"

"I was so excited," she said, dropping her head. "Those pictures online are totally convincing. If you don't know."

Daniel turned his back to her, suppressing his laughter. George paused his playing and smirked.

"Your husband didn't tell you? The cops said he's the research guy. I know it's not my business, but he had to know that thing wasn't up and running. There's no way some guy moving here to study the lake isn't going to inquire about the hundreds of visitors standing around the giant lava lamp, throwing their Rainier cans into the water."

"Except I never directly asked him or anything," she said.

"Yeah, but you shouldn't've had to."

"You're right," she said, standing up. "It's really not your business."

He held up his hands and nodded. "I'm sorry. I didn't mean anything by it."

She squatted next to the boy, swishing her fingers in the muddy water.

"But seriously," he said, squatting next to her, grinning widely, "thank you for that. I really needed a laugh."

"Glad I could help."

George, she realized, had stopped playing and was kneeling in the mud with his hands in his lap, staring up at the plateau.

CHAPTER 15

ESME

Deep in the orchard near the landfill, Esme leaned against an apple tree and hugged her knees, waiting for TreeTop to arrive—to toss her into his wheelbarrow and roll her away, just as he had her father.

Every few seconds, the sound of the falling television crashed through her thoughts. It had happened just this morning, but felt like years had passed.

The day soon disappeared. Darkness crossed the sky, silencing the birds and bringing the cold.

Finally, after nightfall, she heard him coming.

His squeaking wheel was followed by the light of his lantern sliding between trees. Shadows tangled together, black branches crisscrossing the ground.

She scooched into the tree, its bark smooth against her cheek.

And then he was there, emerging from a smudge-pot fog, standing over her, exactly like the cover of the activity book in the library: TreeTop, holding an old-fashioned lantern, his mask clicking as he breathed.

The lantern blinded her as he raised a hatchet above his head. It was time to feed the trees.

es ge up

In the blinding light, TreeTop's towering silhouette peeled away, shrank, divided into three.

"Esme! Get up!"

Daniel was standing over her, flanked by a pair of cops. He roughly shook her shoulder.

"Esme!"

She should have known that Daniel would find her. Back when they used to play outside together, she'd shown him the spot where she'd seen TreeTop—where she'd seen their father's boot.

"Where's the baby, Esme?" he said. "What'd you do with her?"

"Where is Baby Grace?" said the cop with the crewcut. He was the younger, fitter, of the two, but he had tiny yellow corn teeth and his breath smelled foul, so she studied the tag on his shirt: *McDaid*. The other cop, Garza, was an older, heavier man with enormous ears and a moustache that went into his mouth. He looked worried. No: scared.

Daniel explained that there were other cops back at the house with Silas, waiting for Pastor Kurt and Mrs. Trudy to return from their spiritual journey to the promised land of Spokane.

"Esme, this is serious," Daniel said. "Silas said you ran away with the baby. Is Grace here somewhere?"

The cop named Garza shined his light up and down the rows, as if Baby Grace might crawl out from between the trees, palming a small green apple. The cop named McDaid thumbed his belt and stared down at Esme.

Her throat felt raw. All day she'd been reimagining the scene, wondering could she undo it.

"It was an accident," she said.

"They think you *took* her," Daniel said, kneeling next to the tree.

"Like took her *body*?" she said.

"You're gonna fry for this," McDaid said.

Garza sat down and braced his palms on the crabgrass. "We just want to help her," he said, gently. "Do you have her here somewhere with you?"

"Why would *I* have Baby Grace?" she said.

"Silas said you stole her away to raise her on your own."

"What? I *left* her with Silas."

The men looked at each other.

"With Silas?" Daniel said.

"Of course with Silas. When he knocked the TV over, Grace was on the blanket where it fell and I was coming downstairs—"

"Dear god. That's why the TV. Oh, dear god."

"I just ran away," she said, sobbing. "I know I should've stayed, but the TV fell and I couldn't help and I couldn't look. I don't even have my BabySmart certificate so I couldn't give CPR or do stitches or anything. I couldn't even *look*."

"Goddamned Silas," McDaid said, reaching for his radio. "We need to get back over there. Now."

The volunteer firefighter who found Baby Grace curled into the massive flowerpot in the shed behind the church thought he was hearing a puppy as he approached. Pastor Kurt and his flock stored the lawn mowers and snow shovels in that shed, so Silas had access to the key.

"She was so quiet I almost missed her," the volunteer said. "Sounded just like a little puppy, but I'll be damned if it wasn't that baby!"

Not a whimpering pup, but a baby girl inside of a flowerpot, coated in spiderwebs, with a tarp tossed loosely over her head. When the volunteer lifted her out, her diaper was so sodden it almost fell off.

"I knew better than to move her," he said to anyone who asked. "But I was so excited I practically threw her through the roof. Imagine, finding that girl alive! I get misty just thinking about it."

Two days had passed since the television collapsed, but Baby Grace's injuries were mild, all things considered, the same sort that could happen falling off a swing or taking a hard tumble down the stairs: a hairline fracture in her right tibia, and heavy bruising on her thighs and shins from the blunt cube of the television. When Silas pulled her out from under the TV—just her lower half got smushed—her kneecap strained and she suffered scrapes from her hips to her toes, but she was lucky.

In the shed, the volunteer assessed that her vitals were strong, yet she could barely raise her eyelids. She sank into the arms of a medic, and Mrs. Trudy and Pastor Kurt sped to the hospital to be by her side.

The next morning, before the ink on the release form had even dried, Mrs. Trudy was on the highway with Baby Grace in her car seat, speeding toward her family's hog farm in Montana and swearing that her girl would never sleep under the same roof as Silas again.

Shortly thereafter, the real story emerged:

After the TV fell, Grace had been so lethargic she didn't even cry. Silas had assumed she was dead, or close to it. He panicked. Plopped her into a wagon, covered her with a towel, and rolled her through the alley to the church's shed, where he hid her in the flowerpot.

Then he parked himself in a church pew, holding quiet vigil. As volunteers scoured the fields and ravines, he secretly gathered jars of baby food from the community kitchen and fed her peas and potatoes with his fingers, and the occasional squirt of Benadryl to help her sleep.

His plan, he said, had been to leave her in the flowerpot, as if she were an injured bird in a shoebox. He'd bring her food every day, and in a week or so, he'd pretend to discover her crawling out in the desert and be hailed as a hero. Big brother to the rescue.

It was a stupid plan, born of a desperate mind—and it did little to explain the hank of Trudy's clothesline, sliced from its post in the backyard, that one of the town cops had found near the wagon in the shed. Nor did it explain the shiny black garbage bag of bricks sitting next to it, like a kit designed for drowning an unwanted pup.

CHAPTER 16

ABIGAIL

Abigail opened her front door to find Sophia, wearing an American flag bandana around her neck and holding out a dog-eared trio of Sweet Valley High novels.

"Elixir," she said, "for the boredom."

Abigail smiled, unexpectedly touched to have received a gift she hadn't known she'd needed.

Sophia was wearing jeans and a white T-shirt from some 10K Mud Run she definitely hadn't run. In the morning light, her hair was the color of apricots, her rainbow-threaded rattail extra fuzzed.

"Are you ready?" she said, expectant. "The parade?"

"How is it already the Fourth?" Abigail said, squinting at the hazy skies and flagrant sun: nine in the morning and already an oven. The poplar trees along her driveway drooped like sticks of taffy, and she found herself curling inward at the idea of being out in public, on display, especially after finding the boy. "I'm not really feeling it, Sophia."

"Nonsense. You need this," Sophia said, as if it were a prescription. "And bring coins. *Lots*."

"Why coins?" When Sophia didn't answer, Abigail said, "I'll be quick."

The crowds on Main Street were modest, with nearly as many people lining up to participate in the parade as watching from the sidewalk. There were little kids speaking Spanish and old women speaking Ukrainian and leather-clad bikers eating ice cream in the street.

As the two women walked through, the sidewalk practically parted around them and people turned away, suddenly occupied. Abigail wondered if it had to do with her finding the boy, but Sophia walked so fast that she had no chance to ask. She didn't stop until they reached the Healing Lake Hotel and claimed an empty stretch of sidewalk out front.

The hotel's clean, contemporary facade looked out of step with the old-fashioned storefronts, mostly vacant, that lined the street. Ceramic pots and bright squares of pea gravel surrounded its glass door, and farther down, a small fountain dribbled down a slab of basalt.

"I used to work here," Sophia said, "so I'd stand out here and smoke. Perfect spot to watch a parade."

"Work how?"

"Housekeeping. When I remembered to show up. The owners, Mr. and Mrs. Polk, were really good to me. Best coffee in town, too."

In the window, Abigail saw rows of glowing lava lamps and lava lamp T-shirts, like the one Krunk had been wearing.

More people glanced away as they wandered past.

"Sophia? Is it me, or is everyone pretending we don't exist?"

"It's not you. It's me, actually," she said. "I should've warned you. Small town. Small circles. It's like that everywhere I go."

"Because…?"

"Because the people I hung around with when I was an addict despised me once I got clean. And the people who were around after I got clean despise me because of all the rotten things I did as an addict." Her sight drifted past Abigail, and she brightened and lifted her hand in a wave. "Well, except for this guy."

A bald man in a Hawaiian shirt and acid-washed jean shorts was crossing the street, but he halted and grinned at the sight of Sophia, and outstretched his tanned arms. "*This guy* what?"

"This guy...doesn't put up with my crap," she said, embracing him.

"Come as you are," he said, holding her shoulders and taking her in. "Howdy, Sophia."

"Hi, Kurt."

The guy had florid spots on his nose and wore a large silver cross, visible against a nest of white chest hair. Sophia introduced him as a local pastor who hosted recovery meetings at the church over in Quincy.

"For as long as they'll let me," he said, with a self-deprecating shrug.

"Thought you were in Montana?"

"Here this week, there next."

Abigail hung back a little as he and Sophia caught up. He talked about his daughter and ex-wife who lived in Great Falls, and how he'd been trying to get settled over there but was having a hard time finding permanent work outside of the casinos or fracking fields.

"Neither's good for sobriety," he said.

"It'll happen," Sophia said.

In the few minutes that he stood chatting, two women said *hi* to him as they passed, and an old cowboy shook his hand without a word. Before long Abigail noticed him scratching at his razor-burned neck and glancing up the street toward the Basalt Tavern, where a dozen people were outside, drinking beer from plastic cups.

Sophia pinched his shirt. "You okay?"

"Better find my spot before it starts," he said, checking his watch.

"You know how to reach me?"

"Of course."

"Stay clean."

He nodded, and they watched him make his way through the crowd.

"Has to be rough," Abigail said. "Trying to have a normal life with people drinking everywhere you go. The constant lure."

"I can vouch for that," Sophia said, lowering her voice. "But Kurt didn't take off because of booze. He took off because of the Polks. Owners of the hotel."

When Abigail turned to look at the hotel's facade, she saw a middle-aged couple standing in the doorway beneath a dangling dream catcher, peering out of the glass. The man had big gray hair and wore grandpa overalls and a black *BELIEVE* T-shirt. His hands rested on a woman's shoulders, his chin towering above her curly gray hair and purple specs. Abigail scootched over to avoid blocking their view, and they gave her a thumbs-up.

"What's his beef with them?"

"You know about the shooting?" Sophia said, under her breath, looking out toward the street. "Terrible. Maybe eight years ago. The Polks' son was murdered right in that lobby. Just finished high school. On his way to college. Really nice kid."

"Esme's boyfriend," Abigail whispered, recalling how Daniel had called the young man who got shot *the love of her life*. "That's why Esme left town?"

"And why Pastor Kurt avoids this place." Sophia met her eye. "His son was the shooter."

"Oh shit."

"Yeah. And he used Kurt's gun. The whole thing upended his life. Went from owning a house in town to living in a little camper on the edge of an alfalfa farm. Not a surprise that he became a full dipso." Sophia lifted her chin and shook out her hands. "*But*, last I checked we were at a *parade*, Abigail, not a funeral. So can we talk about something else?"

"Sorry."

A group of vets carrying flags set the parade in motion, followed by a glammed-up mom and her tiara-wearing daughter standing in the bed of a pickup, singing gospel songs through a karaoke machine. A family of Mormon kids on unicycles came spiraling behind them, tossing candy, followed by a group of charros stepdancing their horses and charras in colorful dresses, perched on their saddles like flowers.

As the groups filed past, Abigail watched the kids waiting for tossed candy, crouched in the gutter, twitching their fingertips like runners at a starting line. When the treats flew they dove, scraping their knuckles on the street and shoving candy into their mouths and spitting out pieces of gravel.

She was hoping to see George among them, but knew that was unlikely. Before leaving Daniel's home the other day, she'd offered to babysit, and was somewhat surprised last night when he reached out to take her up on it. Grandma had needed a break and Daniel was stuck at work, so Abigail had watched the boy at her house for a few fun, exhausting hours. Daniel's only rule had been to keep him out of the public eye, especially with his mom's killer moving freely through the world.

Maybe through this crowd.

Sophia nudged her gently and pointed up the block. "Ready?"

A battered truck trickled into sight, pulling a flatbed trailer. There was a bedsheet flapping off the side with a single word spray-painted across it:

BELIEVE!

Only when the trailer was much closer could Abigail see the single, foot-high lava lamp bolted to the center of the flatbed.

Based on the crowd's response, it might as well have already been sixty feet tall.

Mr. and Mrs. Polk, the couple in the hotel doorway, came outside and raised their arms and gave a celebratory, *"Yew-yew-yeww!"*

"Aww," Abigail said, feeling a jolt of happiness that caused her to shout, too. "I believe!"

"Coins!" Sophia said, cupping her palm with nickels and quarters.

As the truck passed people lobbed coins and crumpled bills onto the flatbed, contributing to the cause, and a ponytailed guy with a black beret and a gray goatee walked behind, grinning and bucketing the strays. Sophia tossed all of her coins in a single throw, so Abigail did the same. They pinged all over the place, but people hopped off the sidewalk to collect them, and dropped them into the pails.

"Cotton candy," Sophia said, and disappeared into the crowd, leaving her alone.

Watching people rally like this, it occurred to Abigail that she'd thought a lot about what the Lava Lamp would do for her, but not about what it would do for this town. *Build it and they will come*: the spa-era cottages in collapse all around would be scrubbed clean, IKEA kitchens installed, Costco couches placed before wall-mounted televisions. People would be hired to manage vacation rentals, to sell ice cream, to plumb and to wire and to build. And the World's Largest Lava Lamp would glow over this lake like an ancient obelisk.

The lake is the real magic, Eli had said. They would come for the lamp and discover the lake.

"You need a T-shirt!"

She turned to see Mr. Polk, flanked by his wife.

"I've been meaning to get one."

Mrs. Polk was perky and fit, with yoga arms beneath the rolled-up sleeves of her T.

"What's the holdup on the Lava Lamp?" Abigail asked. "Besides money."

"The whole project is an engineer's nightmare," Mr. Polk said, watching the truck fade down Main. "It's one thing to make a lamp work on a bedside table, and quite another when it's sixty feet tall on a lakeshore and exposed to extreme sun and snow and drunk dudes with guns."

Because of the scale, he explained, the temperature of the fluid would have to be extremely high to keep the globules moving. Not to mention the drain on the grid to heat it like that, plus all the lighting and pumps and maintenance. And curved glass thick enough to deflect potshots from every armed asshole in America.

"Which is *a lot*," Abigail said.

"The powers that be thought if they built the base, the rest would fall into place. Some fool convinced them they'd breeze right through the state's mandated studies. Cultural heritage. Environmental impact. Big hurdles. No breezing through."

"And you are officially sorry you asked," Mrs. Polk said.

"For what it's worth," Abigail said meekly, "I still believe?"

"We do, too," Mr. Polk said, putting his arm around his wife. "Fuckinay."

Sophia emerged from the crowd and handed Abigail a pinch of cotton candy.

Mrs. Polk looked back and forth between the two neighbors. "You two know each other?"

"Hi, Mrs. Polk."

They did the awkward dance for a second then embraced. Mr. Polk pulled a strand of pink cotton candy out of his wife's hair and ate it. Winked.

The Polks stepped back and focused on the parade as a few cop cruisers inched past, flashers strobing.

Krunk was in one of the cruisers, chucking candy as he drove. When he saw Mr. Polk he gave a big grin and Mr. Polk stepped forward and pointed at him with both hands, rapid-fire, like a coach congratulating a kid on the court. After a moment he stood behind Mrs. Polk, mumbling, "Good kid, good kid."

Abigail caught Krunk's eye and he tossed a handful of caramel cubes right at her. She gave a fake frown and he tipped his hat.

Sophia stared at her. "You guys buddies?"

"Krunk?" she said. "Why? Is he—?"

"Single? Ready to mingle?"

"No! I just mean *cool?*"

"I only know him professionally," Sophia said, giving a boo-hoo lip and holding out her wrists in the universal sign for wearing handcuffs. "But since you asked, yes, he's single. He was supposed to be getting married to this adorable little peach who works in the city billing office. Blonde, short hair, always looks like she just burst out of a giant cake? I'm a romantic, but she was the mean girl in the cafeteria. No wonder he got cold feet." She tilted her head, suddenly ponderous. "You know, that used to be code for being gay, back in the day—having *cold feet.*"

"No, it absolutely did not mean that," Abigail said, laughing. "You are a font of misinformation."

"Trust me. I'm a librarian."

"Anyway," Abigail said, rattling her head, "I'm not asking about his love life."

"You would be if you saw him jogging past with his shirt off. He's just begging to get kidnapped. Tied to a rocking chair."

"I don't recall that scene in any Sweet Valley High novels."

Sophia squinted up the street and her smile faded. "Ah. Shit. This."

Up the block an uneasy buzz filled the air. Kids scrambled behind their parents, looking terrified, and some began to cry. Abigail's first awful thought was to listen for gunshots.

"Pay attention!" a mother said to her son, swatting the back of his head.

A few of the dads were laughing at the kids diving between

their legs, but most of the adults took a few sober steps back from the street, and some even gathered their things to leave.

"What is happening?" Abigail said. "Sophia?"

"Here we go."

Abigail looked up the block and tightly folded her arms. It was *him*, in the middle of the street: the guy she saw in her window the other night. The tall figure wrapped in white. Her Peeping Ghost.

"Sophia?"

Only he wasn't a guy, exactly, he was a monster, fifteen feet tall and towering over the group of farmers marching below. All of them wore cowboy hats and boots and pearl-button shirts. Some circled around him on nervous, jumpy horses that shat round lumps into the street. A hefty, mutton-chopped man in spangled regalia led the group, rocking on a pony like a ringmaster leading Kong. He wore a white nudie suit encrusted with rhinestones, and when he turned, Abigail noticed a bejeweled apple tree on the back of his jacket, its branches and leaves and perfect little apples creeping around his ribs and up his lapels.

She took a step back and bumped into Mrs. Polk.

"Sorry," she managed to say.

"I get it," Mrs. Polk said, not taking her eyes off the group.

The giant, she could see now, was a man on covered stilts being puppeteered by a few cowboys with thin rods below. His arms were white and strangely long, flowing out from his body and capped with long black gloves. He was wearing a baggy white biosuit that stretched from his shins to the hood on his papier-mâché head. Big dark goggles and a protective mask covered his face. And between the group of men below she could see that, on the bottom of his eight-foot stilts, he wore the black muckboots of an orchard worker.

A crying little girl latched on to Abigail's thigh, before realizing she wasn't her mom and bolting away.

"That's him," Abigail whispered.

"*Him* who?" Sophia said, mesmerized by the street.

"That giant was looking in my window the other night. In Eli's lab. *Watching* me."

Sophia looked suddenly pale. Her fingers stayed on her lip.

"You had a visit from *TreeTop*?"

"Who?"

Before Abigail could ask Sophia what the hell had just happened and who the hell was TreeTop, the masked giant was gone, and a fire truck drove up Main Street, signaling the end of the parade. Its siren blared so loudly that the hotel windows rattled and Abigail's fillings buzzed with pain.

Up and down the street, everyone plugged their ears.

CHAPTER 17

ABIGAIL

Abigail awoke to a text from Daniel, sent at dawn from the orchard where he worked as a crew manager.

at work & george is home with gramma if you want to pop in. no pressure.

Daniel had been reluctant but relieved when she babysat George the other day, so she had a feeling that was a hard text to send. The guy clearly needed a hand, so she had a quick breakfast and walked down the hill, past the gas station and along Main Street. As she was passing the library, she saw Sophia in the parking lot, unloading books from the book drop into a big canvas bag, and it occurred to her that bringing some stories to George might brighten his morning and give them something to do.

"Hey," she said, crossing the lot. "Recommend any books for a four-year-old?"

Sophia scanned the empty street, reticent. Overhead, an American flag drooped in the heat.

"Come inside and you can browse while I get ready to open. But if Miss Nellie comes..."

"She's your boss?"

"Overlord. But she got me this job. Which I need."

"I can just wait until you open," Abigail said.

"It's fine," she said, holding out an armload of books. "Grab these."

After walking from her house in the sun, the library's cool indoor air, smelling of paper and Play-Doh, was a relief. The fluorescent fixtures were off, but the space inside was illuminated by natural light from the windows overlooking the lake. A stepladder leaned against the wall next to the reference books and old celebrity *READ* posters—Nicolas Cage, Whoopi Goldberg—twitched above it. Between the shelves were wooden tables and mismatched lamps. Through the window on the far wall, the World's Largest Missing Lava Lamp cast its shadow over the shore.

Yesterday, on the hot walk home from the parade, Abigail had peppered Sophia with questions about TreeTop, but her friend had been evasive. She kept calling TreeTop the *town mascot*, as if he'd cartwheeled across a Little League field, not peeped through her window, tapping the glass and scaring the hell out of Abigail.

Maybe today she'd open up.

Abigail browsed the picture books as Sophia hustled through her opening procedures. There was something eerie about being in a public space when no one from the public was there, so she was glad when Sophia came over to the kids' corner to fluff the beanbags and wipe down the tables.

"Sophia?" she said, standing in front of her. "Just tell me—should I be worried?"

"Because TreeTop was watching you? That's nothing to fret about. Usually."

"Usually?"

"Whoever was watching you was most likely just trying to scare you, the same way TreeTop always scares people. You saw those kids crying at the parade. That's just how it goes." Then she added, in a near whisper, "Usually."

"But why would someone want to scare *me*?"

"I'm not going to answer that, because I like you," Sophia said. She started to turn away, but nodded to herself and stayed. "You know about the history of the lake, don't you? I mean, what's happening here is pretty freaky. Pretty magical. Mysterious, you know? Not quite the Bermuda Triangle, but *something*."

"You're talking about the water?"

"There's a reason people have been making pilgrimages here forever. Maybe that's why TreeTop came around."

"Because of Eli's work?"

"I don't know what I'm talking about," Sophia said, waving her own words away. "When it comes to TreeTop, it's always best not to overthink it, you know? Fact is, we've got nearly 700,000 acres of fields and orchards to spray with pesticides and herbicides, so every farm in the region has a stockpile of biosuits and goggles, masks and boots and gloves. So it's just not all that rare for old TreeTop to pay a visit. Sure, sometimes spotting TreeTop can feel a little spooky, almost like an omen. Like if you see him crossing your pasture in the sunrise, you might check to make sure your kids are all in their beds, the animals all locked in their pens. Make sure the windows are closed. Take a moment to think about your life, you know? It can be downright ethereal. But it's also pretty awesome when you're a kid, all bored, looking down the orchard rows, terrified that you might have a TreeTop sighting. Or sitting in a baler in the middle of the night, trying to get the hay up before it rains, and swearing you see old TreeTop in the distance, lumbering across your headlights. Instead of worrying about it, maybe you should feel lucky you saw him. Think Elvis. Or Sasquatch. With farm tools."

"Not helping."

"Work," she said, holding up her finger and marching away.

Abigail followed a few feet behind as Sophia pushed power buttons on computers and monitors, tugging chains to light the lamps. She seemed agitated, and Abigail wondered if it had to do with intruding on her at her job.

"I'm gonna duck out, Sophia. I'll come back with George another time. I feel like I'm in your way."

"It's not you," she said, finally giving in. She pressed her palms into a tabletop. "Today is the anniversary. Two years. Since Scotty overdosed."

"Scotty?"

"My guy. He and I were together eleven years, using hard the whole time. I don't know how I manage without him, to be honest."

She scooped a fantasy novel off a chair, pivoted, and found its spot on the genre shelves within seconds.

"Eleven years? My god, Sophia, no wonder. Losing him must've been…"

"It was," she said, sighing. "He was really cool, you know? We planned on spending our whole lives together, but one day I woke up and he was dead on the couch with the TV on and a stray cat I'd never seen before stretched across his lap. I wanted to believe he died for some bigger purpose, to shock me out of the life or something. But he was just getting high, the way we always did."

Sophia said she'd left Scotty's body on the couch, let the cat out, and marched straight over to the lobby of the Healing Lake Hotel. Mrs. Polk embraced her, called the police and, that very night, helped her get into a residential rehab program in Wenatchee.

"I stayed two months. Missed Scotty's funeral, stopped talking to anyone he knew. When I was done I had nowhere to go, so I moved back into the cottage next door to you."

One day, post-rehab, when Sophia was in the library, checking out some of the romance novels that had occupied her adolescence—"*rediscovering joy*, on the advice of my counselor," she said with an eye roll—Miss Nellie pulled her aside and offered to sponsor her in a training program paid for by the state.

"Over a decade of my life was gone, and my family decided they'd rather pray for me than talk to me. Miss Nellie can be bossy and overbearing, but she knew me from around town, used to help me find books when I was a kid. Her help was welcome."

"Sophia, I can't even..." Abigail started to say, but Sophia held up her hand.

"Soap Lake is my home, Abigail, even if some people want to treat me like a pariah. Mrs. Polk was there when I was desperate, no questions asked, even after she fired me for stealing. Pastor Kurt has always gone out of his way to make sure I get to meetings. And Miss Nellie has done everything in her power to help me *stay* clean, starting with giving me this job, which is a better gig than I *ever* thought I'd land. So if you don't mind, let's get your books checked out and get you out of here before I get in trouble."

Abigail smiled. "I'll be quick," she said, and knelt before the shelves as Sophia logged into the computer at the circulation desk. It only took her a minute to gather a colorful copy of Richard Scarry's *Cars and Trucks and Things That Go*, its binding taped and retaped from overuse. George was into anything with wheels, so it was a perfect find.

Sophia was checking the book out when she glanced at the back door and froze. From the parking lot outside came the undeniable thud of a car door slamming.

"I thought she had a meeting!" she whispered. "Go! Quick! Cellar!"

"Why?"

"Miss Nellie's here! Just hide."

Before Abigail could fully register her friend's panic, Sophia had thrown open a door behind the circulation desk and signaled her down a wobbly set of wooden stairs. Abigail grabbed a flashlight bracketed to the wall and descended into the dark. As she neared the bottom, the door closed behind her.

The library cellar was musty and cool, with a dirt floor and walls made of mortar and rock. Abigail wasn't scared exactly, yet she could feel her heart beating faster and her palms were damp and she couldn't shake the feeling that someone was behind her. Her flashlight beam revealed shelves crowded with bins and boxes, furnace filters and LPs, vacuum attachments and dusty art supplies. She ducked under a crusty beam and slipped behind the stairs in case Sophia's boss decided to open the door and peer down. On the farthest wall, next to a defunct boiler, stood a tall metal cabinet. Motes of dust sparkled through her light.

Someone cackled overhead. Not Sophia.

Abigail tugged open one of the cabinet's dented doors and aimed her flashlight inside. At the front of each shelf were jumbled containers of spray paint, linseed oil and paint thinner, plaster and TSP, but behind them sat dozens of mason jars filled with water, each with a crusty lid and handwritten label.

Soap Lake
southeast quad
18m
March 1938

Eli had batches of these same jars in his lab at home. Abigail shook one of them and watched a silver whirlpool form beneath the lid. As she thought about the old hands that had ladled this water from the lake, time itself seemed to dissolve, and her worries seemed to go with it. Maybe this was what Eli felt, studying his ancient water.

It went quiet upstairs, and soon the door opened and Sophia called down softly.

"She's gone. You still there?"

It took all of Abigail's focus to walk up the steps and not run. The carpet and lights at the top were a welcome contrast to the dirt and dark below.

"Turn around," Sophia said, "and I'll check your hair for spiders."

Abigail wriggled.

"What's with the water jars down there?" she asked once she gathered her wits. "Eli has the same ones at home."

Sophia shrugged. "We're supposed to be the town archive, but that just makes us dumping grounds for all kinds of stuff. Heirloom seeds. Soil from the Conservation Service. Tiles from the old spa hotels. Pretty neat, but I don't think anyone's ever organized it. Miss Nellie hasn't been down those steps in years. Too treacherous."

"I can vouch for that."

Sophia glanced at the door where Miss Nellie had come in. "I wonder if she knew you were hiding."

"Miss Nellie?"

"Your book was just sitting right here the whole time," Sophia said, pointing at the Busytown book on the counter. "The way she kept looking at it. She just knows things, you know?"

"Maybe she just likes seeing Lowly Worm drive his Apple Car? Or the Corn Car. Everyone loves the Corn Car."

"Don't think that's it," Sophia said, frowny.

"The Pickle Car?"

Sophia grumbled. Abigail was a little surprised by her reaction, and found it hard to tell how much of it was caution, and how much was paranoia—her brain rewired from years of addiction, and maybe from working under a toxic boss. The benevolent meanies were the worst.

"I'll go so you can work," she said, touching Sophia's arm.

"Sorry. It's just the last thing I need is for her to have something else to lord over me. She's just so unpredictable. Sometimes even cruel. I really need this job, you know?" She bit at the cuticle of her pinkie. "In fact, would you mind leaving the book here? In case Miss Nellie investigates. I'll reshelve it."

"Oh. Sure. Right."

"Maybe grab a different book," Sophia said. "But hurry."

"It's okay, Sophia. I'll come back another time."

Sophia let Abigail out the back door and she made her way to George's house—empty-handed, and unable to stop thinking about those jars.

CHAPTER 18

ESME

Esme sat on a carpeted bench at the Abortion Roller Rink, struggling to unknot the laces of her skate. It was the beginning of ninth grade, six months after the television toppled onto Baby Grace, and this was her first time out for so-called *fun*.

The Abortion Roller Rink was housed in an industrial Quonset storehouse used in the 1950s for packing fruit and repurposed in the 1980s for its current use. The leather rental skates were cracked and old, periodically rejuvenated with Vaseline like old baseball mitts, and their orange wheels dribbled treacherous slicks of WD-40 over the floors. The place got its nickname from the violent antiabortion posters hanging on its walls, courtesy of its owner, Lumpy, a sweet old man with a knotty nose who envisioned kids circling the rink as being trapped in a pro-life zoetrope. Like doughnuts after mass and Mormons raking leaves, the message would roll into the pleasure-center of their minds and make itself home forever.

Esme felt nauseous being in public like this. Her sight fell upon a poster, stapled to the plywood wall, showing a cartoon orca whale holding a protest sign that said *Save the Babies!* in bubbly font. Next to it was a handwritten sign that read, *Gummy Worms, $1 per bag.*

There was little chance that Silas would be here tonight, yet she was anxious about running into him. The last time she saw him was at the Soap Lake Police Department, the night Baby Grace was found in the shed. The cops had interviewed her three times at that point, and she sobbed and told the truth, but they still confiscated her flip phone to see if she and Silas had been communicating about the missing baby. When they gave it back, her mom snatched it and kept it as a punishment. When she saw Silas, he was holding a can of Mountain Dew and sitting in an office with his dad and Officer McDaid, the mean, corn-toothed cop from the orchard. Their eyes met through the glass door and Silas offered her a sinister peace sign. Pastor Kurt dropped the blinds.

Through all the interviews, Pastor Kurt stayed at Silas's side, but Mrs. Trudy was absent and by all accounts, livid. Just before taking Grace back to Montana, she was heard yelling that her baby girl would never set foot in Soap Lake again.

For the next few weeks, Silas faded from view. There was talk of him being tried as an adult and charged with child abduction, child abuse, obstruction of justice and—if the rumors were true, and he'd really created a *drowning kit*, composed of a bag of bricks and a clothesline—conspiracy to commit murder, with combined sentences that could have cost the teenager decades of his life. But Pastor Kurt was insistent the whole thing was a misunderstanding. He countered that Silas, in a state of fear and panic, had stupidly rolled his sister to the church in search of a sanctuary, a quiet place where she could heal, as if the spidery flowerpot were a manger. This whole thing had gotten out of hand. Pastor Kurt assured everyone that Silas had brought the clothesline to use as a makeshift seat belt in case

Grace wobbled too much in the wagon. And the bricks in fact had belonged to Pastor Kurt himself, borrowed from the church garden so he might check their color against his walkway at home for a landscaping project. If anyone didn't believe him, they were welcome to come see the bordered gardens he and Trudy had been designing in their backyard. Pastor Kurt's earnest testimony quieted most of the rumors, especially when it got around that Silas had enrolled in a private counseling group for troubled Christian youth, and was taking weekly drug tests and voluntarily performing three hundred hours of service at the church. No formal charges were ever brought.

It seemed obvious to Esme that Pastor Kurt and Mrs. Trudy were madly in love, despite the recent drama, and like a deranged peacock, all of his efforts were intended to convince her to come back to Soap Lake and create a home with him in which to raise their baby girl. Silas had made a terrible mistake, but he was just a teenager in a floundering family, desperate for love and attention, and not as heartless as he seemed. Despite his pleas, Mrs. Trudy filed for divorce. Pastor Kurt was heartbroken but didn't contest.

When word got out that Silas, after only a few weeks, was not only living back at home with his dad but also *not* awaiting trial, questions of justice emerged: How was it fair that Silas was free when last year, before a grade-school wrestling match, thirteen-year-old Eric Garcia had flashed a butterfly knife at his opponent in the bathroom and was sentenced to thirty days of juvenile detention? And what about fifteen-year-old Sara Zlenko, who stole her stepdad's RV and went joyriding around Spokane until she changed lanes in front of the Davenport Hotel and nearly killed a Gonzaga student on a motorcycle? She spent two years in juvie, and when she turned eighteen, had to finish her sentence at the women's prison in Mission Creek.

How is Silas not in jail? Daniel had asked a hundred times, but made no stink outside of the home. It was better for Esme if it all went away.

With a roller skate in her lap, Esme squirmed on the carpeted bench. Her fingertips were sore and she felt panicky, as if her entire existence were trapped within this impossible knot. Out on the rink, peach-fuzzed boys and lip-glossed girls chased the lights of the disco ball. She really shouldn't be here.

"You look like you could use some help."

When she glanced up, Kevin Polk was standing there, wearing white Cons and khakis, hands trembling as he held out a Swiss Army knife.

"Is this a mugging?"

"With the knot," he said.

His hair was even bushier this year and he wore a white T-shirt and, as always, his John Lennon specs and stamped leather belt.

Kevin had always seemed *different* to her, and it wasn't just his willingness to clean up after her TreeTop tantrums at the library. At the holiday party in fourth grade, he'd given everyone in their class a decorative box of Kleenex that his parents had bought in bulk for the hotel they owned on Main. As he moved down the aisles dispersing them, he explained that *these tissues had real lotion in them*, which was exactly the kind of thing that made other boys twist his nipples at recess. But Esme quietly liked Kevin's odd generosity. When he got to her desk that day, he'd stared deeply into her eyes and said, *They're imported from Spokane.*

Now he was staring at her again, in a way he probably thought was *piercing*. She took a deep breath.

"You're not skating?"

"Nope."

"Me neither," she said, dropping the skates to the carpet and standing up. He was almost a foot taller than her but so thin that she could see the curve of his ribs beneath his shirt.

A group of girls rolled past, giggling at Kevin. They wore so much perfume that Esme felt as if she'd been maced by a florist.

"Can I show you something?" he whispered. "It's about you-know-who."

She-knew-who, so she followed him to the carpeted counter, where wooden cubbies packed with skates reached from floor to ceiling. Lumpy was across the lobby at the refreshments stand, using his sweaty bare hands to pack little marshmallows into sandwich baggies—*mush*mallows, everyone called them, and they were famously delicious, if a tad salty—so they were in the clear.

Kevin walked to the end of the counter and leaned into a small alcove in the corner, mostly hidden, between the carpeted wall and the cubbies. The cubbies had been built from old wooden boxes leftover from when this building was a fruit storage facility, and a few still held stamped images of apple trees and a logo saying *Desert Delite*. Esme knew he was about to show her the familiar words roughly carved into the side of the wood:

The graffiti was low enough to the floor that no one could see it without crouching. Some said the message had been carved at children's eye level as a warning, not unlike the graphic posters pinned around the rink.

"You know about this?" Kevin said.

Esme nodded. When she was little, her dad had pushed her into this corner and, in one of his scary life-lessons, made her reach in and touch the deep grooves of the letters with her fingertips, to feel the words carved long ago. He must have sensed her worry because he screamed *Gotcha!* as if the whole thing were a ghost story, then tickle-clawed her belly and neck, leaving scratches that Daniel called *drunk marks*.

"Everyone says there's a secret number you can call," Kevin said, looking up the wall of cubbies. "Somewhere in here hidden. But I've never seen it."

Across the floor, Lumpy poured soda into Styrofoam cups. Esme lifted Kevin's warm, damp hand out of his pocket and guided it into the tight cranny between the cubbies and the wall. Kevin quivered. There was only a few inches of space back there, but she'd learned long ago that if you curled your fingers around the corner, as if you were trying to pull the shelves toward you, your fingertips would find a series of rough grooves: carvings, it was said, of TreeTop's ancient phone number.

"Do you feel it?" Esme whispered. "His number's etched there."

It was so tight back there that there was no way to see the numbers, so it was something of a ritual for kids to roam their fingertips over the rough wood like a planchette over a Ouija board. In the decades since this rink was built, countless kids had spent slumber parties huddled around landline phones, calling up variations of this indecipherable number and listening to *TreeTop breathing through his mask*—which was likely just the static of a dead phone call.

"No way am I fishing around back there," Kevin said, yanking out his hand and wiping it on his khakis.

Any other boy her age would make a show of not being scared, but Kevin looked like he was about to get hit by a car. She liked that about him. Someday, if the moment was right, she might even tell him about TreeTop wheeling her dad's body through the orchard.

"We should go," she said, "before Lumpy yells at us."

"Think anyone would notice if we just left?" Kevin said.

"One way to find out."

"You're even more awesome in person," he said, gulping.

★ ★ ★

Esme and Kevin drifted into the empty lobby of the Healing Lake Hotel and found, at the front desk, a mug of tea with the bag still in it.

Kevin touched the side of the cup. "Still warm," he said, just above a whisper, as if they were detectives at a crime scene. He peered behind the beaded curtain that led to his home wing. "Let's not rouse Momma Bear."

"Is she mean or something?" Esme asked.

He gave her a look of mild alarm. "No, she's the best. She just *really* likes being a parent."

"Lucky you."

"Yeah, I know," he said, perfectly serious.

Mr. and Mrs. Polk were hippies from the mossy Olympic Peninsula who, when Kevin was a baby, inherited a small wad of cash, grew tired of always feeling damp, and bought the Sundowner Motel on the shores of Soap Lake. Long known by locals as *The Downer*, this compound of hotel rooms and tiny cabins had seen its heyday in the decades around WWII, when visitors crowded the lake by the thousands, making pilgrimages into the desert to soak in the healing waters and be cured of all manner of disease. But that didn't last. In the years of decline that followed, vacation cottages sat empty or became rental homes, and The Downer devolved into a sketchy but affordable waypoint for felons with bus tickets, seasonal workers who couldn't land a hut in the orchards, and a few wobbly senior citizens down on their luck. Within months of buying it, Kevin's parents had kicked everyone out, gave the place a facelift, and renamed it the Healing Lake Hotel.

In fifth grade show-and-tell, Kevin gave a PowerPoint presentation about the hotel's renovation that was more suited for a design class. In addition to giving a virtual tour of the guest rooms, he detailed how his dad had converted one wing of the hotel into the family's living space with windows and doors facing the water, which meant that Kevin's house had *eight* front doors in *eight* different colors, and he had a shower, a safe, and a microwave in his bedroom, like a rich kid on TV.

Kevin led her toward the residential wing, pressing his finger to his lips, *"shhh,"* then ran to his bedroom to grab a pair of frostbitten popsicles that they could nibble as they roamed the hotel's grounds. As Esme waited for him, studying hallway carpet that looked straight out of *The Shining*, she could hear Kevin's mom beyond the walls, complaining to someone about a housekeeper stealing tiny bars of soap. Esme tiptoed out of earshot, feeling like an intruder.

Popsicles in hand, they cut through the hotel hallways. Most of the rooms were vacant, but periodically, Kevin would point to a door as they passed and quietly say the name of the town where the guest was from.

"Walla Walla. Omaha. Corvallis."

Every guest represented a different kind of life, she realized, a fresh path out. No wonder Kevin seemed so different.

"Missoula. Winnemucca. Kingsman."

By the time they reached a walkway lined with solar lights that curved along the beach, the night had arrived in full, and Esme was glad she'd left the house.

"So, is it getting any easier?" he said. "The Baby Grace thing."

After her initial shock, Esme felt grateful that he wasn't pretending nothing had happened like everyone else.

"Avoiding people helps," she said, which was true.

"I know how shitty I would feel in your shoes. But can I just say? Sometimes televisions fall on babies, Esme. You got a raw deal. Not to mention you had no business being in the same house as Silas. The guy's a frickin' wreck."

"Thanks, Kev," she said, and their arms touched as they walked.

They wandered between a group of log cabins facing the shore, and behind them, outbuildings used for laundry and storage. The grounds were dark and still, and soon they passed a cabin with a padlocked door and its own propane tank sitting in a patch of weeds.

"Is this the part where you kidnap me and chain me to a radiator?" she asked.

"How's your schedule?"

"Wide-open. As long as you don't make me roller skate. And don't expect my mom to pay any ransom."

"She could cough up some food stamps."

Esme stopped on the path. Her legs wouldn't move.

"I can't believe I said that," he said, groaning. "It was supposed to be witty."

"It's fine," she said, but she felt a small betrayal. "My mom can't work. Otherwise she would."

"I didn't mean it."

"Daniel says she's *not all there*. Plus booze, although there's a whole chicken-and-egg thing. And my dad, you know, died in the trailer fire."

"Thanks to TreeTop," he said, then looked at his hands. "Just a rumor I heard. That he set the fire."

Esme felt herself jolt. She was never surprised by the reckless rumors of TreeTop that spread through town, yet whenever she heard her dad's death mentioned in the same breath, she worried that *she* might become part of the story.

Eager to change the subject, she shook her fingers and pointed at the padlocked cabin. "What's with this place?"

Kevin explained that his dad had been contracted by the university over in Bellingham to refurbish this cabin for a scientist who received a grant to study the lake. She'd apparently done some research here as a grad student years ago, got sidetracked, and was laying the groundwork to come back and continue her work. Mr. Polk cleared out the cabin for her, set up its propane system and an extra utility sink, and was getting ready to convert it into a lab when the bottom dropped out on her grant. Maybe next year, she'd said.

"Why would anyone want to research this shithole?"

"Are you joking?" he said, and it was his turn to look hurt. "Come here."

On their way to the beach, Esme spotted Kevin's parents through the window, eating ice cream at the kitchen counter. Kevin pretended not to see them. Soon Esme sat with him on the shore behind the motel, their socks balled into their shoes. The muck along the shoreline smelled rank, like the washing machines at the laundromat. Up and down the beach, the lake gently lapped.

"You know what everyone calls this part of the lake?" he asked.

"Crocodile Beach," she said. "Because of all the people with skin disease. Your guests."

The psoriasis and the eczema, the amputations and inflammations, the arthritis and the crusty fingers and toes: people came from all over to pickle their damaged flesh in these waters. From the time she was little, Esme remembered seeing these strangers at the grocery store or filling up their gas tank, their skin red and rashy, weepy and scaly, sometimes melty and burned.

"Calling it that is so *mean*," Kevin said, more upset than she'd expected. "I've made a lot of trips to the store for people who can barely leave the hotel. I've stripped the sheets off their beds and had to throw them out. Because of blood and...you get the idea. But we only have to clean up. We don't have to live with it."

"Fair enough."

"You know it really works, right? This water cures people, Esme. It's shitty how many people don't care."

It took a moment for Esme to recognize the feeling spreading through her. Her shoulders dropping. Her jaw loosening. Her heart opening.

"Amazing things happen here," he said, and turned toward her. "They really do."

The light of a small bright moon made the lake look trapped in a web, and Kevin reached for her hand. As their lips finally met, Esme instinctively opened her eyes and nearly flinched when she saw, beyond Kevin's shoulder, up the dark stretch of beach, Mrs. Polk: standing on her patio, arms crossed, watching. Even from this distance it was clear that she was not pleased.

CHAPTER 19

ABIGAIL

Abigail and George were performing science experiments on her coffee table when she looked out the window to see Krunk jogging toward her porch. He was out of uniform, wearing cutoff sweats and a snowboarding T-shirt. Under his baseball cap his nose was streaked with sunburn and his chin spotty with stubble.

"Just touching base, if that's okay?" he said, as she answered the door.

"George is here," she said. Daniel was staying late at the orchard, fixing a leaky line, so she'd be babysitting late.

"Cool," he said, waving a manila envelope. "I can come back?"

"No, it's fine. Come in."

Krunk followed her into the living room, where George was dribbling red and blue dye into plastic petri dishes. Earlier, he'd dumped his toys out of his backpack and spent a good hour playing *Snake* on an ancient flip phone until it ran out of charge. Then he and Abigail ransacked Eli's lab. They brought up litmus paper, polypropylene tubes, and spread a beach towel on the coffee table to catch the spills. He barely looked up when Krunk said *hi*.

"Are you, like, *on the case?*" she whispered, pointing to his envelope.

"Just a quick look, if you wouldn't mind? A few photos."

Abigail ushered Krunk to the kitchen table, out of earshot of George.

"How is he?" Krunk asked.

"As expected."

"I hear the task force finally came by to talk to you?" he said.

"They didn't seem all that interested in what I had to say, to be honest."

This afternoon she'd been visited by a pair of middle-aged cops, coach-types with graying barbershop hair. The detectives introduced themselves and gave her a card, *Major Crimes, City and County*, a joint investigation unit for small towns in the region, sharing resources, combining expertise, and if necessary, bringing in state troopers. They appeared to be professional at first, until she caught them elbowing each other roughly anytime she glanced away.

As they asked her predictable questions, she noticed they were sharing a thirty-two-ounce cup of soda, passing it back and forth and sipping out of the same straw like teenagers on a date. When they caught her staring, the one with the moustache said in a pouty voice, "Numbnuts here left his drink on top of the cruiser. Fell off." She nodded along sympathetically.

"It was like show-and-tell at Clown School," she told Krunk.

"Sounds like them. The guy with the crew cut, McDaid? He's a real ass. Which means he'll be chief someday."

"He's the one who asked me if I did a lot of drugs. Not, *Do you do drugs?* but *Do you do a lot of drugs?*"

"That's still the angle," Krunk said, wincing. "It fits pretty well. Could explain why Esme didn't reach out to her family about the visit. Just a transaction, in and out."

Abigail's sight drifted toward Sophia's cottage and the mystical unicorn tapestries in its windows.

"I'm guessing you didn't tell them about your visitor? The *Peeping Ghost*?"

She gave him a crusty look. "You mean TreeTop? What's up with you not telling me about him?"

"Busted," he said, hands up, "but I didn't want to freak you out. That guy is scary."

"Yeah, especially when he's tapping on your window in the middle of the night."

"I'm sorry," he said, "but the last thing you need is to get all worried about TreeTop. And trust me, seeing him doesn't mean anything. I dressed up as TreeTop in high school and ran through my ex-girlfriend's pasture, just to freak her out. Crawled around in the principal's yard more than once. Just wait for Halloween around here. TreeTops everywhere. A costume in every barn. It'll curdle your blood."

"But why'd he visit me?"

Krunk shrugged. "You're new, maybe? And you live above a lab full of expensive equipment? He hasn't come back, has he?"

"Not that I've seen."

They sat in silence for a moment, half smiling, until Krunk waved the envelope.

"So what'd you want me to look at?" she said.

"Probably nothing new," he said, pulling out a small stack of five-by-seven photos. "But it can't hurt. In case anything jumps out."

Abigail slid her water glass closer. "Are those...?"

"Nothing too gruesome."

She glanced toward the living room, making sure George was occupied, then flipped through the photos. One showed the boy's yellow pajamas, smeared with blood and dirt, spread out on a table next to his SpongeBob blankie. Another held Esme's jean shorts and gray T-shirt, and something about seeing the little moth hole where the screwdriver had broken through the fabric bothered her more than all the blood surrounding it: her entire life had drained through that lacuna. Abigail shivered and moved through the stack.

"What am I looking for?"

"Just anything different. Maybe you moved something when you found her. Or like something that was in the car isn't here in the photos, that kind of thing."

She shrugged and focused on the contents of Esme's purse and glove compartment as well as the trash she'd gathered from the rest area. She recalled how casual Esme had appeared in the video, wandering up the dark walkway, how her keys weren't even out.

"I don't see her car keys here. Is that something?"

"Don't think so," he said. "If I recall, the tow truck driver made a note on the impound sheet that there was no key when he threw the Cutlass up on his skid. Half the time that just means someone at the scene stuck it under the visor or mat. But I'll look into it."

"Sorry I'm not more help."

She started again at the beginning. Krunk stepped toward the fridge and took in her grocery list, clipped-out comics, and a photo of Abigail on a Florida beach with her mom and Meghan—taken before the wine and belittling began, as they inevitably did—then plucked out a bookmark from behind the picture. It was tan with a light bulb logo, a souvenir from her first date with Eli. She pretended not to notice when Krunk flipped it over and saw the tiny ink heart Eli had drawn on the back.

He stared at it for a few seconds too long, then stuck it back on the fridge.

"Okay if I use the bathroom?"

"Down the hall," she said. As he walked away, flip-flops clicking, she added, "Don't steal my pills."

He halted and shook his head slowly. The way he stared at her from down the hall, he might as well have been inches from her face.

"Your husband is a fool," he said gently, without a trace of humor.

She was glad when the bathroom door closed behind him. She stood up from the table and wagged her hands and sat back down, reminding herself that she loved Eli, her genius husband, and that Krunk had recently broken off his engagement and was vulnerable and sad.

Deep breath. She returned her gaze to the Esme photos. This was why he was here.

The only oddity she could see was that there was only one juice box in the photographs, and she recalled Esme holding two in the video. There was likely an explanation. The juice boxes had been in the front seat with Esme, so maybe, morbidly, her blood had landed on one, earning its own photo in a different pile, right alongside those of the bloody screwdriver.

"Hey, Krunk?" she said, glancing down the empty hall.

A tiny shiver moved through her, as if someone were breathing down her neck. She whipped around and was shocked to find George standing right behind her, with his hands on the back of her chair. In a panic she flipped the photos on the kitchen table—the juice box and bloody T-shirt visible on top—but not before he launched himself into her lap, hugging her tight around the neck. He pressed his cheek into hers.

"Oh, George," she sighed into his thick black hair, smelling his baby shampoo, hugging him with one hand and shoving aside the photos with the other. "You weren't supposed to see those. I'm sorry, buddy…"

She could hear him crying a little as he breathed, and was

completely caught off guard when those sounds became a whisper tight against her ear.

"I dropped it."

His words as hushed as his breath. Abigail froze, unsure of what she heard.

"What'd you say? George?"

With one hand he pointed in the direction of the front door and the desert beyond.

"Out there," he whispered. *"I dropped it."*

"You dropped what, George?"

She heard water running and soon the bathroom door opened.

"Listen, Abigail—" Krunk started to say, then he halted, speechless, staring at George curled in her lap, quietly crying, the photos of his mom's last night spilled across the kitchen table.

Daniel scooped up the sleeping boy from Abigail's couch and overapologized for showing up after dark. His black T-shirt was smudged with mud, and he wore a red bandana around his neck like a film director stuck in a different life.

"I appreciate this so much," he whispered as he stepped out to the porch, cradling George and hobbling across the driveway as if his back were about to go out. Abigail opened the passenger door of his truck, an old Ford Bronco, blue and white, dented and missing some of its trim. Daniel buckled him into the booster and they stepped back so as not to wake him. "I worry about him wandering off," he continued. "Drowning in the canal, or getting picked up by someone who thinks he's a witness or whatever. Plus I can't have him around anyone who might talk shit about his mom, you know? There's a lot he doesn't need to know."

"I'm happy to help, Daniel. He's awesome. Plus I don't know what else I'm doing here."

"You and me both."

He turned toward the Bronco, but she stopped him.

"There's something else," she said, hesitant. "A cop came by earlier and George saw some photos. Stuff that was in the car."

"In the Cutlass?"

"Mostly trash," she said, shaking her head, "but also Esme's bloody clothes. I was looking at them and he came up behind me. It was an accident. I just..."

Daniel blinked, taken aback. He glanced through the window at his zonked nephew.

"Is he *okay*?"

"Not really, no. He was sad. He also told me he dropped something *out there*. I think he meant the desert."

"Wow. Okay." Daniel was quiet for a moment. In the porch light, she could see streaks of dry sweat on his neck. "He said he *dropped something*? He asked about his SpongeBob blankie the other night, so maybe he just meant that?" He squinted, trying to control his reaction. "Why were you even looking at that stuff?"

Abigail told him how the night had unfolded, and he took a long breath, clearly in survival mode.

"It was a mistake," he said, "so we'll just keep an eye on him and hope for the best. What cop is helping you, anyway? Sounds like you're having better luck than I am."

"A guy named Krunk?"

"That makes sense. Abe Krunk's a good guy. Some of the yokels he works with are real garbage, corrupt dropouts, but he's cool. I've known him forever."

"What do you mean, *makes sense*?"

"Because of the hotel?" He must have seen Abigail's confusion because he palmed the side of the Bronco, letting it hold him up. "The shooting. You know Krunk saved Esme, right? When her boyfriend got shot."

"Kevin Polk?" Abigail remembered her conversation with Sophia at the parade, how Kevin had been killed in the lobby of the Healing Lake Hotel.

"Yeah, Kevin's parents own the hotel, so he was working the

desk. Krunk was down the hall delivering a pizza and stumbled right into the shooting. He took a bullet in the thigh. The shooter was about to drop Esme next but Krunk fought back. Lit into him and got Esme out of there. Kind of amazing to be honest. He didn't milk it or anything, but it definitely helped him get a job as a cop. Not sure why he'd want that, but then look at me."

He rattled his shirt and sprinkles of dirt fell off.

"But he and Esme didn't really know each other?" she asked.

"Just from school I guess. I'm sure it's done a number on him. Sure did on her. Sure has on me."

Abigail was breathless. Since that first day out on the canal road, Krunk's pain had been blaring beneath the surface, always behind the shy dude grin.

"What happened to the hotel shooter? He's not still at large, is he?"

"Silas? Nah. Piece of shit. The cops killed him on the beach within minutes of him killing Kevin. At least Esme and the Polks were spared from suffering through a trial."

"Any idea why he did it?"

"There was talk of a drug deal between the three of them, but Kevin and Esme were definitely not the type. I think the shooter had a thing for my sister and was out for revenge when she rejected him. Or just another fried, angry boy."

"That's when she left town?"

"Not that she needed a reason, but yeah. She and Kevin were in love, too. Teenage love, but still. It was the real deal. Shit. *I've* never had that." He noticed her stare because he added, "On that note. I'm tired. Getting loose-lipped." He started climbing into the battered Bronco, but stopped when he saw the look on her face. He raised his eyebrows. "Go ahead. I know what you're going to ask."

"Do you?"

He closed his eyes. "I've never had love like that. In more ways than one."

It took a second for Abigail to catch on.

"Oh. You're...?"

"Gay? Yes. Surprised?"

"Never."

He sized her up, smiling. "But that's not what you were going to ask."

"Nope. But thanks for sharing. I mean, does anyone else—?"

"You're special, but you're not that special." He winked. "I don't exactly hide anything, but honestly I'm never sure who knows. Hardly anyone says a word to me if they do. I was pretty angry in high school. And a few years after. It's amazing how quickly an asshole will stop making *pink sombrero* jokes when his jaw is wired shut."

"Literally?"

"Literally," he smiled, puffing up a little. "I may have gained a little reputation for, you know...protecting myself."

"And Esme, too, I bet."

"Mostly her. That girl was always into something." He shook his head, wistful. "Anyway, small town. I don't broadcast my personal life. Not that I have much of one."

"No prospects?"

"I've met a few guys through work, always passing through, which is probably for the better. Honestly, though, a bigger issue is that I still live with my *mom*. The one person I ever really had something with lasted six months, then he moved to Seattle."

"Not into long-distance?"

"We tried. Or *I* tried. It was easier for him not to, I guess." Daniel shrugged. "Why am I telling you this?"

"Because I'm in no place to give relationship advice?"

"That's the truth," he said. He turned to get into the Bronco.

"As long as we're getting personal," she said, "can I ask you something else? Is your friend in Seattle the reason you want to move there and go to UW?" Daniel blinked and cleared his throat. "Am I being too nosy?"

"A little late to be asking that, J.Jill. And no. It's not because of *him*. How do you even...?"

"I saw the film school catalog on your porch. First day we met."

"Of course," he said. "That was the plan, but I'm not going anywhere. Honestly, I don't know how people do it. I thought life was tough *before* George arrived."

"Maybe there's a way," she said, shrugging.

"According to my handy academic calendar, I've missed the deadline for financial aid and I can forget about merit scholarships because my transcripts are a tragedy. The only reason I got accepted was because of this program for nontraditional students from rural areas. But there will be no full ride for this guy."

"Just wait until they see what you can do," she said.

"How do you know what I can do?"

"I don't," she said. "I guess I just believe you can do it."

"It's a three-hour drive to Seattle and, as you know all too well, I can't leave George for an afternoon, let alone for days."

"They have day care in Seattle, Daniel. Online classes."

"Listen," he said, closing his eyes, "I appreciate your optimism. But you live in a different world than me. When I say it's not possible, please respect me enough to believe that it's really not possible. Sometimes the bootstraps are broken."

Abigail felt the sting in his voice, and knew his words had been gathering momentum for a lifetime. He was understandably discouraged: he'd lost his only sibling and his plans had come screeching to a halt, and nothing she could say would alter that reality. Plus, he was right: Who the hell was *she*?

"Sorry," he said, after a minute. "It's been a long day. And maybe you're right. Maybe the school thing will work out next year."

"Maybe," she said, raising her brow.

"But probably not." He smiled. "What were you really going to ask earlier? Before your driveway turned into a counseling office."

"What happened to Esme's Cutlass? Did the cops give it to you?"

"The Cutlass? I think we're supposed to get it at some point, although…" Daniel didn't finish his thought, but he didn't need to: *although who wants a car stained with his sister's blood?* "It'll go straight to the salvage yard," he continued. "Nice old ride, but I definitely wouldn't want to be seen driving it around town."

"Because it was Esme's?"

"Because it was *Kevin's*," he said, "a graduation present he didn't live long enough to receive. After the shooting, Mr. Polk gifted it to Esme, paid for her insurance and everything. Generous, right? But then she skipped town in it, right after graduation, middle of the night, and I kept feeling like that's what the Polks wanted all along. To push her out of here. Like they *knew* they wouldn't be able to handle seeing her around after Kevin. Solution? One Cutlass, full tank, comin' up."

"I can't imagine what they went through," Abigail said. "Losing their child."

"They were *destroyed*," he said, shaken. "We all were. Why are you asking about her car, anyway?"

"Just wondering if her keys ever turned up. Krunk didn't think they had."

"Keys?" he said, as if it was the last thing he wanted to be bothered with right now. He scratched his hair. "I have no idea."

"Will you let me know if they do?" she said.

Daniel nodded as he started the Bronco. Next to him George stirred.

"Why do I have the feeling that you're not going to need my help on this one?" he said, half smiling as he backed out of her driveway.

CHAPTER 20

ABIGAIL

A plastic birdfeeder that had once been a bong dangled from a hook on Sophia's cottage porch—definitely not sanctioned by the Audubon Society, but the juncos and sparrows still shook with pleasure at its messy abundance of seeds. Sophia came to the door, dipping a piece of beef jerky into a cup of nacho cheese. Except for the rainbow rattail, her hair was a feathery red mess.

"Crime scene?" Abigail said.

Sophia squinted at the sky. It was 9:00 a.m. and ninety-three degrees. Her upper lip glistened.

"This crime scene," Sophia said, "it's not at a swimming pool, is it? An air-conditioned movie theater?"

"More like a snake-infested inferno. And we need to walk there so no one sees Medusa."

"You do realize it's vampire season. No going outside during daylight."

"Even better."

"I'm on Storytime this afternoon, though it's usually just the seniors wheeled over from the nursing home and the home-schoolers dropped off so their moms can finally get to the laundry. Not exactly a picky crowd. Bless their hearts. Think we have time?"

Abigail glanced at the clock on her phone. "Shouldn't be a problem if we start walking now."

"I have a better idea," Sophia said, waving her jerky like a wand.

From the jungle of prickly brush on the side of Sophia's cottage, Abigail excavated a very old, very trashed, very purple mountain bike with turquoise decals that said *Goat Peak*. Once she oiled the chain and pumped up the tires, it was ready to roll. Sophia dragged out a green men's cruiser, then disconnected a tow-along trailer that hadn't hauled a kid in years, but had hauled many bags of groceries from the market and many loads of romance novels from the library.

They rode out of town and climbed a hill between orchards before facing the long stretch of county road that guided them toward the canals. The landscape changed from sleepy streets to fields of onion and alfalfa, from rows of apples to endless shrubsteppe and rock. The cherry harvest was underway, so those orchards were lined with old buses, and dozens of people in hats and long-sleeved shirts dragged ladders between the trees, dumping cherries into buckets awkwardly strapped to their bodies.

By the time they reached the irrigation road where the boy had burst from the sagebrush, the reality of Esme's murder had drained all pleasure from the ride.

"George found me somewhere along here."

They dumped their bikes a short way into the desert to keep them hidden, then meandered nearly a mile through the rabbit brush and sage. Low dry hills scalloped the horizon. Abigail's eyeballs clenched in the light.

"Cutlass was parked way up on that rise."

"I know the place," Sophia said. "There's an old homestead down the hill that burned to nothing back when my dad was a kid. The Rock Shack. Anyone local would know it."

Sophia steered them toward a rough two-track path and then up to a small clearing. The crime scene tape was gone.

"So, remind me again. The boy told you to come out here? What exactly are we looking for?"

Abigail shrugged. "George just said he 'dropped it.' At least I think that's what he said."

She scuffed an *X* into the ground with her foot where the Cutlass had been parked. Then she and Sophia started spiraling out from the *X*, combing the surrounding mustard weed and sagebrush and cheatgrass. Within twenty minutes they made it about sixty feet away from the car, and both of them stopped cold.

In the shadow of a chunk of basalt, a set of keys was tucked into the ground as if trying to unlock the earth. Sophia stooped to pick them up.

"Wait," Abigail said. Daniel had told her that the boy's prints, and no one else's, had been on the screwdriver, but maybe the keys would be different. She untied the red bandana around her neck and pouched them loosely inside of it.

A simple leather *Aquarius* fob, complete with its dozen stars. Two keys for the Olds, two for a dead bolt or door, probably Esme's apartment in Bakersfield.

"She died inside of the car, right?"

"Slowly," Abigail said, "in the dark."

"So her killer threw them from the car to here. Basically trapping her so she couldn't drive away. As she bled."

"Cruel."

"Very cruel."

Based on his dirty pj's, George might have spent hours out here that night, scrambling over the ground in the dark, failing to find his mom's only way out.

Esme never had a chance. Maybe that was the point.

"How did the police not find these?" Abigail said.

"Pigs in town are useless. Plus, she was Esme."

"So you did know her."

"We crossed paths at the library and hotel. What I do know is she was always mixed up in something. Some babysitting shit-show in grade school. Some fiasco with Mrs. Polk. Some drama over drugs between her boyfriend and a local tweaker. Let's just say most people probably weren't surprised when she got killed."

"Because she wasn't the rodeo queen?"

"Small towns aren't the best places to explore your boundaries."

Sophia wiped the sweat off her forehead and handed Abigail her water bottle. They took turns sipping as they walked toward the canal road.

Abigail held up the bandana with the keys. "Worth the trip."

"I guess."

Abigail stopped. "What?"

Sophia plucked a cluster of sage leaves and pressed them to her nose. "You sure the kid said *'I dropped it'*? Because that's not exactly an *it*, is it? Keys are a *them*. Like *Throw 'em here.*"

"He definitely said *it*. But he's four. And he barely talks."

"And why would the kid say he dropped the keys if he was crawling around looking for them? If the bad guy threw them, the kid would have to find them before he could drop them."

Abigail looked in the direction that the boy had run, viewing the world from his perspective, the path he would have taken.

"Maybe we should keep looking?" she said.

The two of them slowed down and studied the ground, zigging back and forth. They saw a horny toad and some stink beetles, and flushed a covey of quail. When they neared the road, they headed in the direction of the bikes.

"A few more minutes?" Abigail asked.

Sophia sniffed her pits. "Why not? No one sits on my lap during Storytime."

They entered the desert again and began walking toward the crime scene, scanning the earth slowly for a few hundred yards, when Sophia stopped.

She was standing over a dusty green juice box poked by a yellow bendy straw.

"We're going to need more bandanas at this rate," she said, tugging a crumpled one out of her back pocket and tossing it at Abigail. "Like a goddamned magic show."

Abigail softly cupped the juice box in the bandana. Its waxy cardboard was printed with a smiling red apple against a green background, and the smudges of blood on the front looked like falling autumn leaves.

"Maybe Esme told George to take this and run," she said, quietly. "While she was...bleeding."

The top corner of the box was folded back, giving it the appearance of being closed, but when she squeezed, the box popped open. She and Sophia looked at each other. Abigail loosened the opening, ready to plunge her pinkie inside.

"I wouldn't do that," Sophia said. "Scorpions. Black widows. Jerusalem crickets."

"The desert is such a welcoming place."

"Just peek first."

Abigail squeezed the box open, letting the sunlight in.

"Something's there. Not a scorpion."

She pulled out a plastic bindle, larger than a golf ball, full of pale yellow, crystalline powder. The powder filled a quarter of a sandwich bag, looped over itself and tied into a knot.

"That's not candy," Sophia said, bobbing a little as she leaned over it. "I'm not sure what it is, but I'm pretty sure what it's for." She pressed sweat away from her eyes. "You know, I could take it and ask around."

Sophia's jaw shuddered, and Abigail could see that she wanted to carry this package home and nail shut her door and not re-enter the world until it was gone—to find her god in the dark.

The drug thing fits pretty well, Krunk had said, *if she was meeting someone here who was connected.*

"I don't think so," Abigail said, shaking the bindle and sighing. "Esme was muling after all."

The powder shimmered in the sun, and Abigail felt her stomach drop. As crass as it was, she wanted Esme's death to be more grandiose, somehow, more deserving of the girl she kept hearing about. The one who flipped off the rodeo queen and carved her own path out of the desert. But there was nothing exceptional about this. She was just like everyone else, hungry for money, trying to stay afloat, seeking any means of escape.

Abigail certainly didn't blame her, yet she couldn't help but see it as a failure of Esme's imagination.

PART 2:

THE TREETOP ORACLES

CHAPTER 21

ESME

One summer night after they'd been dating for nearly a year, Esme led Kevin out to the spot in the apple orchard where she'd seen TreeTop pushing his wheelbarrow. They set up camp under the stars and zipped together a pair of sleeping bags. Kevin was in science-fair mode, jotting notes and listening for TreeTop's squeaky wheel. But outside of a coyote loping past and being awakened at dawn by sprays of irrigation water, nothing eventful happened.

The next day at the library, Esme led Kevin to the middle-grade nonfiction books and showed him the biography of Jackie Robinson that had terrified Daniel as a child. All summer, they had been prowling the town in search of TreeTop graffiti, most decades old, seeking patterns that might have evaded them during childhood. The graffiti was still there, for the most part—*TreeTop Kills*, written on picnic tables and playground equipment, locker-room walls and bathroom stalls—but that had been about the extent of it: it was just *there*, with a distinct lack of purpose…

Which was more than could be said about the scribbles in the Jackie Robinson bio. As they skimmed the book, they discovered that the entire page in question had been sliced out, taking with it half of an outfield and a chunk of Robinson's late career as well as the message about TreeTop. They shouldn't have been surprised, nor should they have assumed its absence was nefarious. This sort of erasure happened sometimes under Miss Nellie's watch, when characters got a little too sexy on the page, or someone's privates popped up in an anatomy or anthropology book and needed to be neutered. The sign she taped above the copy machine said it all: *Not in My Library!*

Esme and Kevin should have been relieved that the graffiti was gone, but it was hard not to feel disappointed. As a kid, each TreeTop etch had felt like an invitation to a world of gravity and consequence. But her childhood had been receding these years in all sorts of ways, and it seemed now as if her quest for TreeTop had been hardly different from a kid playing Monster. The same held true when she thought about her dad whispering about the secret TreeTop messages around town. Each year, as he faded into memory, alongside old toys and hiding places, he seemed less like a humble crusader, and more like an ineffectual alcoholic and pothead who'd told ghost stories as if they were history.

At one point, she quietly returned the *J* encyclopedia he'd stolen to its shelf at the library. It still reeked of smoke.

Adulthood was creeping toward Esme in other ways as well. During high school, she began working at the Dairy Freeze on the highway, spiraling cones for families passing through on their way to visit the Grand Coulee Dam. And Kevin, when he wasn't attending club meetings or studying, began working at the hotel, landscaping and running the desk, which meant Esme began spending a lot of her time there, too—

At least until one freezing night in their sophomore year when Mrs. Polk—Kevin's turbocharged, attack-helicopter of a mom—

came bursting into the lobby and caught Kevin squirming on top of Esme on the communal couch, fully clothed, tongues locked. Mrs. Polk had a great fake smile and sometimes rubbed Esme's back when she and Kevin were snacking at her fancy kitchen counter, but it was clear that she saw Esme as an unwanted distraction in her only child's life, and it was no surprise that she got strict: from that moment on, Esme was banned from visiting the hotel whenever Kevin was on duty. Which was a lot.

Mr. Polk took a different approach: he secretly gave them condoms.

If any other adult had tried to give her birth control, Esme would've assumed that all they saw when they looked at her was a bad mother in the making. But Mr. Polk understood that it was easier to get meth in Soap Lake than condoms, and she appreciated his gesture even if she and Kevin weren't quite ready to use them. Though this was the twenty-first century, sex ed at the high school amounted to a one-hour abstinence talk hosted by the evangelical gym teacher, and unless you wanted to run the gauntlet of grandmas at the grocery store cigarette counter, there was only one place in town to buy condoms: for $1.25 in quarters from the vending machine in the rancid bathroom of the gas station, which also sold Hot Sex Oil guaranteed to blister the flesh and some kind of penile pleasure ring that looked a lot like Cthulhu.

Mr. Polk had arrived in Esme's life just as the shine around her dead father had begun to fade. He seemed genuinely taken by her, and was downright enthusiastic about the ways she was bumping Kevin out of the tight lane he'd always occupied. He was a tall hippie with a nest of gray hair and a beer belly, and a big fan of overalls, lined with flannel in the winter, cut into shorts in the summer. He built remote control airplanes in a little cabin he'd converted into a workshop, and he liked to fly them low over the lake, often getting so tipsy on Irish stouts and Belgian ales that the planes nose-dived into the shore. Kevin claimed it was all part of a self-perpetuating cycle that got him outside of the hotel and away from Mrs. Polk.

You crash the planes, Kevin said, like a monk, *you rebuild the planes.*

Hakuna matata, Esme said.

Despite the pressures of growing up, Esme's life was relatively drama-free compared to most of her high school classmates. Silas continued to keep a tight grip on his anger toward her, as if it were the one thing he could count on, but he'd stopped going to school a while back and she hardly ever saw him around town, so his spite rarely reached her. For a long time, this made him easy to ignore.

That all changed one afternoon in the August before her senior year, during a lunch break from Dairy Freeze, when Esme was speed-walking over to the lake to eat the turkey sandwich she'd brought from home, and a kid with a crew cut stepped in front of her on the sidewalk.

"You Esme?"

He was nine or ten, wearing cutoff jeans and no shirt, and his chest was stained with orange popsicle drips.

Esme smirked. Main Street was empty. The kid had bare feet, and she was wondering how he was able to walk on the concrete in this heat. And where he had emerged from.

She bent to meet his eye. "Yeah, I'm Esme. Who wants to know?"

"Silas is going to murder you," the boy said, then slapped her face so hard that her ears rang. Before she could react, he ran across the street and vanished between buildings.

Esme stood on the sidewalk holding her cheek, looking around for Silas, and thinking the little misfit had probably just earned his popsicle.

She dialed Kevin's number right away but hung up before he answered, and when he called her back she texted **at work,** though by then she was sitting on a rock behind the library in tears. She threw her sandwich at some seagulls.

If she had told Kevin about the slapping incident, he would've gone into Sherlock mode and enlisted his dad and the police to pay Silas a visit, or even enlisted Daniel to kick his ass. But Esme had always felt a little protective of Silas, maybe because she could see that he was acting exactly as everyone should expect him to, given how he'd always been treated.

Plus, in a weird way, she felt as if she deserved it.

That night after work, she snuck into the hotel lobby and found Kevin at the reception desk, staring down at a pile of college catalogs.

"You okay?" Kevin said, looking up.

She was still wearing her trucker's hat, black jeans and Dairy Freeze shirt, complete with the streak of strawberry syrup that had shot all over her at work. In that lobby, with its aromatherapy machine and gentle tunes, it was hard not to feel self-conscious.

"Sure," she said. "Just spent eight hours scooping ice cream."

The bell on the door dinged and Kevin sat up straight, wearing his robotic cheesy smile. Esme stepped aside as he checked in a young couple whose toddler had scallopy rashes on her arms and legs.

"Look at the colleges my mom flagged," Kevin said after the family was all checked in. "She needs to realize I'm not going anywhere without you."

It sounded like a cast-off comment, one of his many idealistic proclamations, but Esme felt a familiar panic. Kevin was going away next year, somewhere serious, somewhere new, and no matter how many times he'd vowed his life to her with stars in his eyes, there would be no room for her on his journey.

Last Esme checked, she had a 2.46 cumulative GPA, which meant she'd have her pick of in-state community colleges and, if she got lucky, one of the lesser-known state schools. She'd just never given college a ton of thought.

"It'll work out," she said, but her words felt as hollow as her heart. "Just wanted to say 'hi.' I better go."

They kissed quickly and as she turned to leave, Kevin made a show of holding the catalogs high in the air, then dropping them into the trash can next to the reception desk.

She knew he'd dig them out as soon as she was gone.

On her shortcut home, as she was strolling along the path that cut between the hotel's rental cabins, Esme heard footsteps, followed by a faint knocking coming from the maintenance sheds.

Not knocking. *Banging.*

Tiny moths spiraled around the garden lights. Esme followed the sounds.

Thunking. Accompanied by a muffled shout.

"Hello?" she said, hesitant, as if she were being lured into a trap by the little misfit.

"Yes, yes, hello?"

Esme moved toward the voice. "Hello?"

"Don't go. Please. Can you hear me?"

"Barely?" Esme walked past the laundry cabin, thinking with horror that some kid was trapped in a dryer. "Hello?"

"Over here. In the cabin."

On the farthest edge of the property was the cabin that Kevin and his parents called the Lake Lab. It had a separate walkway, barred windows, and its own private capsule of propane.

"The door is really stuck. I've been trying to open it forever. This is what I get for forgetting my phone at home."

Since late spring, Kevin's parents had been leasing the retrofitted cabin out to a limnologist named Dr. Carla, a tall Black woman with flecked brown eyes and tiny gray coils in her fade. She'd come to town on a research grant and brought with her a pair of twin toddlers and a stay-at-home husband.

A theoretical *husband,* Mr. Polk liked to say, because though *Mister Doctor Carla* had been seen pushing a double stroller around town, no one had actually met him. Mr. Polk speculated that he lived in a tank of oxygenated gel next to the water heater in their cellar.

Though Dr. Carla worked in her cabin lab every day, Esme had only met her once, when she'd appeared in her biology class and gave a presentation on the lake as part of her grant requirements. Dr. Carla drew a map of the lake on the whiteboard, then circled one large section where vents reaching twenty-eight meters deep were home to colonies of *extremophiles*—the lake's *inexplicable microbes*, thriving in a toxic mineral soup that was the consistency of syrup.

"For centuries," she'd said, lifting her chin and going into full lecture mode, "indigenous people gathered here each spring, to forage and trade and heal in these powerful waters. The early white settlers followed their lead and soaked their sore limbs and diseased livestock in it, too, and soon their settlement transformed into a thriving spa town. Veterans from the Great War came to be cured of the maladies and infections that plagued them. It worked well enough for the government to build a VA hospital way out here. It's a nursing home now, but still—how wonderful that this is your backyard! How lucky you are to live here!"

Then Dr. Carla lowered her voice. "It may be hard to believe, but someday, your little lake might make a whole bunch of industries irrelevant. You heard it here first."

Esme and Kevin looked at each other across the classroom and grinned. Most of the speakers who visited their class told them about the devil in music, or the devil in video games, or the devil in Harry Potter, and a lot of their classmates grew up mocking the lake, saying they wouldn't be caught dead swimming in it without a Band-Aid over their bunghole. But Esme and Kevin believed that something magical was happening here, a warp in the fabric of this desert.

Maybe this wasn't a shithole after all.

"Dr. Carla?" she said, leaning into the cabin door. "It's Esme."

"Kevin's friend? Oh, good! Can you get Mr. Polk? Tell him to bring, I dunno, a crowbar? The door is really stuck. I'm starting to feel buried alive."

Esme jiggled the knob and stepped back. On the outside of the door was a beefy hasp locked shut with an even beefier padlock.

"It's not stuck. The lock is locked."

"That's not possible. I'm holding the padlock right now. I always bring it inside with me."

"There's definitely a big lock on here," Esme said, rattling it against the hasp. "Maybe someone didn't know you were in there. I'll get help."

Dr. Carla didn't say anything for a long time.

"Hello?" Esme said, pressing her ear against the door.

"Please do. And have someone call my husband. He's probably worried sick." And then she mumbled, *"Or not."*

As Esme relayed the message, Mr. Polk gathered some tools and Mrs. Polk called the police. A patrol car arrived and some overeager young cop gripped the barred windows with both hands and climbed up on the propane tank to see if they might get Dr. Carla out through the vent in the roof. When Mr. Polk saw him using the propane regulator as a foothold, he yelled at him to get down before they had a gas leak to deal with on top of all the rest. It only took a few tries with the crowbar to pop the hasp off the door, and when Dr. Carla emerged, she seemed embarrassed.

"Thanks for the rescue," she said to Esme.

"Easy peasy."

Mr. Polk was holding the busted padlock in his palm. "Never seen this in my life."

"Meth heads?" Dr. Carla said.

"Or a prank?" Mrs. Polk said, hopeful.

"The pranks around here, my god. Not funny."

In the porchlight, Esme noticed a scattering of burned matches on the walkway, just alongside a bed of dry cheatgrass that grew up against the cabin's log walls and propane tank. She was about to guess something horrific—matches, grass, propane, padlock—but stopped herself: this was a place of healing. Maybe Dr. Carla secretly took smoke breaks.

Dr. Carla was clearly shaken and Esme needed to get home, so she walked at Dr. Carla's side to Main Street. A horned owl bobbed on a light post above the barbershop, and some coyotes yipped on the cliffs above the water, but otherwise the town was quiet.

"Remember this moment, Esme. While I was locked in a cabin, my husband was at home on the couch smoking a joint and popping who knows what else, and probably watching lesbian porn or a documentary about Nikola Tesla. Tells you everything you need to know about men."

"Not my man."

"Kevin? Ah, you're probably right. Just don't forget *he's* the lucky one."

As they parted ways, Dr. Carla called out.

"I owe you dinner! Friday night okay? Six o'clock?"

"I'm kind of—"

"Great!" she said. "I'll set it up with that perfect boyfriend of yours."

Even under the dim streetlights, Esme could see her wink.

CHAPTER 22

ABIGAIL

Abigail stood alone in her kitchen, staring at Esme's keys and drugs and the bloodstained juice box the boy had dropped. Her first inclination had been to go straight to the police, especially given the possibility of DNA or prints on the little carton, but decided that Daniel should be the one to make that call. After all, those detectives were inept at best.

She opened her spice drawer, bagged the juice box, bottled the powder, and tightened the bandana around the keys. Then she stashed it all in the back of the drawer.

She was heading for the shower to wash the desert out of her hair when her phone pinged with a text from Eli:

babe you have time for vid chat? going insane over here.

She replied right away: Of course! You okay?

just work stuff. can you go down to lab? need to check some water. 5 minutes? xo

Down in the lab with her laptop, she waited for the digital trill of Eli's call. She'd hardly been down here since TreeTop's peeping visit and it seemed now as if the space belonged to a stranger. Three microscopes under plastic covers. Bins of cables and wires and sensors. Shelves of dishes and beakers and binders. Fridges full of jars.

She recalled how careful Eli had been about protecting those canning jars of lake water. They had originally been collected by an amateur scientist, a signal corps veteran from Seattle who'd come home after World War One with a case of trench foot that devoured his flesh and left him immobile. He'd been so moved by the lake's power to heal him that he'd hopped the train over the Cascades several times each year, taken samples, and stored them in his basement in Seattle. After his death, his family had donated the jars to the university, who'd passed them on to the researcher Eli had replaced, Dr. Carla Something. When the university delivered the samples to Eli, he'd spent days transferring as many as he could into plastic Nalgene bottles to reduce the risk of contamination from the canning lids, and relabeled them so there was no chance of the dates or depths fading with time. Abigail had never seen him so reverent.

She remembered how good it felt to be in the vicinity of a passion she didn't possess herself, yet it nagged at Abigail that she'd been observing it all quietly, and from a distance, like an intern shadowing a genius. So when spring came around and it was time for Eli to sample the lake on his own, she made a conscious effort to get more involved.

One morning, as he'd loaded his little fiberglass hopper boat atop Medusa, Abigail climbed into the car and told him she'd be joining him on the lake. Eli was enthusiastic, but once they hit the water he grew quiet and hyperfocused, jotting down temperatures and depths and cryptic abbreviations on a waterproof notepad. Here and there he smiled as he rowed, saying next time he'd leave his work behind, like a proper gentleman.

As the lake lapped beneath her, she'd felt herself disappear.

Eli had checked his GPS and shoreline features then lowered a black-and-white disc into the lake and waited for it to fade from sight, measuring the murk of the water. He snapped together pieces of a probe that looked like a mechanical rolling pin. When he dropped it into the depths, his eyes seemed to glow.

The whole time they were out there, Abigail felt like she was getting in his way. When she offered to help with the equipment, he politely explained the risk of contamination, so she pressed her knees together, curling into herself, and tried to enjoy the water's greenish color against the stark crags of the shore.

After a time, Eli asked her to keep the boat steady as he reeled in the samples. She'd gripped the oars and, when he finally got the last canister onboard, felt the boat drifting. In a panic, she cut the oar to the right and knocked the canister out of his hand just as he was unscrewing the lid to transfer its water. They both watched as the sample spilled all over her sandaled feet. It was cold and felt like baby oil.

"Does that count as contamination?" she said, wiggling her toes.

"For what it's worth, I'm glad you came. Just you being here." He raised his hands and swiveled, taking in the lake, and she could see herself reflected in his glacier shades. "But who's ready for chicken fried steak at the diner?"

"Tell me," she said, rowing them toward town. "Do I have your little sea monkey fellas all over my feet right now?"

"*Extremophiles* is the correct term," he said. "And believe it or not, I haven't actually established their exact size. Right now I'm just tracing their DNA and verifying the composition of the water they live in, so that when I study them in the lab I'll have a baseline of their environment. But they are definitely a lot smaller than sea monkeys. You could probably fit a few million of these little guys on your foot."

She stretched her arches. "Ew."

"Imagine how they feel, having evolved in that soup for millennia, and suddenly they're flopping around in a film of lilac bodywash. Battling toe fungus."

"So that really was *the* water?"

"That water we just spilled has been trapped in the lake's deepest vent for thousands of years. It has *never* moved. It has never been touched by light or air, let alone human skin. It'd be hard to find a fluid on earth that's more rare than that water, but those vents aren't going anywhere. There's more. We'll be fine."

"Maybe I'll be able to run really fast now."

"You'd be surprised," he said, widening his eyes. "We have no idea what that stuff could lead to. You should see the chat room talk about this lake. It's like superhero fan fiction. 'One teaspoon of the stuff down deep and your lungs fill with yellow foam that lets you breathe underwater.' It's a whole different planet down there—"

"And there's life on it!"

"Are you mocking me?"

"Definitely."

Eli leaned forward and grabbed the oars so she had to stop rowing. They drifted sideways and bobbed gently under the sun.

"I'd dump it *all* for you, Abigail, get a job teaching high school science. You know that, right?"

She believed that he would. But she also knew she'd never ask that of him, that his research was too important, too integral to his happiness and identity—and no matter what Eli said, she knew he knew that, too.

Down in the lab, Abigail's laptop trilled, and Eli was suddenly on-screen. His hair was dark and curly, noticeably longer.

"Babe," he said, leaning forward with his hands pressing into his cute, plump cheeks. "You have no idea how *good* it is to see you."

"You okay over there, Eli? Your message…"

"I'm fine. My work, though…ugh."

Eli told her that there was only so much testing he could do in his home lab, which was why, before leaving for Poland, he'd shipped some lake samples to a private lab in Berkeley. They broke down the elements, tested them for a range of chemicals and microbes, and sent Eli the digitized reports. It was cost-effective, far cheaper than buying all the equipment and setting up a more advanced testing facility. She knew all that.

"You saw me ship those samples before I left, right?" he said. "Wrapped each one in a cold-pack, boxed it up? Well, the lab in Berkeley claims to have tested exactly what we sent them. But the results are *wrong*. It's weird."

She positioned her laptop on the stool so Eli could see the lab, then he guided her to one of his refrigerators. Each sample was labeled with depth, location, and date, going all the way back to the 1930s.

"Somewhere on the lower shelf," Eli said, "see if you can find *June 18, 1968.* Should say *Northwest quad, 27.4 meters.*"

As she hunted through the samples, Eli explained that he was still in the process of creating a historical baseline of the lake and isolating any variables that could affect its microbial life. Once he verified the lake's composition over time, he could begin what he called his *real work*: mapping the genes and attributes of the extremophiles living in the vents, and determining what miracles they might perform.

But in the process of establishing that baseline, everything had gone to hell.

"I wish I could just go down to the lake and start over. Problem is we know what Soap Lake looks like *now*. We need to know what it looked like in the *past* to have a baseline for my work."

Abigail held up a plastic liter of water from the fridge's bottom shelf.

"*June 18, 1968*. Straight from the Summer of Love. Now what?"

"Does the bottle look okay? Lid is on tight and everything? Let's pour it into something."

She emptied it into a graduated cylinder and the water was slightly murky, as if clouded by a dribble of milk. As it settled, he explained that eight years ago, Dr. Carla—the previous researcher—had tested the water from that same sample.

"I have her results right here. On paper, it looks similar to the other samples taken around that time—1967, 1969, 1972. In terms of its composition and whatnot, they're all pretty close."

"Because the layers in the lake don't move."

"Exactly—*meromictic*. But here's what makes no sense at all. I sent a vial of that same water to the lab in Berkeley before I left. It seems redundant but the testing is a bit more accurate now, and it's a way to validate Dr. Carla's findings so I don't have to double-check everything she did, just enough to show that the tests she ran were done correctly. That her results match mine."

"Only they don't?"

"Not at *all*. My results came back with a different composition than hers. I don't mean like slightly off. I mean like 80 percent off. Like *different*. It's not the same water."

"Maybe Dr. Carla messed up somehow. Because didn't she basically bail on the grant?"

"She took off and left everything unfinished," Eli said. "I spent weeks trying to decipher all the stuff she threw into boxes. I found her name on the website of a community college in Seattle and emailed her to see if she could catch me up. She never replied. I just figured she was embarrassed about her shoddy work. But then I found this."

He shared his screen and pulled up a pdf: a report from the lab in Berkeley that included a long list of elements and minerals found in the sample he'd sent.

Sodium. Carbonate. Sulfate. Potassium.

"What am I looking at, Eli?"

"In theory, this is the composition of the lake, circa 1968. All of its elements are on this list, but the concentrations are really low, like I said, about 80 percent off. Plus there are some others that can't be in the lake. See it?"

Abigail read down the list.

"Arsenic?"

"Yes, but that's not it. Its levels are really low and it occurs naturally. Keep going."

And then she saw it: "Fluoride?"

"Bingo."

"Which is added to tap water?"

"Bingo again. Fluoride's natural, but not like this. These numbers are through the roof."

"Which means what?"

"Guess what year Soap Lake began adding fluoride to their tap water, as a way to prevent tooth decay in children?"

"I'm guessing after the Summer of Love. And please don't say 'bingo.'"

Eli smiled. "Five years later. In 1973."

"So the water in the bottle from 1968 is not water from 1968."

"Not a chance. Someone diluted these samples with tap water, as far as I can tell. Traces of chlorine in there, too. *All* of them."

Abigail found herself staring at the window, now shaded by a miniblind, where late on the night of Esme's murder, TreeTop had been watching her. Something she had yet to share.

And she thought about a time months before, when she and Eli had stood on the lakeshore for the very first time.

"Eli? Remember right when we got here, how surprised you were that no one in the industry had set up shop in town? That there were no *biotech vultures.*"

"Not to mention fossil fuels. Maybe pharma. What about it?"

"If whatever is happening with your microbes could change so much, wouldn't there be industries who'd want to kill the research? I mean, it's all great when something new comes along, but usually when that happens—"

"Something old has to die," he said, distantly. "Sometimes an entire industry."

"And all the money that goes with it," she said. "When did these jars get corrupted?"

"Who knows?" he said. "Sometime between when Dr. Carla was here and the day we shipped the samples to Berkeley. Could've been eight years ago or five months ago."

"I guess that doesn't narrow it down."

"The saddest part of all of this," he said, after a moment, "is that those two fridges behind you hold every drop of Soap Lake water we have from the past. And they've *all* been ruined. I mean, I may still be able to use some of Dr. Carla's research, but I can't count on it to be reliable. Now I'm wondering if someone in the industry bought her off. Because it's starting to look like she sabotaged the whole project on her way out the door. Like a big *F-you* to the town." Eli shrugged and shook his head. "I can still work on parts of the grant, and I've been able to find traces of the extremophiles' DNA, even with the sabotage. But it's hard to put into words how bad this is, to have no baseline for my work. It's like the lake's history has been erased, one bottle at a time."

They looked at each other on-screen, across the planet, and Abigail smiled.

"What?" he said, smiling back. "Please tell me they're looking for a produce person at the grocery store."

She picked up the beaker from the counter and swiveled it around. "Eli, don't get your hopes up. But I might know where to find more old lake water."

CHAPTER 23

ABIGAIL

"I need your help," Abigail whispered at the library circulation desk, poking her head between a pencil sharpener and a coffee can of pens.

Sophia beamed at the arrival of her friend. Not that Abigail was much of a sight: she was still wearing the dusty clothes she'd worn for this morning's excursion into the desert, and still had sunscreen crusted around her face. But Sophia was like a new person—a person who worked at a cosmetics counter, perhaps, or handled PR at a megachurch. She'd showered since the ride and was wearing deep red lipstick and a frilly white blouse. Her rattail was threaded into a tight French braid and tied at the end with a huge red bow. Her posture was amazing.

"Please say *crime scene*," Sophia whispered.

"Water jars this time."

Sophia pointed at the floor. "In the cellar? Those water jars?"

"They're in need of rescuing, if you catch my drift. After work. In the name of science."

"I catch your drift," Sophia whispered, nodding. "Yes I do. Your drift has been caught." She continued to nod as Abigail drummed her fingers on the counter. "Also, I heard something that may be useful. About the stuff in the juice box."

"Already?"

"It may not look it, Abigail, but this is where the action's at."

In the corner, two old men in sweatpants worked together on the *TV Guide* crossword. At a table in the YA section, a group of swearing teenagers played Dungeons & Dragons. On a beanbag in Kids, tots ate board books.

"Oh, it looks it."

"Apparently there's been some talk of a drug coming that could get you high for a year. It could be related."

"High. For a year? That's a terrifying thought."

"Is it?" Sophia said, cockeyed. She added that she'd been thinking about Esme's angle: Esme hadn't been carting that much product, so the meeting in the desert could have been just a taste, what she called "a test run before the milk truck." It was low-risk if she got caught, which might have explained her willingness to drive it up here with George in the car. It was possible, too, that she tried to game the system and it backfired, but Sophia thought it was more likely that Esme was collateral damage—that whoever she'd met didn't like the product, or killed her simply to relay a message up the chain.

"So Esme herself may have had little to do with it," Abigail said, and Sophia shrugged.

"Just a guess."

The two were standing in silence when the back door to the parking lot swung open. Sophia mouthed, *Miss Nellie. Risen from the grave.*

Bit by bit, Abigail had learned all about Sophia's unhealthy relationship with Miss Nellie.

On the one hand, at the most vulnerable point of Sophia's life, when she'd lost Scotty and was struggling to stay clean,

Miss Nellie had offered to sponsor her in the state's Bridge to Tomorrow program, ensuring that she'd have a steady part-time paycheck and twenty-four months of job training at the library. On the other hand, Miss Nellie never let an hour go by without reminding Sophia of what a *loser druggie* she'd been, and how pickled her brain was as a result, how diseased her body, how rank her breath, and how thoroughly grating her voice was each time she stammered through a phone call to patrons who just wanted *a gosh darned library book, not a brush with the Grim Reaper herself.*

Sophia took it all with a bowed head, especially when Miss Nellie swore there was no guarantee of a job for her once the program was complete. She dangled that possible job in front of Sophia with such capriciousness that Sophia could never tell whether she had a real shot or was chasing a dream. Her reaction was to hunker down and work twice as hard.

Miss Nellie didn't come in, so Abigail leaned across the desk far enough to spy her standing in the doorway, chatting with a plump older guy in red suspenders.

"That's her big brother, Hal," Sophia whispered. "He's a hog with a hard-on. Always hits on me. Licks his chin."

"Ew."

"And he smells like pumpkin."

"Okay."

"Innards, not muffins."

"Got it."

Sophia began zapping books, head down...clearly upset.

"Sophia? When you say he's *hitting* on you, what do you mean, exactly?"

"Forget I said anything."

"Because you know you don't have to take that, right? If he's bothering you we can do something about it. Even call the cops."

"He's *buddies* with half the cops," she said, then closed her eyes. "I have to work here, Abigail. *Live* here. So please don't make a thing of it."

"Just trying to help."

"Well, don't."

The door back there closed, shuttering the sunlight, and Miss Nellie started coming their way. Her brother was gone.

"I'll let you get back to your work," Abigail said loudly, touching the back of Sophia's hand before drifting toward the shelves. "Thanks so much for your help!"

Abigail wandered through the stacks until she reached the window that looked out to the lake and the World's Largest Missing Lava Lamp. She spent a minute feeling conflicted, and attempting to convince herself that whatever that guy had done to Sophia, doing something about it was her decision, no one else's. But the conversation wasn't over.

She passed the shelves that led toward the restrooms and was surprised to come upon an alcove with a small wooden table, entirely covered with a paper map. A dented silver suitcase sat next to it. No one was nearby, but draped over the back of the chair was a bright red winter coat—hooded and familiar.

A man coughed behind the wall and a toilet seat clacked the rim. He was in the bathroom.

Abigail may have shaken off her curiosity and let this wandering dude exist without intrusion, but there was no ignoring how often he walked past her house, jotting on his map—which, she told herself, justified a *little* snooping. She stepped closer. The map detailed the entire region, with rivers and lakes and highways in black, and a tight gridwork of property lines and roads in red.

Oddly, it was covered with tiny green doodles.

Her first thought was that the guy had been using this to track his meandering walks. But when she reset her focus she saw that the green doodles were actually green symbols: ampersands and fish, waves and spirals, scarabs and chevrons, moons and omegas, stars and forks—dozens of simple green glyphs, marked all over the map.

She dragged it to the side and discovered piles of printed documents beneath.

A few were articles about the Lava Lamp, including one from the travel section of the *New York Times* and a report from the county tourism commission. Others came from peer-reviewed scientific journals, and one from an old issue of *WIRED* highlighting the decade's most promising innovations.

The other articles were from regional newspapers, dating as far back as the 1960s. And in the upper left corner of each was a tiny green symbol.

A hand: "Fireworks Found on Playground, Child Loses Digit."
A fish: "Field Hand Injured in Baler Mishap."
A wheel: "Packer Killed in *Desert Delite* Storehouse Accident."
A flame: "In Close Vote, Dairy Workers Reject Union."
A spiral: "Person of Interest Sought in Gas Station Assault."
A flower: "Wandering Toddler Found."

The tiny green symbols on each article corresponded with those scrawled across the map. He was clearly tracking the locations of the incidents, and maybe the homes or businesses of those involved. Some of the plats held only a single symbol, but others were piled with them, as if more than one event had happened in those places.

Abigail's head was spinning and the tangy smell of the coat didn't help, but her thoughts stopped cold when a toilet flushed behind the wall.

Focus: her fingertip touched the lake and began tracing the road uphill to her home. Green symbols speckled her street. She was thinking she could count out the plats to find her house, only that became unnecessary when she saw without question which place was hers: the one scrawled with a small green eye. As if she were being watched.

Faucet off. Ratcheting paper towels. Footsteps on tile.

Quickly, she lifted her phone high above her head and took a bird's-eye photo of the map.

"Not in *my* library!"

Busted: it was Miss Nellie, carrying a tote bag full of jigsaw puzzles on her forearm. She wore a Seahawks *12th Man* T-shirt over a blue frock, and her thick gray hair was tucked into a bun and pinned by a yellow pencil. The set of keys looped over her finger held a stabby black self-defense key chain *and* pepper spray, as if one weapon were never enough. She was clearly on her way out, and clearly about to murder someone. Namely Abigail.

Before Abigail could fumble through a response, the bathroom door opened and the red coat guy rounded the corner. He was tugging up his grimy jeans when he caught sight of Abigail standing next to his table. His sun-bleached beard was thick but not long and his hair was trimmed close, with some gray hairs in both. His green eyes widened and she thought of course of his map.

"Have you been watching me?" Abigail said, taking a step toward him.

"Leave him be," Miss Nellie said sharply, and then to him, "Don't mind old snoopy here. You take your time. Everyone knows this is your table. She knows that now, too. Don't she?"

Abigail flinched as the guy yanked his coat off the chair like a matador and whipped it onto his body, zipped it up, raised the hood. As if it were a ward, of sorts, a dreamcoat to protect him from harm.

"I need to know," Abigail said, "if you were looking in my window. Is that why you drew an eye?"

Miss Nellie glared at her as he expertly folded the map and zipped it into his coat pocket, mumbling gibberish, then packed the articles into his suitcase.

"You take all the time in the world," Miss Nellie said to him. "This table is safe. She just didn't know."

She gripped Abigail's elbow and steered her toward the front.

"Stay put until he leaves," she said, tapping the seat of a wooden chair. "And don't snoop like that again."

On her way to the desk, she pointed to a handwritten sign taped above the printers: *Not in My Library!*

Abigail sat, concentrating on the old Michael Jordan *READ* poster hanging across the way. She felt chastened, yet respected the way Miss Nellie protected those who sought solace within these walls.

Before long, the guy marched through the shelves, snapping shut his suitcase as he walked. He stopped in front of Abigail, leaning close enough that she could see the dirt around his tear ducts.

"It was *TreeTop* watching you!" he said, shaking all over. "TreeTop!" Then he left.

A minute later Miss Nellie emerged, holding her tote bag and her stabby keys.

"Just give him a little more time before you leave. They don't tell you when you choose a library career that you have to be a rabbi, therapist, and referee." She rubbed her chin. "Scratch that. They actually do."

"What was he doing back there, anyway?" Abigail said.

"Tracking Sasquatch. What business is it of yours?"

"Someone was looking in my window. Into my husband's lab, middle of the night. And my house is marked on his map. So it actually *is* my business."

"You're Sophia's *neighbor*," Miss Nellie said, nodding as it dawned. "She's a bit dim, isn't she, our Sophia? You know, when she first started working here, she thought we called our library patrons *patients*. 'I was helping a *patient*,' she'd say, or 'That *patient* needs me.' As if this were the ER."

"That's sweet," Abigail said.

"No. That's *drugs*." She jangled her key chain. "Listen, I live alone, too, so I get it if you're worried about being watched. But him out there? He's just damaged, not out to harm anyone, no matter what he's marked on his—what does he call them? His 'Oracle Maps.'"

"Oracle Maps?"

"Says he's mapping the past to see the future. Like a time traveler. Does that make any sense? Swear he should be on Wall Street."

"But why is he singling out my house?"

"Don't make you special," she said, with slight scorn. "He marks everything on that map. Has for years. His son went missing and he's been doing that ever since. Just a toddler. He eventually turned up, but in the meantime his marriage collapsed and I think he did, too. Even though it turned out to be a whole lotta nothing."

"So his son was okay?"

"Kid wandered into the desert for a night or three. That's scary, sure, but not quite the same as being abducted by a bad guy in an orchard, which is what Daddy swears happened."

Abigail was feeling loathsome about this tendency of hers to gaze outward rather than in, as if viewing all of her experiences through a broken mirror—when Miss Nellie turned a fierce eye toward her.

"I know who you are," she said. "I wasn't going to say anything, but you know what? The way you were *violating* that man? You need to hear it."

Abigail gulped.

"The two of you actually have quite a lot in common," Miss Nellie continued. "His name is Preston? Ring a bell? His wife used to be a researcher here, studying the lake. Yeah, let that sink in. Changes things, don't it? She's the one your husband replaced."

"His wife was Dr. Carla? It was *her* son who was taken?"

"Who got *lost*," Miss Nellie said.

Eli had talked about Dr. Carla abandoning her research eight years ago, skipping town and leaving a shoddy trail behind. Only that wasn't why she left.

"His wife has custody, then?"

"Not exactly. Preston refuses to leave town, even just for a visit to Seattle. Hasn't seen her or their kids since they moved out. Says he's *guarding* the lake. That his project demands his full attention."

"Poor guy."

"Poor guy indeed," she said, giving Abigail a chilly stare. "Just don't forget that in a few years, you could be *him*."

In the lot behind the library, now closed, Abigail and Sophia loaded the last box of canning jars into the back of Medusa. Now that they were out of the dark, webby cellar and drenched in the evening light of summer, Abigail studied one of the jars. Its metal ring was crusted shut and she read its brittle label as if it were a bottle of wine.

Soap Lake
Northeast Quad
21m
Oct 1951

The water inside looked like canning syrup with a splash of mud—like it had actually come from the lake, not a faucet. Eli would be over the moon that she'd unearthed samples that hadn't been tampered with. From here, the plan was to hide them in his lab fridge and padlock its door.

"You sure you're okay with this, Sophia? I don't want you to get in trouble."

"You said it was important," Sophia said. "I just hope Miss Nellie...you know."

"For what it's worth, I filled out three different comment cards on you. *True expert in the romance genre. Brings fresh energy to the library.* She needs to know what a badass you are, especially with the way she treats you."

"Yeah, well, she's earned the right."

"No, Sophia. She hasn't. Neither has her brother."

"I wouldn't be anywhere *near* this library if it weren't for her. Guarantee I'd be using. Or collecting worms."

"Maybe, but you still don't deserve—"

"I appreciate it, Abigail, but everything is part of a trade-off."

"Okay," Abigail said, holding up her hands. "But first chance you get? Promise me you'll push Miss Nellie down those stairs."

Sophia stared at her, nodding.

"Kidding, Sophia. I'm *kidding.*"

Sophia gave a cryptic wink.

Abigail was about to start the car when she glanced through the windshield at the lake. The shore was empty except for a few sandpipers—and the guy sitting on his suitcase in the sand.

"Oh shit."

"That coat," Sophia said, tapping the dashboard temperature: *106.* "If you ever see him walking, offer him some water. Really. It's a collective effort. Miss Nellie usually makes him drink from the water fountain before he goes outside. Krunk gives him bottles of Gatorade right out of his little cooler. Guy's gonna keel over."

"Do you know him pretty well?"

"Not really," Sophia said. "We crossed paths in a few pretty horrendous living rooms."

"Dealers?"

"And a cook, as I recall. But that was a long time ago. As far as I know, he dabbled and moved on. Got clean. Found other things to occupy his time."

"Clearly."

Sophia rummaged in her lunch and retrieved a can of orange juice. "Be right back."

She raced over to the shore and gave the drink to Preston, who popped the top and chugged the whole can. They had a quick exchange, and then he lifted his suitcase, ducked his head, and sprinted along the shoreline.

"That was nice of you," Abigail said as Sophia climbed back into Medusa. "What'd he say?"

"Something about your *time capsules*," she said, pointing to the boxes of jars behind them.

"Time capsules," Abigail said, recalling Miss Nellie's words about his Oracle Maps: *tracking the past to see the future.* "You think he knew about the lake water? That it was in the cellar?"

"As far as I can tell," Sophia said, biting her thumbnail, staring at the empty shore he'd left behind, "that guy knows *everything.*"

CHAPTER 24

ESME

"Preston probably has *no* idea you're here," Dr. Carla said as she led Esme and Kevin into her home. "I told him it was a dinner party a hundred times, but he's been watching a *Shaun the Sheep* marathon with the twins. Pretty into it. He's probably high. As long as they aren't drinking bleach." And then she parked her hand on her hip and said, "You know, he didn't even notice I was *gone* the other night. I was three hours late."

"The locked-in-lab night?"

"Don't ever get married," she said dryly.

Dr. Carla was self-assured and gorgeous, with hardly any makeup and a chunky seashell necklace with red beads that Esme couldn't stop staring at. In the kitchen, she handed them each a glass of red wine, as if Soap Lake were Copenhagen and that whole Drinking Age thing didn't apply. Dr. Carla must have noticed Esme's hesitation because she said, "You didn't drive, did you?"

"A car?"

She smiled. "You are adorable. I love that you chop your hair."

She spun around, her batik blouse rippling, and took a baking dish bubbling with carroty white sauce out of the oven.

They sat around the table and Kevin began chatting about the Young Scientist scholarship he'd been working on, something about the lake levels fluctuating with precipitation and evaporation. He was dressed just right in one of those striped dress shirts that came with little envelopes of spare buttons. Esme was so nervous about being underdressed in her black blouse and jeans, big silver hoops, that she zoned out from all the scholarship talk and drank her wine in three big heartburning gulps. Dr. Carla caught her and smiled.

"You're our first guests," she whispered. "Preston hasn't met anyone. He tried to do some art class for kids at the library and not a *single* parent showed up. Broke his heart! But enough about that." She leaned toward Esme. "What college are you going to?"

Esme had just eaten a piece of salami and had to swallow the rubber-band thing that was around it, so again Kevin took over. He told Dr. Carla about how he was polishing the final rows of his transcript and drafting admissions essays, but wishing he'd had more opportunities growing up that he could plug into those empty slots in the application.

"He dominated the science fair six years straight," Esme said, and Dr. Carla laughed as Kevin humbly explained that most of his competition was from kids making potato-cannon flamethrowers or blasting phone books with shotguns to test the depths reached by different gauges of shells.

"Bill Nye meets Ted Nugent," Esme said.

"That sounds *amazing*," Dr. Carla said, her teeth purple with wine. "Number one, you need to write what you just said to me all over your college applications. Here's the pitch—rural *wunderkind* in underserved region makes the best of scarce opportunities. Got that? And number two, you're coming to work for me."

"For you?" Kevin said.

"Congratulations, young man, you've just been awarded a highly competitive internship in a university-sponsored research lab. And it should make that scholarship proposal a breeze."

"Awesome. What do I do?"

"You follow me to the basement, of course." She led them into the hallway and opened a narrow door.

"You have a basement?" Kevin said.

"Preston is expanding the root cellar. Refinishing it to make a playroom for the kids."

"Handy," Esme said.

"As long as the whole house doesn't collapse. I don't even want to *think* about what this place would look like without me. He's a wonderful guy, but if he had his way he'd be pulling a wagon full of crap everywhere he went, if you know what I mean!"

Esme didn't, but she still followed Dr. Carla down the steps into a large root cellar with low ceilings and walls made of crusty rock and cinder block. Some lumber and five-gallon buckets of tools sat in the corner. The floor was stacked with old boxes holding canning jars.

"I have more in the lab, but this is the best storage I could find for overflow." Dr. Carla spun around and handed Kevin a glass jar with a rusty lid and a peeling label.

Soap Lake
SWquad
14m
July 7, 1978

"I've got over two hundred containers full of old lake water that need to be transferred and documented, and half their lids are crusted shut. Part of my grant includes cataloging the stuff and storing it under better conditions. So. Let's see what you got. Open."

Kevin hugged the jar against his body twisted the lid off.

"Good technique. You're hired."

"They don't call me The Claw for nothing," he said, flexing his fingers. *"And all this time,"* he added in his best B-movie voice, *"I thought it was a curse."*

"Oh my!" Dr. Carla said, sloshing her wine.

Esme was buzzed and relaxed by the time Preston, Dr. Carla's shaggy-haired husband, tiptoed into the kitchen in bare feet and a Hendrix T-shirt, whispering about how he had to crawl out on his belly while the twins were glued to *Shaun the Sheep*.

"Let's eat before they show up and ruin our meal," he whispered.

Kevin disappeared to the bathroom and Dr. Carla disappeared into the pantry, leaving Preston and Esme standing at opposite ends of the table. He fidgeted with his wedding ring, she with her silver bracelet. His eyes were bright green and some of his hair was so long that it fell into his face and stuck to his stubble. He reminded Esme of her mom, in the way he put more effort into withholding his words than into speaking them.

Esme smiled and filled the silence. "Sorry about your kids class."

"That library," he mumbled.

"What do you mean?" Kevin said, arriving just in time. They all sat.

Preston started to speak but Dr. Carla came in, clutching bottles of salad dressing. "Don't get me going on that library," she said.

Dr. Carla told them about how Preston had gone in with the kids one day and inquired *"offhandedly*, mind you," about any studies they might have on the region's groundwater contamination or arsenic levels in the lake.

"The librarian—you know *her*—threw up her hands and said, 'Don't ask me!' I'm pretty sure they don't teach that response in library school."

"Why'd you want to know about arsenic?" Kevin asked, transparently fishing for a scholarship topic.

"It kept turning up in my samples, but it was a false lead from the start. Minuscule numbers. Plus it exists naturally in the lake. Erodes from rocks."

"And apple seeds," Preston blurted.

"That's cyanide, sweetie," Dr. Carla said, and caressed the back of his hand. "I was just working through some variables. You start down one path, cross it out, start down another." She took a glug of wine and for a moment seemed exasperated. "I'm crossing out a lot these days."

"Is it not going well?" Kevin said.

"Of course you'd ask that," she said, pensive. "You know how when I visited your class, I talked about researching the lake back when I was a grad student? It was all preliminary and sloppy, but had so much *potential*. That was something like fifteen years ago."

"Seventeen and a half," Preston said, glancing up from the pile of cherries he was pitting and dropping into bowls for the tots, his fingers stained deep red. "Pre me."

"Couldn't have had that much potential if it took that long to come back," Kevin said.

"On the contrary," Dr. Carla said, shaking her head. "My findings could change the *world*."

When she was in graduate school at UW in Seattle, Carla spent a week assisting Dr. Felix Raymundo, an award-winning mycologist, on his annual research trip to Soap Lake, where he was doing fieldwork on a species of lichen that lived on the basalt around the lake.

On their first day, Carla rowed them along the shore, holding the boat steady as Dr. Ray scraped lime-colored lichen off the rocks. Then he directed her toward the lake's deepest vents—

where the good stuff is—and began unreeling canisters into the depths.

Back at camp, Dr. Ray handed her a sample of lake water to study and pointed her toward a portable chemistry closet inside the RV bathroom. He cautioned her that she was on her own with her experiments, and that at the end of the week *nothing* was to come home with her.

"Researchers are welcome. Prospectors are not."

Carla borrowed a microscope and agar dishes, set up in the corner of the table, and immediately began testing the water's salinity and acidity. If anything of significance were to turn up, she knew it would never hold up to peer review, at least until it was replicated under controlled conditions, but she was nonetheless thrilled when she began to see signs of microbial activity. As she siphoned drops of that rare, slick water—water that had been eternally immersed in the dark, with the same pH as ammonia, highly sulfidic, lacking oxygen—she knew that any creature that could live in such an extreme environment had to be exceptional.

Like a lot of breakthroughs, hers began with an accident.

Carla was introducing a gentle dye to her samples, hoping to isolate any microbes without compromising them, when something went wrong. Each time she added a drop, the water fizzed and turned milky yellow. She found a thicker dye in the chemistry cabinet and stirred it into a cold beaker of lake water. Her intent was to slide a drop under Dr. Ray's powerful microscope to see if she could view the cells, but the little beaker also began to fizz, and within minutes a yellow foam the consistency of shaving cream had settled on the surface. She siphoned it off and saw no traces of the dye, as if it had metabolized.

Dr. Ray didn't say a word.

Carla put away the dyes, assuming that she'd messed something up.

"Any PCBs in here?" she said, standing in front of Dr. Ray's supplies.

"Some used motor oil out in the storage, pre-1979, that's old enough to have PCBs. But I've got something stronger if that's what you're after," he said. "Chlorofen. Third shelf. Highly chlorinated biphenyl. Decades old and definitely illegal. Produced in rural Poland, in a town where you wouldn't want to fill your water bottle or eat a carrot."

"I won't pour it on my salad."

Dr. Ray groaned as she stirred three hundred milliliters of Chlorofen into a water sample. This time, when she siphoned off the yellow foam and dolloped it into a clean beaker, she couldn't resist touching it with her finger—and it gave her a small electric shock.

It didn't seem possible, but her first thought was that she'd found an exoelectrogen—a microbe capable of passing concentrated electrons through its cellular walls.

A living battery. Powered by filth.

She tested a swab of foam for trace PCBs and it came back clean. Her hands were shaking as she rummaged for a micro voltmeter, grounded one probe and dropped the other into the beaker. The dial settled into a reading: 28,088 μV.

All night she was awake, wondering what she'd done wrong.

But if she hadn't—if this was real—the foam was evidence of a transformation: the microbes had neutralized the toxins. And created electricity in the process.

When she asked Dr. Ray about it, he grumbled about bioprospectors and cautioned her to "beware those who mined the natural world for profit!"

When Carla continued to pepper him with questions, he finally lost it: "If this is *that*, you're not ready for it. Hell, I'm not ready for it. And neither is this place!" Sensing her frustration, he took a breath and tapped her canister of lake water. "If this becomes your path of study, you'll be back when you're ready. But now is not the time."

On their last morning at the lake, Dr. Ray went out in the boat alone and told her to pour her samples into the RV's waste tank to destroy them, as they'd agreed. With destruction on her mind, Carla stooped into the storage compartment and gathered a quart of red transmission fluid, a bottle of blue sewage tank treatment, and an ancient milk container holding used motor oil, circa 1975, polluted with PCBs.

Then she poured a splash of each into her sample. The liquids bobbed around the water like colorful ball bearings before blooming into yellow balls of foam. Bubbles churned through the dark gray soup.

Within minutes, the water in the beaker showed no sign of black oil, nor red fluid, nor blue liquid—just water, as pure as light, with yellow foam settled on top.

It zapped her finger when she touched it, and the hair on her arms lifted into the air.

"That was seventeen years ago," Dr. Carla said, glopping creamy pasta onto Esme's plate. "You would've been a baby."

"Why'd it take you so long to get back here?" Esme said.

"It's ironic how much we know when we're young, and how little we know when we're old. Dr. Ray was right. I wasn't ready for a discovery like that in grad school. Even today, I don't know exactly what I found."

"But you're back."

"I spent nearly two decades studying extremophiles and meromictic lakes, but I was more than a little hesitant to return. And then, maybe six years ago, I received a call from a colleague who knew I'd done some research here telling me that someone had donated several hundred jars of old Soap Lake water to her university, and asking did I have any interest in them? You saw them in the cellar. I applied for grants and got ready to restart my research. But we'd just gotten married and—"

"I hit rock bottom," Preston said, raising his hand. "Rehab. Long story."

"But we made it, finally. Is the research going well? No, but it *continues*, which is the best you can hope for in this line of work. It's a slog."

"On that note," Preston said, and they all went politely silent. He clearly thought she'd shared enough.

Kevin faked a laugh. Esme stared at her pasta. And the lull was broken a few seconds later when, somewhere deep in the house, one of the twins barked loudly and everyone smiled.

"Preston gets nervous when I tell people," Dr. Carla said, touching her glass. "I've managed to map the microbe's DNA, so I know it's there, and I have other evidence of the colonies. *But*. And this part you cannot repeat, even to your folks."

"Carla," Preston said. "They aren't interested."

She ignored him, and he huffed and began scarfing his pasta.

"I'm sure you've seen me out there in the boat, taking samples, but for the life of me—"

"You know how to row a boat?" Preston said to Kevin, still chewing. Kevin nodded. "There you go. He can row, you can focus. Problem solved."

He picked up the crusty bread loaf, ripped off a chunk, and passed the rest to Esme.

"At this stage I'm testing for remnant DNA to pin down their exact location. But I don't know." Dr. Carla's plate was untouched. She was bereft. "You spend your life waiting for this one thing, and then just when you're close, it becomes elusive. *The best laid plans*, as they say."

Kevin nodded. "So you're unable to repeat the experiments from grad school?"

"It would help if the meth heads would stop breaking into

her lab," Preston said. He stabbed some pasta and mumbled as he ate it. "Tweakers or whoever."

Esme and Kevin stopped chewing and glanced at each other. She knew he was thinking exactly what she was: *TreeTop*.

"Preston thinks someone is messing with my samples," Dr. Carla said, "diluting them or something. Which would sound totally *bonkers* except for the fact that someone *did* lock me in my own lab, right?"

"And maybe," Esme mumbled, "tried to set it on fire."

"You saw that, too," Dr. Carla said, nodding intensely. "And there's been this *zombie* hanging around the hotel lately. I've been meaning to ask your dad about him, Kevin. This morning he banged on the cabin door and asked what I was cooking. I hadn't even had my coffee and there's a guy standing at the door in rags, looked to be maybe twenty? Long brown hair. *Missing teeth*."

Esme felt her stomach drop. Kevin looked at her.

"Silas," he said. She nodded.

"I've seen him on the lakeshore a few times," Dr. Carla continued, "just staring at the water. The first time I honestly thought he was a sack of dirty laundry or something."

"He's had it rough," Esme said, somewhat defensively. "He's been doing all these programs. To get better."

Dr. Carla shook her head. "Whatever programs he's in? They don't work."

She was right. As far as she could tell, Silas's main therapy the past few years had been to get fucked-up as often as possible. Pastor Kurt kept trying to rescue him, spending money he didn't have on yet another private Christian rehab, but it was never long before Silas was back, digging his own grave.

"Is he dangerous?" Dr. Carla asked.

Kevin looked at Esme, who was sneering without realizing it. But before either of them could answer, the twins, Ali and Alan, stormed into the dining room and soaked up all the focus.

A while later, Esme was assembling a letter *A* out of sliced cheese on Ali's plate when she caught Dr. Carla smiling at her. She asked if she'd be interested in babysitting.

"I know it's shitty to offer your boyfriend an internship and give you the babysitting scraps. Real progressive of me. But I'd pay you well. And his is volunteer."

"Esme is amazing with kids," Kevin said.

"I can see that," Dr. Carla said.

"I love 'em," Esme said, which was true, and was something she hadn't said to anyone in a long time.

"Well, good," Dr. Carla said. "Let me know if you need to pad your college applications, too. Though something tells me you don't need any help."

"Deal," Esme said, and it took her a minute to process what Dr. Carla had just implied: that Esme seemed smart, college-bound, just like Kevin. Guilt by association, she supposed.

When Dr. Carla and Kevin moved into the living room to discuss his internship, Esme and Preston cleared the table. As soon as they were alone, he whispered, "I saw your face when I mentioned someone messing with Carla's lab. So? What am I missing?"

Esme was alarmed for a moment. "I don't know," she said.

"Well, someone does," he said, harsh enough to spit, then he squeezed the sides of his head. "Sorry. It's right *there*. I just need somewhere to start."

In the other room, the twins were dragging cushions off the couch.

"Have you heard of TreeTop?" she said.

He tapped his stubbled chin, nodding. "I've seen the graffiti. *TreeTop Kills*. What's that all about?"

"My dad thought something bad, like *bad*, was happening here. Since before he was a kid."

"Think he'd talk to me?" he said.

"He's dead."

Preston nodded slowly, and the way it sank in, the way he just kept nodding, she could tell what he was thinking: that her dad's death had something to do with TreeTop.

"Listen," she continued, "I don't know what it all means. But people have written it all over town. In secret. For years. *Tree-Top Kills.*"

"I saw it at the playground, right? And where else?"

"Behind the cubbies at the roller rink might be a good place to start. There, and maybe under the bathroom sink at the grocery store. And—"

"Wait!" he said. He tugged a smeary finger painting off the fridge, flipped it over, and pressed a pen into her hands. "Here. Slow down. Draw me a little map."

CHAPTER 25

ABIGAIL

Stepping into the air-conditioned lobby of the Healing Lake Hotel with George holding her hand, Abigail felt as if she'd entered a basement, circa 1977: orange-and-red fractal carpet, Styx playing in the background, and a gumball machine filled with black eight-ball gum. George stared wide-eyed at the KISS pinball machine in the corner, and at the shelves displaying lava lamps in a rainbow of colors: *BELIEVE!*

For the next few days, Abigail would be babysitting George while Daniel made the drive down to Esme's apartment in Bakersfield, a thousand miles south. The trip was mainly so that Daniel could go through his sister's belongings, chat with her neighbors, and finally have some time to wrap his head around her death. But he also planned to have breakfast with the cop down there who'd been helping the task force, hoping she'd have something more to contribute to Esme's murder than had the local jokers here.

On his way out of town this morning, when he'd dropped

George off at Abigail's house, she handed him the keys she'd unearthed in the desert, still wrapped in a bandana. She'd considered sharing them with Krunk first, but decided that Daniel should make that decision, not her. When Daniel saw them, he shook his head and pointed out the sheer holy freakishness of her finding the keys to Esme's apartment right as he was prepping to go there. He said he'd be careful with them in case there were fingerprints and probably give them to the cops when he got back.

When she tried to give Daniel the bottle of yellow powder, he took a step back and asked her to bury it for the time being.

"The second the cops see that, this investigation is over. Or *more* over."

Back to her spice drawer it went.

Abigail rang the bell on the reception desk. They were there to buy matching Lava Lamp T-shirts, part of her plan to make George's stay feel more like a slumber party than a babysitting gig. She'd been conscious of keeping his presence low-profile, yet as they were standing in the empty lobby, she glimpsed a framed photo of a young man with round wire glasses and messy brown hair, and realized she'd inadvertently brought George directly into his mother's past. Below the photo, an inscription read:

Kevin M. Polk
Gentle Be Thy Slumber

It occurred to her that there wasn't a single place in town where more threads of this mess converged.

Esme would have been here all the time with Kevin.

Dr. Carla had a lab in one of the cabins, which meant Preston would have been here, too.

Krunk was delivering a pizza here when Kevin was shot in this lobby.

Sophia used to clean these rooms, make these beds, vacuum these halls.

And the boy Abigail was charged with protecting was right now staring at a photo of his mom's murdered boyfriend. She gently spun him around to leave, but before they reached the exit, a *yoohoo* voice chimed through the lobby.

"Help you?"

Mrs. Polk stepped through the clicking beaded curtain and leaned across the reception desk. She appeared open and friendly, with springy gray hair and oversize grape-colored specs.

"Oh, it's you!" Mrs. Polk said, slapping the counter. "From the parade. You decided to stay."

"More like *still here*."

"And who's this guy?"

Mrs. Polk wore the eager smile of someone who adored kids but didn't see enough of them, yet her face fell apart when she figured out the boy was George.

"I hadn't realized at the parade," Mrs. Polk whispered, "that you're who—" But she was thoughtful enough to stop speaking: *found him.*

"It was the other way around. And George here is really smart, and he has ears."

"Of course," she said, before turning to face him. "You're about four, aren't you?"

Her words arrived in an odd, accusatory tone, so it came as little surprise when the boy moved on to stare at the peace lilies and spider plants on the windowsill. A brown leather belt stamped with symbols and letters hung from a single nail alongside.

"We just came to grab a couple T-shirts."

"Of course," Mrs. Polk said, fumbling along the shelf behind her. Then she turned.

"He is *beautiful*," she said, speaking through her hands. "It's like she's right here. The resemblance. I'm just plummeting through time right now. *Whew.* Worse than a hot flash."

George bumped his forehead into Abigail's thigh, acting shy. She was about to send him off on a distraction—*Did you see the lava lamps?*—when he stepped toward one of the many photos of Kevin hanging near the window. It showed Kevin in a hammock as a pimpled teen, looking over the top of *The Hitchhiker's Guide to the Galaxy.* In a singsong voice, George whispered, "Night, Kevin."

Mrs. Polk went pale. "What did you say? You know about my Kevin?"

The boy fell back into Abigail, but he didn't need to answer. It was clear that Esme had kept a photo of the love of her life somewhere prominent. And maybe she and the boy had said good-night to him every night, just as they had to photos of Daniel and Grandma. Part of their nightly ritual.

Night, moon. Night, Daniel. Night, Gramma. Night, Kevin.

"Let's get you a gumball," Abigail said, moving toward the eight-ball gum, but Mrs. Polk intervened.

"Yeah, don't eat those," she said. "Older than that record." She excavated a shoebox from under the counter and lifted the lid to reveal a bright assortment of candy bars. "My husband's stash. Take as many as you want."

The boy picked a Milky Way.

"Good choice," Mrs. Polk said.

As Abigail steered the boy toward the lava lamps, Mrs. Polk shifted her attention to the T-shirts, mumbling about finding an elusive extra-small. "Now, you are looking for lava lamp shirts, not the ones with the town's so-called mascot. You-know-who. Makes me shudder, the crocheted dolls and PEZ dispensers. Part of why the Lava Lamp is so important—cancel that monster out. Should be coffee in the pot for you while I'm rummaging."

Abigail was glad she changed the subject. George had enough to terrify him without giving him a lesson in TreeTop.

"I've heard it's the best coffee in town," Abigail said.

"Things taste better when they're free." She winked. "Mr.

Polk roasts the beans himself. Between us, he'd be bored to death without all the cops and volunteer firefighters dropping by for refills. Cheapest security system around, plus if the hotel ever catches fire they'll be *caffeinated*."

Abigail attempted to buy two *BELIEVE* T-shirts and a bottle opener shaped like a lava lamp, but Mrs. Polk insisted on giving them to her. George had meanwhile migrated to the KISS pinball machine, its board lit with dudes in Kabuki makeup, crotching out.

Mrs. Polk gave him quarters and soon his silver ball jacked the bumpers and dropped the targets and colorful circles lit the board.

Abigail strayed to the wall of framed photos, all of Kevin. As a tot on a beach. As a grade-schooler, standing next to an owl. As a teen, wearing a lab coat and displaying a crusty jar of lake water.

She startled when she felt Mrs. Polk suddenly inches from her side, speaking quietly.

"I have to tell you. My reaction earlier. Seeing him?"

"It's okay," Abigail said, taking a step back.

"No, it's not," Mrs. Polk said, gripping Abigail's wrist. "The boy is four. We know that now. But when we heard there was a child, a survivor, we had no idea how old he was." It took Abigail a second to realize where she was going with all of this— and why she was tearing up. "After Kevin died, Esme practically disappeared overnight, so when we heard she had a child, we were hopeful. They were sexually active, you see? We wanted to be grandparents. But he's around *four*," Mrs. Polk continued, as if the number were the most heartbreaking word in the world. "Our Kev has been gone for eight years…"

They'd been hoping that Esme had left town in such a hurry after Kevin's murder because she was pregnant with his baby, and that it was their grandchild who'd burst out of the desert that day, right into their lives. But the math didn't add up.

"It just never made sense why anyone would want to hurt

Kevin." Mrs. Polk pressed her fingers into her cheeks, wiping them dry. "They say the worst thing in the world is to lose a child, and that's true, without question. But you lose their future children, too..."

She glanced over at George, who looked up from his game.

The beads clicked behind the desk, and Mr. Polk came in, towering and glum.

"They're just getting T-shirts," she said.

He looked at Abigail with recognition. "You're married to the researcher, right? The guy in Poland?"

Abigail did her best to not appear jarred by the question. "That would be Eli. My absentee genius."

"Thought so," he said, attempting but failing to smile. "Can I show you something?"

"We actually need to get going," Abigail said.

"Just a few minutes down at the lake," he said, holding his wife close. "We've got a nice little beach. Please."

He squinted at her in a way that Mrs. Polk couldn't see. A signal. So she agreed.

As Mrs. Polk skipped ahead with George, Mr. Polk handed Abigail a cold can of tea and led her to a pair of Adirondack chairs along the shoreline, where they took a seat.

"Esme called me," he said.

"Esme called you?"

He ignored her, his gaze drawn to a couple of hotel guests sitting at the water's edge, their bodies smeared with drying gray mud. Beyond them, a pregnant woman knelt on all fours in the shallows, soaking her hands and feet. Her belly sat in the lake like a bowl.

"See that kid out there?" he said, lowering his voice.

A bit farther out, a young man in shades was floating on his back in the water.

"He's going away to college soon," Mr. Polk said. "University of Hawaii. Marine biology. He's been here all week, a going-away gift from his mom."

When the young man stood she could see that his chest, shoulders and back were covered in scabby boils.

"He's not a superficial guy," Mr. Polk said, "but he wants to be able to take off his shirt at the beach, you know? Told me he wears a thick hoodie everywhere he goes, even on the hottest days, because otherwise it all seeps through."

"Is the lake helping?" she said, her words struggling to get past the bubble in her throat.

"It sure seems to, especially in conjunction with the change in diet and climate. Twice a day he swims out with a bucket and a rope and collects mud to smear on his skin. And soaks in the water in between. The inflammation is down and he's definitely less embarrassed about it. That's the most important thing. Kid could barely get two words out when he first got here. Now he lets me put mud on spots he can't reach."

Abigail was watching this young man but thinking of Kevin. Mr. Polk was helping, she thought, but he was being helped as well.

"This is why you're here," Abigail said.

"The lake takes away our pain, too."

He looked down the shore at Mrs. Polk and George, carving channels in the mud.

"You'd think the end of a person's life would mean the end of their story," he said, "but that's not always how it works. Sometimes the story has no end. Sometimes it just keeps going."

She could tell he was talking about Kevin, and maybe even liked how centered he seemed, but wasn't sure why he was sharing. Until—

"Your husband is doing valuable work here," he said. "Not to mention the care you're giving to that child. The last researcher—"

"Dr. Carla."

"Why am I not surprised you already know about her? Her lab was just there, the cabin farthest from the hotel."

"It's nice she let Kevin work with her. I saw the photo in the lobby. Of him wearing a lab coat."

"She was pretty great with him. Gave him an internship, helped him with a scholarship." He glanced around. "But the whole time she was here, doing her work on the lake—"

"Things happened?" Abigail said.

"Yes, they did."

"Like her child disappearing into the desert?"

"Exactly like that," he said.

"And visitors coming around for a peep through the window?"

"You, too, huh?" He leaned in and grew serious. "I don't know what to tell you except to be cautious, but try not to worry too much. The power structures here are monstrous and invisible. But they can generally be avoided if you're smart."

Abigail felt woozy and planted her palms on her knees. "Esme really called you?"

"She did."

"What did she say?"

He shrugged and sipped his tea.

"You haven't told your wife," she continued. "That's why you looked at me like that in the lobby."

"I haven't told anyone," he said. "I thought it would've gotten out by now. There's an investigation underway, last I heard. If it can be called that."

"So why on earth are you telling *me*?"

He watched Mrs. Polk and the boy, playing by the shore. "I can't begin to express how much it meant to me, peeking through that beaded curtain today and seeing Esme's child playing pinball with my wife looking on. It's one of the most beautiful and unexpected things I've seen in my life. Oh hell." He grunted and squeezed his hands together as if in prayer. "She tries so hard to get past what happened. She's got a library on grieving. Goes to workshops in Spokane. Constant podcasts and more than a few gurus. Once a year Pastor Kurt, the shooter's dad, comes around to do this reconciliation walk around the lake, just the two of them, as an attempt at healing. Forgiveness."

"You don't go with them?"

"I tried once. Made it about fifty feet before ducking out to be alone. It was too much."

"I can only imagine."

"Nothing against Pastor Kurt. But his kid, Silas, the one who murdered Kevin? He was trouble his whole life. Ruined his dad's marriage, broke up his family, weaseled his way out of court. I can't help but think Kevin would be alive right now if they just would've locked that kid up instead of trying so hard to reform him. It's not a nice thought. But goddammit, nothing fills the void."

Abigail thought about how hard it would be, in the face of such loss, to forgive.

"One night this past spring, I was asleep at the front desk at three in the morning and the phone rang. I assumed it was a guest in need of Tums or my world-famous Indica Cupcakes with melatonin frosting, but it was her. 'Hi Mr. Polk. It's Esme.' As if we spoke all the time."

"What'd she say?"

"She said she was living down near Bakersfield and that she was thinking about coming home. I didn't pry, but I could hear sadness there. Desperation. I told her I'd help her in any way I could, maybe give her a job and a room at the hotel if she needed it, though I can't imagine she would've wanted to spend any time on the premises. Given Kevin. She listened for a minute then said she had to go and hung up."

"That was it?"

"Not quite. She called me late at night over the course of a month or so, maybe half a dozen times, well into May. We mostly reminisced about Kevin. She kept circling back to the shooting like she was stuck on it, you know? Struggling. A lot of trauma there that she'd never dealt with. No therapy or church or anything. I could hear the homesickness in her voice. And we talked a little about how sometimes when you go away you miss the things you didn't think you'd miss. The people. Hard to imagine her out there all alone."

"So you were surprised she wanted to come back?"

"Even with the loneliness I couldn't make sense of it. She was calling me like clockwork and then one week the phone didn't ring and I never heard from her again. I assumed she'd changed her mind or maybe took my advice and found a counselor. But the whole idea of her coming back here never sat right. Until I read about George in the newspaper. The boy made it make sense. How did I never ask her whether she'd had any *kids*?"

"What do you mean?"

"Having a child changes everything. It's hard to raise a kid, especially broke and alone, so I'm guessing she finally got desperate for some help. And missed her family, of course. It suddenly added up, her coming back."

Near the water's edge, George splashed his palms into muddy puddles.

"It's probably good no one here knew of his existence," he said. "Whoever killed her? If they had known she had a kid, they would've looked for a kid in the car. Small towns have long memories. A lot of people blame her for what happened to Kevin, among other things, though I sure don't."

"Does Mrs. Polk?"

Mr. Polk looked out over the lake. "She lost her only son."

"Is that why you haven't told her that Esme called?"

They watched Mrs. Polk and the boy emptying yogurt containers full of water into a hole in the mud. The boy was laughing as he poured one on Mrs. Polk's drizzling hair, and she pretended to be upset, which made him laugh even harder.

"She lost her only son," he repeated.

CHAPTER 26

ESME

Esme came home from the high school for a quick lunch, tossed her backpack to her bedroom floor and was about to collapse on her bed, when she noticed broken glass spread across her comforter. The curtains were open and the window above held a splintering crater surrounded by jagged fragments.

She yelled for Daniel and he came running into the room, holding a half-eaten PB&J stained with Doritos fingerprints. She pointed at the window.

"Is that a—?"

"Gunshot," Daniel said, and pulled out his phone.

Fifteen minutes later, Esme and Daniel stood in her tiny bedroom with a local cop she recognized from years ago: McDaid, the crew-cutted asshead who'd cornered her in the orchard after Silas stashed Baby Grace in the flowerpot. He was a little older now, still crew-cutted but paunchy, with even more swagger than he'd had back then. The kind of cop who always rested his palm on the top of his holstered gun, even when talking to a classroom of kids.

McDaid leaned over her bed, studying the cratered window and shards of glass.

"You sure your mom didn't hear a shot?"

"I'm sure," Daniel said.

Before long, Kevin came rushing in from a math club tournament. He hugged Esme and asked in a panic what he could do.

McDaid brightened at his arrival. "Bring any of that famous coffee?"

"We don't deliver," Kevin said, chuckling, as Daniel and Esme rolled their eyes.

McDaid studied her closet door with his flashlight, then rubbed his finger over a small hole. "There we are." He illuminated a scuffed dent on the closet wall, and picked up a lead bullet with a slightly flattened head from the carpet below.

"Looks to be a .38." He dropped it into his pocket, as if that were crime scene protocol. "The question is—"

"Silas," Daniel said.

"Definitely," Kevin said.

"No way," Esme said.

Lately it seemed that everyone she ran into found it necessary to report how *roasted* Silas was these days, and all the hateful things he spouted about her: he was gonna drown her in the lake, make her swallow her own eyeballs, drop a TV on her head. And of course there were his visits to Dr. Carla's cabin and the little misfit he'd enlisted to slap her. But despite those threats, and against her better judgment, she still had a soft spot for the guy. He'd never had a chance.

"I guarantee the department isn't paying for any ballistics analysis," McDaid said. "I could fill out a report, but unless someone saw Silas firing a .38 Special this way, it's only going to create paperwork. We don't even know if this was a crime. People shoot guns. Bullets go astray. Especially this side of the lake." McDaid turned toward Esme. "If you actually got shot, that would be a different story, of course."

"Next time," Daniel said flatly, and Esme smirked.

McDaid glared at him. "You done?"

Daniel stared back for a second, then gave up and spun away. A few seconds later the screen door flew open and he could be heard under the ash tree out front, throwing blows at his boxing bag.

"We'll talk to Silas," Kevin said, perfectly agreeable, as they made their way outside.

"I wouldn't advise that," McDaid said, stepping off the porch. "Silas has had a tough go. I think it's best to give the kid some space. Let him cool off. If I see him, I'll have a word. We go way back, me and him."

"I bet you do," Esme said under her breath, then crossed the lawn to stand with Daniel.

After Officer McDaid was gone, Daniel insisted that Kevin take Esme to the Lazy-A Diner while he cleaned up the broken glass in her bedroom, and duct-taped some cardboard over the window until he could replace the pane.

Esme began feeling nauseous during dinner, but wasn't sure if it was the all-you-can-eat spaghetti at the diner—delicious during the first plate, repulsive by the third—or that she was more than a little sick of everyone talking about the same two things: Silas's threats and Kevin's college plans. Against Kevin's objections, she walked home from the diner alone, hoping the fresh air would help settle her gut.

It did. But her nausea returned with tidal force when she approached her home in the late dusk light and saw Pastor Kurt sitting on the top step of her porch, wearing jeans that used to fit and a Hawaiian shirt bouncing with lemons and limes.

"I'm not here," she said, head down, marching toward her front door.

"I heard what happened to your window," he said. "You okay?"

"I'm fine."

"Good. Because we need to talk. It's about Silas."

In his forties now, Pastor Kurt had gone half-bald and his moustache was bristled and white, and it was hard to believe that he was the same man who'd brought his infant daughter into the library for Esme to hold that day. She still felt horrible about what happened with Baby Grace, but saying *Sorry we dropped a giant-ass television on your sweet little Tater Tot!* had never felt like the right thing to do.

Esme begrudgingly led him to the lawn chairs under the ash tree.

"I never see Silas anymore," she said. "No idea what he's up to."

"Well, I can tell you that lately he's up to meth and oxy and heroin, when he can get it, and being agro and sick when he can't. Of course it's no help that we live in a town where drugs are easier to find than pencils. You don't know where he is, do you?"

"Not my scene."

He checked his watch, one of those stretchy silver bands, and Esme noticed that his hairy wrist had been rubbed bald around it. Somehow that was grosser than being hairy.

"I don't know for sure that Silas shot out your window," he said, "but he has said some things. He tends to blame others rather than reflect on his own choices."

"Is this about Baby Grace?"

"Yes."

"And he blames me is what you're saying?"

"And Trudy. Honestly, it's taken me a long time to get past blaming you, too. But I have."

"Mostly," she mumbled.

"Mostly." He smiled lightly.

"What changed?"

"You mean why is he focusing on you? Maybe it was all the failed rehab, revisiting his past. Add a lot of chemical paranoia. Plus it won't come as a surprise that he's always liked you. *Like* liked. So you and Kevin being all perfect probably stings a little."

"Perfect? Please."

"He broke into the church," he said, moving on, "and stole some things. Emptied the coffers with a crowbar. And my house, too. He figured out the code to my gun locker. Took my .38."

"So it was him."

Pastor Kurt shrugged, tight-lipped.

"How'd he get the combination?" she said.

"Right there in needlepoint on my living room wall," he said, shaking his head. *"Father Forgive Them. Luke 23:34."*

"So, 2-3-3-4?"

"I thought I was being clever. He also got my generator out of the garage, so it may be that he's just trying to pawn the stuff, as usual, and I'm overreacting."

"But the pistol—?"

"Changes things. Trudy is taking it very seriously. When I told her about your window she made me come here. To let you know it may not be over."

"She's still in Montana?"

"She and Grace both," he said, brightening a bit. "That's the other thing. I've decided it's time to start exploring a way out. I've been getting over to Montana to visit Grace every month anyway, so I'm not around as much. Grace is a wonderful little girl. Trudy remarried but it didn't work out, so I'm trying to be more present. Make sure Grace has the love and support she needs."

"Your work with Silas is done, in other words."

All light left his face.

"I don't know what he's doing or who he's staying with,"

he said. "He's more distant than ever. Trudy isn't taking any chances. She carries a gun everywhere she goes."

"That's just Montana," Esme said.

Pastor Kurt shook his head fiercely. Esme's mouth went dry.

"I understand this is the last thing you want to be thinking about," he said, "but Silas's world fell apart the day the TV fell, even if it was mostly his own damned fault, trying to cover it up like an idiot."

There it was again: *mostly.*

"We were just kids," she said.

"Doesn't matter. He'll never be able to separate *you* from what happened. Grace, too. She's lucky to be alive. And Silas is lucky he's not in jail. I'd like to keep it that way."

Pastor Kurt pulled out a folded slip of paper with his phone number in Great Falls.

"Please call me if you learn where he's staying. If I'm not in town, I can be back here in a day. Or if you ever need an ear. I mean that, Esme."

As he neared the road she shouted, "I'm sorry about what happened!" She was as surprised to hear it as he was.

He stopped and turned. "I know you are, Esme. I appreciate that. But it changes nothing."

CHAPTER 27

ABIGAIL

From the way George ran into Abigail's house with knees pinned together, she knew his bladder was as taut as a water balloon. He raced to the end of the hall and disappeared into the bathroom, carrying the grab bag of Happy Meal toys she'd just bought him at the thrift store.

This was George's third day without Daniel and last night's dinner of frozen quinoa bowls with teacups of tap water had been bland enough to make him pouty, so they'd been out and about for the past hour, loading up on frozen chicken and pizza, yogurt and peaches. Next, they swung by the thrift store and scored a stack of battered board games held together by rubber bands—Life, Mouse Trap, and a *Back to the Future* tie-in. They were sure to be missing half their pieces, but they could combine them into a hybrid game or something, where the giant mouse attacks the little Life cars before getting run over by Doc's DeLorean. At least they'd be occupied until Daniel came home tomorrow.

Abigail halted as she set the grocery bags in the kitchen. Three of her cupboards were open, a can of Eli's baked beans was on the counter, and the spice drawer was fully extended, its bottles shuffled into a mess.

Down the hall, her bedroom floorboards creaked.

"Eli?" she said, recognizing the delusion as soon as it left her lips.

Whoever was there stopped moving.

Abigail's vision tightened as she crept down the hall, threw open her bedroom door and spotted Sophia, sitting on the floor. She was still wearing her white frilled work blouse but it was half-buttoned, exposing her threadbare tan bra. Next to her was a scorched piece of foil and a lighter.

Her hand was bleeding as she held out the small spice jar, Esme's yellow powder inside.

"Esme's drugs," Sophia said, "aren't *drugs!*"

Abigail set George up in the kitchen with a snack and his new toys, then closed the bedroom door and slid to the floor next to Sophia. She'd been crying, and the colorful threads of her rat-tail were so unraveled that she looked as if she'd been sprayed with Silly String.

Sophia handed her the small jar of powder. The boy's presence down the hall was helping Abigail stay calm.

"Is the cut bad?"

"Gah. Scraped it when I was climbing in your stupid window."

"You broke into my house and took the powder because you wanted to be high for a year. Is that what this is?"

"Nothing happened," Sophia said. "I had a pinch and a smoke, but stopped myself before booting it. I felt *nothing.* Other than a horrendous headache." She dabbed at the blood on her hand. "Esme wasn't muling."

"Then what on earth is that?"

"Could be anything," Sophia said, glum. "Ground-up animal horn. Some experimental pesticide. Since Bakersfield is farm-land. I don't know."

"Makes as much sense as a drug that gets you high for a year."

The two of them stared at the bottle for a moment, before Abigail tucked it into the pocket of her shorts.

"Sophia, I know you don't have to have a reason to relapse, but—"

"Miss Nellie found out about us stealing the water jars. I got fired."

"Oh shit," Abigail said, palming her eyes. "Sophia! How'd she even...?"

"She went off on me when I showed up for Storytime. It was humiliating. I had the book picked out and everything. Frog and Toad? The one with the melting ice cream?"

Abigail sighed. "I love that story."

Sophia explained, in her fitful way, that Eli had apparently contacted the university, requesting to amend the grant because the integrity of his water samples was in question. When he'd heard about the old jars in the library cellar, he told them to disregard his request. But it was too late.

"The grant committee reached out to the city to verify the existence of the jars. It got back to Miss Nellie that we broke in. She claimed she hadn't even known they were there and that I should've stuck to sharpening pencils. Preston was there, too. He seemed really worried."

Abigail recalled how he'd watched them from the shore that day as they loaded the jars into Medusa, and the way he'd called them "Time capsules."

"We'll get your job back, Sophia. You helped out a desperate patron on an important errand. Maybe Eli can call—"

"I don't need you to *save* me, Abigail," Sophia said. "But thanks anyway."

They sat in silence for a while, like friends at a wake, and Abigail took it as a good sign that Sophia didn't storm away.

"I should've known," Sophia said, fingertips on her forehead. "Esme wasn't the type. Maybe a little weed, but not the kind of deal that gets you killed in the desert. And she definitely wasn't naive enough to scam someone."

"People change," Abigail said. "Plus, isn't that what got Kevin Polk killed? He and Esme crossing that tweaker?"

"That made even less sense," Sophia said, shaking her head. "Little Kevin, star of the science fair, slinging with *Silas*? That dude had meth for breakfast and washed it down with cleaning products. Kevin knew better than to get in with him."

"Maybe the shooting wasn't over drugs, or didn't happen the way everyone said it did. Just because the guy was an addict, you know?"

Sophia craned toward Abigail, her nest of hair dropping across her face.

"You're pushy, you know that? And you're batty. And you need to get a job or a dog or something before you get in trouble. But you're also not the first person to say that to me."

"Who was the first?"

"Silas's dad. Pastor Kurt."

"The guy I met at the parade? In the Hawaiian shirt."

"That's him. He swears Silas wouldn't have killed Kevin over drugs or anything else. Kind of makes sense, too. Silas was a basket case, but he had plenty of ways to get high without having the class valedictorian hook him up. Kurt is adamant that there was never any drug deal. Says that Silas might have threatened Kevin, tried to scare him, but never would've pulled the trigger. They'd known each other since preschool."

"Do you believe him?"

Sophia shrugged and looked at the cut on her hand. "I believe Kurt's a good guy carrying a huge burden, doing his best to stay sober and cope. He does have a point. But I don't know, Abigail. Pastor Kurt's entire life imploded because of Silas. Seems like he might be looking to offload the blame."

Abigail could hear the compassion in Sophia's voice, but her skepticism was clear. Of course Pastor Kurt didn't want to believe that his son had murdered a classmate in cold blood, whether it was over a drug deal or something else, like a grudge or a crush. If he accepted that, he'd also have to accept that he was, at least in part, responsible.

After all, he was the kid's father. And the owner of the gun.

Before long the bedroom door opened and George was there, holding out Mouse Trap as if it were a peace offering.

"Give us five minutes and we'll play, okay?"

"I call green," Sophia said, pointing at him and sniffling.

He backed out of the room and closed the door, and the two women sat in silence as his footsteps padded down the hall.

CHAPTER 28

ESME

kid is missing

Sitting on the rocks by the lake, huddled within her hoodie, Esme reread Kevin's text.

kid is missing

Her phone glowed through the darkness as she replied.

Kevin what's that mean, kid missing?

Usually Kevin and Esme found it fortuitous when they texted each other from opposite sides of the lake: Esme sitting on the shore near her house, looking across the water at the Healing Lake Hotel, where Kevin was either on the reception desk or looking out his bedroom window toward the settlement of tiny

homes where Esme lived. They often sought moments of connection like this, when they felt the sizzle of fate in the air, the
world-behind-this-world peeking through. It made them feel
meant-to-be.

But this seemed bad. Kevin finally replied.

hang on something weirds happenin

Between school and her shifts at Dairy Freeze as well as
Kevin's jobs at the hotel and rowing Dr. Carla around the lake,
it had been tough to find time to see each other at all. When
they did, their conversations revolved around Kevin's incoming
acceptance letters (UW, Western Washington University, and
University of Chicago) and navigating their future as a couple.
His latest plan was to quietly burn the Chicago acceptance—
he'd only applied to appease Mama Bear—and begin making
plans to go to school in Bellingham, where Esme could shape
up her grades at the local community college before joining
him at Western. For as much as Esme loved Kevin, she hated
the idea of following him wherever he went, even Bellingham,
which seemed like a dream-come-true of trees and people.

whats weird kev? is this real, kid missing?

Kevin replied right away.

SERIOUS weird. Get home NOW.

Across the lake, the streetlights along Main Street were joined
by blue-and-red flashers as a police cruiser sped west. A few
seconds later, more flashers tumbled through the dark.

Esme thought she might be sick as she stood from the shore
and made her way home.

The closer they came to graduation, the more menacing

this town became. The misfit slapping her face and the bullet through her window had been bad enough, but lately the sinister vibes were even reaching Kevin. A few days ago at the library, while he was helping Miss Nellie fix a printer jam, someone stole his flash drive right out of the computer he was using. Kevin of course blamed Silas, without an iota of proof. He had no backup and lost half of his work, including his entire Young Scientist scholarship application. The scholarship was a long shot but Dr. Carla had been helping him, providing access to her textbooks and binders of data, plus passwords for a few research databases where he could download scholarly articles. When the flash drive disappeared Kevin had still been in the gathering stages, but beginning to explore a possible link between field runoff and fertilizer contamination in the groundwater. But now, given his crappy luck and the impending deadline, Dr. Carla had convinced him to focus on something easier, like evaporation and precipitation patterns in the lake.

The theft had seemed dramatic, yet it paled in comparison to a missing child. The second Esme walked into her house, her mom muted the TV and said that a toddler had disappeared while playing near the canal, though they didn't know yet whether the water had gotten him.

Within minutes, a hotel van skidded in the dirt out front. Out popped Kevin and Mister Doctor Carla, who was holding Ali to his neck as he jogged across the yard. She was crying. Her twin brother wasn't with her.

"Guys?" Esme said from the porch, shot through with fear.

"It's little Alan," Kevin said.

"We don't know where he is," Preston said, then practically threw Ali into Esme's arms. Ali squirmed and reached back for him, grabbing a fistful of her dad's hair, and Esme had to loosen her fist and prevent the kid from dropping. She turned Ali around and bobbed with her under the porch light. Her little barrette bounced atop her head.

"Remember me?" Esme said. "I'm your mom's friend. Hi!"

Ali hugged her tight but kept crying.

"Dr. Carla wanted her with you," Kevin said, as they got back in the van. "I'm helping Preston."

"Okay. Of course."

"Alan's been gone for hours," he said, sounding destroyed. "They found his shoe by the canal, crammed into the fence. We're hoping he didn't climb over. Just stay here with Ali. I'll text."

"Okay. Yes."

"This fucking *place*!" Preston screamed from the passenger seat, punching the dash as the van sped away.

CHAPTER 29

ABIGAIL

Daniel leaped out of his Bronco and jogged across the orchard lot, where George and Abigail were waiting. He spun the boy over his shoulders like a propeller, and the boy laughed and sandwiched his uncle's cheeks between his palms. Abigail wandered past stacks of wooden apple boxes and into the shade of a storage building, giving them space.

On his drive home from Bakersfield last night, Daniel had called Abigail to ask her to bring George to the orchard because he'd be driving all night and going straight to work from the road. A pump had gone out, so hundreds of trees had been watered by hand for days. Daniel put up a good front for his nephew, but he was clearly stressed and weary.

He handed George a brown paper bag with a lukewarm cheeseburger and fries, and an orange soda in a Styrofoam cup. He dropped the tailgate and sat him there to eat while he caught up with Abigail.

His face changed when he caught sight of Sophia, sitting in

Medusa, rereading *A Date for Doris* with her bare feet on the dash. After her break-in and relapse, Sophia had told Abigail she couldn't be alone, and apparently had actually meant she *couldn't be alone.* She'd been quietly hanging around ever since, eating chicken nuggets and popsicles with George, bumping into Abigail in the hallway.

"How is he?" Daniel said, gesturing to the boy, who was ripping open a ketchup packet with his teeth and squirting it down the length of each fry.

"He seems okay. Should I not ask about Esme's apartment?"

He shrugged. "I'd been hoping to find a journal or something, but the cops were right, there was basically nothing there. Hardly any food. Milk crates for shelves. She was so broke. I should've done more to find her."

"You were letting Esme be Esme."

"I guess," he said. "She was worried, though. A butcher knife by the front door. Pepper spray on top of the fridge, next to her bed, in the shower caddy. I did learn some things."

Daniel had spoken to a few of her coworkers and neighbors and pieced together that Esme had a babysitting arrangement with another single mom in the building. The woman was a stripper with a three-year-old and a shopping addiction who was always pushing Esme to give the pole a spin. The cash had to be tempting, but Esme wanted a regular schedule for George, so she stayed on the day shift filling orders at an auto parts warehouse.

One night last spring, Esme came home after work and nobody answered when she stopped by the other mom's place to pick up George. She figured the mom had taken the kids to the playground, but when she got to her apartment George was sitting on the couch with the other toddler, watching TV and eating a box of fruit leather. The two kids were all alone, surrounded by snacks, with a gallon of milk parked between them.

There was a note on the coffee table from the other mom: *Emergency! Sorry!*

She'd been called in for a bachelor party. The kids had been alone for six hours.

When the other mom came home in the middle of the night, she and Esme fought so loudly that the landlord had to step in.

"That had to be when she started thinking about coming home," Daniel said. "She had no one to help with George. Whatever she faced coming back here, it must've been worth the risk, to gain a little security."

Based on the mail and printouts in her apartment, he figured out that after that night, Esme had been looking into apartments in safer neighborhoods, day care options, Head Start wait lists— and running into dead ends at every turn.

"As far as I could tell, the bills were piling up and she had no consistent day care, no money, and no one to turn to for help," Daniel said. "She worked full-time but got behind and couldn't catch up. Every month she was at risk of getting evicted."

"So she needed to come home," Abigail said. "Get some help from her family. George recognized you and your mom from photos, so she must have been laying the groundwork."

"She was so desperate. The drugs angle starts to make sense."

"Except it wasn't drugs in the juice box," she said. "Or if it was, they don't get you high."

She glanced at Sophia, boiling in Medusa, four doors open.

"Wow," he said, pointing. "She?"

"Yep. A snort and a smoke."

"Is she okay? I mean, besides not being high."

"She has a nasty headache."

"I guess I owe her one," he said, shaking his head, letting this information settle. "That's, uh, good news. But if it's not drugs, then what?"

"No idea. Nothing worth dying over."

"Yeah."

They watched as a brindled old mutt emerged from the orchard to drink from a small ditch. Behind him, apples had begun to pinken on the chalice-shaped trees.

"Do you want me to pass the powder to the cops, then?" Abigail said.

"I'm too tired to think about that. Just sit on it for now."

She patted Daniel's shoulder and left her hand there for a moment. He stood stiff at first, nodding, then pressed his own hand into the back of hers.

"I'm glad you're back," she said.

"Me, too. I missed him."

Over on the tailgate, George opened and closed his cheeseburger, as if chatting with it.

"I found some other stuff," Daniel said. He pulled an envelope out of his back pocket, opened it, and handed her a folded pair of postcards. "These were on her fridge, right next to photos of me and Mom and Kevin." He gestured toward George. "So they'd be familiar."

One of the cards held a black-and-white photo of the town's Fourth of July parade, circa 1960. In it, a group of men on horses towed ropes attached to a giant figure of TreeTop. He was propped on a rolling cart, wearing a dark rubber jumpsuit and a lopsided gas mask strapped to a wooden mannequin head.

"Cuh-*reepy*," she said. "That was on her fridge?"

"A little reminder of what she'd left behind," he said. "You know Esme left town the night of her high school graduation, right? Middle of the night, I'd come in from baling hay and found her rushing around, throwing her clothes into a backpack. It was a rough time. She hadn't left her bedroom since the shooting. When I came in, she kept saying that TreeTop had been watching her sleep. She pushed me aside and sped away in the Cutlass. I thought she'd be right back, that this was just more grieving over Kev. I drove around all night looking for her. That was the last time I saw her."

Abigail turned the TreeTop postcard in her hand. "So seeing this every day was a reminder not to let her guard down. Especially with the pepper spray and the knife."

"This one, too," Daniel said, trading it for a postcard of the

Healing Lake Hotel. "At first I was thinking it was a reminder of Kevin, of the good times they'd had."

The postcard held images of the lake and hotel, with its name in the bold red font of roadside attractions.

"The hotel looks different here," she said, tapping it.

"That's important," Daniel said. "After the shooting, right around when Esme left town, the hotel went dark for a year, like a black hole in the center of Main. Yet another spot in this town whose past was more important than its present. Everyone was waiting for the Polks to disappear to Costa Rica and start over."

"But they stayed."

"And gave the place a facelift. An homage to Kevin. And one thing they did when they renovated was change the phone number of the hotel. Made it something more memorable and publicized it in holistic health magazines. *1-555-HEALING* or something. Look at the back."

The back of the card was blank, except a phone number in tiny black handwriting.

"That's Esme's penmanship," he said. "And that's the hotel's *new* number. Which the Polks didn't set up until long *after* she left town. So why did *she* have it?"

"Because Esme called the hotel," she said.

"Exactly. Called someone there in the months before she died."

"It was Mr. Polk," Abigail said, her face warming at the betrayal of his secret.

"Or possibly Mrs. Polk. Or someone else who works there."

"No," Abigail said, "it was Mister. He told me. While you were away."

Daniel pressed back his hair and stared at her. The bags under his eyes were thick.

"Mr. Polk told me about the calls," she continued, "but he hasn't told anyone else—"

"And you didn't think to call me?"

"I'm telling you now?" she said, hunching her shoulders.

Abigail explained what happened on her visit to the hotel with George: how Mrs. Polk broke down once she realized he was Esme's son, and the way that, sitting on the lakeshore, Mr. Polk choked up as he talked about Esme calling.

"His wife doesn't even know Esme reached out to him. So it's delicate."

"Why would she call him?" Daniel said—but didn't add, *and not me.*

"It makes sense, doesn't it? She wanted to make sure she'd be safe coming back here. She had some bad history in this town, but years had passed, and maybe she hoped things had changed. She needed reassurance. To get a read on whether she'd be safe before springing it on you and your mom. After all that happened with Kevin, it makes sense she'd ask Mr. Polk. That he'd be clearheaded about it."

"Unlike me," Daniel said. "I can't believe you took George there."

"It was just a place to buy T-shirts for our slumber party. I'm sorry. I didn't..."

"It's fine," he said, shaking his head in a way that signaled it really wasn't. "It's good to have it verified, I guess. The calls. Reinforces this."

He showed Abigail a series of photos on his phone: a phone company log, a dozen pages long, with so many redacted numbers that it resembled a CIA document.

"Esme had no phone registered in her name. She used the payphone at the grocery store across from her apartment building. These are its records."

"How'd you get those?"

"That breakfast I had with the cop who's handling the investigation down on that end. A judge granted her limited access to ninety days' worth of call records from the Bakersfield payphone. There were apparently calls to Idaho, Montana, and Oregon, all redacted. Mexico and Guatemala, too. But the ones visible here were all made to and from *this* area code and *this* prefix."

"The detective just gave these to you?"

"Sort of?" Daniel said. "I bought her a Grand Slam breakfast and was asking about the murder investigation. She implied the cops up here were blowing her off, and eventually she came clean. She'd already sent three copies of these records to the task force. Didn't hear a word back, and when she called to follow up, the receptionist said that maybe they got jammed in the fax machine. Clearly slow-walking."

"What does that mean?"

"It means that once the local cops here learned drugs were involved, they stopped putting resources into Esme's case. She said it probably doesn't help that our last name is Calderon."

"That's messed up."

"Good news is that when she went to the bathroom, she left these call records on the table. You know, *wink-wink.* So of course I took photos of them," he said, pointing to his phone. "It's right there, over and over."

The number of the Healing Lake Hotel. The number Esme had written on the postcard.

"You know, Mr. Polk seems like a great guy," he said. "Esme really liked him, and definitely some father-figure vibes. But *Mrs.* Polk is an uptight hippie, trying to be all loosey-goosey but really full of scorn. A lot of people looked down on Esme, didn't know what to do with her. But Mrs. Polk *hated* her. Always behind a fake smile, which made it worse."

Out on the road, a white pickup drove slowly past, blasting Waylon.

"Just doesn't seem right that my sister is dead," he continued, lowering his voice, "and Mr. Polk is over there working on his toy planes and conveniently forgetting to tell anyone that he and Esme had been calling each other before she died."

"Wait," Abigail said. "Not *calling each other.* Esme called him. Not the other way around."

"And he called her."

"According to Mr. Polk, Esme called the front desk, middle of the night, maybe half a dozen times, then she abruptly stopped. That was it."

Daniel stepped close enough to Abigail that their arms were touching, then scrolled through his phone, cupping his free hand over the screen to shield the sunlight.

"These in red are outgoing calls *from* the Bakersfield payphone to the hotel. Seven calls, last April and May. About thirty minutes each. Except the last one, which was only eight minutes."

"Maybe Mrs. Polk walked in so he hung up," she said.

"But these in black are going *to* Bakersfield, from the gas station payphone on Main to the grocery store payphone across from Esme's apartment. Six calls total. All between fifteen and thirty minutes."

"Payphone to payphone," she said, "they'd have to be scheduled."

"Every Monday and Thursday at 3:30 a.m. for three weeks, according to the records. She was there waiting for the phone to ring. And walked George there with her so he wouldn't wake up alone in the apartment. Night clerk at the grocery store said the boy would sit on the curb, half-asleep, drinking chocolate milk while she was on the phone. He gave him a fidget-spinner to help him stay awake."

"Mr. Polk didn't say anything about calling her," Abigail said. "And if he did, why would he walk down to the gas station and use a payphone instead of just using the phone at his desk?"

"Maybe he didn't want Mrs. Polk seeing the bill and asking who he's been calling in California at exactly three-thirty in the morning—the same number, over and over. Whatever the reason, he definitely didn't want his conversations with Esme traced back to the hotel."

The two of them looked at each other, then over at George, who'd wandered to the edge of the orchard and knelt beside the brindled mutt, patting his freckled belly.

CHAPTER 30

ESME

The night that Alan went missing, Esme read Ali a dozen fairy tales and let her snuggle with the crocheted crab Kevin had given her for Valentine's Day. Ali soon crashed but Esme was up all night, checking her phone every five minutes to see if there was any news about Alan. She couldn't stop thinking about his gray-green eyes and the way he wouldn't stop patting her back when they hugged goodbye after Dr. Carla's dinner party.

In the morning, before his shift at the orchard, Daniel went to the store to grab some Cheerios and returned with four bags of groceries and, strapped to the roof of his Bronco, a blue wading pool covered with starfish. Still no news about Alan.

Kevin called at one point and told her that, since the boy's shoe had been found by the canal, he and Preston had been driving slowly up and down all the irrigation roads, searching, but getting nowhere.

"They were talking about bringing in divers, but the flow is

so high the canals are like a giant blender right now. Dr. Carla
is insisting they shut off the irrigation to help the search."

"Fat chance," Esme said. "Every farmer for fifty miles will
raise hell if they kill the flow."

When Daniel came home on his lunch break, Esme asked
him to take her and Ali to the Abortion Roller Rink. He stayed
in the Bronco with the tot as Esme slipped inside, ignoring the
CLOSED sign on the propped open door. No one was at the
counter but the restroom doors were open and someone was
slapping a mop around the women's. She stood before the cubbies of rental skates, glad for the carpet silencing her footsteps.
Being here felt stupid and the smell of feet was making her nauseous, but when she stooped low enough to see the words carved
into the side of the cubbies, right where they'd been since she
was little, her certainty returned.

Countless times as a girl, Esme had cupped her fingers around
the corner between the wall and the shelves, searching the
cramped space behind the cubbies for TreeTop's scratched phone
number. Back then she'd wanted to know the number without
really wanting to know, like screaming away before ever checking for the monster behind the door. It was enough to sense it
was there, felt but unseen. In that way, she was like everyone
else in this town: knowing without knowing.

Esme wasn't sure what she'd find as she pressed her shoulder
into the cubbies and reached behind, letting her fingertips find
the gouges in the wood, like tracing the path of a chomping
termite. But she'd come prepared: she retrieved from her back
pocket a small makeup mirror and pinned it against the wall,
just opposite the carving, and used her free hand to shine her

phone light. Amidst the long light and shadows, the wood was gouged with sloppy digits.

Everything was backward in the mirror—*5* or *2*? *4* or *9*?—and muddled by the fact that the phone number had been scored into the wood decades ago, when it was a storage box for fruit, long before it had ever been repurposed as a skate cubby. She did her best to duplicate the number on the back of her hand with a Sharpie.

Someone flushed a toilet as she left.

When Esme hopped into the Bronco, Daniel stared at the scribbled number.

"Is that what I think it is?"

"Drive."

Without a word he headed into town and pulled into the lot behind the gas station. Opened his ashtray and slid out a few quarters.

"You really think it's real?" he said. "TreeTop."

"About to find out."

"Make sure no one sees you."

On the ride over she'd been studying that number on her skin, wondering if any slumber party kids had ever made it this far. The first three digits were hard to read, until she realized they resembled the region's area code, *509*. But that couldn't be right: Why would a seven-digit number begin with an area code?

Because sixty years ago, she reasoned, when these digits were first scored into the wood, phone numbers followed a different system.

Every day for years on their walk to school, she and Daniel had passed the decades-old sign painted on the side of the brick laundromat. It was one of many such murals in town, faded by the sun, remnant of a thriving town in a different era:

Soap Lake Mud Baths
God's Gift to the Sick!
Tel. SOA 4214

Sometimes she and Daniel would read the sign aloud like carnival barkers, finding it hilarious that their forgotten town was *God's Gift* to anything.

Back when telephones were still a novelty, each town used letters as the prefix, not numbers. Which meant it wasn't *509* carved into the cubbies, but *SOA:* Soap Lake's old telephone exchange.

The equivalent of *246* today.

She dropped the coin into the payphone and dialed.

Her first attempt led to a dead end recording: *The number you have dialed...*

She was studying her hand, beginning to press various interpretations of the last four digits, wondering if she'd transcribed something backward, when the little letters embossed into the payphone buttons jumped into her mind with the answer:

8
T U V
7
P Q R S
3
D E F
3
D E F

She knew it was going to ring even before punching that last
3. And it did. Rang and rang until someone picked up. They
didn't speak, but she could hear breathing. She bunched her
T-shirt over the receiver and muffled her voice, like a kid pretending to be a kidnapper.

"Please let the boy go," she said. *"Pretty please?"*

She hung up and climbed into the Bronco, and Daniel sped
out of the lot before she'd even shut the door.

"Can't hurt, I guess," he said, which made them laugh because they knew it very much could hurt. "Don't tell anyone
you just did that. Not even Kevin."

In the back seat, Ali said, *"Shhh."*

After scrambled eggs for dinner, when Ali was getting drowsy,
Kevin texted **Headsup** and within a minute a small silver SUV
pulled up to Esme's house. Seconds later, Dr. Carla rushed inside, holding Alan on her hip and lifting Ali into a tight three-
way hug. Alan was crying and wearing nothing but shorts and
his face was a rashy mess. Dr. Carla couldn't stop moving and
seemed out of it.

"Oh, thank *god,*" Esme said, hands over her mouth. She
hugged Alan uncontrollably. He smelled of garbage and his
feet were bleeding. "Is he okay?"

"I don't know," Dr. Carla said, holding out his legs and studying his bare feet, as if it only now occurred to her that he might
be hurt. "Some landscaper found him. Wandering the landfill."

The landfill, Esme thought, that bordered the orchard where
she'd once seen TreeTop.

"No shirt or shoes. Overheated, crying his eyes out." Dr.
Carla pressed a water bottle to Alan's mouth. "Keep drinking
that, sweetie."

In her sputtering voice, she explained how a landscaping
crewman was dumping grass clippings when he heard Alan's

cries. Good thing he was bawling, the guy said, because the piles of trash were so high he never would have seen him.

"I only just got him a few minutes ago," Dr. Carla continued. "Cops think I'm on my way to the station to meet a medic and debrief, so I don't have much time. I just kind of turned when they went straight."

"You bailed on them?"

"Hell yes I bailed." She cradled Alan's head and lowered her voice. "You should've seen the way Alan reacted when the one cop came over to talk to me. Practically climbed over my head to get away."

"Cop with a crew cut?"

"Could be nothing. But felt like something." She walked to the screen door and looked out. "Anyway, you have no idea how much I appreciate you doing this and just *everything*." Dr. Carla gave her a ferocious hug, full of kids' limbs and bumped heads. "Help me get them in the car, please?"

When they reached the SUV, Dr. Carla double-checked that no one was hiding in the pile of bags and crates stacked throughout the vehicle. She looked up and down the road as Esme buckled in the twins.

"Are you—?"

"Getting the hell out of here and never coming back? Definitely. I *hate* that I have to leave, but what choice do I have? Look me up sometime. And you didn't see me tonight."

"I thought the cops said he just wandered off."

"No reason to think otherwise," Dr. Carla said in a mock macho voice. "Yeah. Except for his sneaker stabbed into the chain-link fence three feet higher than Alan could possibly reach. It took some real elbow grease to get it out, too. Ten feet from that rushing canal. Tell me that's not a message."

"Somebody *took* him?" Esme said.

"They want to mess with my water samples so I can't progress with my research? Okay. I don't get it, but I'm a stranger in a strange land. And maybe a Black woman in a town where the bigwigs are all white men. Maybe I need to be more gentle when I lambast them for neglecting the lake. Fine. I'm not a social worker, but I can try. They want to lock me in my lab and almost burn me alive? Going a little far, but okay. But steal my *baby* from his front yard? Drop him naked in the landfill and hope he finds his way home? No mom puts up with that shit. If I don't get on the interstate right now, I'm gonna end up in jail for murder."

The twins wailed as she hopped in behind the wheel. Esme leaned into the passenger window. "Do you want me to move some stuff so you'll have room for Preston? It's gonna be a tight fit."

"Preston is staying in town," she said. "Said he's not finished, whatever that means. Fine. But as soon as I get settled, he's no longer Mister Doctor Carla. Oh, and I wasn't here. Did I already say that? Say bye-bye, kids."

The twins wailed.

"Don't take Main Street," Esme said, and told Dr. Carla about the shortcut between the orchards that would dump her outside of town limits. Just in case.

Dr. Carla put the car in gear, but held her foot on the brakes and looked Esme in the eye. "This is the most magical place on the planet, Esme. You're lucky to have been born here. And this place is lucky to have you. But *please* be careful. And look me up if I can ever do anything."

As Esme watched Dr. Carla's SUV grow smaller, she wondered if her payphone call had made any difference at all, if the figure on the other end was even real, or if it was just another way for her to feel like she was doing something when all of the power was locked high and far away, beyond the likes of her.

As soon as Dr. Carla was gone, Esme ran to the bathroom and scrubbed her hand until the numbers written there were gone, and her skin was pink with welts.

CHAPTER 31

ABIGAIL

Daniel and George disappeared down the orchard rows to fix the broken pump, and Abigail parked Medusa in the shade of the storage buildings and sat scrolling through her phone. Sophia snoozed so deeply in the passenger seat that she wondered if maybe Esme's powder had been narcotic after all.

There it was, on-screen, the photo she'd taken in the library of Preston's Oracle Map.

She'd intended to delete the image days ago and felt a tug of guilt at seeing it again, dappled with Preston's green glyphs.

Then again, he *had* drawn an eyeball on her home—a home she shared with her lake doctor spouse, who happened to have replaced *his* lake doctor spouse—all of which gave her permission to look more closely at the map.

Starting with the Healing Lake Hotel. Mr. Polk was a good guy, but Daniel's suspicions over the phone calls and Mrs. Polk seemed valid, too, and Abigail wanted to verify something simple: if Preston was mapping crime, then maybe the hotel would be covered with green icons.

But the hotel's spot on the map was clean except for a single doodle: a green revolver, smaller than the gun from Clue, likely denoting the town's most notable crime: the shooting of Kevin Polk. Seeing it reassured her about her faith in Mr. Polk.

She continued to scan the map and noticed that, although plenty of the doodled places were within town limits, those marked the most were outside of town, on county roads with rural addresses.

Distant orchards and farms. Epicenters of violence.

Except for one.

She tugged Sophia awake, and the *Doris* novel slid from her lap.

"Sophia? You know anything about this?"

Sophia wiped her chin on her shirt and leaned over the phone with half-lidded eyes. "I'd guess it has to do with Preston? You know, based on the completely *insane* doodles all over it. I do work at the library, Abigail." She rattled her head. "Enh. Shit. *Did.*"

"He's mapping violence."

"Just delete it," she said, attempting to stretch in the confines of Medusa. "Let the poor guy chase his tail. We all have our balms."

Abigail pointed to the spot on the map, just off of Main, that was so covered with Preston's pictograms that she couldn't recognize the location beneath.

"What's this place?"

Sophia peeked and shook her head. "*That* place I want nothing to do with. Spent more time there than I care to remember."

"What is it?"

"City Building," she said, crossing her arms and closing her eyes. "Home of the Soap Lake Police Department."

The walls of the Soap Lake police station were decorated with dusty animal heads, buck and badger, and a deranged coyote with a missing eye. Beyond the front counter was a small quadrant of desks with outdated monitors and electric typewriters and more paper than Abigail had seen in years, except perhaps in Eli's lab. Every chair but one was empty.

A full-figured woman with cropped brown hair sat at the high counter near the door, humming into a headset phone. She had chaw in her lip and long, painted nails, and a row of rings lined her fingers like brass knuckles.

Mmm-hmmm. Mmmm. Hmmm.

Ignored, Abigail read the bulletin board notices about feral cats and local prowlers. She'd tried texting Krunk a short while ago, but he hadn't replied. Now she tried to focus on what she'd say when she saw him.

She'd look him in the eye and say, simply, *Set me straight—*

About Preston's Oracle Map, and whether this police department appeared on it because so many criminals filed through here that its cluster of green glyphs was inevitable; or whether something sordid was afoot, as evidenced by the task force cops dragging their feet rather than finding Esme's killer.

And *set me straight* about why Esme, who by all accounts was a caring mother, would bring her boy to a drug deal that wasn't a drug deal, and why the killer had thrown her keys into the desert and made her slowly die like that—an act of pure cruelty, not a deal gone wrong.

And about Mr. Polk, who'd been speaking to Esme but keeping it secret, yet he'd never been questioned; and Mrs. Polk, who despised Esme for the love she stirred in Kevin, and who was also somehow above suspicion.

The woman on the stool hung up her phone and spat chaw drool into a plastic cup.

"Don't tell me you found another Mexican in the desert," she said.

Abigail opened her mouth but couldn't speak.

"Hang out in the desert long enough," she continued, "out

come the Mexicans, carrying gallons of water. Tell me I'm not right."

"The boy is American?" Abigail stammered. "And even if—"

"If this is an emergency, hang up and dial 9-1-1," the woman said, pointing to a white courtesy phone on the wall. She dabbed her drippy chin with a Kleenex.

"It's not."

"Well," she said, shuffling papers, "he's not here. And, anyway, you're married."

"He?"

"Officer Krunk? That is who you're *after*, isn't it?"

Abigail was flummoxed. And could feel herself about to lose it.

"Listen," the woman said, scanning Abigail from top to bottom and back, "his fiancée may not be some astronaut, but she's a good woman, *very* cute, and she's been trying hard to patch things up? So just stay away from him."

It took a second, but Abigail realized this woman was calling her a home-wrecker, referring to that *adorable little peach* that Sophia had said worked in the city billing office: *Blonde, short hair, always looks like she just burst out of a giant cake?* Krunk had broken off his engagement with her before Abigail had ever met him, not to mention that nothing had happened between them.

Your husband is a fool.

"Is Krunk here?" Abigail said through her teeth. Now she was pissed off, and the woman must have sensed it.

"Most everyone is over at the nursing home doing shooter drills. Should be there all day."

"I'll come back," she said.

"Try to have an *official* reason next time," she said, scraping spit into her cup. "This is a police station, not a singles bar."

When Abigail spun to leave, she bumped into a wire rack. It tipped over and pamphlets fanned across the floor: "Preventing Home Invasion." "Your Lost Pet."

She was on her knees, hands shaking, righting the rack and gathering pamphlets, when the woman just had to add, "Maybe I'll see you at Ladies' Night. Bring your friend, too. The gay one, not the junkie."

Abigail froze. Stood up. Faced the woman.

"Excuse me?"

The woman sat straighter on her perch, a trace of regret in her pursed lips.

Before she could stop herself, Abigail raised her hand and slapped the woman's chaw cup. The woman flinched as it tumbled toward her, spilling brown goo across her keyboard and splattering the front of her blouse.

Abigail speed-walked into the lobby and rounded the corner toward the restrooms, eager to escape the receptionist's curses. She was rankled and thirsty, proud and ashamed—and somewhat regretful she'd only slapped the woman's cup. The water at the drinking fountain was lukewarm and tasted like pipes but she held herself there, breathing and drinking, until the woman's outburst faded and she felt herself begin to calm.

Into the quiet came a murmur of voices.

Across from the police station was a solid wooden door that said *Agriculture Appreciation Office* in gothic gold letters. The door was wide-open and a yellowing American flag was pinned to the paneling inside. A giant map of the region papered the wall beyond it.

As she stepped inside, she could hear men laughing and talking behind a closed door. And she could see that the map on the wall was a scaled-up version of Preston's, missing his green glyphs, but holding red roads and a black grid of property lines.

"What can I help you with, miss?"

She was surprised to turn and see a white-haired man sitting at a desk to her right. His gut pressed against a pearl-button shirt with glitzy stitching and muttonchops dropped from his cheeks.

Something about him was familiar, maybe because he could've been an extra in a Western, the mercantile guy in suspenders with a wall of jawbreakers and flour behind him.

"Just noticing the map," she said.

"There by the door we should have some freebies," he said. "Not as big of course, but they're good maps. Cover the whole region." He leaned forward as if to get up, but the effort strained him and he decided he liked his chair. He pointed to a wooden rack on the wall. "On second thought, looks like we're due for a refill, don't it? Field trip came through yesterday and raided our racks. Kids on the way to the Grand Coulee Dam. I got some free coloring books in the back, too, which I hear are all the rage these days. Adults. Coloring. The Apocalypse is upon us. You farm?"

The question threw her off. She tried to place where she'd seen him before, but felt like she was staring too long, so she craned around and looked out to the lobby, at the sign above the main doors: *Municipal Offices*.

"Isn't this the City Building?"

"We're not officially part of the city. Maybe that's why they hide us back here with the pigs and the dumpsters."

The man's eyes narrowed and he looked down at his desk. It was clean and tidy with pens and a calendar pad, but no computer in sight. An old landline phone—avocado green, with square digits—sat in its center.

"If you're looking to pay a bill you gotta go around to the other side of the building. Want me to show you?"

Abigail thought about Krunk's *very cute* ex-fiancée, working over in the billing office, and couldn't respond fast enough.

"No thanks."

"Well, okay, then," he said. "So you don't farm and you don't need help paying your trash bill. And you're staring at that map like you're a kid lost at Disney. So are you?"

"Lost? Not like that." She pointed to the map. "Okay if I look at it for a minute?"

"That's what it's there for," he said, winking.

She stood in front of the map and soon the man's presence faded. She touched a little red star with the tip of her pinkie. *You Are Here.* She tried tracing the road she'd walked from her house up into the desert where she'd found George, but the red line her finger was tracing hit a curve out by the pump station and branched away from the road.

She took a step back. She could feel the man watching her.

"Is this accurate? I don't recognize these roads."

"Red lines are water, not roads."

"Water?"

"Canals, big and small. It's an irrigation map. That's why we're here."

He meant this office itself, but also the town, the region—all these people living year-round in the desert. It was the area's existential refrain: *That's why we're here.*

"All that water," he continued, "flowing from the Canadian Rockies into the Columbia River then out to the fields and orchards and pastures. Nearly 700,000 acres. Nearly a trillion gallons a year. Mostly moved by gravity. Isn't that something?"

"Ah," she said, pointing at the door. *"Agricultural Appreciation Office."*

"We handle public relations. Education. Let the engineers do the engineering and leave the gabbing to us. Keep everything running smoothly. And of course we educate people such as yourself how the water in those canals eventually turns into food on the grocery store shelves. Even your organic Honeycrisps at the Crunchy Co-op over in Seattle have probably grown fat on *our* water. See, we give our talks each year at the schools, but since you aren't from here, you probably missed some of those facts. But I can provide you with a map and a coloring book—"

"How do you know I'm not from here?"

"Oh, let me count the ways," he said, fluttering his eyelids. Then his face went flat. "I know who you are."

The room grew suddenly hot. "What do you mean?" she muttered.

He grinned at her discomfort. "Small town is all."

Behind the door the voices went silent, and Abigail found herself looking in the direction of the empty lobby and the police station beyond it.

The man stood from his chair, punching out a fart in the effort. "You ever been up to the Canadian Rockies? They get so much snow up there they can practically ski year-round. Not literally, but point being all that snow melts and flows straight down to the Columbia—"

"You were in the *parade*," she said, cutting him off and feeling her eyes go wide with recognition: the Fourth of July parade, jostling on the back of a pony, wearing a nudie suit with a rhinestone apple tree creeping across his back.

Leading TreeTop down Main.

"TreeTop," she muttered.

He studied her with a coldness that made her shudder.

"That would be us," he said. Then he clapped his hands. "Let me get you that map and coloring book."

He opened the door to a long, well-lit storage room in the corner and the first thing she saw was a rhinestone jacket hanging on a hook, like it was Hank Williams's dressing room. Beyond it, two guys with barbershop haircuts held Styrofoam coffee cups.

"Outta my way, ladies," he said. "Worse than goddamned hens, drinking my coffee and eating my doughnuts."

They laughed. "You don't need no more doughnuts, Hal."

The parade guy disappeared into the room and she could hear cardboard boxes sliding around.

Hal. Alone in the office, it took Abigail only a second to connect that name to Miss Nellie's big brother, the *hog with a hard-on* who made a habit of harassing Sophia at the library. Her first instinct was to march through that door and tell him to stay away from her friend, but she knew how badly Sophia wanted her job back, so held her tongue.

She glanced at the exit, tempted to leave, but was drawn back to the giant map. She opened up the photo of Preston's Oracle Map on her phone and zoomed into the green pile he'd drawn atop the police station—a shamrock and a fish and a raindrop and a flag and a bishop and a bike and many more—and wondered whether Preston wasn't pinpointing the police department, at all. Maybe he was marking this office, the *Agricultural Appreciation*—

She smelled pumpkin. Innards, not muffins.

"Well, shit!" Hal said, standing just behind her shoulder, loud enough to make her jump. "You got a map right there on your phone!" She could hear him wheezing as he shoved forward a paper map from the stack in his hands, its black plats and red canals visible even while folded. "But you need one you can actually read, without all that doodled craziness getting in the way." Then he made his way to the rack by the door and refilled it. "Hell. Forgot my coloring books. Be right back." He disappeared into the storage room again.

This time he closed the door behind him, and she could hear the murmurs of men.

All that doodled craziness.

Abigail was flustered, as if she'd been caught doing something wrong. Hal probably knew all about Preston's maps, given that his sister was his ersatz guardian at the library. She pocketed her phone and map and tried to shake off the worry moving through her.

She found distraction in the timeline of framed black-and-white photos hanging on the farthest wall.

The first showed Soap Lake back in its heyday, when the streets were crowded with hotels and spas, the shores brimming with visitors swaying on wooden crutches, many wounded by war.

The next photo, circa late 1930s, showed the mammoth construction site of the Grand Coulee Dam, fifty miles northeast, big enough to clog up the Columbia River and, in the process, drown thousands of acres of tribal lands and homes, submerging eleven towns and diminishing native people's access to salmon. None of that was on the placard beneath, which bragged instead about how the dam created enough electricity to fuel two million homes each year, and how part of the project involved diverting a river of fresh water into these canals, creating *An Oasis in the Desert!*

The next showed a sunbaked family near rows of fruit trees, their hands collectively touching a water pump, as if drawing from its power: *Irrigation Has Arrived, 1952.*

Next, a wrinkled fruit picker standing on a ladder, dropping apples into a burlap sling. The camera had caught her glancing down and grinning, as if she couldn't imagine a happier fate than long days in ungodly heat doing manual labor for low wages.

And then she came upon TreeTop: photos of the mascot through the years, starting sometime in the 1950s, she'd guess. The first image of him resembled a soldier on a World War One battlefield, with his cartridge mask and tinted goggles and black rubber jumpsuit, standing before sprawling young fields.

His outfit changed from photo to photo, decade to decade, as did the tools he wielded and masks he wore.

In one photo he held a pruning saw. In another a scythe.

In another he aimed a fat nozzle at the camera, spraying a ghostly fog.

By the time she reached the last few photos, the line between myth and performance had thoroughly blurred, with TreeTop standing on hidden stilts in the annual Fourth of July parade. He still wore tinted goggles and black rubber gloves and boots, but now he wore a sleek mask and a white biosuit, fabric instead of rubber, with its hood tight around his forehead. And he was fifteen feet tall.

The door partially opened and she could hear the men speaking inside.

"Did we not try?" Hal said to them. *"Were we not patient?"*

"We did, boss. We were."

"That's it, then. And stop being so casual. Acting like goddamned Girl Scouts."

He closed the door behind him and stood next to Abigail, nodding at the photos, wheezy from his walk. His breath held the minty rank of a recent chaw.

"That there's my favorite," he said, tapping the photo of TreeTop decked out in black rubber, floppy cartridges hanging from his chin like tentacles. "That's the original mascot. I was just a kid and *god* he gave me the heebie-jeebies. Vintage gas mask straight from a vet. Ironic thing is most people spraying the fields didn't wear masks at all. Breathed it all up and died young. I think they just needed a way to make him—"

"Terrifying?" she said.

"Universal," he said, "like he could be anyone. They thought he would be inspiring, you know, all that patriotic worker stuff like the goddamned Soviets were doing. He just kind of took hold, TreeTop did. See, people *needed* him." He grew animated and she could tell this was part of his spiel when he visited schools and such. "Times were *tough*, you know? Soap Lake had seen its heyday with the spas, people packed onto the beaches and on Main. But gradually most of those tourists just disappeared, off to amusement parks, zoos, and shiny places closer to the interstate. The town started to get *real quiet*." He paused, then perked up, eyes wide. "But the canals—they could change all that, give this whole region a new purpose! We had good soil, endless sun, lots of space, but don't think for a second it was easy. The scale was enormous. Bigger than anything. Hundreds of thousands of acres irrigated by a single river. Imagine the labor. Surveying the land. Scraping rocks out of the desert. Setting up watering systems that would mostly run on gravity. Working in this heat. People, many of whom had never grown a carrot in their garden, carved farms and orchards into the earth. And everyone was counting on that water. I tell you, it was brutal. A lot of early farms didn't make it. Hell, a lot of *farmers* didn't. Imagine the stresses of putting their entire lives into this grand endeavor. More suffering than you or I could ever imagine." He caught Abigail's eye for a second, and she tightly crossed her arms. "The suffering. Those towns that got swallowed up by rerouting the river were just the beginning. All that tribal land buried under water? Just the beginning. All those men who died on the job—"

"Just the beginning?" she said.

"But look at us now, feeding the world." He pointed to the giant map on the wall and lifted his chin. "Without suffering, there is no bounty. Can you see that? Of course you can. So we embrace it. Honor it."

"With TreeTop," she said, though she could scarcely get the words out.

"People needed a mascot. Someone to remind them of the greater good. We got *him*."

He waved a coloring book in front of her and smiled when she took it. The cover held an image of a gargantuan TreeTop in full silhouette.

"That'll keep you up at night, eh?" he said. "Especially if you're alone."

She took a step back.

"Are you TreeTop?" she said, and her mouth was so dry it came out as a whisper.

He shook his head, smiling. "Now, if you were a little kid and you asked me that, I'd get all spooky and say, *No. TreeTop sleeps high up in the branches above your head...so watch yourself!* But since you're all grown-up and showing such interest in our traditions, yeah, I guess you could say I'm TreeTop. Though there's a bunch of us play a part. Takes quite a lot of practice with the stilts and the puppeteering, and about twenty years ago I just sort of became the leader when the last guy, well..."

"I don't mean in the parade," she said.

The man's smile dissolved and it was his turn to take a small step back.

"TreeTop is pretend," he said. "You do know that, right?"

He touched her forearm and she felt goose bumps rise. He nodded at the coloring book, rolled in her grip.

"You can read all about TreeTop right in there," he added with a wink. "Some puzzles for you to solve, too. Since you seem the type."

As soon as the man lifted his fingers, Abigail briskly walked out, taking one last glance at the map on the wall—at its deep red network of canals encasing the region like a web.

As Abigail waited for Krunk to get out of his training at the nursing home, she sat at a picnic table on the beach, eating a shrink-wrapped salami sandwich from the grocery store. On the drive over in Medusa, she'd tried to talk to Sophia about Hal, but her friend just stared quietly out the window. When they arrived at the lake, Sophia found a spot to lie in the sand and escaped so deeply into *Doris at the Dance* that she didn't seem to care she was getting a savage sunburn on the back of her thighs, nor notice when Abigail draped them with a towel.

Between bites of sandwich, Abigail flipped through the "Tree-Top Activity Book," beginning with a page called *Origins*.

TreeTop was born deep within the waters of Soap Lake.

After World War One, soldiers came from all over to heal at this magical lake in the desert.

Their diseased and rotting flesh, along with their terrible memories of war, thickened on the bottom of the lake, swooshing around and clinging together and forming the loose figure of a monstrous man: TreeTop. He crawled through the slurry of mud and minerals, breathing the curative water and absorbing the pain the men had left behind.

TreeTop could feel the suffering of the soldiers, every moment of their agony, and he wanted to help those who had helped them—to give back to the town that had given him life.

Swimmers reported feeling his muddy fingers grasp at the bottom of their feet, as if he were begging them to pull him out. A few times people who were known to have done hateful things were yanked straight down into the lake, never to emerge again.

When the canals filled for the first time, the sudden onslaught of water allowed TreeTop to rise from the depths of the lake. He crawled up the shore to a nearby farm and hid in a collapsing outbuilding, leaving a muddy trail behind, eating chicken eggs and barn kittens and waiting to emerge.

Soon, the land was carved with fields and orchards, but the desert was hot and unforgiving, and the farmers were desperate to get their plants to thrive. So TreeTop crept between outbuildings, gathering whatever he could find.

A pair of black rubber pants and a hooded rubber jacket.

A gas mask, left behind by a soldier.

A rusty wheelbarrow with a squeaky wheel.

A lantern. A shovel. A handsaw. A hatchet.

In the middle of the night, TreeTop slipped into the orchards and began to work, doing all he could to enrich the tiny town on the lake that had softened the suffering of so many others. During the day he stretched out in the branches above and slept, waiting for darkness when he could work the land again...

Abigail set down her sandwich. Barn kittens?

She flipped through the crosswords and dot-to-dots, the word searches and the mazes—until the sound of a police siren broke her trance.

"Sounds like they're done with the training," Sophia said, lifting her head from the sand.

"Not sure I want to go back to that police station," Abigail said, fiddling with the activity book. "Especially with the creepy farmer den across the hall."

"I think technically it's a *dell*, not a den."

"We need to get you back on that library desk, *stat*," Abigail said, staring. "Like now. I'm texting Eli. Telling him it's time to raise hell on Miss Nellie."

"Don't count on her changing her mind."

"Eli's got a good argument. That water is necessary for his research, so when he heard there were jars archived in the library, he demanded you bring them to his lab. You would've asked permission but Miss Nellie was off, I dunno—"

"Yanking lollipops out of baby's mouths," Sophia said.

"Exactly."

Abigail opened her phone and spotted the text that Eli had sent early this morning:

so think medusa will make it or should I look into other options?

She'd answered him while drying off from the shower—whatr you talking smack about medusa?—and hadn't thought about it since. She'd been occupied, to say the least.

Now she could see that she'd missed his reply.

yr kidding right?

That was their whole exchange. She still had no idea why he was asking about Medusa, so she began to text him back when she stopped and opened her email. It had been days, she realized, since she'd checked it. Six, to be exact.

And there, before the clothing sales and the latest conspiracy theory her crazy mom had sent, she found a message she'd missed from Eli.

Subject: Itinerary.

She thought about their last call, how it had been brief because he was *pushing to get everything done.* On the phone he kept saying, rather sweetly, that he couldn't wait to see her again: *We're going out, first thing.*

She'd assumed he was being abstract, expressing a sort-of desert island fantasy about what restaurant they'd visit come December, when he returned to the States.

But she could see now that those were plans, not abstractions. That Eli was being literal.

His email showed an airplane logo. Date and time and flight number. Warsaw to Seattle.

It didn't seem possible that the day could get any hotter, but she sweltered in the shade.

Eli was coming home.

never doubt medusa, she texted, fingers quivering. cant wait...

Until when? Day after tomorrow. Morning.

When she looked up, Sophia was squinting with concern. "Something the matter?"

"Nope," Abigail said, stunned. "Just Eli's coming home."

"Eli who?"

"Funny enough, that was my reaction. I'm picking him up in Seattle. Day after tomorrow. Good news is he'll be here in person to help you get your job back."

"So what's the bad news?"

More sirens from across the lake began filling the air. Another cop and an ambulance.

Sophia and Abigail stared at each other.

"I think I know where we can find Krunk," Sophia said, looking pale.

CHAPTER 32

ESME

Esme stood on the dark walkway outside of Dr. Carla's lab, waiting for Kevin to show. Before long he came jogging up the walkway and quietly punched in the key code on the lab door. He seemed nervous as he pulled her inside and kissed her. He smelled a little ripe, with a touch of lime deodorant.

"I've been helping Preston since yesterday," he said. "He's losing it. Said he was going to walk around the landfill, looking for clues. Find out who took Alan. He didn't seem to register that his wife and kids are *gone.*"

Esme had only been inside this cabin once before, on the day Kevin started working for Dr. Carla, and even that was brief. The place was bland but functional, tidy but overstocked: shelves of glassware and instruments, swabs and droppers, binders and gloves.

"I can't believe Dr. Carla left all this behind," Kevin said, leaning into her crowded desk. "Her whole professional life is in this room."

"At the moment she's not exactly interested in her professional life."

The windows were covered with blackout blinds and Esme moved to open one.

"Don't," he said.

She stopped. "Kevin, why'd you want to meet me here? If your mom sees me..."

"Bear with me," he said, the desk lamp creating warped shadows on his face. "Remember those jars of old lake water Dr. Carla was storing at her house? Last night, middle of the night, Preston asked me to help him move whatever was left of them over to the library. We hid them in the basement. He taught that kids class there so he knew the code for the door, and he thought it would be safer stashing them there than at home. He said they were dangerous. That someone took Alan because of them. And whatever else Dr. Carla was up to."

Esme pointed toward a tall shelf on the far wall that held a few dozen Nalgene bottles of lake water, labeled in Kevin's old-lady penmanship. "You missed some."

"Apparently someone already ruined those." He tugged on the chain at the eyewash station. "There's something else. After the library last night, Preston said he was going to walk home, so I went to bed. But then a little while later my dad caught him right out there, outside the lab, all alone, middle of the night, trying to break the lock on the door."

"Trying to get in here?"

"But my dad wouldn't let him in without Dr. Carla's permission. I guess before she left town she told him that *no one* was allowed inside, and mentioned Preston by name. I'm supposed to be keeping an eye out in case he comes back." Kevin peered out the peephole in the door, then glanced around the lab. "The university will send someone to get all of Dr. Carla's stuff, eventually. In the meantime my dad wants me to box it all up before anything else is corrupted. Or stolen."

"Stolen?"

"Like my flash drive?" he said, meeting Esme's eyes for an instant before moving behind Dr. Carla's desk. He stared at the binders and manuals stacked on the shelves, probably obsessing again about the research he'd lost: all that data on aquifers and groundwater flow, fertilizer runoff and precipitation shifts—gone in an instant. He'd had to start again from scratch.

"Kevin. What are we doing here?"

"You know who they began looking for," he said, opening and closing the same desk drawer, "the *second* they found out Alan was missing?"

"Who?"

"Silas. Makes sense, too. He's been out there on the beach every morning. Plus his history, hiding Baby Grace in the shed. And his drowning kit."

"That wasn't anything like Alan's disappearance," she said, aware of how defensive she sounded.

"Turns out it couldn't have been him, though, because he was busy failing a piss test when Alan went missing. But did you know that Silas stole a revolver from Pastor Kurt's gun locker?"

With reluctance, Esme told him about Pastor Kurt's visit to her porch, when he'd warned her about the stolen gun. And, finally, about the little misfit who'd slapped her on the sidewalk.

"So can we finally agree that it *was* Silas who shot out your bedroom window?"

"I'm fine, Kev."

"You still feel like it's your fault. Like you deserve how he's treating you. Can't you see he wants to hurt you?"

Intent on ignoring him, Esme dragged her fingers through a box of black rubber dropper caps.

"I talked to my dad about a restraining order," he continued, "but Silas isn't exactly scared of getting in trouble. And the cops claim they can't do anything until he *does* something, which is, like, beyond logic, especially with his history. Esme, we're supposed to be moving out of here in a *month*. It just feels like a deadline."

"So we leave in three weeks instead," she said.

"All this stuff with Alan," Kevin said. "It's got me thinking about how *precarious* everything is. Why haven't we been more worried about Silas? More *proactive*, you know?"

From a high shelf, between a set of binders, Kevin retrieved a small silver key and used it to unlock Dr. Carla's bottom desk drawer. Esme considered asking him how on earth he knew about some hidden tiny key, but then he'd spent enough hours scanning the binders and books on those shelves that it made sense. From the drawer Kevin tugged out a stack of notebooks and set them on the floor, then pulled out a bundled-up Seahawks T-shirt. It was clear from the way he held it that something was wrapped inside.

"Tell me that's not a gun," she said, feeling slightly lightheaded.

Kevin cleared a space on the desk and carefully unfolded the fabric, revealing a brown paper lunch bag crumpled to the size of a softball. From inside the paper bag he pulled out another bag, this one clear, plastic, and half-full of crystalline yellow powder. He set it under the desk lamp and it looked as if it glowed.

"Kevin? Is that—?"

"Yeah."

"Why on earth does Dr. Carla have *that*?"

"It's not Dr. Carla's."

It took a second, but she soon had the answer: "It's Preston's?"

"He's an *addict*, Esme. Think about it," Kevin said, sounding grim. "His refusal to go with his own wife and kids when they left town? The way he was trying to break in here last night the *minute* I left him alone? Plus all that talk of rehab and hitting rock bottom when we went to their house for dinner? It totally adds up."

"But why would Dr. Carla...?"

"Maybe she doles it out to him or something. Helps to wean him off." He stepped back and pointed at the powder. "I mean, look at it. The way it's hidden. Packaged. Plus isn't heroin this shade of yellow sometimes?"

"You're asking *me*?"

"All I know is Dr. Carla had it stashed like this for a reason. And she clearly didn't want Preston getting in here."

On the corner of the desk, just beyond the bag of yellow powder, was a photograph of Ali and Alan as infants, lying together on a quilted blanket in the grass, their tiny hands grasping each other. Esme clutched her stomach, worried she might be sick.

"Kevin? What does this have to do with *us*?"

"This stuff," he said, meeting her eye, "is going to keep us safe from Silas. At least until we can get the hell out of Soap Lake."

Esme stared. "Silas."

"He's convinced you ruined his life, Esme. I mean, it's not like he listens to reason. But he might listen to this."

Esme huffed. "Kevin. We are *not* selling drugs to Silas."

"Not *selling*, Esme. *Trading*, I guess. For safety."

"You mean *bribing*."

"I mean making it worth his while," Kevin said, meeting her eye, "to never aim a pistol at you again."

Esme crouched behind a poplar tree in the lakeside park, watching Silas in the distance. He'd been on the shore since early this morning, just as he had every day now for a while, sitting cross-legged in the sand, wearing a shredded trench coat and chunky boots. The rising sun flooded the lake in a warm glow.

As much as Esme hated to admit it, Kevin was right: trying to barter for Silas's good will was a better option than waiting around for him to hurt her. Because inevitably he would.

They had no plan B.

On the shore, Kevin held out the glass vial of powder they'd scooped from the bag in the lab. He looked around as if worried about being seen, then worked his way through the script that he and Esme had been practicing all night like drama class psychos.

"Do you know what this is, Silas?"

Silas was about to yell at him, but instead he leaned way over and took the vial. He flicked it, then held it up to the sky, as if to decipher its contents: yellow crystalline powder that looked as if it had been harvested from the sunrise.

"You cannot tell *anyone*, Silas. I found it in one of the hotel rooms and I know exactly who left it. This Alaskan guy, an old bearded biker. A cop came into the hotel to refill his coffee and the biker panicked and left in a hurry. He forgot this in his shaving kit. That was, like, three days ago. He's not coming back."

Silas popped the top off the vial, licked his pinkie and took a taste. He scowled a little and squinted at Kevin as he pressed the lid back on. He held it up to the light again. Mumbled something.

"I don't want money," Kevin said, shaking his head. "I just want you to leave Esme alone."

Silas balked, mumbled again.

"You're right," Kevin said. "*Us*. Leave *us* alone. Please. Just stop with the threats. No more shooting windows or anything else. If you do that, it's all yours, totally free. There's even more. You just have to promise. And if you get caught, you didn't get it from me."

Silas bowed his head and stared at the sand for a second. Then he jumped to his feet and stumbled backward, as if his legs were asleep.

"Silas? Deal?"

He didn't respond, just stuffed the vial into the pocket of his trench coat and limped down the shore like a movie monster.

"Silas? Promise?"

He raised one arm in a horrid thumbs-up.

CHAPTER 33

ABIGAIL

As Abigail drove north along the curve of the lake, an ambulance and a few cop cars were blocking a lane.

"Something bad," Sophia said as Medusa trickled through the scene, past a few gathered cops.

Blood streaked the barren road for a hundred feet or more, and down feathers twitched in the weeds. A cop wearing latex gloves opened a large evidence bag and dropped a shredded red winter coat inside.

"Is that?" Sophia said through her fingers. "No. *No.*"

"Preston's."

The ambulance drove away—no lights, no siren, no rush—and they knew he was dead.

Abigail stared ahead, gripping the wheel, rolling slowly along, glad she and Sophia were together, far from her friend's preferred escape. Sophia nodded intensely and pulled a fresh yellow paperback out of her tote. On the cover, a crimp-haired blonde girl in a striped sweater chatted with a preppy boy.

Sweet Valley Twins and Friends #15: The Older Boy.

She chewed her finger and leaned into the page like a fiend.

In the bloody oval where Preston had died, the downy wisps were sopped and still. Abigail drove past a brown Datsun pickup with a sunbaked woman sitting on the tailgate as a cop took photos of her hands. Abigail parked Medusa at the edge of the scene and got out.

Krunk was sitting on a guardrail, legs crossed. Across the road, basalt cliffs rose toward a hazy sky. Behind him, a slope of loose rock dropped into the lake. As she approached he rested his cap on his knee and swept his hair to the side, but couldn't manage a smile.

"Want to sit?"

She pointed at the road. "Don't you need to...?"

"Cones are doing my job just fine. You knew him?"

She nodded, staring at the bloody patch where Preston had died. A spirograph of tire treads faded in and out of it, like bike tracks through a playground puddle.

"Bystander pulled him to the shoulder," he said, looking toward the Datsun, "but someone nailed him long before she got there, and looks like another someone after that. Before we arrived more cars drove through, ruining the tread patterns. So we've got a lot of work to do tracking down whoever hit him. And even if we do, with the way he wandered these roads, no shoulder, looking at his maps, the coroner will call it accidental. Ill-advised behavior."

"Another win for hopelessness," she said, and he looked at her, as earnest as a Little Leaguer.

"You alright?" he said.

"You serious?"

They sat in silence, kicking at the ground, and she realized this was the second time they'd hung out near a crime scene. He seemed too fragile for this job.

"Was he alone?" she said. "When he died?"

"No," he said, forcing himself to sound professional. "Hey, do you mind if we...?"

He raised a leg over the guardrail and swiveled around. It took her a second to figure out that he wanted to look out at the lake, rippling peacefully in the sun, and not the bloody road.

"First car," he said, "hit him on the tight side of that curve and dragged him to here. His arm must've got twisted into the axle. Followed immediately by the second. Both hit and run. Fifteen minutes later, that woman in the Datsun saw him and stopped, pulled him to the shoulder. Called 9-1-1. Said he was a pretzel. By the time we got here he was already gone."

"You mean dead."

"I mean dead."

He stooped and pulled a little feather up from where it was snagged in the cheatgrass. He offered it to the air and it drifted west until it became invisible.

"She covered his face with that coat of his," he said, "which seemed..."

"Poetic?"

"Sickening."

Over in the bed of the Datsun, the woman was rubbing baby wipes over her hands, dropping the pink crumpled sheets behind her.

"Did he say anything?"

"Nothing useful. He was holding a piece of a map, though nothing new there."

"Where's the rest of it?"

"Blowing down the highway, I imagine."

Abigail wiped her palms on her thighs and thought about Hal in the Ag Office catching sight of Preston's map on her phone, and the timing of him being run down within hours of that moment.

She hardly knew Preston, yet she felt hollowed out. It was

the shock of it, to be sure, and the tragedy of the guy's spiraling life. But mostly she just felt guilt.

"Was that why you came looking for me at the police station earlier?" Krunk asked.

"Some lady told me you were out. And when I say *lady* I mean *warthog.*"

"That would be her."

"She called me a home-wrecker."

"About *me*?" he said, surprised. "I didn't realize I had a home to wreck. Why were you looking for me?"

Speaking to Daniel in the orchard lot about payphone records seemed like ages ago, and her words felt half-hearted. "I wanted to ask you about the Polks."

"Patron saints of the lake. I love the Polks."

"And Esme. I was just wondering if they'd been questioned about her death."

"Because?"

"Because Esme had been calling the hotel in the weeks before she died."

"Okay," he said, looking at her sideways. "I guess I didn't realize you were still…"

"Detecting?"

"Snooping," he said. "For clarity, *someone* was calling the Polks' hotel from a payphone near Esme's apartment. And *someone* at the payphone here was calling it back. We've got all that from the cops down in Bakersfield. But between us, the task force is looking into all kinds of calls made to and from those payphones, all over the west, even out of country. Could be that she set up a chain of deals along the way and this one just went bad."

"It's not drugs," Abigail mumbled, but didn't elaborate: Daniel's wishes.

Krunk glanced at her and continued. "As for Mr. Polk, he's not some kingpin, which puts him in the periphery of the investigation. It's not illegal to talk on the phone."

"It just seems like they should be digging into those calls more."

"Think about Daniel," he said, and lowered his voice. "And Esme's mom. She's hanging on by a thread already, and then her daughter reaches out to the Polks after all these years and doesn't call her, not even to say she's coming to town for a visit? Doesn't call her own brother? On top of that no one knew she had a child? There's no need to rub their noses in all of that unless it helps the investigation. Right now it doesn't."

She must have glanced over at Sophia, or maybe it was the mention of drugs, because Krunk was looking at her, too: lounging in Medusa, one bare foot hanging out the window.

"Is your friend on the nod?" he said.

"Sweet Valley High."

He arched his brow. "Think she might answer some questions about the drug angle?"

"Please don't," Abigail said, shaking her head. "She's in a bad place."

"Often is," he said, but he sounded sincere. "Try not to agitate the Polks, will you? Esme's death brings up a lot of pain for them. Because of Kevin."

"For you, too, doesn't it? Because of the hotel."

"Sure, I guess," he said, after a moment, staring at his hands.

It was clear he needed no encouragement, just a simple ear. "What happened that day?"

"The shooting? Shit, I've been trying to answer that question for years."

"Yeah?"

"I didn't know Esme and Kevin well, or anything, I was just delivering pizza. Second month on the job, I'm whistling down the hotel hallway and see my classmate get his head blown off. Then *pow*. I get shot, too. I really thought I was going to die." Krunk seemed surprised at himself, at the way he was carrying on. "I should've been in therapy, but instead, as soon as my leg was better, I rented a depressing apartment in Seattle and played video games alone. Barely explored the city at all and spent all my savings in no time. Talked to no one but a few bartenders and the janitor at the laundromat. Had to come home to my high school bedroom and start over. That's when I got this." He tapped his badge. "Not my dream come true. Though every day at this job motivates me to get out of here even more. I'm saving up to do it right next time, but you know how that goes. Might be here forever at this rate. So yeah. It's all good."

Abigail could plainly see that being in the hotel that day had messed him up more than he let on. He'd been too late to help Kevin, but not too late to drag Esme up from the floor and away from the gunman and finally to safety, despite getting shot himself. It explained a lot.

He'd saved Esme's life once, but hadn't been there in the desert when she'd needed him to do it again.

"Did Esme ever talk to you about what happened that day?" she said. "Raise doubts or anything?"

"What do you mean?"

"About Silas, I guess." She explained how Sophia and Pastor Kurt were in recovery together, and how he didn't believe drugs were involved. Nor that his son would ever have killed Kevin.

"Pastor Kurt's kid pulled the trigger, so it makes sense he doesn't want to believe it," Krunk said, patting his thigh. "But I've got a bullet hole and a lot of trauma that would argue otherwise. And it messed Esme up enough that she couldn't live in her hometown. Still, I wouldn't want to be in his shoes. His son. His gun. I get it. It's tragic."

"Yeah," she said, and stood from the hot guardrail, feeling a tightness in her chest. "Is someone going to tell Preston's wife?"

"Ex-wife," Krunk said, cocking an eyebrow. "She lives in Seattle. Used to work in biotech but now is at a community college. I'll make sure someone tracks her down."

A few tufts of down bobbed on the surface of the lake, close to shore. She could feel Krunk watching her.

"I should go," he said, and reached out and lightly squeezed her palm.

When he lifted his fingers away, she wanted them back.

As he walked toward the cones, she heard a *hissss* and turned to see one of the cops spray-painting the asphalt to document the scene. She watched him spray bright green arrows and dashes, then trace the oval where Preston's body had finally ripped free of the vehicle. When he was finished, he stepped back to size up his work, like a baker decorating a cake—or a man scrawling symbols on a life-size map.

CHAPTER 34

ABIGAIL

Abigail biked to Preston's house, certain his place would be empty in the wake of his roadside death. She'd left Medusa at home and waited for nightfall, assuming that the police would be here all day, but there was no seal or paperwork on the door, and the porch was scattered with junk mail, so clearly they hadn't. She wasn't sure what she might find, but with his maps of violence and archives of crime, Preston, if anyone, would have something to reveal about Esme's murder.

He'd been run down for a reason.

Stinky sumac sprouted all around his house, nearly blocking it from view. The other homes on the street were quiet, with tidy yards. No one was outside.

Abigail lifted the doormat in search of a key and a spider ran over her hand. The top ledge of the doorframe was empty except for dead bugs, but when she tipped over a clay planter, a tarnished key sat on the concrete beneath.

The house inside was hot and stuffy, its windows lined with

black garbage bags. Boxes were spread throughout the living room, and every surface was covered with bales of information: articles from newspapers and magazines, pamphlets and maps and legal documents. Printed photos of people and homes, fields and streets, patches of empty land.

She walked a figure eight through the room, reminded of Preston's table in the library.

In his bedroom, piles of paper instead of a bed.

In his kitchen, piles of paper on the counter, plus a corded yellow wall phone next to the fridge. She picked it up and was surprised to hear a dial tone. The room smelled so rank that it quickly became a taste—rotten potatoes or broccoli—so she hopped back down the hall.

She opened the door to what must have been Ali and Alan's room. A half-finished game of CandyLand sat on the rug next to the bunk bed, with a pair of plastic gingerbread people posed on the path. Pajamas and socks were deserted on the floor. Winter coats and rain jackets hung tightly inside the narrow closet. And that was it. The whole room was a Pompeii of childhood, a museum abandoned by his kids in an instant a decade ago and untouched since. She imagined him fooling himself into believing they were in here playing board games, and not estranged tweens living two hundred miles away.

The guy was a hoarder caught in a loop. She supposed she should've expected this, deleted his map for good and focused on her own problems—the impending return of her husband, for one. Yet she was wary of leaving.

Maybe because Preston's house seemed to hold all information, and no interpretation. Data without conclusion or analysis. All these piles: he'd given up his family in order to turn his home into a giant storage cabinet. Collection was distraction. It allowed the journey to never end, like the roads he walked each day. The real tragedy seemed to be his inability to do something with all of this information. To make it all add up.

If he'd been predicting any future in this life-size oracle, she thought, it was hers.

She was about to slip out the back door when a tiny question gave her pause: Where had Preston *slept*? She'd just snooped through every inch of his house and, outside of the kids' bunk beds, there was nowhere for the guy to climb under the covers and shut out the world.

Back in the twins' room, she took one last peek at the bed-covers, seeking the shape of a man. But the sheets and rails were thick with dust, undisturbed, so he hadn't been sleeping here. With a flood of sadness it occurred to her that Preston might have curled into a ball and slept on the closet floor each night, like a scared child.

She opened the twins' closet and took one last look inside. A draft of cool air drifted in, causing a jacket to twitch, as if someone were hiding behind it. She pressed her hand through, parting the coats, fearful yet skeptical, but her fingers kept reaching, and with a rush of vertigo she almost fell forward. No one was there—

But neither was the back wall of the closet. She shoved aside the hangers and discovered that the floor continued through a framed opening in the drywall, down a set of wooden steps, and into an enormous room. Motion-sensor lights blinked to life as she waved her hand.

"Hello?"

Nothing. The updraft was cold and soily as she descended the steps, looking back halfway down as if someone might lock the closet door behind her. She worried she might find a person down there—an abducted coed, a banker in chains—but as her eyes adjusted to the brightness she realized that this was more likely a dungeon of the mind.

Yep.

The room was the size of a large bedroom and braced with wooden beams. With the amount of light it could have been a grow-room, but every inch of the corkboard walls was plastered with documents in Spanish and English: newspaper articles and chat room transcripts, official maps and handwritten notes, church bulletins and grade school menus, fliers for missing farmworkers and lost pets, and a shocking number of autopsy reports and obituaries. Artifacts in bags were tacked between it all: broken eyeglasses and dog collars and cocktail napkins and shoelaces and candy wrappers and burned matches and popsicle sticks and half a denture and a blue latex glove covered in blood—and so on.

But the strangest, most striking things in the room were the strands of colorful yarn pinned to the walls, hundreds of them, maybe thousands, overlapping and crisscrossing as they linked image to image, page to page, one part of the room to another. Each strand passed through the middle of the room before being pinned to a different spot, so the center was a cat's cradle of yarn, hovering in place, spoking outward like an exploded rainbow.

"My god," she whispered.

In the middle of the room, directly below the colorful star of yarn, was a yellowing mattress, a lumpy pillow, a gray blanket. Preston's bed.

Upstairs was a staging area for this room. And this was interpretation, not just information.

She'd found the meaning of his map.

CHAPTER 35

ESME

Esme entered the Healing Lake Hotel lobby from the street, silencing the strap of bells on the door as she slipped inside. At the desk, Kevin was wearing a loose turquoise tank top with a Healing Lake logo. He saw her and immediately peered through the beaded curtain behind him, on the lookout for his folks.

Despite Mrs. Polk's adamant wishes, Esme and Kevin were moving to Bellingham together in less than a month—Kevin on a scholarship to WWU, Esme to a community college until she raised her grades—yet she was still banned from visiting Kevin while he was on the clock. She'd never earn his mom's approval.

They kissed over the counter, a quick peck that Kevin pulled away from. He squeezed her hands.

"I'm worried about Silas," he whispered, biting his lip the way he did when he was feeling insecure.

"Me, too," she said. "I hardly slept."

"Linen guy earlier told me Silas had some episode at the gas station last night, three in the morning, acting all possessed.

Trashed the bathroom. Poured out a bunch of soda. Stomped on bags of chips. Totally berserk. The cops came and everything."

"What? Was it, like, a *reaction*?"

"To the powder? No idea. But I did a search and it's not the way you're supposed to act on heroin. I just hope he's sleeping it off in a jail cell right now. And not somewhere…"

Dead, Esme thought. She unclasped his hands and clutched her elbows.

"Look," he continued, "we don't know anything. The gas station stuff could just be another Silas implosion. Him raging at the world."

"But he probably had the vial on him."

"Probably."

"Which means the cops got it."

"That's my thinking, too. A cop car drove past a bit ago, but they do that anyway. I couldn't see who was driving." He looked out toward the street, where a seagull was pecking a pork rind in the sun. "If Silas tells them it came from us? You know, it was *a lot*. In terms of dealing or possession or whatever."

Esme's panic became denial. "He wouldn't tell them it came from us."

"He would if it got him off. I was thinking we should get rid of the rest of it. Find somewhere to ditch it. Because if the cops come here to search…"

"Dr. Carla could go to jail."

"I was actually thinking more about *us*," he said. "But yeah. Her, too. Feel like sneaking over to the lab?"

"I think I remember the combo."

"Dad's running errands. Mom went back to bed. But if she gets up and sees you, tell her you're boxing up stuff for Dr. Carla."

Just then, the bells on the lobby door jangled. Esme could feel her shoulders hunch and she closed her eyes, tense about the possibility of a visit from Mrs. Polk.

"Just the mail," Kevin said, and the carrier left it on the desk.

On top of a hospitality catalog and a few credit card solicitations was a full-colored envelope addressed to *Mr. Kevin Polk* from the University of Chicago.

"Apparently they can't take 'no' for an answer," Esme said. "Hotshot."

The glossy collage on the envelope included images of the Windy City skyline, a high-rise residence hall, and a dorm room, complete with chuckling roommates.

A round sticker on the outside said *Welcome to Campus North #309, Kevin Polk!*

"That's weird," he said, but his cheeks were blooming red.

Esme's hands flattened on the counter. She felt herself fade. *Oh.*

Earlier, when she saw Mr. Polk out by the lake, he'd given her a hug and told her he was going to miss her when school started, but was glad she'd still be in state.

Bellingham is like five hours, he'd said. *We'll still be seeing a lot of each other.*

Now she realized he wasn't talking about Kevin and Esme; he was talking about Esme alone.

Because Kevin was going to Chicago to live in his fancy new dorm.

And Esme was staying in state. Maybe even in town. With Silas.

"Please don't be mad," Kevin said, grabbing her wrists.

"I'm actually not *mad*," she said, unpeeling his fingers and holding up her hands. "More like...bummed. When were you going to tell me, Kev?"

"Mom really wants me to go to Chicago," he said, tapping the envelope, "so I told them yes. But I'm still thinking about Western."

"You can't do both," she said.

"It's a hard decision, Esme. I'm just keeping my options—"

"You're keeping Mommy happy," she said, quietly. "I get it. I'd probably do the same thing. Just please stop dragging me along."

"I love you," he said, dipping his knees in a way that was totally irritating and heartfelt. "You know I do. Besides, we're visiting Bellingham next week, just the two of us."

"If we're not in jail."

"If it doesn't feel right," he said, ignoring her, as if incarceration couldn't possibly interrupt the perfect path of Kevin Polk, "maybe we both go to Chicago. Same plan, different place."

"I can't afford that, Kev. And I need to be able to get home for my mom. It just sucks that..."

"Wait," he said, holding up his hand and squinting toward the street. "Cop. *Cop.*"

Esme turned. Out the lobby window, a cop cruiser slowed down long enough for her to see Officer McDaid behind the wheel, looking toward the hotel. Then he hit the gas. Someone was in the back seat. Long hair. Black T-shirt.

"Was that Silas with him?"

"Oh shit," Kevin said. "It was."

"I guess that means he didn't OD," she whispered. "That's a relief. Sort of."

"McDaid would've stopped if he was coming in here, right? He always parks out front."

"Look," Esme said, fighting back tears, "I don't know how I feel about anything right now." She took a step back and gathered herself. "I think you should go to Chicago. It makes sense."

"Esme."

She actually was angry, she realized. Or so hurt she couldn't tell the difference.

"It'll be fine, Kevin. Go to Chicago."

"We're not breaking up, Esme."

This time, somehow, she yelled. "Just *go*, Kevin! Okay? Go!"

Down the long hall of guest rooms, a pizza guy in a red shirt and black jeans was making a lunch delivery, propping an insulated maroon box on his palm. He must have heard her yell because he tugged his black cap down over his eyes and studied the room numbers as he walked.

"Hey, Abe," Kevin said, low energy, and the pizza guy raised his free hand without looking toward the lobby.

"Hey, Abe," Esme said, and she wondered if Kevin thought she was mocking him.

It was Abe Krunk, from the forgettable dream that was a high school hallway. He was a harmless guy with pained eyes, pretty cute, really into gaming and cars.

Kevin was looking at her. She sighed and smirked.

"What?" he said, lightly, her brown-eyed boy.

"I should get to the lab," she said, plucking the front of his turquoise tank over the reception desk, as if trying to hang on to him before he rocketed away. "We'll talk about it..."

She stopped midsentence when the lobby door opened behind her and the strap of bells clacked the glass.

Esme felt herself shrink, dreading the possibility that it was Mrs. Polk, roused by the sounds of arguing teens. Esme wasn't even supposed to be on the premises.

She closed her eyes and took a breath. A hot draft slid through the open door and across the back of her legs. Behind Kevin, the beaded curtains clicked.

"We'll figure it out, Kev," she whispered, and opened her eyes.

Only Kevin was looking past her, unblinking. Pale.

"*Oh shh,*" he said, barely audible.

Behind him, down the carpeted hall to his left, Abe was about to knock on a door when his knuckles paused midair. He, too, was staring past her, and slowly raising the pizza box to his face.

"*Esme go,*" Kevin said, and at first she was sure it was a bomb, the gunshot. Because her face was sprayed and stinging, and she couldn't catch her breath through the blood.

★ ★ ★

Kevin folded to the floor next to the desk and somehow Esme was on her knees alongside him. Silas was by the door, hair in his face, moaning and studying the revolver in his grip. His mouth moved and he shook all over and he looked like he might walk backward out to the sidewalk. Or use the gun on himself.

Esme's throat creaked as she struggled for air.

You okay, Kev? she tried to say. *You okay?*

On the carpet Kevin was clutching her hand and—

No. *She* was clutching Kevin's hand, but his hand wasn't doing anything.

A few feet away, the beaded curtain seemed to breathe and she could feel him in the air.

Tick-tick.

Feel him leaving, her brown-eyed boy.

Go.

Silas was blubbering now. Walking toward her in his baggy black shorts, his baggy black shirt. Acting all possessed.

What'd you do to me, Esme?

He was closer now, looking at the pistol, looking at her, but her ears were ringing from the gunshot and the static of Kevin in the air—

es ge up

Abe was screaming her name from down the hall, peering over the top of his pizza box, as if it were a shield.

esme get up

esme run

Run!

Silas swiveled like a machine, aimed toward the hall and squeezed the trigger. Abe jumped into the wall and dropped to the carpet holding his thigh in the air, pizza box flopped to its side.

Esme's teeth chattered. Her face dripped. Her hands were slimy wet.

Silas was above her now, the revolver quaking.

What'd you do to me, Esme? What'd you do?

She saw it coming out of the corner of her eye but Silas clearly didn't: the stool cracking him on the face. That sound: a big rock hitting a small puddle. By the time he hit the floor his temple was bleeding and Abe was on top of him, spit falling from his mouth, tears from his eyes, pant leg blooming, pizza hat gone, pounding him with his fist. Over and over.

Silas gripped his pistol, veins bulging on the back of his hand, and Abe squeezed his slippery wrist.

Getoff me! Silas screamed. *Getoff dude!*

Abe lifted his body into the air and kneed Silas hard in the sternum and for the first time in a minute the lobby went quiet. Abe hobbled to his feet and twisted Esme's collar into his fist and ripped her off her knees.

"Run!" he screamed in her face, and threaded her arm through his, and together they blundered violently over Kevin and out the door to the beach.

Glass exploded behind them. Another gunshot. Silas was up.

As they ran Esme waited for a second pop, for everything to go dark, but the bullet never came. Abe tugged her into the sunshine, his leg drizzling blood behind them.

No one was around, not even on the lakeshore. Maybe they'd heard the shots and hid.

She knew the combo, she kept saying, but Abe tried to steer her away from the cabins—

"Up the beach," he said, "behind the library."

She shook her head. Silas would cut them off. He'd been on these walkways so many times that he could glide through them like a cat. Esme dragged Abe to the far side of the property, directly in front of Dr. Carla's lab.

She punched the code into the keypad. The lock opened with a *beep.*

Inside, Abe locked the door and leaned his back against it,

sliding to the ground. He was breathing hard and pressing his palm to his thigh.

"What is this place?"

"Shh!"

The windows were blacked out and Esme's vision was clouded so it was impossible to see anything except the lens in the door, hovering above them like an eye.

She peeked through it. Silas wasn't out there.

Somehow Abe fumbled with his phone and dialed the police and was surprisingly calm as he whispered.

Esme felt as if she were coming off a sedative. Her hair was stuck to her forehead. She felt sharp little splinters in her cheeks and had to kneel to slow the onslaught of vertigo.

"Is Kevin?"

Krunk stopped whispering into the phone and nodded.

She thought about the powder she and Kevin had given to Silas, and the blunt foolishness of believing they could ever cross into his world and return unscathed.

What'd you do to me, Esme?

It definitely wasn't heroin. Whatever it was, it had invited death into their lives. Silas had taken some and lost his mind and got arrested, and the second the cops dropped him off, he came to the hotel for revenge. Even the cops wouldn't believe him now, not after the shooting, but they still might connect the powder to Kevin and Esme, and even to Dr. Carla.

She wiped her eyes and told herself that she'd be okay dying right now but she was *not* going to jail for this. And Kevin was *not* going to be remembered as the kid who gave bogus heroin to Silas. Because this was not that. This was always about Baby Grace. This was Silas killing Kevin to finally and totally eviscerate Esme.

Successfully.

"They want to know if we saw another shooter," Abe whispered, holding the phone against his chest. "Or just Silas."

Tick-tick.

Esme turned toward Abe and a gauzy fog cleared from her mind. His red pizza shirt was ripped from the tussle. He was still palming his thigh.

"Esme?" he whispered. "You didn't see anyone else, did you? The cops need to know."

"Just Silas," she mumbled.

"Just Silas," Abe said, nodding into the phone.

Across the dark room, Esme reached up and felt around the shelves, between Dr. Carla's binders, until her fingertips found the key. Then she knelt and unlocked the bottom desk drawer and tugged out the bundled Seahawks shirt with the bag of powder folded inside.

If it wasn't heroin, what was it?

"What're you doing?" Abe whispered, holding the phone away, but she was on the ground behind the desk so he couldn't fully see. "He's still out there, Esme. So if there's a rag for my leg or a weapon?"

Esme unbundled the package and tossed the T-shirt to Abe.

Was this bundle why someone stole little Alan and ran his mom out of town?

She took out the plastic bag, a quarter full of yellow powder, then locked the desk drawer and returned the key to its shelf. Her hands wouldn't stop quivering.

"They want to know if you're hurt," Abe whispered, but then he saw the pain in her eyes and realized it was an absurd question and went back to mumbling into the phone.

They heard more gunshots.

Abe froze. Stared at her.

Then came more: *pop-pop-pop-pop-pop.*

Abe asked who was shooting and nodded into the phone as the dispatcher spoke.

"Out on the lakeshore," he said to Esme. "The cops shot Silas. Sounds like he's dead."

Esme stood to her feet.

"We're supposed to wait," Abe continued, his voice breaking. "In case he wasn't alone." He looked down at his thigh. "Could you at least help me with this?"

Without a word, she threw open the door and blinding sunlight blasted into the cabin. She heard muffled yelling on the hotel beach and sirens over on Main. The lake glimmered so brightly it hurt.

"Esme?" Abe said, finally collapsing into sobs. "Will you help me? Please? Esme?"

On her way out, she cupped the bundle in her palm, with nothing more to give.

CHAPTER 36

ABIGAIL

It wasn't a murder *board*, exactly, that Preston had constructed in his basement bunker. More like a murder *cube*. A murder *polygon*. A murder *rhombicosidodecahedron*.

Murder being the operative word.

As Abigail took in the room, the colorful beauty of its nucleus was muted by the images and articles all around her, many so grim that she felt like a visitor to a museum of atrocities.

One section of wall contained a newspaper article ("Wandering Toddler Found") about Preston's tot Alan, who'd gone missing for two days before turning up at the landfill, barefooted and alone. Around the headline were maps of the neighborhood and photos of the landfill and the skeletal orchards around it, with the most striking image being of a child's shoe stuck in a chain-link fence above the canal. Each piece was pinned with its own strand of yarn that stretched through the colorful bolus in the center of the room before splaying out to other articles about other children, missing forever or found alive or discovered dead, and other incidents that occurred at the landfill and around the canals. A lot, as it happened.

Already Abigail was overwhelmed, but she wandered along, drawn to certain photos—a row of women holding shovels, a stone labyrinth with a black bell in its center—until one image halted her cold: a folded white biosuit on an evidence table.

TreeTop's uniform. Speckled with blood.

High above it were two pieces of weathered scrap wood, screwed to the wall, as if to cover a rodent hole. She stood on her tiptoes and saw they had once been part of a vintage apple box, roughly cut apart and scored with a messy combination of numbers:

On one piece, below the stamped logo of the Desert Delite fruit storage company, a familiar phrase was carved into the wood:

She glanced around the room, overwhelmed by its complexity and scope, as Preston's reality settled in: *everything* here was TreeTop.

Beginning with the uniform, she followed a spoke into the weave and back out again. An article about a woman killed in a vehicular homicide connected to a photo of a food processing plant connected to a mugshot of a scowling cowboy connected to an autopsy of a dead inmate connected to an industrial accident report connected to a shriveled apple core in a sandwich baggie, tacked to the cork...

Abigail found her rhythm, snapping photos with her phone and moving between strands, feeling like she could hop from thread to thread forever. Preston had been trying to get ahead of it all like a storm chaser, attempting to predict whatever was coming next, but his mental health had clearly been eroding. That much had been clear when she'd first seen him wandering the streets of Soap Lake, tattered map in hand, or hovering over his crowded table in the library, but this space revealed even deeper levels of suffering and delusion. There was logic at work here, to be sure, yet the arrangement was manic, even frantic, as if Preston had begun to mimic a classic murder board he'd seen on TV, and along the way had lost control—as if the board had begun controlling him.

She pinched the colorful web, waiting for the strands to vibrate, unsure if she was the spider or the fly.

On a far section of wall, she found the article from the local paper about Esme's murder, complete with her high school photo, and the word *walker* circled in red. A series of strands stretched from it into the taut star at the center of the room.

Abigail traced one strand to a batch of old newsletter articles about a group of dairy workers' failed attempts to unionize. Organizers had pledged to try again despite the fear tactics management had used to discourage undocumented workers from voting their support. Next to the articles were copies of citations for labor and safety violations, and the obituary of a man in his thirties, wearing a filthy Mariners cap. Other strands headed from this collage back into the center of the room before plunging out to other parts of the walls, and though a story began to emerge, a causal chain, like gazing at the stars and seeing constellations, she saw no direct connection between any of this and the article reporting Esme's death.

Abigail made her way back to the article on Esme and followed another strand to a postcard of the Healing Lake Hotel, surrounded, not surprisingly, by articles covering the shooting of Kevin Polk. Part of the wall was dedicated to Kevin's accomplishments, with ribbons and certificates, and a packet detailing a Young Scientist scholarship he'd been awarded—third place, posthumous—for a proposal he'd written about groundwater flow and fertilizer runoff.

Abigail was taking photos of it all when the taut pieces of yarn dragged against her arm and she was suddenly awash in panic and had to close her eyes to stop the feeling of being tangled up in these strands. For a horrifying second, she felt as if she'd fallen into something from which she'd never emerge.

In Preston's hibernaculum, there was no time.

This was the reality that Abigail faced when she finally climbed up through the closet, down the hall to his kitchen, and saw a blinding sunrise through the gaps in the back door. She'd been downstairs for hours.

She pulled the collar of her T-shirt over her nose, filtering out the worst of the smells, then grabbed the corded phone off the wall. In her other hand, she gripped a photo she'd unpinned downstairs of the Last Payphone on Earth: the scratched and dented phone behind the gas station on Main Street.

The payphone someone had used to call Esme in the month before she died.

The photo was one of a dozen that Preston had tacked around a simple map of Soap Lake. The array of photos pinned around the map represented specific spots in town: the payphone, a picnic table, bathroom stalls, the side of a dumpster, a playground slide, a napkin dispenser, a school desk, and more, including the base of the World's Largest Missing Lava Lamp. Preston had vandalized each spot with the same phrase, in the same shape, almost of an eyeball:

He'd been writing the same message all over town: *TreeTop Kills*, so *Kill TreeTop*. He'd even managed to decipher the numbers from the chopped-up fruit box and add them to the center of his scribbles, as tiny as a pupil, as if to say, *And here's a phone number to get you close.*

Then Preston had snapped these photos of his own graffiti before the lower half was painted over or scratched out, presumably by the powers that be, so that all that remained was this little reminder:

Flagrantly left intact by those in power because raising people's fear fed straight into the myth.

In Preston's kitchen, Abigail squinted at the photo of the payphone graffiti and punched the number into his yellow wall phone.

It rang a few times. Then someone picked up.

Wheezing. Not talking.

"I'm looking for TreeTop?" she said, hesitant.

No answer, but a faint, breathy acknowledgment: *Mmmhhh.*

"TreeTop?" she said, louder this time.

"We're listening."

A man. Gravelly.

She hesitated. She heard a squeaky exhale.

"I need TreeTop."

"For who and why?"

She didn't respond, and as the seconds dragged to nothing, her hand grew damp on the receiver.

"Girl," he said, followed by a breathy pause. "You just committed suicide."

She heard the receiver slam into its cradle and quickly become a dial tone. She, too, hung up.

A minute passed as she stood in the kitchen, hand over her mouth, wondering what had just occurred. The photo she was holding dropped to the ground.

She'd found a way to plug herself into the system—tapped into TreeTop—and was trying to process what that meant, and to reconcile it with the web Preston had created downstairs—

When the sound of Preston's ringing phone hit her like a punch in the face.

It rang. And rang.

And it suddenly seemed like a very bad idea to be standing in front of this phone, looking a lot like someone who'd just been on it, so she sprinted out the back and started biking toward home, until she could no longer hear Preston's phone ringing behind her, as if tolling from the grave.

CHAPTER 37

ABIGAIL

Abigail was grateful to see Daniel standing in her driveway, leaning against his battered Bronco. She was breathing hard and her neck ached, both from craning around to see if anyone was following her and from spending half the night crawling through Preston's colorful web.

"I'm so glad you're here," she said, as she leaned the bike against her house.

Daniel held his finger to his mouth and pointed to the car's front seat, where George was sleeping. Daylight had arrived, and the coolness of the night dissolved around them like a mist.

"Was I supposed to watch him?"

"Nah. He was up at four wanting McMuffins, so we took a road trip." He gestured to the bag on his hood and picked up two cups of coffee, handed her one. "He insisted we bring you breakfast. Then he fell asleep in the drive-through. Kids are so lame."

"All talk."

"Plus their IQ's are, like, seven. Are you just getting home?"

he said, smiling. He stepped back to take in her gray T-shirt smudged with grime, and her ponytail, lopsided and springing leaks. "Let me guess. Cowboy Tinder? Lava Lamp Rave?"

"I wish." She wiped her hands on her shorts and realized they'd been trembling ever since the phone rang in Preston's kitchen twenty minutes ago. She took a deep breath and clenched and unclenched her fingers. "Can I trust you?"

"Abigail," he said, growing serious.

"I need to know when Esme left town. Back in high school. The specific date."

"Grad night? Summer, 2011. June 15, I guess. Why are you...?"

She explained how she'd spent the night at Preston's house and found a secret basement he'd dug through the closet in his kids' room, like Narnia gone wrong.

"You broke into his *house*?" he said, eyes wide.

"Just for a look. And to snap some photos," she said, waving her phone. "Plus the guy is dead?"

"I heard."

"This is why."

She could feel his stare as she opened the photos and began swiping, describing the bunker that was like a manifestation of Preston's wounded brain.

Daniel leaned in, halting on a photo she'd taken of the room while standing on the steps.

"Why are you asking about Esme? Don't tell me Preston was involved in her murder."

"I spent all night trying to figure out if what Preston was doing *really* makes sense or if it just makes sense in that conspiracy-theory way, because it feeds some deep hunger. Fills a void."

"Like his scientist spouse dragging him to the middle of nowhere and leaving him alone?" Daniel said, shaking the sleeve of her T-shirt. "That kind of void?"

"I know," she said, shaking her head with mild shame. "I was actually thinking it was about his kid going missing. His life fell apart, so he created this elaborate mythology to make it make sense. But when I came across this…" She zoomed in on a police evidence photo of TreeTop's outfit displayed on a table. "Don't ask me how he got it, but this is from a murder case that never made it to trial. Twenty years ago." On her phone was a photo of a woman with big brown eyes and straight black hair. "*Her* murder."

Daniel studied the photo quietly. "Go on."

One late night in 1997, she explained, this woman was working the graveyard shift at a potato processing plant in Quincy, twenty-five miles away. She was concerned about the amount of time she and her coworkers were spending handling frozen spuds on the packaging line without a chance to warm their hands, so she skipped her dinner break and spoke to her boss about it.

"Their fingers were cold," Abigail said. "She wasn't a crusader or Erin Brockovich or anything, just a single mom with three little kids at home, but some of her coworkers were undocumented and they were afraid to say anything. So she stepped up."

Her boss claimed they got a warming break and it was called *dinner*, and the flimsy gloves they used were fine. He brushed her off, so she went up the chain, and when the company did nothing she finally complained to the state's labor department.

"Ah. Whistleblower."

One night, a few months after she reported it, as the changes the workers wanted were in process, cameras outside of the plant captured a truck speeding across the lot and plowing into her, and clipping two other workers in the process. The driver slammed the brakes after bouncing over her, and when he was backing up to run her over again, one of her coworkers jumped into the cab and dragged him out, pinned him down until the police came.

"The driver was dressed as TreeTop," she said, pointing to the photo of the outfit, speckled with blood, probably from when the guy had been wrestled to the ground.

He was a middle-aged white man, a soft-spoken orchardist who lived forty-five minutes away, just outside of Soap Lake. He had no connection to the processing plant or the whistleblower, yet he'd plowed a stolen pickup into her on her dinner break.

"She died before the ambulance arrived. Her three kids, born and raised here, had to be taken in by their grandparents in Mexico."

The orchardist who ran her down died, too: hanged himself with a piece of wire in the county jail the following day, while waiting for his arraignment.

"Apparently he was an upstanding member of the community," she said, scrolling to a photo of him, pinned by strands of yellow and green yarn. "Church every Sunday. Donated apples to food banks each harvest. Yet he dressed up like TreeTop and murdered a twenty-two-year-old single mother who was raising her kids in a trailer. Because her fingertips were getting frostbitten at work and she made the mistake of saying something."

"And you're sure that's why the guy did it?" Daniel said. "Like it wasn't some kind of a love triangle or unpaid debt or something?"

"Right? And the orchardist looks squeaky-clean. Except..."

On her phone, Abigail showed a newspaper photo of a semi-truck tipped on its side, surrounded by apples. "A little over a year *before* the woman was run over, the same orchardist was being sued by a trucking company. There was an accident out on I-90 and they spilled a load of Fujis. There were medical bills and cleanup costs, not to mention the loss of the fruit, and when it was determined that the orchardist had fudged the weight on the paperwork to save a few bucks on transport, he became liable for *all* of it. Of course he refused to pay so the trucking company filed suit. The guy was already deep in debt and close to losing the year's harvest, on the brink of financial ruin—but lucky for him, eleven days after the lawsuit against him was filed, the owner of the trucking company drank himself to death. All alone in a motel room in Soap Lake." She swiped through her phone until she found an image of Preston's Oracle Map, then traced her finger to a tiny green bottle that had been scrawled atop a building just outside of town limits. "Motel Five. Autopsy said alcohol poisoning from four liters of gin. No receipts. No witnesses."

"Let me guess—the trucking company pulled the lawsuit."

"And the orchardist didn't have to pay a dime. His business fully recovered."

"This was a year before he ran over the mom? What's the connection?"

"The connections go on and on," she said, tracing her finger along Preston's map to a plat in the countryside, marked with a trio of tiny green ripples. "Totally different incident, okay? Six months *after* the woman was run down, a teenage boy who lived on this farm drowned while swimming in the Columbia River."

"Okay?" Daniel said, eyes wide, clearly intrigued.

"In March. In his underwear. A stranger who happened to be driving by, miles from home, saw the boy splashing out in the river, pulled over and swam out to rescue him. Only while he was fishing him out, the kid apparently panicked and gouged at his neck and face, and the stranger had to let him go. The boy went under and never came back up. Sixteen years old. A sophomore at Soap Lake High School."

"I vaguely remember that," Daniel said. "Though hearing it like that sounds sketchy. Kid swimming in the Columbia that early in the year, all alone?"

"And the bystander getting all scratched up while trying to save him? Almost like he wasn't there to save him at all, but to drown him, right? Especially when you find out that the Good Samaritan happened to be in management at a certain potato processing plant in Quincy."

"The same plant where the woman got run over."

"He was head of safety. He didn't lose his job when the

woman blew the whistle, but suddenly the state was doing random inspections. The guy was demoted from safety lead to line manager. And the company was fined."

"I bet," Daniel said. "So who was the kid who drowned?"

"That, I don't know. Preston took some photos of his parents' alfalfa farm, including of the kid's dad screaming at him from behind a barbed wire fence, which means he probably tried to interview him about it. As far as I can tell Preston was trying to figure out whether the drowned kid's parents had crossed someone, threatened to disrupt the system, and paid the price. Just like the whistleblowing mom. And the trucking company guy. Someone went after their son—"

"Just like they went after Preston's," Daniel said. He scrolled through the phone all the way back to the evidence photo of TreeTop's outfit, worn by the orchardist. "So it's some kind of loop. And we're only talking about it because the orchardist got caught. Wearing this."

"That's how Preston made his way in, I think. Then it was a matter of finding the links between all these different people and places and incidents."

"*All?*"

"All the ones in the basement," she said, opening her phone to an image of the entire sprawling colorful lair. "As far as I can tell, there are hundreds of crimes and accidents and deaths down there, and Preston found a way to connect them. I think he was hoping to get ahead of it, like predict the next move." Abigail's heart sank as she thought about that streak of blood on the roadway, and Hal in the Ag Office peering over her shoulder at the map. "He's been mapping this stuff for years, but he must never have been a threat until now. It's like he finally got too close."

Or I did, she thought—but shook the idea away.

Daniel zoomed through the crosshatched web on her screen. "All of this *bloodshed*," he said, somberly, "disguising itself as TreeTop."

"Hiding behind the boogeyman. Mostly it seems for ag."

Daniel looked up. "Why'd you ask me when Esme left town?"

Abigail hesitated, then showed him a photo taken of an old washhouse on a farm. The photo was taken at night, with a spotlight illuminating a dead man slumped against a stone wall, shotgun in his lap, blood sprayed behind him. Above his blasted head were wooden shelves lined with jars of canned fruit, some exploded from the shot, with gloppy plums and syrup oozing down and mingling with his bloody hair. His neck was bent forward as if he were staring into his lap. An antler-handled knife sat on the floor next to him. And he was dressed as TreeTop.

"That," Daniel said, looking away and shaking his head, "is *scary*. Who *is* that?"

"Arthur someone. Took his own life on his family farm. But he doesn't matter."

"Cold-blooded, J.Jill. I like it. Go on."

"What matters is that he's another dead TreeTop, right? Which makes this the second time in as many decades that someone who was dressed like *that* took his own life."

"Okay," Daniel said. "The orchardist who ran over the mom hanged himself in jail. And poor Arthur here."

"Preston was able to pinpoint two incidents in sixty years when TreeTop failed," she said. "Those are the key. Two men dressed up as TreeTop botched their jobs. In failing to get it done right those two men cracked open the system so Preston could find his way in."

"He linked the two guys together?"

"Yeah. When I first saw it I was wondering why he'd do that if the two incidents were literally years apart. But then I saw the date that this Arthur dude shot himself. Summer, 2011. June—"

"June *15*?" Daniel said, tensing up. "Abigail?"

"The night of Esme's high school graduation. The night she left town."

CHAPTER 38

ESME

In the hospital after the hotel shooting, Esme had been pre-scribed a sedative, but once she was back home in her bedroom, middle of the night, it wasn't nearly enough to erase the con-stant memory of Kevin's face, or the frenzied look Silas wore as he realized what he'd done. Daniel had left a pipe and some in-dica next to her bed, but smoking it only made her cry, so Fri-day morning—three days and counting without Kevin on this earth—he brought her a white noise machine that he'd picked up at the health food store in Wenatchee.

Daniel had meant well, but Esme still thought it was the stu-pidest thing she'd ever seen: a machine that created static, like the broken clock radio in their mom's room. Still, she plugged it in next to her bed and clipped shut her curtains and soon she felt herself being erased by the hushed sounds it created: ocean waves, pouring rain, tumbleweeds in the wind.

Outside of a few oblique comments at the police station, no one knew anything, as far as she could tell, about her and Kevin trying to bribe Silas with the powder. Even when McDaid was taking her statement in the hospital, she basically nodded along, *yep, just like that,* glad that the sedative was making her so agreeable. When she mentioned the way it all felt like a dream, McDaid stopped writing, squeezed her hand and shared that Silas had been *on something bad.* He told her how he'd picked him up for trashing the gas station in the middle of the night, held him at the department until morning, then dropped him off right on Main.

"Thought he was okay, you know?" McDaid said.

She nodded, perfectly agreeable; anything that would get him to unclasp his slimy trout of a hand and let her go back home.

Once there, Daniel brought her soup and tea, and whispered the same thing each day: "Take all the time you need, Esme, just don't turn into *Mom.*"

Her mom said little about the shooting, but she kept straightening the photo of Kevin on top of the television, dusting its floral frame, and she insisted on giving Esme a shampoo and a haircut, which was so sweet it made Esme cry.

Pastor Kurt came by at one point, tennis shoes squeaking as he lamented the loss of Silas. She stared at the wall as he told her he didn't really blame her for Silas's death, but that forgiveness would take time. He said it wasn't easy losing a child, even one who was the architect of his own doom. His life was falling apart but his daughter, Grace, filled him with hope. He said he'd pray for Esme and would send her money at the drop of a hat if she ever found herself in need, so there was no call for lawsuits over the gun or anything.

"I've helped a lot of wounded people," he said as he left, "so reach out if you ever want to talk. I'll be ready to forgive you someday, Esme. Just not today."

She continued staring at her wall long after he squeaked away.

Mr. Polk came by twice, all alone. The first time he sat on the edge of her bed, facing away from her, and tried to speak but just cried his eyes out. A few hours later he came back and this time he told her what happened to Kevin wasn't her fault, and that the pure love his boy had for her was still there, even if Kevin wasn't.

"If you close your eyes you can feel it," Mr. Polk said, and he was right.

Mrs. Polk was obliterated, but he was adamant that she held no ill will toward Esme.

"Not a drop, you understand?"

Once that was off his chest he said the first wink of sleep they'd had *since Kevin* was when the police told them they'd wrapped up the investigation, that it was *one of those bad good things* that Esme and Krunk had witnessed the shooting because it allowed everyone to begin finding closure. They were going to shutter the hotel for a while, but she would always have a place in their lives.

Before he left, he said there was a car parked out front for her, an old maroon Cutlass that was supposed to be Kevin's graduation present. He'd transferred the title over to her and paid the first six months of her insurance so she could still go to Bellingham for school if she was so inclined. Or not. But it was all hers. And if she ever needed *anything...*

Kevin had been slotted to give the valedictorian speech on graduation day, but they let Abe Krunk give it instead. He stood there on crutches, sweating in the sun, quoting famous people he'd never heard of, and at one point ditched the speech, saying there was a fine line between being inspirational and hosting a pity party. He received a standing ovation.

Esme gave zero thought to moving away in the fall, and she had no idea what to do, if anything, with the baggie of yellow powder she'd taken out of Dr. Carla's lab after the shooting and hidden behind the propane tank.

And then of course *he* made those Big Life decisions for her, just as he always had.

★ ★ ★

The night of graduation, when her classmates were all driving their rigs into the desert and burning their textbooks and doing Prairie Fire shots, Esme fell asleep before sunset and woke up hot in the dark. She'd been sleeping on her back lately, sheets up to her chin, pillow over her eyes, breathing fresh air from the gap in between, so her mouth was parched and it was hard to swallow. She stumbled to the bathroom and refilled her water jar. The only light in the house came from the television, a *Full House* rerun on mute as her mom snored in her chair. Back in bed she glimpsed her phone—12:14 a.m.—and saw that Daniel had texted after work that he was helping a coworker bale the second cutting of hay, making some midnight dollars, and he'd try to stop in during a break or just see her in the morning.

She cranked up the volume on her white noise machine and stillness became sleep.

She sensed him before she knew he was there, yet her sleep was too deep, her body too heavy, as if she were pressing through herself. His rubber boots flattened the static as he crossed the bedroom floor and stood over her.

Her mouth was open and she dreamed of an ice cube on her tongue, and then she snapped awake. A man was pressing the flat side of a knife blade into her mouth, as if it were a tongue depressor. Her hands shot up and gripped his rubber-clad wrist.

"No," he said, and his knuckle pressed her chin. His hand was quivering, which scared her even more. A drop of his sweat hit her cheek.

He was shining a light into her face, but she caught a glimpse of the knife's antler handle, and she could smell the tire-y tang of his gloves. Her eyes were tearing up and she couldn't see much—hooded white biosuit, goggles crooked, gloves black this time—but between the waves of noise she could hear the familiar sound of his mask clicking in and out. Breathing hard. Maybe panicked.

"Some kind of dust?" he said, so quietly that it took her a second to decipher what he wanted. He sounded as scared as she was.

He slid the knife out of her mouth. She swallowed and coughed.

"I don't know," she whispered.

"Listen," he hissed, *"whatever it is, I need it. Otherwise. Please. Just tell me where."*

"I don't know."

"You don't understand," he said, pointing the knife at the cup of her throat, and she was thinking it was time to finally be free, she and Kevin together again—

Then she heard Daniel's Bronco rolling up out front, his headlights casting branchy shadows through her window. For a split second the room went still—and then Esme threw up her hands and spun off the mattress, dropping hard to the floor, half-tangled in her sheets, and when she scrambled under the bed TreeTop grabbed her calf and then her heel, but she screamed and kicked like crazy.

She must have still been screaming when Daniel stormed inside because their mom was in the hallway, staring out the open back door. TreeTop was gone, and Esme was in her bedroom, dumping textbooks out of her backpack and filling it with jeans and T-shirts and deodorant and, finally, grabbing the keys to the Oldsmobile Cutlass that would take her past the lake and out of town, out of this desert, out to the interstate, and deliver her full speed into whatever remained of the rest of her life.

CHAPTER 39

ABIGAIL

Daniel's hands were shaking as he yanked Abigail's phone from her and zoomed in on the dead man in the washhouse, trying to see his face through the slop.

"This is the guy who tried to kill Esme the night she left town?" he said, gritting his teeth, as if he were going to exhume and interrogate him about what he'd done to his little sister.

"Within hours of Esme leaving, this guy took his own life," she said.

"Dressed as TreeTop," Daniel said, squeezing shut his eyes. "When she told me he was there in the house, I thought Esme was just being Esme again. She was so out of it after Kevin. And she'd been saying that shit her whole life about TreeTop visiting her. I should've believed her. Should've *done* something."

"Maybe he really tried to kill her that night, but—"

"He messed up," Daniel whispered, nodding.

"He messed up," Abigail said, "because you came home. And Esme got away."

"Until she didn't."

He hardly seemed to notice as she took the phone out of his hands.

"She'd gotten away from TreeTop once," she said, "but that didn't mean she was free forever. Maybe that's why she called Mr. Polk at the hotel before coming back here. She needed to come home, needed help from her family, but had to find out whether things were settled with TreeTop. Somehow she believed she was safe. That it was all in the past. And, Daniel? There's something else."

He looked at her through half-lidded eyes. "About Esme?"

She opened her photos and found the article about Esme's murder, pinned to Preston's wall. Daniel zoomed in on the four strands tethered between it and the rest of the room.

"What did these connect to?" he asked.

"First one was the hotel shooting."

"When Silas killed Kevin," he said, shaking his head. "That wasn't some TreeTop conspiracy, just a broken dude with a life-long grudge." He tapped the screen. "So maybe not everything in Preston's web fits. What about the others?"

"One strand connected to an article about a missing baby that hadn't been missing at all." She held out her phone and Daniel glanced at the image of a yellowing paragraph from the local paper, dated April 2006.

"Esme's babysitting fiasco. With Silas."

"Looked to me like Preston was trying to link that incident to his own missing kid, the one found at the landfill."

"Alan."

"But as far as I can tell it didn't go anywhere."

"Makes sense he would connect it to Esme," Daniel said. "She experienced all kinds of fallout from that." He told her about what happened with the falling TV and how Silas hid Baby Grace in the shed. "There were rumors Silas was waiting for his chance to drown her. But Grace was fine, all things considered. And honestly, Silas's behavior kind of makes sense, in retrospect. His dad was strict, newly remarried, brand-new baby taking up all his attention. They didn't even trust him to babysit. Kind of doomed, if that's how your parents see you." He shook his head.

"Poor Esme, getting caught up in that."

"Yeah. She just wanted to make a little cash babysitting like other girls her age." Daniel took a deep breath, gathering his focus. "What else did Preston dig up?"

"One of the strands connected to a real estate ad for my house," Abigail said. She opened a photo of Preston's Oracle Map and zoomed in on the eyeball he'd scrawled over her home. "Maybe because I found Esme?"

"Let me see?" he said, and began scrolling around the map, studying the spots piled with green where TreeTop operated. She showed him the photos of the *Kill TreeTop* graffiti that Preston had scribbled in various spots around town, along with Tree-Top's phone number, which she herself had called this morning. And she told him how she'd ended up in the Agricultural Appreciation Office yesterday.

"Preston had that office marked on his map more than any other place in town," she said. "He clearly thought it was important."

"They do all the TreeTop stuff," Daniel said. "Of course it's them. Everyone knows it, too. Without actually knowing it."

"But the thing is," she said, "there was no proof down in that basement that TreeTop killed Esme. I'm thinking she was on his wall because he was still figuring out whether she'd fallen victim to the system. Or *hadn't*."

"You said there was one more strand?" he said. "Something Preston connected to her death."

"From decades ago," she said, shaking her head. "Seemed random. Esme would've been pretty little. Like second grade."

She brought up the collage of images and articles about the

dairy, especially the workers' failed attempts to unionize. Daniel studied them for a second, then looked at her.

"Abigail." He swiped and leaned in, as if he were tunneling through his own thoughts. "Are you *kidding* me?"

"What?"

"Esme was right," he said slowly, dazed. "She'd been saying it ever since we were little."

"Saying what?"

"That TreeTop killed him," he said, staring at her with wide, intense eyes. He turned the phone sideways and zoomed past the maps of the dairy and photos of the cows, and finger-tapped an obituary photo of the scruffy man wearing a stained Mariners cap. "Abigail, this guy's my *dad*."

CHAPTER 40

ABIGAIL

As Abigail scooped up Eli from the Seattle airport, she was overcome with a spiraling dread. The city felt relentless and sleek, with zippy cars and gleaming high-rises, concrete tunnels and everywhere the distant sparkle of the Sound. She hadn't had a haircut in months, and in her Lava Lamp T-shirt and Chaco sandals, she felt like she worked at a pet store. Yet she believed Eli when he kissed her cheeks and told her she was beautiful. He, too, wore the slovenly uniform of travel, but he'd grown an ample head of hair and damn it looked good.

Eli was sweet and rambling with his affection, but the prospect of getting reacquainted not just with him, but with the person she'd been four months ago, was overwhelming. His absence had brought a lot to the surface, she realized: resentment over the way he prioritized his profession, most notably, but also a quiet clarity about her own shortcomings. Ever since they began dating, she'd been so mesmerized by the glow of his path that she'd neglected to seek a path of her own. And his arrival drew attention to something she'd been trying for weeks to avoid: how inexorably her daily life had become connected to Esme's death.

Even here, two hundred miles from Soap Lake, in the midst of a reunion she'd been dreaming about for months, Abigail was preoccupied by images of George running in terror and Esme slumped in the Cutlass, of Preston on the road and the man's voice on the phone: *Girl, you just committed suicide.* And she couldn't shake the wounded, angry expression on Daniel's face yesterday as he'd processed the connections between Tree-Top and his father, who'd died in a trailer fire years ago. She worried about leaving him alone.

"Can we grab a coffee before driving back?" Eli asked, resting his hand on her thigh. "I want to slow down and hear what's been going on. I feel like I've missed so much."

"I need to focus on directions," she said, squinting at her phone, "if that's okay? We're almost there."

"Almost...where?"

In five hundred feet, turn left, her phone said.

Soon she steered Medusa onto the campus of a community college north of town and parked next to a food truck selling *Giant! Corn! Dogs!* Its presence seemed an omen. The day was warm and a gentle rain misted around them. Finches and chickadees sang and chirped in the trees. Eli looked around but said nothing, and she wondered if he thought the single dorm building in the distance was a hotel.

Now that they were parked, he faced her and held her hands. "So? What's up?"

"We should go," she said, pointing at a row of low gray buildings. "We're actually late."

Eli took in the wide lawns, the concrete benches, the walkways shaded by ginkgo and fir. Everything was quiet with summer.

"Late for?"

"Trust me?" she said, pulling on a sweater and tucking her hair into an elastic band.

The campus was an unassuming mix of painted cinder block buildings that looked like a prison complex and modern struc- tures with colorful accents that looked Scandinavian. They wan- dered down a hallway, passing a few students, some young and fit and carefully dressed, others in pure survival mode, with sweat- pants and giant sodas, shooting texts between classes to the sitter.

Inside the elevator, Eli stared at a poster announcing *Career Day*. The sponsor's logo was a white circle with blue waves swirl- ing over a single word: *Hydrolicon*.

"I know that company," he said. "And why have I heard of this college? Tell me this isn't a job interview, Abigail."

"It's not," she said, and for the first time all day, she stopped moving. "You know the guy I told you about who wandered all over town in his coat, even when it was a hundred degrees?"

"Sure, I remember him. Guy with the map."

"Well, he died the other day. Someone ran him over by the lake. Hit and run. We're meeting his wife in three minutes."

"His wife?"

"Ex-wife, actually. You'll have a lot to talk about. She used to have your job."

Eli's laugh ponged through the elevator, but when he saw the expression on her face he went silent. "Dr. Carla?"

"It was hard to convince her to see us," she said, "until I told her I knew Preston."

"Preston is the coat guy?"

"Her ex. I'll explain everything, Eli, but for now let's just..."

The elevator doors opened, but Eli just stood there, hands on hips, more annoyed than bemused. "Abigail. I trust you, but c'mon. What am I stepping into here?"

"It's not about you, okay? Or mostly not."

He stared at her, then pressed back his hair and gestured out. "Lead the way, I guess."

At the end of the hall a door opened and a doe-eyed dude

in a Red Sox cap stepped out, looking forlorn as he tugged on his backpack.

A tallish Black woman emerged from the office behind him, graying curls loose behind a tight red headband. "Monday," she said to the student's back. "Not a day later."

The guy lowered his head as he passed.

Lazy piece of shit, she mouthed, pointing at his back.

A cluster of students holding laptops and drinks appeared from an adjacent hallway and surrounded her like chirping baby birds. She held up her hand and cut them off.

"This is my lunch hour," she said, smiling but stern, "so unless you want to lose a limb, you need to come back at noon. I don't even want to smell you until then."

She wore an amused grin as they scattered down the hall.

"Please," she said, holding open the office door.

"Dr. Carla?" Abigail said.

"None other," she said, not unfriendly, but not extending a hand. She looked exhausted. "My turn for summer quarter. Because what else would I possibly have to do?"

"Sorry," Eli said, plucking his *POLSKA* T-shirt. "Just got off a plane."

"You'll fit right in."

Dr. Carla's office was crowded but not messy, with a series of framed black-and-white photos of different lakes that immediately caught Eli's attention. Soap Lake was noticeably absent.

Abigail had been expecting a nerdy mouse in a lab coat—a woman she could picture marrying Preston years ago—but Dr. Carla was pure vitality and power. She wore glossy red lipstick and a beaded yellow necklace over a loose orange blouse. A small diamond adorned her ring finger: remarried.

Dr. Carla locked the door behind them, and pulled a cup of yogurt from a lunch bag.

"You live in Soap Lake," she said, paddling her spoon into the yogurt. "Still no lava lamp, I take it?"

"Just the base."

"Oh god. That's even sadder."

"I believe," Abigail said, raising a limp fist.

"Well, good for you," she said, deadpan. "Say hi to Jesus for me when you die. So, you knew Preston?"

"More like Preston knew me," Abigail said, hesitant. "He wasn't exactly—"

"No," she said, sharply, "he wasn't."

Abigail thought about the streak of feathers and blood on the highway, and his ubiquitous map missing from the scene, and she wondered how much Dr. Carla knew about the circumstances of his death.

"I brought you this," Abigail said, digging into her bag for the newspaper she'd scooped from her driveway early this morning. "It has an article about what happened. In case you…"

Dr. Carla barely glanced at the paper before sliding it back. "That's not necessary."

Abigail tucked it away.

Every few seconds the monitor on Dr. Carla's desk displayed and dissolved photos of her twins: a stunning boy and girl, bobbing in a canoe, posing in front of an aquarium, leaning into each other at an ice cream parlor. Preston's kids.

"I don't think I mentioned it in my message," Abigail said, "but Eli here has your old job. He's a limnologist."

"Excuse me?" Dr. Carla said, slightly smiling.

"He's researching the lake on a grant."

"I've got some of your old binders and samples," he said, sitting up and clearing his throat. "I reached out months ago. But you're clearly very busy."

Dr. Carla's sight tracked between them.

"You're not here because of Preston?" she said, setting down her spoon and tensing up, genuinely afraid. "When did you begin researching the lake?"

"We moved there this past winter—" Eli said, and she held up her hand.

"Do you have kids?" she asked, cutting him off with an urgency that completely changed the tenor in the office.

"Kids?" Abigail said. "None."

"Thank god for that. So what'd they do to you? Boil your pet rabbit on the stove?"

Abigail gulped but didn't speak. Eli appeared confused.

"I assume that's why you're here," Dr. Carla continued. "They got to you somehow. Want my advice? Don't go back there. Have a Realtor put your house on the market and arrange a moving truck. Walk away. *Survive*."

Eli closed one eye as he spoke. "Doesn't that seem kind of extreme?"

"Eli's been in Poland for four months," Abigail said. "He's missed a few things."

"I can see that," she said, looking him up and down. "*Extreme*, Eli, is kidnapping a three-year-old boy then dumping him half-naked at the landfill two days later." She pointed at her monitor, where her young twins posed on a sledding hill. "Ask my Alan about *extreme*."

"I'm sorry," Eli said, his voice reflecting the gravity in the room, "but is that why you left midproject? Because someone did that to your kid? I assumed you left, at least in part—"

"Because I'm Black? You wouldn't be the first."

"Small town," Eli stammered, "rural west. Had to feel conspicuous."

"It was TreeTop," Abigail said, and Dr. Carla shot her a surprised look.

"You've been talking to Preston. How'd they get to you?"

"Where to begin?"

"Maybe with Esme," Eli said, quietly. "Finding her body. Out there."

"Esme *Calderon*?" Dr. Carla said, gasping. "Of Kevin and

Esme? Esme's *dead*?" She shook her head gently. "I thought she'd fled the state, my god."

"She was living in California," Abigail said. "Stabbed in the stomach with a screwdriver on the night she came back to town. Her little boy was with her, but he escaped."

"She had a baby?"

"Her brother, Daniel, has him now."

Dr. Carla sighed loudly. "*That* is alarming news. Esme? I'm surprised Preston didn't call me. Or maybe he did and I hung up. She was such a…" Her words trailed off and she dabbed her nose with a Kleenex. "I really liked that girl. Her poor family. Why would someone kill *her*?"

"The detectives are saying drugs," Abigail said, "but the detectives aren't interested in anything else."

"Like TreeTop?" Dr. Carla said, tilting her head in a way that made Abigail wonder about her sincerity.

"Maybe. I spent a night this week in Preston's basement and I *swear* he was onto something. It's not all some psycho conspiracy theory."

"Oh, is that what this is? You're here to teach me something about the father of my children? Please, go on. It'll be a good follow-up to your husband's TED Talk on being Black in the rural west."

Abigail felt her face glowing as red as a siren light and she knew she'd never show up late to class if Dr. Carla was teaching. Eli clasped her hand.

"I'm sorry," Dr. Carla said, eyes closed, palms up. "It's been a hard few days. I've known for years that Preston would die there, but the reality of it, you know? Of course he was onto something. I could've told you that the day I fled town."

"Was that the day your son disappeared?" Eli said.

"Actually, two full days *after* Alan disappeared, which was when he turned up at the landfill, all sunburned and wandering around in his underwear. His feet were bleeding. The local cops claimed he'd been hiding in a dishwasher when it got picked up by the trash truck, rode it to the landfill like a stowaway. I didn't believe it for a second. I scooped him up and we left for good. Didn't even stop for a tetanus shot until we got to Seattle. We haven't been back and never will. He was *three* and they did that to him, and who knows what else? Imagine what they do to adults."

"We don't have to imagine," Abigail said, glancing at the newspaper sticking out of her bag.

"You're right. We don't." She took a deep breath before adding, "I was a researcher, you know? Not a goddamned mafiosa. I just wish I had left sooner."

"But Preston stayed."

"Yeah," she said, "zipped up his technicolor dreamcoat and stayed. He'd call the kids once a month, but eventually all he wanted to talk about was *the oracles*. That's what he called our son being ripped out of his front lawn by some redneck thug while Daddy ran inside the house to hit the pipe. I understood him feeling guilty, creating his own personal purgatory for his failures as a parent. We all do." She glanced at her office door. "But move on. Raise your kids. Don't abandon your family because you want to get to the bottom of something that was going on long before you were born and will continue long after you die. Sometimes I think this whole thing was pretty convenient. Gave him his chance to disappear."

"If that basement is any measure," Abigail said, "he succeeded."

"You really went to the house?"

"Two nights ago."

Dr. Carla's face softened and she gave the smallest of nods.

"The twins' room was exactly the same," Abigail continued. "He made it so you have to crawl through their closet to get to the basement."

"I figured something like that was coming when he began digging out the old root cellar."

"It's like its own think tank down there."

"Problem is," Dr. Carla said, "Preston was the one doing the thinking. He used to call me and ramble about TreeTop. Said there was no one left he could trust with that stuff. I never knew what was real and what was a delusion. Was he still leaving graffiti all over town?" She spoke in a faux spooky voice. *"TreeTop Kills!"*

"That was him?" Eli said.

"Apparently there were others before him, way back in the day, trying to break the system or what have you. Preston picked up where they left off. Took it to a new level."

"He was after the truth," Abigail said.

"Oh, believe me, he got it," Dr. Carla said, wide-eyed. "The truth will *not* set you free. The truth gets you run over by a pickup truck."

"You're really not surprised about his—?"

"Can we just call it murder?" Dr. Carla said. "I mean, the Medical Examiner's Office said whoever plowed into him dragged him for over a hundred feet before slowing down. That's not the same as bumping him off the road by accident and getting scared and driving away. Followed immediately by another vehicle finishing the job. The only question I have is, *Why now?* I mean, the guy's been pursuing this stuff for years. Everyone could see that he was mentally ill. Harmless. He always had free range, as it were. But something must have changed."

Abigail studied the back of her hands, avoiding the question. In TreeTop's mind, Preston's oracles had been innocuous—disregarded as scribbles of his illness—until a photo of his map was spotted in Abigail's hands.

After all, she was the *walker* who found the boy. The lake doctor's wife.

Which, for some reason, meant that Preston had to die.

"Doesn't really matter," Dr. Carla continued, perhaps noticing Abigail's confusion and discomfort. "And if I don't seem that upset, you could say I'm late in the stages of grieving. I've been waiting for this since the day he decided to stick around Soap Lake instead of moving over the mountains with us."

Dr. Carla rolled her chair to the espresso maker behind her. "Coffee?"

Eli nodded, bright-eyed. Abigail declined. Dr. Carla poured water into the machine.

"Is Mr. Polk still perfecting his roast?"

"He is," Abigail said. "And still a sweet guy."

Dr. Carla laughed. "Back in the day, I'm pretty sure his wife thought we were having an affair. Outside of a handful of industry prospectors trying to spin gold out of microbes and molds, Mr. Polk is one of the few people I know who was genuinely interested in my work on extremophiles. When you get back there—what am I saying? You're not going back there! Isn't that what we decided?"

The coffee stopped sputtering and she poured it into a white espresso cup for Eli. He tried to sip it like an old Italian man, with the napkin and the pinkie, but just looked like he was doing a shitty imitation of Queen Elizabeth.

"You know, when you first called and mentioned Preston," Dr. Carla said, "I expected to hear that his house had burned down. That a lamp had shorted out, catching his newspapers on fire. It'll happen soon if it hasn't already. His life's work will be gone. The cycle will continue. Just don't tell anyone you were exploring his basement and maybe you'll survive." She took a calm breath. "What I'm still trying to figure out is why you're *here*. You haven't shared anything new about Preston. You didn't have to see me in person to tell me about Esme's death. Which leaves...the lake?"

"Eli's research is tanking," Abigail said.

"Of course it is," Dr. Carla said.

"I sent some of those old water samples to Berkeley," Eli said, perking up, "the jars from the '50s and '60s? Everything was off. Fluoride through the roof, which just screams tap water, right? And sodium way down, which made no sense. I thought I must've corrupted them somehow. But of course it wasn't me."

"Diluting the samples with tap water is one of the many things they did to disrupt me," Dr. Carla said. "I managed to complete some tests, but nowhere near enough. That water was irreplaceable, too, like ice cores from a glacier that's melted back into the earth. I should've kept quiet once I figured out it was happening. Instead I went around fuming to anyone who would listen. Farmers on the irrigation board. City council members. I told them that whoever was sabotaging my work was too late, I already had *all I needed*. Of course I was exaggerating, but they didn't know that."

"Is that when?" Abigail said.

"They took my boy. Yes, but only after they sabotaged more samples. Tried to burn down my lab with me padlocked inside. Even stole the flash drive where Kevin collected research for some scholarship proposal. Depleted aquifers. Groundwater flow. All of it gone, so the kid had to start over from scratch. I eventually got the message. One of my tasks for the grant was to use the jars I'd inherited to establish a historical baseline for the lake. But without them—"

"Its history would be erased," Eli said. "No going back. Only forward."

"I never quite figured out why someone was so opposed to my work. Still haven't."

"At least you saved those other jars," Eli said to Abigail.

Dr. Carla's cup halted near her lips. "What other jars?"

Abigail explained the cache of canning jars she and Sophia had smuggled out of the library cellar, and how Preston had been on the shore, watching her load them into Medusa.

"'Time capsules,' he called them. We stashed them in Eli's lab."

"Preston," Dr. Carla said, with a rueful smile. "While I was searching for Alan, he told me he needed to get the jars out of our house. That they were the source of the problem, as if they were cursed. I could've killed him. I had no idea he pulled it off. Does anyone else know?"

"I made a few calls," Eli said, shaking his head. "Cat's out of the bag, as it were."

"Just don't be surprised if the samples were ruined the second you left town," Dr. Carla said. "And be glad you weren't there to get in the way."

"Is that why you've never published your findings?" Eli asked.

Dr. Carla stared at him, unmoving, as if he'd touched a sore spot.

"Between your notes and those early publications," he continued, "it seemed like you were heading toward some big revelation about extremophiles in the lake. The clear genetic lines. A microbe no one had ever studied thriving in such a hostile environment. I've always been surprised you just stopped."

"They chased me out before I could sample the right vents. I was terrified."

Eli seemed puzzled. "But you mapped the microbe's DNA. And I saw your drawings and photos and notes."

"Finding trace DNA in the lake wasn't the issue. It was all over the samples. Yours, too, I imagine."

"Of course. Lingers in the water for ages."

"But everything else was based on the time I spent there as a grad student."

"Wait. *Everything?*"

Dr. Carla looked between them for a minute, hesitant about what she was about to share. Then, in a pensive voice, she told them about her research trip to the lake, back when she was a doctoral candidate, long before she'd ever met Preston or given birth to the twins. About watching the extremophiles squiggle around under the microscope, and her realization that they'd never been classified. About the simple tests she performed and the surge of yellow foam that was created when she added toxins to the water. And the way the microbes metabolized the PCBs, detoxified the water, and created microvolts in the process.

"A *lot* of voltage, too," she said, "relative to their size."

"Exoelectrogens?" Eli whispered, leaning so far toward Dr. Carla that Abigail thought he might fall to a knee and propose. "I suspected that, but it was such a long shot." He turned to Abigail, stammering as his thoughts outran his words. "Micro-organisms. Creating electricity. To be harvested. By humanity."

"Potentially," Dr. Carla chimed in. "My experiments showed that the microbes knew exactly how to maintain their environment deep within that lake, protect it from any intrusions that might disrupt their harsh little ecosystem. As far as I could tell, the more toxic the intrusion, the more ferocious their metabolic reaction."

"And the higher the voltage," Eli said. His knee was bobbing and Abigail could tell he'd give anything to sit here and mine Dr. Carla's mind for the next few days. "But you weren't able to re-create the results?"

She shook her head.

"So what became of the foam you saved? The by-product of the process. At least you had evidence. Somewhere to start."

Dr. Carla traced the rim of her coffee cup, clearly wary.

"It traveled with me everywhere I went for years, like a cat or a houseplant. It lost all of its charge, of course. And didn't stay in its colloidal state, but rather settled into a crystalline yellow powder. I knew it was important, but outside of the most rudimentary testing—you know, viability, voltage—I left it alone, figuring I wouldn't really be able to do much until I got back there and had new samples to work with. It was the only proof on the planet of what I'd discovered."

"An organic battery," Eli said with reverence, as if it were only now sinking in. "A living energy source…"

"Fueled by *waste*," she said, nodding so eagerly that Abigail wondered if she'd ever shared her findings. "Who knows what those creatures could do if scaled up? There'd be a lot to figure out, of course, but you can imagine the applications. A perpetual energy source, cultured on-site. Homes powered by vats of microbes in the cellar. Sewage transformed into electricity. Power plants running on toxic waste. Electric cars with living chargers under the hood. Superfund cleanup sites feeding the grid."

"The death of fossil fuels," Eli said, and Abigail stared at him—excited by the prospect, yet worried about what it could bring into their lives.

"*Potentially,*" Dr. Carla repeated. "But I was a grad student with too much on my plate, totally unprepared for such a find. If you had asked me at the time, I would've said I was savoring it, waiting until I could really focus and figure out who to approach for mentorship, if anyone."

"Or sponsorship?" Eli said. "Hydrolicon?"

"It was tempting, but I didn't last long in industry. I wasn't willing to share." She paused, studied her lap. "In retrospect, I'm ashamed to say, I think I may have been hogging the discovery for myself." She sat up tall, took a breath. "Anyway, life happened. I sat on it quietly for years."

"Seventeen?" Abigail said.

"That's how long it took me to get back to the lake. I had a proper lab this time, a cabin right on the shore, and had learned a thing or two. That was going to be *my* time, when I could begin culturing the microbes and re-creating the process in a controlled setting. I did everything I could, but when they snatched Alan, I didn't think twice about leaving it all for someone else." She glanced at Eli. "I divorced Preston. Raised our kids. Remarried. And I took a job helping people who actually *need* my help. Forget industry. Community college is where the action is at." She planted her palms on her desk and glanced at the clock. "Which reminds me. I'd like to take a walk before my dear hobgoblins start biting my ankles again, so if you'll excuse—"

"Who else knew about the powder?" Abigail said, not even gesturing to move.

"Well, Preston, of course. And Kevin. Not that I ever showed it to him, but the kid was a snoop. I didn't mind, though. Part of his curiosity. Kevin told Esme everything, so she probably knew as well. They were so cute, the two of them, sharing pie at the diner. Very *Twin Peaks*. Kind of sweet."

"All of them are dead," Abigail said bluntly.

"Excuse me?"

"Everyone you just mentioned who knew about the powder? Preston, Kevin, Esme—they're all dead."

Abigail retrieved the little jar of powder from her bag and set it on the desk between them.

Dr. Carla gripped the arms of her chair and leaned back, as if the jar might explode.

"I don't know what I was expecting when you came in here today," she said, staring at the powder, "but it was definitely not *this*."

She picked up the jar and turned it like a kaleidoscope, and seemed to fade from existence: she was Sam Spade ripping excelsior off the Falcon, Belloq prying open the Ark, Vincent gazing into the shimmering briefcase. It was hard to tell whether this reunion was stirring up greed or reverence or fear within her. But unquestionably there was recognition of the power contained within this little jar.

"Just seeing this again," she said, clearly moved. "Sometimes it feels like this discovery was akin to the first human finding fire." She almost smiled. "When I look at it, I'm reminded of the *hope* I felt back then. Things were going *so* badly with my research. I wasn't being a very good mother. The town was creeping me out. My marriage felt like a bad grade school dance. And then I met Kevin and Esme. I had them over for dinner one night, and looking across the table at the two of them, bright-eyed and awkward but throwing themselves at life anyway, which I *loved*, I remember feeling this great sense of relief. Of peace. Here was the future, you know, young people who *cared*. They could have ducked their heads and faded away, but instead they chose to *care* about people and the planet and science and each other..." She sighed.

"Sounds encouraging," Abigail said.

"Well, sure. Except. What good was hope like that when pitted against the kind of people who would take a *child* in order to disrupt the truth? Those people would rather kill than give up power. They look at innovation and they don't see hope. They see a threat. For those people, there is no tomorrow. All they can do is *devour*..."

Dr. Carla flicked the jar and watched it roll across the desk. It stopped in front of Eli.

"How did you find them?" she said.

Eli was caught off guard. "Find them?"

"The microbes," she said, pinching at something on her shirtsleeve. "You can imagine my questions. The vents, for starters. How did you figure out where to extract the samples? Kevin and I must have gone out in the boat a dozen times and never once found the colonies. You must have included a dive team in your grant? Not to mention which contaminants you used to create the foam. I don't even want to guess how you managed all this from Poland."

Eli stared, confused. "I don't know anything about that," he said, pointing at the jar.

"This was from Esme," Abigail said, and Dr. Carla looked as if she couldn't catch her breath. "She had it with her when she was killed. I'm guessing she swiped it from your lab after Kevin was shot."

Dr. Carla gasped. "Esme had this? My lord. Is this why someone...?" She closed her eyes without finishing her thought: *killed her*. "This is the batch. My grad school batch."

"The *only* batch," Eli said, "from the sound of it."

Dr. Carla looked between them and scooted her chair back. "So it *was* you," she said. "I should've known it was all too coincidental, your insistence on meeting me today. You know, I didn't respond to you for a reason."

"I'm not following," Eli said.

"I have *no* interest in putting you in touch with someone in industry. I left Hydrolicon years ago. I work here by choice."

She spun and lifted her mouse, waking up her computer, opening her calendar.

"Take your powder and go," she said. "I have students waiting."

Abigail and Eli exchanged a look.

"There's been a misunderstanding," Abigail said.

"We're not *prospectors*," Eli said, a tinge of hurt in his voice.

Dr. Carla appeared confused for a moment. She turned again to face them.

"We're really not," Abigail said.

"You didn't email me some weeks ago," she said, flicking the jar, "proposing to sell this?"

"I emailed you yesterday," Abigail said, "about meeting today. About Preston. That's it."

"Then I'm guessing you also didn't leave a message with Mary, my work study?"

"Not us."

"I thought the email was spam at first," Dr. Carla continued, wiping a speck of paper off her desk, "because it had been sent from one of those accounts with all the ampersands and dollar signs. But then the subject line said, 'Bugdust.' I knew exactly what it was referring to. I blocked the email address. Then a week or so later someone called and left a message with Mary, my work study. All her note said was 'Urgent!!' which is pretty normal for her. She's a bit high-strung. The printer jams and she braces for war, you know? She wrote down a number with a Soap Lake prefix and a precise time to call. Middle of the night. I did a quick search and of course the number was for a payphone."

"Behind the gas station," Abigail said, and Dr. Carla nodded.

"I never even asked Mary about the message, just threw it away. You might say Preston has conditioned me well on how to respond to creepy messages from the Inland Northwest. So when you brought out the powder..."

"You thought we were behind the messages," Eli said. "And now we were here to extort you in person."

Dr. Carla opened a desk drawer. "I do have Mary's number somewhere."

"Was it three weeks ago they called?" Abigail said. "That would've been—"

"You think it was Esme?" Dr. Carla said, clicking open her calendar and scrolling back. "Mary would've got the call on the afternoon of... June 29 or 30."

"Esme was murdered on the thirtieth," Abigail said. "She could have been planning to be there by the payphone in town, waiting for your call. Hoping the cash she earned from selling you the powder would relieve some pressure. She was broke. Things weren't going well."

"I would've helped her," Dr. Carla said, as if asking for forgiveness. "I could've given her some money or got her set up in school. She didn't need to *extort* me. Ah, *Esme*."

After a minute, Abigail stood and slid the jar back across the desk.

Dr. Carla studied it, as if considering the path her life might have taken were she to have continued to pursue its microscopic world. Her reverie was interrupted when a student tapped on the door.

"What are you going to do with it?" Eli asked.

She opened a desk drawer and tossed the jar in, alongside red pencils and dirty yogurt spoons. "Keep in touch, Eli. Maybe between us we can figure something out. In the meantime, duty calls." She sat up straight and folded her hands on the desk. "Kindly lower the drawbridge on your way out."

CHAPTER 41

ABIGAIL

Eli dropped his suitcase on the porch with the depressed relief of a salesman home from selling vacuums. Abigail put her arm around him and they started kissing, planning to make their way inside for some much-needed sex. But their teeth clacked, and they both seemed distracted and out of sync, so they hugged and awkwardly shrugged it off.

"Lab?" she said.

"Lab."

As Dr. Carla had predicted, the door to the lab had been forced open, its jamb splintered into a violent wooden star. The fridge that had been holding the library jars was toppled on its side, surrounded by broken glass. A chalky crust stained the tiles—evaporated lake water—so it had been hours since the break-in.

"Should I call the cops?" Eli said, moving slowly through the room.

Abigail thought about the police department's convenient

location, right across from the Ag Office, and how futile a call
would likely be. But mostly she thought about the specter of
Eli meeting Krunk.

Your husband is a fool.

"I'm thinking not."

He stared at the shattered jars for a long time before saying,
"Are you going to tell me about this TreeTop thing? Whatever
happened while I was away?"

On the three-hour drive from Seattle, Eli had asked her this
same question, but she'd been exhausted and irritable, and fell
asleep against the window.

Her reluctance felt justified. She'd spent the past months seeking and gathering and feeling, and now she was protective of that
time, as if it were integral to the person she was becoming…

Yet she also knew that if there was to be any hope for them
as a couple, the boundaries of her solitude had to end, and her
marriage had to begin. Right now she wasn't even sure if she
wanted that, but she still opened her phone to the photos of
Preston's basement and handed it over to Eli, then explained as
he leaned against a counter and scrolled.

The boy, his mom, the Cutlass. The lab, the peeping, the
trash. The library, the map, the jars. The keys, the juice box,
the powder. The murder of Kevin Polk and the exodus of Esme
Calderon. Preston's rainbow room and the graffiti he'd scribbled around town.

It was easier than talking about herself.

Eli showed quiet interest, but she caught him studying her, as
if trying to determine how badly she'd lost her mind.

"I'm not making this up," she said.

"That's what scares me. Here I thought you'd be bored to
death alone."

"Yet you left me anyway."

He didn't bite. Instead, he hunkered into her phone and didn't
interject again until he saw an old newspaper photo that showed

a group of grinning white women of all ages posed atop a wall of sandbags, legs crossed as if they were a USO group visiting a base during wartime. They wore dark skirts, white shirts, and meticulous lipstick, and each held a shovel over her shoulder. The gray disc of Soap Lake was visible in the background, as were members of the Moses-Columbia tribe in full ceremonial dress. Water lapped against the burlap bags, and the playground and picnic tables were partially submerged behind them. A caption scratched into the photo read, *Calamity Prevented, March 1952*.

"Why would Preston have this?" he asked.

"No idea."

"But that is Soap Lake? And those are sandbags?"

"Definitely."

"There's not a single mention of a flood in any of the documents I've read," he mumbled, shaking his head. "Spring of 1952. Can't be right."

"Is that the rainiest year on record or something?"

"I've looked at a century's worth of precipitation charts. Rain didn't cause that flood. Had to be groundwater." He yanked his laptop out of his bag and wiped the dust off a worktable. They sat on stools next to each other as he toggled between websites and glided between documents, including a survey of the region's aquifers and groundwater flow, Bureau of Reclamation reports, *Wenatchee World* newspaper articles, and a 3D-topo map that showed the rise and fall of the land around Soap Lake.

Eli was humming to himself, immersed, as if he were still across the planet. So she took a few slow laps around the neighborhood, the stars above crisp and bright like none she'd ever seen.

When she went back inside the lab, Eli lifted his head. "Hear anything about the Lava Lamp while I was away?" he asked. "Like why they stopped building it."

"I guess there've been engineering and financial snags. And I heard something about tribal heritage."

"That's what I'm seeing here. A lot of letters and comments in the newspaper claim the project was halted because the town didn't budget for an archaeological dig. The lake is sacred to the Colville tribes, so the state required a Cultural Impact Study. Looking for flint knapping and mat fibers, traces of human occupation. Making sure they don't desecrate the site."

"With the World's Largest Lava Lamp? I could see that."

"But the weird thing is," he said, tapping the top of his screen, "the state's official status report on the project shows that the heritage study was completed a few years ago. The town received the go-ahead for the next phase—an Environmental Impact Study. To assess the project's effects on the lake."

"Because the Lava Lamp would be built so close to the water."

"The EIS was supposed to be complete before the town moved ahead with construction, but with the base already built, they either somehow missed that little detail or tried to get away with skipping it. But *that's* why the project was halted. They never completed the environmental analysis. Still haven't."

"Then why are people blaming the heritage study?"

"Spotted owl," he said. "Create a scapegoat."

"Someone didn't want the lake studied. Environmentally."

"Looks that way."

Above Eli's screen, their eyes met for a second before he clicked back to the photo of the sandbags.

"Groundwater," he said, then turned to face her, gesturing with his hands as if he were giving a report. "Spring 1952. Fresh water from the Columbia River was diverted from the Grand Coulee Dam and released into the canals for the first time. As soon as they turned on the tap to begin irrigating all those new fields and orchards, river water began seeping through cracks in the canal, following gravity through the ground until it reached the lake. So much seeped through that first year that it nearly flooded the town. Hence the sandbags."

Abigail shuddered as she recalled the origin story she'd read the other day in the "TreeTop Activity Book": *when the canals filled for the first time, the sudden onslaught of water allowed TreeTop to rise from the depths of the lake...*

"To deal with the groundwater they installed intercept wells," Eli continued, pointing to a map on his screen, with crosshair symbols at different points around the lake. "These wells keep the lake volume about the same. The water seeps in, the lake gets high, the wells pump it out and prevent the lake from breaching its banks and flowing into town. They figured out early on how to stop the canals from flooding the lake, but not how to stop them from *diluting* it."

"Diluting?"

He shook his head. "Those canals are part of the biggest reclamation project in America. They irrigate almost 700,000 acres of farmland. Even with the wells, with that amount of water flowing through..."

"Some of it is going to seep into the lake," she said.

"It's the mineral content that makes the lake special, you know? Sacred."

"Healing."

"Yeah. That and it being meromictic. Because the water on the bottom stays on the bottom. It never turns over. The water in those vents didn't change for millennia."

"Until the canals came," Abigail said.

"Right. River water seeped through the ground and changed the lake's composition. Its equilibrium. For the first time ever, the layers inside the lake began to *move*."

"Which means...?"

"Those canals are turning it into a freshwater lake, slowly destroying the very qualities that make it special."

Eli closed his eyes and she knew it was even worse than he'd imagined.

"And your...microbes?" she asked.

The extremophiles, he explained, had found a way to thrive

in some of the harshest conditions on the planet. They evolved to survive deep within those vents, in that hostile water, to devour toxins and, as a by-product, to pass electrons to the outside of their membranes: *an organic battery run on waste.* Then humanity turned on the tap and diluted their world until it wasn't as *extreme* anymore.

"The microbes were there when Dr. Carla was in grad school," he said, sounding more morose by the minute, "and she had the powder to prove it. Years later, after getting married and having kids, when she went back to study the lake, she found traces of their DNA, just like I did, but couldn't find the actual microbes. She assumed she wasn't sampling from the right spot. That she kept missing the vents. She thought she'd somehow *failed.* But I've looked at her logs. She hit the right places. She couldn't find the microbes because—"

"The microbes weren't there," Abigail said, quietly.

"Because they've gone *extinct.*"

Eli closed his laptop and pressed his hands over his mouth.

As a grad student, Dr. Carla had been lucky enough to sample one of the last living colonies, to catch the end of their existence as a species. By the time she went back seventeen years later, the composition of the lake had changed. It was no longer their world.

"Those microbes evolved down there," Eli said, sounding stunned, "untouched for thousands of years. Then Progress came along." He snapped his fingers. "Wiped them all out."

The terrible permanence of Eli's words left Abigail envisioning the beautiful Bamiyan Buddhas, blasted out of existence by the Taliban, or the last white rhino on our planet, blasted out of existence by a poacher. All the lost tribes and species, the lost languages and libraries, and the insistent myopia of man.

Of TreeTop.

Eli glanced at the glass shattered on the floor of the lab.

"Those jars could have proven what the lake was like *before* it became diluted. So they destroyed those, too."

Abigail spoke into the silence.

"Is that why Esme was killed?"

"She had the powder," he said, "which was the best proof out there of what the extremophiles were capable of. And maybe the best indicator of what irrigation has done to that lake. But it wasn't just her who got killed over it. The boy from the hotel, too."

"Kevin Polk. What about him?"

Eli pointed vaguely to his shelves of binders and notebooks. "Dr. Carla said she gave him access to all of her research on groundwater flow. So if he was digging around those aquifer maps and flow charts? He could've easily stumbled upon the fact that the canals are seeping into the lake. It's all right there. Maybe without even knowing it, the kid got too close."

"Close enough to be murdered," Abigail whispered.

According to Sophia, Pastor Kurt swore that Silas wouldn't have killed Kevin over drugs or anything else.

"I think we should take Dr. Carla's advice and leave Soap Lake for good," Eli said, standing up, slowly nodding, as if to convince himself.

"I don't follow," Abigail said.

"The microbes I was sent here to study are *gone*, Abigail. And obviously people are getting murdered over this stuff. Agriculture is ruining this lake, and anyone who can prove that is a direct threat to the region's economy. No wonder TreeTop is willing to kill to silence the research. I didn't sign up for this. You *definitely* didn't. I feel like a teacher getting trained to handle a shooter. No thank you. I'll go back to stacking apples."

"What about Esme?"

"Esme's dead," he said. "We're not. *Yet.*"

From her spot on the stool, Abigail watched Eli cram some folders into his laptop case, but she was thinking about Esme:

not her body in the Cutlass, but Esme as she'd been in the surveillance video, holding George's hand and walking him to the
bathroom. Pausing to look at the stars.

"Take Medusa if you want to leave," Abigail said, and began
unspooling the car key from her key ring. "I'm staying in town.
At least for now. I'm not finished here."

"Abigail," Eli said, nearly pleading. "I'm obviously not going
to leave you, but c'mon—"

He was interrupted by a knock on the open door.

Sophia stepped into the room, wearing a sleeveless Def Lep-
pard T-shirt, taking in the broken glass and toppled fridge, poking at a splinter on the doorjamb.

"What a mess," she said, giving Abigail a hug. "Welcome
home." Before Eli had a chance to introduce himself, she blurted,
"You'll talk to Miss Nellie for me?"

"I'll what?" he said.

"The library," Abigail said, raising her brow.

"About your *job*," Eli said.

He was distraught about the jars, the microbes, and Abigail's
refusal to leave, but that didn't stop him from stepping around
the broken glass and placing his giant hands on Sophia's frail
shoulders. He had sweat on his temples and his enormous curls
were leaning to one side like a wave about to crash.

"I'm sorry about all that," he said. "First thing tomorrow we'll
go see that goddamned Miss Nellie. We'll get your job back or
we'll take the whole town to court. Okay?"

Sophia nodded. "Okay." She shook her head at the mess and
gathered a broom from the closet.

Eli stood over the broken glass.

"As long as we're here," he said, then mumbled to himself
about the possibility of *scraping up the evaporated solids as an alter-
native form of* something or other.

"Thank you," Abigail whispered, touching his back.

He picked up a label that clung to a few broken shards.

"May 1957," he said. "As if killing the lake wasn't enough, they had to also kill its history."

"Because?" Sophia said, leaning on the broom.

"Just without these jars, there's little evidence of what the canals have done to the lake."

"Which is what?"

"Oh. Diluted it with river water. Obliterated a very rare species of microbe."

"Now I'm thinking I should've checked the labels," Sophia said. "Been more choosey. About the vintage or whatever. Before I took them."

Abigail froze. "Took them?"

"It's just the one box. Twelve jars, maybe fifteen? I didn't check the dates or anything."

Eli straightened up. "You have jars of *old* lake water?"

"From the library," Sophia said. "Preston's *time capsules*. In my fridge next door. Behind a ton of carrots. I swear I'm turning orange."

"Why, Sophia?"

"When we were unloading them from Medusa, the fridge was getting full? Plus it made sense to not hide them all in one spot. Good call, I'd say, especially after what happened to Preston. Rest in peace. And your door."

"You have them in your fridge? Right now?"

"I figured they'd be safer there because people generally see the state of the place and stay away." She leaned toward Abigail and winked. "Well. Except *you*."

CHAPTER 42

ABIGAIL

Abigail couldn't sleep, probably because she could hear Eli working in his lab, deciphering the next steps of his research. So she grabbed the old mountain bike off Sophia's porch and rode in the dark to the Healing Lake Hotel.

When Abigail entered the lobby, Mr. Polk was dozing at the desk. He shot up and looked around, blinking hard, as if trying to discern where he was. Big gray hair coiled over his ears.

"Not who I was expecting," he said, scratching his stubble. "What time is it?"

"Maybe three?"

He touched his box of key cards. "Everything okay? Need a place to crash?"

"Just to talk, I guess."

"Sounds like coffee," he said, standing slowly from his stool, revealing a black T-shirt with a thin red outline of a lava lamp. He moved with such tightness she could practically hear him creaking.

"I saw Dr. Carla earlier today," she said.

He was filling a mug from a warm carafe when his hand froze, mid-pour.

"Am I still asleep? *Dr. Carla?*"

"She praised your coffee. And you. But didn't have much kind to say about her time here."

"Understandably," he said, as he handed her a mug of silky coffee. "Daniel did mention you were picking up your husband over in Gomorrah. Nothing about Dr. Carla, though."

"Daniel was here?"

"Mrs. Polk offered to watch George and he took her up on it. Poor guy is desperate." He gestured past the beaded curtain. "The boy is actually sound asleep on our couch right now. Daniel is pulling long hours at the orchard, so we've watched George twice now. It's been nice."

Abigail smiled, glad that Daniel felt comfortable reaching out, but also unsettled that George was being made vulnerable to the dark whims of this town.

"Keep a close eye on him, will you?" she said. "It's just that whoever killed his mom is still out there, and after what happened to Preston—"

"He's in good hands, Abigail."

She nodded, reminding herself that the Polks knew loss all too well.

"Did Daniel ask about Esme's phone calls? I'm sorry. I had to tell him."

"Ah, don't apologize," he said. "That's what brought him around here in the first place. I thought he was here to raise hell on me for keeping the calls secret, but he's such a sweet guy. He just wanted to hear what his sister had to say, how she'd been doing, that kind of thing. We had a good talk. Sad, but healthy. And Mrs. Polk got a babysitting job out of it, so it worked out." He paused and looked at the floor. "Given the circumstances."

Standing in the stillness of the lobby, colorful lava lamps

churning through the night, Abigail understood why Esme had reached out to Mr. Polk, of all people, and why Daniel had trusted him enough to leave the boy in the Polks' care: he was calm and empathetic, but there was an intense pain there, too, just beneath the surface, that made him especially receptive. He gave comfort freely to others, and welcomed their comfort in return.

"Did he ask if you ever called her from the payphone down at the gas station?"

"Yeah," he said, looking confused. "Payphone to payphone? What was that all about? I haven't used a payphone in years. I got a phone right here."

"It's probably nothing," she said.

"Usually when people say that, it's probably something," he said, but let it go. He settled onto his stool and flicked a small moth off his notepad.

"Can I ask?" she added, hesitant. She thought she was here to ask him if he knew anything about the powder that Esme had with her on her return to town. But something else was troubling Abigail. "Did something happen between you and Dr. Carla? Her lab was, what, a hundred yards from this desk. You must have known her pretty well. Yet you hardly asked anything when I told you I saw her."

"Got me there," he said, lowering his voice. "No bad blood or anything. Certainly nothing Carla did. But if you must know, there was some *interpersonal* drama between us."

"You two were…?" She raised her brow.

"Nothing like that," he said, smirking. "When Carla first came to town, I felt like such a groupie. I helped her get set up and showed her these websites I'd been following for years. *Einstein's Garage. The Hobo Biologist.* I was always scrolling the chat rooms for random innovations, but my main interest was mineral lakes. Stuff for marketing, like anecdotes about how Soap Lake had saved great-grandpa from an amputation. So it was inevitable that Carla and I would bump into each other deep in the forums and chat. Middle of the night, me sitting here, Carla sitting there, over in her lab. She was going online instead of going home, probably because even then Preston was a little bonkers. Plus you know how this town can be. Both of us were a little lonely. And I think she liked having someone nearby who was excited about her work rather than treating her like an invader."

"Until Mrs. Polk found out?"

"She felt threatened by my friendship with Carla. I guess I didn't hide my excitement very well."

Abigail smiled. "Should I dare ask what was so exciting?"

"Extremophiles, believe it or not. Kinky stuff." He wagged his eyebrows. "Carla's work was interesting, my god. And she appreciated that I was interested in it. Nothing more."

"So you knew about the powder?"

"The billion-dollar bugdust?" he said, impressed. "I'm a little surprised she shared that with you. Though I suppose it helps you're married to a limnologist. With me she hinted at it, teased a little, but never came right out with her findings. I'd seen mentions in the chats before, though. Industry gossip."

"A drug that could get you high for a year?"

"Whatever you were looking for," he said, "that's what the powder did. My favorite was this amniotic yellow foam, one teaspoon lets you breathe underwater. The US Navy would pay top dollar for a canister of that stuff, eh? With the bugdust, rumors were out in the world long before your husband started his work here. But only if you knew where to look."

She considered asking whether he, like Pastor Kurt, thought there was something suspicious about Kevin's murder—that, contrary to the town narrative, Silas hadn't killed Mr. Polk's son. But with the framed photos of the boy enshrined all around this lobby, she couldn't find the words.

"Here comes Krunk's little *hello*," Mr. Polk said, pointing at the window. "Watch for it…"

Out on Main Street, under a sodium yellow streetlight, a cop cruiser drove past and quickly lit its flashers—a short bright blast that blared red and blue lights through the lobby. By the time Abigail finished blinking the cruiser was gone.

"He's probably heading back to the gas station after watching for DUIs out on the highway," Mr. Polk said. "He'll swing by here in a few minutes for his coffee. Poor guy. You know your life sucks when you're turning to me for entertainment."

"He comes by every night?"

"It's my duty to bore him to tears with my hobbies. Design ideas for remote control planes. Model engines that run on French fry grease. All my Soap Lake chat room stuff. He thinks I'm a real kook, yet every shift he shows up. Pretends to listen. Between us, I think it's a bit compulsive. Trauma, you know? Circling back each night to the scene of the shooting, like those sandhill cranes who return to the same fields each spring. Like he's got no choice."

Abigail could picture Krunk leaning against this desk, within sight of the hallway where he'd been shot by Silas and a few feet away from where he'd scooped Esme off the floor, dragged her over Kevin's body, and helped her survive the shooting.

"This one's his," Mr. Polk said, reaching an overhead shelf and retrieving a coffee mug that held a cartoon pig dressed in police blues: *World's Okayest Cop*. "Isn't that great?"

"It suits him," she said, smiling. "I should go before he gets here."

"Probably a good idea," Mr. Polk said, smiling. "With your husband home and all."

"You've heard the rumors," she said, and he nodded. "Apparently I'm quite the home-wrecker. At least according to the troll at the police station."

"Don't pay her any mind," he said, brushing the air with his hand. "Just bad timing, Krunk dumping Rebecca right around when he met you."

"Rebecca is…?"

"*Was* his fiancée. A meanie cheerleader who waltzed straight into a job at the city. Krunk is better off without her."

"You really don't like her."

"Let's just say I wasn't surprised when he called off the wedding," he said. "And no offense, but it had nothing to do with you. Just—"

"Bad timing," Abigail said, repeating Mr. Polk's words, and thinking, for the first time, about that timing: Krunk had dumped Rebecca right around the time he'd met Abigail in the desert, at the scene of Esme's murder—

Which meant Krunk had dumped Rebecca right when Esme had come back to town.

The spots from his flashers still hovered in her vision.

Krunk hadn't left his fiancée for Abigail, she thought, but maybe he had for Esme.

PART 3:

THE RECKONINGS

CHAPTER 43

ESME

It had been eight years since the last time Esme had driven over Ryegrass Pass, heading west on the interstate, then south along the coast, and eventually stumbling into a new job and a new life. Landing in Bakersfield had felt at first like a dead end, but work was easy to find and no one there was sliding knives into her mouth as she slept. To keep it that way, she vowed to never own a smartphone or log in to social media. She'd thought she'd leave at some point, but when George came along (coworker drinks, one-night stand) she no longer felt the need to go anywhere else; her life had come to her. At least for a while.

She blew her bangs from her lower lip and checked the rearview. George was watching *Cars* on a mini-DVD player for literally the fifth time since leaving California. He caught her looking at him and blew his bangs, too.

"That's how it is, huh?" she said.

"That how is, huh?" he replied, and they both cracked up.

The Cutlass glided over the interstate, through the desert,

through the darkness. She kept her speed at sixty-five, knowing how screwed she would be if she were to get pulled over in an old car in the rural west with brown skin and a juice box full of a powder so rare not a cop on the planet could identify it.

She thought about calling Mr. Polk again, knowing if she showed up at the hotel and dropped George off—*By the way, had a kid, could use a sitter*—he'd embrace the moment and probably comp her a free room, a can of ale, and a frozen pizza. But she couldn't leave George alone like that—he wasn't great with strangers—especially if *Mrs.* Polk was anywhere within range. That woman could judge with the worst of them.

She also thought about dropping George off with Daniel, but he and Mom didn't even know there *was* a George, let alone an imminent homecoming. How many times had she stood in front of the payphone, ready to call her family to share the news of her child? It had always felt like the kind of call that would have repercussions, create vulnerabilities, even cost lives. They meant well, but her mom couldn't even grab a meal at the diner without telling the waitress about her cat's latest hairball. And with a single phone call Daniel would have puffed up his chest and gone into caveman mode, vowing to *make sister safe*. Then they'd start sending her money they didn't have and, along the way, news of her and George would seep into the town.

Still, it was almost enough to make her whip the Cutlass around—

At least until she reminded herself how unsustainable daily life in Bakersfield had become. Relying on neighbors to take care of George each time she went to work. Always having to choose between groceries and rent, an oil change or the electric bill. Never knowing whether the warehouse manager was about to hit on her or yell at her.

And she and George doing everything alone. The boy needed some family. After eight years away, she did, too.

It was easy to forget that was the purpose of this trip, with the truth of the shooting looming.

She skirted town and drove deeper into the desert, dodging pelty lumps of roadkill. Soon the county road reached the turnoff that led to the Rock Shack, the place they'd arranged to meet.

She knew she was going to feel nervous, coming back to this area, but hadn't expected the impending feel of the world closing in. A tightness in her chest.

Be smart, she reminded herself, as she pulled over and killed the lights. This place has a long-ass memory.

She was TreeTop's unfinished business. To hurt her, they'd hurt George, just as they'd hurt Kevin.

She'd been hanging on to to Dr. Carla's yellow powder for eight years now, tucking the same plastic bag into an old sock and moving it from one drawer to another, one apartment to the next. After that horror show with Silas, her initial plan had been to protect herself from incrimination by destroying it— that is, until the night of the white noise machine, when she'd been roused awake by TreeTop, asking, *Some kind of dust?*

He hadn't even known what he'd wanted, the maniac, but he sure left an impression on her. That powder was worth a lot to someone.

Ever since that night, she knew it would someday come in handy, like an emergency button she could push in a moment of desperation. A way to buy her safety.

She'd been reassured that things would be fine—as long as she brought the powder.

She took a few deep breaths and turned on the dome light.

George was wide-eyed in his booster, licking a flat-fruit wrapper.

She shook his Cookie Monster slipper and tried to appear calm.

"You think you can hide while I meet with someone?"

His brow furrowed.

"It's like when you used to come to work and you'd have to sit against the warehouse wall and be quiet. It's just for a few minutes and I'll be right outside the car. Can you do that?"

George nodded.

"What if I cover you up with your blanket?"

He gave her a thumbs-up.

"Are you scared?" she asked.

"Nope."

"Are you sure? Because if you are we'll figure out another way."

"I'm not," he said through half-lidded eyes.

Of course he wasn't: at every turn, he went out of his way to make her life better. He made it easy, being a mom. Well, easier.

"Get on the floor behind my seat. In a ball."

He watched her tighten the fold across the top of the juice box.

"Wha's that?"

"This," she said, wagging it in front of him, "is our special ticket. It keeps us safe from any baddies. It's *really* important. We can't lose it, okay? Remind me not to throw it out."

"Don't throw out," he said, pointing.

"Thanks."

"Can I hold it?"

"No. Just pretend it isn't here."

As George curled into the floorboard behind the driver's seat, Esme stirred the juice box into the trash on the floor next to him.

"Ready?"

She dropped George's SpongeBob blanket over the curve of his back, then tucked it in here and there, loosened it until it looked natural.

"Make yourself small," she said. "Smaller!"

Then she dropped some of the trash on top of him as he giggled.

She hovered above him for a few seconds, watching as he

stuck his arm out and spidered his fingers over the maroon carpet, maneuvering past the hump and through a chips bag and a soda can, searching for the special juice box. She tickled his hand and he cackled and yanked it back.

"Quiet. Really."

Outside, the cool air hit her skin as she pushed his booster seat into the trunk. She considered stashing the juice box back here, too, alongside the spare tire and the tangle of jumper cables. And maybe George, for that matter. The trunk would be less—

But it was too late: a car was approaching, the headlights shifting through the dry grasses and casting long, comblike shadows into the sage.

CHAPTER 44

ABIGAIL

Abigail left the hotel lobby and found Krunk sitting in his cruiser behind the gas station.

"Can we talk?" she asked.

"Hop in," he said, popping the lock.

Out where Main met the highway, a blinking red stoplight quivered on its wire. She leaned the bike against the peeling wall that held the Last Payphone on Earth, and slid into the passenger side of the cruiser. She had to move his black boots off the seat and shift his small cooler of Gatorade to make room for her legs.

"Sorry about that," he said, pushing his cooler aside. "Usually no one rides up front."

From this vantage, he had a clear view of drunk drivers and speeders on the highway, if any, but far more likely of blowing tumbleweeds and spiraling plastic bags and the occasional loping coyote. She couldn't imagine a lonelier way to spend each night. No wonder he wanted out.

"So, what's up?" he said. "I wasn't expecting to see you, now that your man's home. Shouldn't you be making casserole or something? That's not a euphemism."

"You park here a lot?"

"I have my spots," he said.

"Right in front of the payphone someone was using to call Esme. So you must've seen his phone number. Before someone crossed it out."

"His?"

"Theirs? I don't know. TreeTop's."

Krunk nodded, chewing his gum.

"Are you here about Esme? Because I would *love* to be able to bring something to the task force that wasn't related to drugs. I mean, the TreeTop stuff would be a hard sell, but if we could connect it to an individual, with evidence, and not have to tell some ghost story about a boogeyman with a screwdriver? I'm all ears."

In the glow of a fluorescent light, the payphone appeared flat and cinematic, like a Hopper painting, or a shot in a horror film.

"*TreeTop Kills,*" she said, "written right there. Same thing all over town. If you look closely, you can see they crossed out the phone number and the rest of the message—*Kill TreeTop.* You'd think they'd cross it *all* out."

"I imagine leaving it up helps spread the myth," he said, wiping his hands on his pants. "Plus *TreeTop Kills* has been a thing forever, like Soap Lake's version of *Kilroy Was Here.* It scared *all* of us when we were kids. Our parents when they were kids." He looked around the parking lot, checked his rearview before shifting to face her. "Listen, Abigail. Whatever you've been digging up about TreeTop, just be careful. Sounds like you made your way to the inner circle, so to speak."

"Not my crowd."

"Not mine either," he said. "You do know that, right? The downside is I can't help much if you get in over your head.

Though I did vouch for you at the department the other day, in case anyone was listening."

"Like the detectives who interviewed me about Esme?"

"*Yes*, actually. McDaid, at least. I don't know where it begins and ends, okay? I've made it my business my whole life not to get involved in that stuff. Call it a survival technique."

"Lovely traditions around here," she said.

"Without farming, this place dies."

"And without irrigation, farming dies."

"Most of it, yeah."

"But *with* irrigation," she said, "the lake dies."

He raised an eyebrow, as if confused and determined to stay that way. "Part of me, maybe the part of me that grew up here, sees how fragile this place is. So when something threatens an entire way of life, you know, it's like a single cancer cell entering a healthy body. The body needs to eradicate it. Before it spreads and brings everything else down."

Abigail stared.

"Okay," he continued, noting her dissatisfaction, "think of it like this. Growing up, I always heard about the glory days of the lake. Native people coming to cleanse their spirits and their bodies in this water. Grand hotels. Soldiers in agony being cured, for real, when Western doctors couldn't help them. Wall-to-wall tourists. And then entire generations watched most of that disappear. If the ag economy ever goes belly-up the way tourism did? We're talking about this town disappearing from the face of the earth. But with the shift to ag, people have been able to make a living and feed millions while they're at it. Point being, all of that makes it easier to look the other way. Is the logic, anyway. Not that I'm part of it."

"So murdering people is okay as long as it keeps the canals flowing."

"Can't farm in a desert without irrigation," he said, looking out his window, "and who said anything about *murdering* people? Maybe you're right, though. Maybe TreeTop is behind Esme's death. It wouldn't be the first time something like that happened." He peered through the windshield and held up a steady hand. "Hang on a second: duty calls."

A teenage couple with matching skeleton hoodies walked hand in hand across the street and into the gas station lot.

"I should get them for curfew," he said. "But they'll probably buy an energy drink, then use the change to buy a condom from the grody machine in the men's room. So if I interrupt them, they'll go home without the condom and in sixteen years I'll be harassing their future child for a curfew violation."

"You'll still be here?" she said. "I thought you were itching to get out."

"That's the kind of philosophical garbage that occupies me most nights. Does that count as a koan? Mr. Polk loves those. You know, like one hand clapping."

"One cop evading," she said.

"Right," he said, turning toward her. "You were saying?"

"You know how there've been rumors about us? Romantically speaking."

Krunk tightened his lips. "Sure. Not my favorite topic. But sure."

"That's because you dumped your sweetheart—"

"Rebecca."

"Right around when we met, so some people thought you did it for me. But that was just bad timing, right? Coincidence. On the way over here from the hotel, I actually *thought* I had it all figured out. When you dumped Rebecca, called off the wedding and broke her heart, it was because you were in love with Esme, and somehow you figured out she was coming back to town."

"Oh. Huh. That's creative."

"Only I was wrong. You weren't in love with Esme at all. You just saw an opportunity and took it. Esme had your ticket out."

Krunk finger-tapped the steering wheel. He looked out the

window at the teenagers and sighed heavily. "The guy's pants are falling down on purpose. Doesn't get sadder than that."

Abigail was undeterred. "Esme began calling the hotel from a payphone in Bakersfield, reaching out to Mr. Polk for advice. She was desperate to come home but needed to know whether she'd be safe, and she trusted Mr. Polk to be discreet. But then out of the blue, she just stopped calling him. He was baffled. It made no sense. At first I thought Mrs. Polk had to be involved with the way she resented Esme. I figured she must have answered the phone one night and scared her off. Because who else would have been there while Mr. Polk was off on a cookie run or napping in the back? It would have to be someone who hung out in the lobby a lot. Someone who stopped by for coffee so much that he'd have his own mug. *The World's Okayest Cop*."

"What are you getting at, Abigail?"

"You answered the phone when Esme called Mr. Polk," she said, and she could hear the hurt in her voice. "I mean, we could look at the call records and pinpoint the exact day, the exact minute, maybe even correlate it with the location of your radio. Point being it *had* to be you. You got the number she was calling from, then came down here and called her back on this payphone. Where you'd be safe. Isolated."

Krunk worked his tongue around inside his cheek.

"And," Abigail continued, "when I asked you about Dr. Carla the other day, you told me that she'd left her job to teach at a community college. Why would you know that unless you'd reached out to her? At first I thought Esme had sent her the anonymous email, trying to sell the powder and make a quick buck. But I was wrong—it was you all along. Esme's *bugdust* was your chance to get out. Isn't that what you called the powder when you emailed Dr. Carla to try to sell it to her? Isn't that what you figured out from Mr. Polk? All those nights, listening to him talk about the lake? Maybe he even showed you the rumors about the powder in the chat rooms?"

He shrugged.

"You were there when Kevin was killed," she said, softening. "You attacked Silas and saved Esme's life. You're probably the only person in town she would've agreed to meet. You nearly died together that day. Of course she'd trust you."

"And I'm a cop," he whispered. He took the wad of gum out of his mouth and plunged it against the dashboard. "I'm a *cop*, so I could help her land home safely. But it's not what it looks like, Abigail."

"It looks a lot like you…" But she stopped herself from saying it, maybe because she wanted so badly to be wrong, to feel safe sitting with him in his cruiser in the middle of the night. She wanted to believe he was incapable of murder.

Krunk whipped around, clenching his jaw.

"Like I what, Abigail? *Killed her?* Really? You're saying that to *me?*"

"I want to know what happened."

He shook his head and looked away. "You sure about that?"

Before Abigail had a chance to answer, he hit the flashers and sped out of the lot. She gripped the handle inside the car door and felt her guts spread through her back like a sprawling octopus as he gunned it to sixty down Main.

CHAPTER 45

ESME

The cruiser stopped on the side of the dirt road, swirling dust through its headlights. Esme's gut was swimming, but she told herself that George was fine, that she had little choice but to come home, and that it was okay to need help. She'd done everything she could to pave the way, including agreeing to this meeting.

But still: her desire to have an answer to Kevin's murder had been replaced by a mild self-loathing at how quickly this trip had morphed from a chance for her to get some support, and for George to finally know his family, to a quest for answers she hadn't even known she'd wanted. Here she was, making her little boy hide in a dark car. If this was the situation she was putting him in, maybe it was better not to know.

"Just me," Krunk said, all chirpy, leaning out the cruiser's door.

"Eight years and no *hello*?"

Krunk hopped out. Locked his cruiser but the lights stayed on.

"Yeah, sorry," he said, "I'm just. Hi."

As awkward as ever Krunk flailed his arms, contemplating the appropriateness of a hug, then stretched for a handshake. She'd been expecting him to be wearing a uniform, but he was dressed like any other sporty white dude. Cargo shorts and running shoes and a red T-shirt. That didn't ease her nerves.

His hand was clammy. This was weird.

"They really let you drive that thing?"

"Sort of don't ask, don't tell," he said, looking at the cruiser. "My landlord loves when I park it in front of my place. Keeps the trash away."

"Mmm."

She reminded herself that she trusted Krunk, a boy she'd known her whole life.

Who'd been there when Kevin was killed.

Who'd attacked Silas and saved her life.

Who was now standing inches away from her, wiping his hands on his shorts.

"So, what's the plan?" she said, rocking in her sandals.

"Sorry," he said. "Thought I explained this on the phone. We'll take your car, head up past the Rock Shack. Somewhere we can talk where we definitely won't be spotted. Somewhat touchy, me being here."

She looked at the Cutlass, imagining George bundled in his blanket behind the driver's seat, hiding like a champ, and wondered if he'd fallen asleep. She was expecting this would all be outside, a leaning-on-the-fender kind of thing. It wouldn't be the worst thing to let Krunk know the boy was in there, but it wouldn't be the best thing either, especially since not a soul in town knew of his existence, and she wanted to keep it that way until she was certain they were safe. If this all went south, nothing would be sacred, not even a child. Just ask Dr. Carla.

"Let's just talk here instead," she said.

Krunk shook his head. "We really don't want anyone seeing your car parked out here next to mine. In case it's tequila night at the old homestead? With all the drunken bonfires, a cop car parked on its own is normal up here, but parked behind another car it's just asking for gawkers. And California plates, especially on a car that the Polks gave you? It would make for a loud reentry."

"I don't want that," she said.

"Call it an abundance of caution. The stakes are pretty high."

"Right," she said, opening her car door, feeling less nervy already, and even impressed by how seriously he was taking this.

She sat behind the wheel, looking into the rearview. As Krunk walked around to the passenger side, she whispered: "Just like when I'm at work. Don't move. Be quiet."

On the floor behind her, George, the little turd, said, "Okay!" in his regular voice.

"Shh!"

Krunk didn't appear to hear them.

She started the car. Didn't buckle in. Glad she'd thought of the trash.

CHAPTER 46

ABIGAIL

"Where are you taking me?" Abigail said, clenching the door handle.

Krunk shook his head as he drove through town, past the library and the lake. "You mean, 'Where are we going?' I'll take you back to your bike right now. Just say the word."

And end my incessant questions, she thought.

"I'm good," she said. Though she began to feel less good when Krunk drove past the high school and between the orchards, then up the steep canal road carved into the hills above the lake. He parked on a small overlook. Behind them, the oily black canal slithered like a mamba through the night.

Abigail followed as Krunk led the way with his Maglite. In the cheatgrass his light paused on a deteriorating pair of men's bikini underwear, patterned with stars and stripes.

"Come here often?" Abigail said, nodding toward them.

"Don't look at me," he said.

They reached a steep embankment, not far from the cruiser.

He'd left the parking lights on, so a yellow-orange aura glowed in the distance behind them.

"You're not going to push me off, are you?" she said.

Krunk went limp.

"You do know you're safe with me, right?"

Abigail was strangely trusting of Krunk, until it occurred to her that a few miles farther along this gravel road was the spot where George had burst from the sagebrush and, later, closer to town, the spot where she'd first encountered Krunk. He'd seemed so broken that day, and only now did she wonder if what she'd really seen was the guilty afterglow of murder.

You do know you're safe with me, right?

Maybe he'd said the same thing to Esme.

"The payphone isn't the only place I park," Krunk said. He pointed to the rocky plateau across the lake, where the first trace of daylight created jagged silhouettes. "Sun's gonna rise soon. It's pretty cool when it comes burning over those cliffs and hits the water."

Abigail's hand wormed deep into her bag. Esme's yellow powder was across the state in Dr. Carla's drawer of dirty yogurt spoons, so its fate was out of Abigail's hands, and Esme's keys were now with Daniel. Preston's incriminating rainbow murder room was indistinguishable from the manic debris of a hoarder, and if Dr. Carla was right, his whole house would soon burn to the ground. Which left just one more piece of evidence to clear out of her life.

She pulled out the empty juice box from her handbag, still sealed in a sandwich baggie. She'd been carting it around since she'd packed for Seattle, thinking it would be safer in her bag than left alone in her empty home. Except for the splatter of blood across its cartoon front, it resembled something exhumed from a diaper bag.

"What is that?" he said, hitting it with his Maglite's beam.

"You don't recognize it? From the video you showed me of Esme at the rest area, digging through the trash?"

Krunk found a sudden need to look away, to shine his beam far behind them, on the rabbit brush along the canal.

"That's where Esme had it hidden," she said. "Krunk, I found the powder."

"What-are-you-talking-about?" he said too quickly, as if it were one word.

"It was tucked inside the juice box, probably in the back seat of the Cutlass with all the other trash. The boy took it with him when he ran. He dropped it in the desert."

"I'm confused."

"No, you're not," she said. "That's why you showed me the video of the rest area, isn't it? The photos of trash, too. Since I'd been the first person at the car, maybe I could help you figure out where it had ended up. Or was that whole thing so you could get a minute alone with the boy? See his reaction. Make sure he didn't recognize you."

"Haven't you figured out," he said, "that I came to your house to see *you*?"

"That's not the only reason."

Huffing, he took the juice box from her hands. "It's a piece of trash."

"With Esme's blood on it. The powder isn't in there anymore. Obviously."

She watched him closely, waiting for words that never came— *Then where is it?*—but he just tossed it back and she caught it against her stomach. He stuck the Maglite under his arm and stooped to tie his bright blue running shoes.

"I don't know what you're talking about," he said, coldly, "but it sounds to me like more evidence of drugs. I can pass that on to the task force and they may want to pursue it—"

"Krunk."

"Though there's also the risk of charging you with withholding evidence, obstruction—"

"What'd you *do*, Krunk? Fuck, man. What'd you do to her?"

He stopped, nodded. After a minute he said, sharply, "I was delivering a *pizza*, Abigail."

She could feel spittle hitting her face and knew the conversation had finally changed. Krunk looked out at the horizon and began to speak.

"I was delivering a pizza."

That day had been playing through his mind in an endless loop, beginning with the scaley old dude who'd called the pizza shop, promising a big tip for a *piping hot* delivery. That tip was the only thing on Krunk's mind as he sped to the hotel and parked, then hustled down the hallway, holding the pizza aloft and arriving just in time to hear a gunshot coming from the lobby and to watch an explosion of blood as his classmate Kevin dropped to the carpet. Esme knelt beside him like a ghost as Krunk's entire life spiraled into an image of Silas staring at the pistol in his hand, looking first confused, then terrified, spit stringing from his rotten teeth. At some point he glanced up and his eyes met Krunk's. He raised his pistol and fired.

The moment the bullet hit, Krunk buckled and spun sideways in the air. The insulated pizza box landed on his head.

"I didn't know how badly it messed me up," he said, looking away from Abigail, "until months later, when I was alone in Seattle, trying to start over. I couldn't sleep. Couldn't talk to anyone. I felt nervous all the time unless I was drunk, so I drank every night. Everything was so expensive. Parking. Laundry. Cable. Food. I tried to give it a real shot, living there, but my savings were gone in no time. I had no choice but to come home. I got a girlfriend, felt pretty okay, I guess. But when I got this job, the first night I was alone in the police station, what do you think I did?"

Opened the restricted report from the Healing Lake Hotel shooting to see if somehow it made sense.

"I thought the answer to *me* might've been in there," he said. "They got the bad guy. Silas was dead. But it didn't feel over, you know?"

Late at night in the police station, Krunk skimmed the incident and toxicology reports, the autopsies and witness statements. He studied the floorplans of the hotel and traced Silas's path to the shore and his site of expiration.

In one of the police interviews, a tweaker nicknamed Tesseract—one of Silas's known associates, lately said to be living under a viaduct in Yakima—mentioned that some new drug was the real reason Silas had shot Kevin. She didn't know what it was, but heard it was the color of gold and got you high for a year.

Bugdust or some shit.

Reading that phrase stirred something in Krunk. For one, it reminded him of being in the hospital on the night of the shooting, when a trio of guys he'd assumed were with the cops showed up at his bedside. He was sedated but answered what he could, and after the interview was complete, a good ol' boy named Hal came back into the room, saying he'd forgotten his hat. Krunk didn't know him but he'd seen him around town. They were all alone and he rested his hand on Krunk's bandaged thigh and said, *One more thing.* Then he asked Krunk if Esme had mentioned anything about whatever Dr. Carla had discovered in the lake.

Some kind of dust?

Through the warm fuzz of the pain meds, Krunk thought about how he'd hidden in the lab with Esme after the shooting, and had watched her dig something out of Dr. Carla's desk and take it with her when she left. But before he could say anything he felt Hal's hand pressing on his bandaged gunshot, sending a jolt of pain up his spine. Krunk squirmed, anxious about how excruciating things were about to get, but then the guy snapped his fingers, thanked him for his heroics, and left the room.

Krunk didn't fully grasp what had just happened, but he had a feeling it had to do with *you-know-who*, and if he'd learned one thing from growing up in Soap Lake, it was this: those people stopped at nothing.

He put all of that behind him until one night, years later, when he was a cop and Mr. Polk was showing him some wacky chat rooms. That same term popped up again, ringing a bell deep inside: *bugdust.*

"Turns out," Krunk said, "there's a lot of chatter online about some organism in Soap Lake that could change the world. And it got me thinking about the day of the shooting, how Esme knew just what to grab when she left the lab. I didn't know if it was a drug or what, but I knew it had to be valuable."

"So that was the end of your digging?" Abigail said.

"Not exactly."

A year passed. Then two.

And last spring, during yet another graveyard shift, Krunk went to visit Mr. Polk in the hotel and found his chair at the front desk empty.

Mr. Polk was off on a cookie run, or somewhere sneaking a nap. So Krunk poured a cup of coffee and played pinball, killing time, as he always did.

On ball three, the phone rang. Krunk waited before picking it up.

"Healing Hotel," he said.

He was plucking a pen out of his shirt pocket to take a message when a woman's voice emerged on the line.

"Everything there okay?"

"The owner stepped out," he said. "What room you calling from? I can have him—"

"Is this Abe Krunk?" she said. "Mr. Polk said you'd been around."

Krunk scanned the lobby, certain Mr. Polk was pranking him.

"How do you know my name?"

"I never had a chance to thank you," she said. "For getting me out of there."

Not since he'd been shot had Krunk felt so ready to collapse into a pile of bones. He planted a hand on the desk to hold himself up but ended up dropping into the chair behind him.

"Esme? Is this you?"

"This is me."

"Are you *here*? In town?"

"Not yet," she said, followed by a hiccup of regret.

"So you're coming home?"

"Maybe. But you can't say *anything* to *anyone*."

"Why would you do that?" he said, aware of the disdain in his voice.

She laughed and changed the subject. "Can I ask if you were okay after?"

Krunk's mouth was dry and he was surprised at how close he was to panic.

"You were there," he said. "You know."

"All too well."

He was unsettled by the feelings heaving through him. At the relief, but also how much more he had to say. And finally someone to say it to.

Except a door somewhere closed. Mr. Polk coughed beyond the beaded curtain.

"I can't talk here," Krunk said. "Give me the number you're calling from."

Before hanging up, Esme shared the number of the payphone across from her apartment in Bakersfield.

Within minutes, Krunk was behind the gas station, cruiser parked, using the payphone to dial the number he'd just jotted down.

Main Street was still. Middle of the night. A whistle of wind through the budding trees.

It took a dozen rings before Esme picked up. In the background on her end, Krunk could hear truck traffic passing and a car door slamming: she was outside, also at a payphone, somewhere with a 661 area code.

"Esme?"

Silence.

"If you're serious about coming back here, we'll have to arrange it like this. Payphone to payphone. You can't call Mr. Polk anymore. Calling the hotel is too risky."

"Because of Mrs. Polk?" she said.

"Who else?"

She didn't respond.

"Did he tell you I became a cop? I can help. I'm the one you need to be talking to."

She still didn't respond.

"There's something you should know," he continued. "I don't know if I should share this. But it's about Silas."

He could hear the quickening of her breath.

"I can't get into details over the phone," he said, "but I've been looking into the shooting. No one else knows. But I have some doubts, Esme. I don't think Silas killed Kevin."

He could hear the receiver drop, swinging and clacking against the payphone base, as somewhere far away, Esme fell to her knees.

On the dark ridge above the lake, Abigail watched Krunk scrape grime off the lens of his Maglite.

"What did you mean it wasn't Silas who killed Kevin?" she asked.

He looked away from her. "I had some doubts. Turned out Esme had doubts, too. Long before me."

Krunk and Esme spoke five or six more times, late-night calls on a specific schedule, always payphone to payphone.

"I told her that I would pave the way for her return, since I'm a cop, in case there was any blowback. Of course Mr. Polk had no idea."

In their first few calls, Esme shared details from the shooting that felt like they didn't belong, anomalies she'd always written off as the effects of trauma: the way the beaded curtain *ticked* right when Kevin got shot, as if someone had been behind it. The way Silas looked at the gun in his hand, terrified and confused, as if that powder had possessed him, or the shooting had happened without him. And the question the cops had asked as she and Krunk were hiding in the lab: *Had Esme* seen *another shooter?* Not, Was there *another shooter?*

Esme pled with Krunk to share whatever he'd gathered from the police files, and he dropped a few hints—*the way the report had us positioned in the room isn't at all how I remember it*—but insisted they meet in person for any more than that, so they could come up with a plan.

"Because frankly, Abigail, if I told Esme everything I'd uncovered and she got scared, decided to stay hidden in California, then I'd be the one with a target on my back. All she'd have to do is tell one person. Daniel, her mom, Mr. Polk. Hell, someone at the FBI. And I'd spend the rest of my life waiting for TreeTop to chop me up and feed me to the trees."

It was only on the last payphone call, after Esme was packing her Cutlass, primed for revelation, convincing herself that she was going back home for family and support, not to discover the truth about the shooting—only then did Krunk even mention the powder.

"So this is kind of weird to ask," he said, head ducked into the payphone, palm planted on the gas station wall, "but it would make my job a lot easier if I could get whatever you took out of the lab that day. Something to use as leverage if things go south, or to stash in an old evidence box, ease some tension. A little insurance. Don't worry, no one knows you took it."

Krunk squeezed shut his eyes and waited, worried he'd just botched his escape.

"Except you," Esme finally said.

The next morning, Krunk created a fake email account and anonymously sent a message to Dr. Carla, hoping to cash in and get out of town, once and for all.

Subject line: **Bugdust.**

CHAPTER 47

ESME

Esme didn't see anyone at the Rock Shack when they crept past in the Cutlass, but Krunk still insisted she drive farther along the narrow two-track path that snaked between brush and rock.

"Head over the rise in case anyone decides it's a good night to party."

Seemed like overkill, Esme thought, but Krunk was clearly concerned about how mingling with the town pariah might impact his job.

Fighting nausea, she drove into the desert, sagebrush scraping the sides of the car like the fingernails of a witch. She wondered what George was thinking, hidden under the blanket in the back seat, if he was even awake. He didn't make a peep.

She parked in a small clearing and killed the engine and the lights. Spooked by the dark and the quiet, she turned on the dome light, dim and yellow. Then she turned on the radio, something low that would blur out George's shifts and sounds, but also blur out her conversation with Krunk. Her hand roamed between stations and settled on squelchy butt-rock: "Welcome to the Jungle."

Krunk rolled down his window and scanned the dark.

"You do have the powder?" he said, sounding nervous. "Because the powder's what makes this doable."

"Does Mr. Polk know we're out here?" Esme said.

Krunk sighed. He'd gotten more uptight, she noticed, since high school. More jumpy.

The shooting maybe, or the job.

"It's better he doesn't know the details at this point."

"Details of his son's murder, you mean?" She raised her brow and glanced out at the desert. "I thought you were going to bring files or something."

"I'm going to need that powder, Esme. That's where we start."

"With the powder."

He couldn't sit still and his words sounded scripted. Esme's anticipation chilled to paranoia. Was it possible Krunk was acting in an official capacity, using the shooting to lure her here, to somehow entrap her? She felt like she'd walked into a sting.

"Are you recording this?" she said, too loudly.

He lifted the front of his T-shirt. "We're in *your* car, Esme. Jeez."

"But are there other cops out there?"

"What? No. Of course not."

"If the powder is some kind of evidence," she said, lowering the temperature, conscious of George in the back, "the last thing I want is to cast a shadow over Kevin. Or self-incriminate. Is that why you want it?"

"You're fine," he said, smiling gently. "This is *way* under the radar, Esme. I'm sticking my neck out, and the powder might be the one thing that protects me. *Us.* Do you want to know what happened to Kevin?"

"At what cost?" she said, catching his eye.

Krunk didn't answer. Instead, in a calm, assured voice, he told her what he knew.

Beginning with his time exploring the police files, which documented how Silas had trashed the gas station the night before the shooting. How, according to the cashier's statement, he had been seething about some golden dust that Kevin had given him, stuff that was either so potent it was scrambling his brain, or so bogus it was sending him into a rage.

What'd you do to me, Esme?

"Take one guess who the reporting officer was."

Esme looked up. "McDaid?"

After the incident at the gas station, Officer McDaid brought Silas to the police station. Only he didn't arrest him, nor did he document what they talked about for nine hours, just kept him on a bench in the back all night so he could cool off and sober up. It was all informal, McDaid said in a statement, "trying to keep the kid out of jail." Something he'd been doing for Silas since junior high.

"There was no record of it, but McDaid *had* to have taken possession of whatever remaining powder Silas had on him," Krunk said. "And Silas must have confessed he got it from Kevin. All off the record. Silas left the department that day in a rage, blaming you and Kev. And McDaid was right at his side."

Silas was already falling to pieces, probably going through withdrawals, and McDaid preyed on his weakness: riling him up and planting the idea of going after Kevin, maybe Esme, too, assuring him he'd be there for him if things went south, just as he had in the past. Minutes before the first shot was fired, McDaid dropped Silas off on the shore behind the library, right up the street from the hotel. Silas never knew where he'd be sleeping, so he'd stashed a backpack with some clothes in the bushes behind the book drop—along with the .38 he'd stolen from his dad.

"But we were there," she said, picking bits of plastic off the

Cutlass's steering wheel. "Everything pointed to Silas being the shooter."

"It still does," Krunk said, "which is exactly how they got away with it."

"*They?*"

Instead of responding, Krunk expressed surprise at the weight that had been given to his and Esme's witness statements, when in fact they were unreliable at best.

"Neither of us admitted to *seeing* Silas shoot Kevin. We both saw Kevin get shot. We definitely heard it. And we saw Silas standing there with his dad's revolver."

"We didn't need to *see* him fire the gun to know it happened."

"That's right," he said. "Because we heard the shot, and we saw him panic and shoot me, and there he was, a little while later, dead on the beach, holding a revolver full of empty casings. All of which meant there was no need for an external ballistics report."

The evidence appeared undeniable, Krunk explained, which allowed the crime scene analysis to be completed in-house: mapping the trajectory of the gunshots, the positions of those in the room, the spray and drip patterns. In a detailed ballistics report, the individual bullets would have been matched to the microscopic grooves in the barrel of the gun, like fingerprints. But in this case the evidence was undeniable, with two eyewitnesses, a dead shooter with a history of violence, and no trial on the horizon. The department only had to complete an internal ballistics report. Nothing external required.

"Is that normal?"

Krunk shrugged. "Not normal, but legal, and definitely cheaper, as long as the rest of the evidence is indisputable. It gets better. I don't know if our statements were doctored or if you and I were so traumatized that we didn't pay attention to whatever we signed off on, but the way it's portrayed in the report is *not* the way it happened, Esme. It's just not. The report has Kevin facing a different direction when the bullet hit and Silas standing about six feet closer to the desk than he actually was. It also states that Kevin leaned toward Silas to prevent him from shooting you, which explained the odd trajectory and spray pattern. You know that didn't happen."

"What are you saying?"

"The shot that killed Kevin was fired from the northwest quadrant of the room. Behind the desk."

Behind the beaded curtain.

"Silas was on the other side of the lobby. There's no way he fired that shot. See..."

Esme could still hear the beads of the curtain *ticking* together in the wake of the gunshot, a sound she'd first attributed to Kevin's soul passing out of the lobby, and later to Mrs. Polk leaving the doors to their residence open to allow air from the lake to flow through the building.

She didn't want to be thinking about this anymore, *reliving* it, and for what? It represented all that was bad about this place, and nothing that was good. As Krunk continued speaking, she envisioned opening the car door and quietly walking into the desert and away, heading back to Bakersfield and an invigorating career as a pole dancer. But of course, there was George.

"I get it," she said quietly, hoping Krunk would shut up.

But Krunk was on a roll, explaining how the .38 Special was the firearm most commonly used by cops for decades. After McDaid dropped Silas off, he could easily have made his way into the back doors of the hotel, armed with the same type of gun. He'd goaded Silas into going after Kevin, then waited behind the beaded curtain as an insurance policy.

"Silas hesitated, or wouldn't pull the trigger—so McDaid did."

After Kevin dropped, Silas could see his own doom. He shot Krunk. Then went after Esme.

Maybe it was the smells of the desert at night, smoky sage and dust, or maybe it was hearing all of this from a kid she'd known forever, but Esme was reminded of how boxed in she'd always felt growing up here. The way people pinned their problems atop her life when she was just trying to navigate the world.

"I can't do this again," she said.

Krunk paused. "What does that mean?"

"All of this. I can't do it. I mean, am I supposed to be *surprised* it wasn't Silas?"

Krunk's palms were flat on his thighs, calm except one tapping finger. "I guess not."

"Thanks anyway, but I gotta go," she said, and started the car. "Can you help me turn around? I don't want to hit those rocks."

In an instant, Krunk yanked the keys out of the ignition. The music died. Esme heard a small gasp behind her, but in the jangle Krunk gave no indication that he'd heard it.

"Dude," she said.

"Powder."

"What?"

"*Powder.* Give it to me. These people don't mess around, Esme. We've come too far. You know how this works."

Esme nodded, biting her lip, focused on containing her anger. George had seen her pissed-off enough that she knew he was back there curling tighter into his ball, covering his ears beneath the blanket, the way he always did. A heavy shame consumed her. Not a good intro to his new town.

"I just wanted someone to tell me it would be okay," she said, nearly whispering. "That coming back here, my life would be *nice.* That's why I called. I thought you were here to help me."

In the silence that followed Esme told herself that it would smooth things over to just give him the powder and be done with it for good. She was considering how to delicately reach behind the seat to find the juice box when Krunk popped open the glove compartment and began frantically scooping everything out, napkins and forks and straws, a few tools, some fuses and brake bulbs.

"Please don't do that," she said. "Give me my keys. C'mon. Please."

He ignored her. Esme found herself leaning back and thinking that this was the exact situation she'd always promised herself to avoid: alone with an angry man. Her baby out of reach, probably hugging that all-important juice box to his chest.

The last thing she wanted was for Krunk to start rummaging around behind her.

"I'll get the powder," she said, quietly. She turned her whole body to face him, her back against the door, her skull resting against the cool glass of the driver's-side window. She stuck out her hand. "Keys. We have to drive to get it. I don't have it here."

Krunk looked at her, his eyes yellow in the dome light. She thought he'd finally come to his senses. The keys were on the seat, pressed into his crotch, but rather than grab them she watched as he changed in an instant from frantic to something altogether worse: the guy was scared.

"It's okay," she said gently. "I'll give you the powder."

But Krunk was still staring, unmoving, unbreathing, which felt far more sinister than anything else tonight.

"Let's just go," she whispered, and that was when she realized Krunk wasn't looking at her, exactly, but past her shoulder, through the window behind her head—

And then she could feel the car door fly open behind her and she tipped backward, arms and legs flailing, and he was there, after all these years, of course he was. Her back thudded on the hard dirt between his boots. His gloved hand came swooping down from a high arc and buried the screwdriver into her stomach, one deep plunge under her ribs, then he twisted away and disappeared, as always, into the dark.

TreeTop.

CHAPTER 48

ABIGAIL

Though it was mostly dark, the first birds of the day were singing in the desert. As Krunk spoke, Abigail could feel her feet press into the crusty earth. Horrified. Ready to run. But also desperate to know.

"So you can see why I needed the powder, right?" Krunk said.

Abigail could barely get the words out. "To fund your escape?"

"It was more than *that*," he said, agitated. "Yes, selling the powder to Dr. Carla would get me the cash I needed to get out and start over. She'd give me a finder's fee or something. And if not her, someone in industry would. It only got urgent because I decided Esme deserved to know what really happened at the hotel. The *second* I told her that Silas wasn't the shooter, I gave up any possibility of staying here. I had to get out fast, preferably under the radar."

"Because of TreeTop?"

"Who else? You think I could've hung around town after

exposing a conspiracy within the police department? A staged murder. Falsified reports. Not to mention linking it all to Tree-Top? Selling that powder was my only way out. If I seemed desperate, it's because I *was*."

He shut off the flashlight, maybe to hide a surge of emotion.

"I can tell you don't believe me," he continued, "but that's always how it is with TreeTop." He sniffed. "Maybe that's why I'm still alive. Because I did the smart thing and stayed out of their way. I've been a real good cop, catching speeders instead of blowing the whistle." He sighed. "But always waiting to be next? Abigail, it gets to you."

She nodded, still struggling to speak.

"They killed Kevin for passing around that powder," he said. "It's the only thing that makes sense. Whatever it is, whatever it does or proves, they killed him to keep it buried. It's worth that much."

"Silas, too," Abigail said.

"Yeah, sure," he said. "Silas, too. Though he really did shoot me, you know? That part of the report was accurate. About the only part."

He turned on his light, illuminating the cheatgrass, the rocks, the sage.

Abigail believed him when he said TreeTop killed Esme in the desert that night. And she believed him when he said the powder was the only way to guarantee his own safe departure, even if he had no idea what it was or what it could prove about the ruination of the lake. And she believed him about the dangers he faced were he to expose the system. As Mr. Polk had said, *The power structures here are monstrous and invisible.*

But treachery came in many forms, and none of that made Krunk innocent.

CHAPTER 49

ESME

Esme slammed her head back into the dirt and shrieked at the starry sky.

"What'd you do?" she yelled at Krunk. *"What'd you do!?"*

Her feet flailed up near the steering wheel and the screwdriver bobbed painfully with each kick. She could hear Krunk hopping out of the passenger door and suddenly he was behind her, *ohgod*, spitting and panting, gripping her armpits and struggling to lift her back into the Cutlass.

"It's okay, Esme. He's gone. There's some headlights down the hill. A truck. Driving away. Listen."

She heard the whine of a pickup shifting in the distance, but had dirt in her mouth and her whole body was shaking and she felt no relief.

"Esme, try not to move. Let's get you up. Cross your arms. Grab your shoulders."

Leaning over her, straining to lift her into the Cutlass, Krunk looked in horror at the blood blooming on her T-shirt. The reality of what he'd done was settling in, she was sure.

He had set her up: led TreeTop right to her.

In the dim dome light, George's little fingers crept over the back of the seat.

She snapped alert. Pushed herself past the pain. George shouldn't be here, even in hiding. And she didn't trust what Krunk might do.

She took a breath, and everything stopped.

And then she clutched Krunk's T-shirt in her fists, pulling him toward her so he couldn't move, and roared like she'd never roared in her life:

George, run! Run! Run!

And she continued to roar as the rear door flew open and George, her sweet smart boy, burst out of the Cutlass and scrambled into the darkness. His blanket fell to the dirt.

Krunk toppled into the open door and nearly dropped her. "Who is *that*!?"

He's my son, she tried to say, but her words grew clotty in her mouth and she felt the skin on her stomach tighten.

"He's my *son*," she whispered.

"Your *son*?" he said.

He looked into her eyes and it was clear he understood something big, something new.

"Should I—?" he said, but stopped. "It's not as bad as it looks. Don't worry. It's not as bad."

Krunk was panting as he lifted her into the driver's seat and took a step back.

"I'll get help. My kit. First aid in the cruiser. Don't *touch* that and don't *move*!"

He slammed the doors and was gone. She was alone up front and George was out there somewhere. She cranked down her window to listen but it hurt.

Her breath was clapping, her heart punching. Her shirt was growing heavy on her belly.

Someone scrambled through the cheatgrass. Or an animal.

"George?" she whispered.

She maybe heard him cry.

"Hide until I call you," she whispered. "Wait until it's safe."

In a little while, maybe she and George could crawl to the road together.

Except she could feel it now, scraping her spine like a stick on a fence—

The back door opened and the overhead light came on.

"George?"

But it wasn't George. It was Krunk.

Crawling on the floorboards. Looking for the powder.

She could hear her keys jangling as he moved.

"Krunk? Give me the keys. I can maybe drive."

He squeezed her shoulder from behind.

"Just stay put," he said. "I'll get help. Just don't move...*it*."

Then the door slammed shut and the car shook.

The pinch in her belly hurt slightly less, which was hopefully good.

And it was good that Krunk was getting a first aid kit out of his cruiser.

Maybe there was no need to worry.

He would patch her up and drive them to the hospital.

This would all be chalked up as a mistake someday, a failed attempt at coming home.

Yet another TreeTop nightmare she'd survived.

This time was different, though. This time—

When the screwdriver came down and TreeTop's sleeve shifted, she'd seen a strip of pale skin just above his black latex glove.

CHAPTER 50

ABIGAIL

The sun was rising and a faint blue light radiated over the lake. As Krunk spoke, he kept looking around, as if expecting Tree-Top to come crawling out of the desert toward his cruiser. Abigail felt hellish and wary. Her image of Krunk as a wounded friend was eroding, replaced by a figure of callousness and manipulation.

"You *left* her in her car?"

"*I* didn't hurt her, Abigail. Plus I couldn't report it."

"You let her bleed to death, Krunk!"

He nodded intensely, as if this was the first time that reality had occurred to him.

"I was there to *help* her, okay? To give her some peace about Kevin. I did the right thing, telling her. I know I did."

"Just not when she got killed."

"I did the right thing," he said, but this time his voice caught. "Once TreeTop was gone, I was going to get help—"

"Was that before or after you threw her keys into the desert?"

"That. Okay, *that*. Was because out of nowhere this *boy* took off running? She sent her little kid out there, middle of the night? All alone?"

"She probably thought you'd hurt him, Krunk. She wanted to make sure he was safe."

"So what was I supposed to do? If I gave her the keys, as soon as I went after him, to try to bring him back, Esme would drive off."

"And leave George alone in the desert with *you*?"

"I didn't think it through," he said. "At one point I heard him crawling around out there, so yes, I chucked the keys in his direction. I heard them hit the dirt, but didn't hear him pick them up. So it could've been an animal. Or maybe TreeTop came back. I don't know. I didn't think it through."

"You already said that," she said. She wondered if Krunk could even hear what an ugly liar he'd become, or if his self-delusion ran too deep.

"I was trying to come up with a plan," he said, splaying his hand for emphasis, "to get Esme to the ER, but I couldn't leave the kid alone out there. She wasn't that bad, injury-wise, as long as she didn't move. I *told* her not to move."

"And that you'd get her help?"

Krunk was resistant, but his shoulders sank and he finally gave in.

"Everything just kind of *happened*." He sputtered an achy laugh. "Does that ever happen to you? I mean I was delivering a *pizza*, Abigail. I answered the *phone* to help Mr. Polk. And suddenly I was in the desert with Esme's blood all over my hands, hearing little sounds and waiting for this maniac boogeyman to come running out of my childhood to stab me?"

"So you went to your cruiser," Abigail said, trying to remember, amidst the stringy sympathies she was feeling for Krunk, that George's mom was dead.

"I sat behind the wheel holding the radio for maybe half an

hour. I was *scared*, okay? I couldn't make myself go back up there. I should have, but I *couldn't*."

"You couldn't make one call?" she said. "One call and she'd probably be alive."

"Or both of us would be dead."

"You said TreeTop was gone."

"He was. But, you know, TreeTop is never *really* gone."

"It looks a lot like you set her up." He turned sharply toward her as she continued. "*Meet me in the desert and bring that priceless powder…then she gets killed?*"

"Maybe I *did* set her up. I didn't mean to, but maybe I led him right to her. I don't know how. I didn't tell anyone we were meeting, but Esme might have."

Abigail closed her eyes. Another layer of self-delusion, she thought.

"I just needed out," he said, and she was surprised to hear him sobbing. "Do you have any idea how hard it is to leave a town like this? Then to have *TreeTop* after me if I stayed? He's probably watching me right now, Abigail. He probably knows I was digging around in the police files and the only reason I'm alive is because he's keeping me close like he always does, waiting for the right moment…"

She thought about Preston being overseen at his table in the library, Dr. Carla and Eli overseen in their labs, and knew in that regard Krunk was probably right: everyone was safe until they threatened the proper order of things. And she couldn't help but notice that Krunk didn't speak of TreeTop as a network of solipsistic assholes clinging to their power, afraid of change, justifying their atrocities with propaganda about the *greater good* of the town; no, he spoke instead of TreeTop as a towering monster who kills children and feeds them to the trees, as if he were still a scared little boy.

Abigail could feel herself wilting, forgetting about Esme for a moment and seeing only Krunk.

"Hey," she said, gently shaking his shoulder. "Whatever happens next, it's going to be okay."

He stopped sobbing and roughly wiped his face.

"*Whatever happens next?* Nothing is going to happen, Abigail. I didn't kill her."

She pulled her hand away.

"You might've had your reasons. But you left her out there to die."

"No," he said, firmly, "that's not what happened. She had a serious injury but she would've been fine, probably for another day or two. Only—"

"Don't," Abigail said, stepping away from him. "Krunk. *Don't*—"

"George killed her, Abigail. It's tragic, but that little boy pulled out the screwdriver and she bled to death. Must have been blocking an artery is what the medical examiner thought. I told her not to touch it. Multiple times."

"Krunk."

"I mean, no one would ever hold him accountable or anything, but that boy killed his mom. I think we both need to just let everything go, you know? Otherwise, you can imagine him, his whole life, carrying that..."

And *that*, she knew, was the ugliest excuse of them all: the worm that would rot his soul.

"You're better than this, Krunk."

She could feel him watching her back as she aimed her phone light at the ground and began walking toward the road.

"Don't go," he said, raising his voice. "We can figure this out, Abigail."

She walked faster, her light casting a synthetic glow on a flattened cigarette pack, an empty foil of cold meds, sparkles of broken glass—but not fast enough to get away from his words.

"What would you have done, Abigail? What would *most* people do? Because I'm the so-called hero and what did I do?"

Although she had no good answer, and could identify with the way certain moments *just happened*—taking a walk, finding a boy—she also knew he'd made the wrong choice, then doubled down, making it worse. He might have been delivering a pizza or stepping up to answer a phone, but the abyss he stared into was of his own making.

"You're better than this, Krunk!"

"Am I?" he shouted. "Abigail? Please don't leave me alone! I've got no one! Abigail?"

And though she could hear the remorse in his voice, she continued marching toward town, accompanied by the lonely, familiar sounds of gravel crunching underfoot.

CHAPTER 51

ABIGAIL

In the crisp sunrise light, Abigail parked the bike in the rack at the Soap Lake police station. It had taken her over an hour to walk back to town and gather the bike from behind the gas station, and she'd spent most of that time checking over her shoulder for Krunk.

Over on Main, a few dudes in Day-Glo vests climbed into a work truck with bags of gas station doughnuts, but otherwise the town was barely awake. Abigail remained cautious. She was at the police station to see if she could quietly find out who was on the task force investigating Esme's murder, but beyond that she had no plan. She thought if she had the name of a detective from out of town, a state cop from a distant place who could assure her safety, then maybe she'd hand over the bloody juice box, shed it from her life, and share what she'd learned about Esme and Krunk in the Cutlass, Preston's murder, and TreeTop's diabolical web. And if he hadn't already, she knew Eli would soon be shouting from his professional rooftops about the ca-

nals diluting the lake and decimating the miracle microbes, and
the real reason the World's Largest Lava Lamp hadn't risen beyond its base.

She was wary of being seen by the guys in the Ag Office, but
the building outside was eerily still except for a few perky sparrows flitting between trash cans. As she approached the entrance,
she glanced up and startled when she saw a figure at the edge of
the parking lot, half-crouched between city vans.

She covered her mouth and stifled a scream: it was TreeTop,
wearing a white mask and hooded biosuit. He didn't seem to
notice her standing against the building, but she noticed him,
especially when he pivoted to slip around one of the parked vans,
revealing a rope of blood on his chest and sleeves. He stumbled
over the curb, knuckling the asphalt as he caught himself, then
sprinted out of the lot and across a field of cheatgrass, in the direction of pastures and orchards and miles of open desert. Then
he was gone.

Abigail reluctantly walked toward the door. The walkway
below held small, dark smears, and inside the lobby, near the
drinking fountain, sat a metal irrigation pipe glossy with blood.
She stepped around it and pushed open the door to the police
department. On the far side of the room, a pair of middle-aged
cops were holding coffee cups and gabbing. Neither turned when
she entered. No Krunk in sight.

"Help you?"

Abigail recognized the voice. She turned to the desk where
the nasty receptionist was seated on her stool, wearing a telephone headset.

"Oh. You." She shifted her butt, lifted her chin. "That little mess you made with my cup? You're lucky I'm feeling nice.
Anyway, he's not here."

"What?" Abigail said, mouth dry, feeling like she might be
sick.

"Officer Krunk," the woman said, "your *bestie*? He called in a bit ago. A deer fell into the canal up above town. He's gonna try to steer it out."

"What?"

"A deer. Fell in. To the canal," the woman said, pursing her lips, taking her time as she sipped from a pink to-go cup. "Happens a lot. They wander in from the fields and fall in while getting a drink. Then just float along until they can't anymore and *bloop*, they drown. If she's a doe she's screwed, but a buck? Krunk's got this way of getting on his belly and reaching down from the maintenance bridge, then grabbing his antlers and dragging him to the side so he can scramble up the concrete and get out of the water. I mean most people would just let them drown, you know. Let nature take her course. If the canals are nature, I mean." She leaned forward. "You alright? You look pale."

"I think something happened," Abigail said, pointing toward the lobby, her words faint. "There's blood out there. Something *happened*."

"Oh hell," the receptionist said, turning toward the cops across the room. "Why didn't you say so? Cole! Cole, we got something here. Owen! She says there's blood out there."

She pointed toward the door. The pair of cops set down their coffee and glanced at Abigail with matching furrowed brows on their way into the lobby.

"Stay put," the woman said, adjusting her headset and punching something into her keyboard. But Abigail didn't stay put. She followed the cops into the lobby and watched as they stepped around the bloody pipe. Its end was mottled with hair and, on the floor next to it, a shingle of gray scruff: a piece of a man's crew cut. The cops' hands slid to their guns and one of them opened the restroom door, checked inside, gave the all clear. Next they moved across the lobby to the Agricultural Appreciation Office and gently opened the door.

"Soap Lake Police! Hal? You in here?"

Ah, Jesus.

One cop moved deeper into the room and yelled into the storage area as the other approached the desk. Abigail peered inside and saw Miss Nellie's brother, Hal, the *hog with a hard-on* who led TreeTop in the parade. He was sprawled across his desk, temple gashed and dripping, and the phone cord was wrapped around his neck. The cop searched for a pulse but Hal clearly wasn't coming back.

She stepped deeper into the room. On the floor next to the desk, she could see a ripped irrigation map, doodled in green and spattered with blood. A stack of TreeTop activity books were scattered around the checkered tile, and in the doorway of the storage area, another man was on the floor, face down, his gray crew cut soaking red. One of the cops stood over him.

"*Jesus-H.* We got McDaid here. He's gone. How many times I say this shit was gonna get him killed?"

"That's enough of that."

"Right," he said, bowing his head. "You're right. Sorry. Sorry. So how you want to play this?" His hand was poised on his radio, contemplating who to call—then he spotted Abigail watching from near the door.

"You need to not be here!" he yelled at her, face red, spit stringing from his lip.

She turned to walk out of the room, but not before taking one last glance at the photos hanging on the wall in tribute to Tree-Top, ancient mascot, hero of this magical, godforsaken town.

CHAPTER 52

ABIGAIL

After ignoring the receptionist's frantic shouts and slipping out the side door of the City Building, Abigail biked straight home. The streets were quiet and her driveway empty except for Medusa. She was surprised the cops weren't there, waiting to take her in for a statement, and surprised to see Eli's suitcase still buckled shut on the front porch, where he'd left it last night. She sat next to it for a while, fending off a panic attack and sobbing into her hands. She thought about leaving town, and about calling the cops on the cops, but when she spotted a tiny bloodstain on the side of her sneaker, remnants of traipsing through the lobby, she got scared and wiped her eyes and erased the photos of Preston's basement from her phone.

After a while she went inside to take a shower and saw that her bed was still made. No wonder then the suitcase: Eli was still in his lab, unaware she'd been gone half the night.

Downstairs, the lab was unexpectedly lively. Eli was on the phone with Dr. Carla, pacing as they discussed Sophia's salvaged jars. He paused just long enough to kiss Abigail's cheek, but not long enough to notice the weariness in her eyes or the stain on her sneaker. A pair of water jars from Sophia—*1959* and *1986*, according to their labels—sat on a table, next to his laptop and an assortment of sensors, beakers, microscopes, and solutions in tiny bottles.

He had his microbes, she supposed, and she had her murders.

Her phone *pinged*. A text from Daniel.

you free for a little George help this morning? sorry at work in a pinch.

She took a breath and texted him back.

of course! what's up?

The Polks apparently had to prep for an incoming wedding party, so they'd dropped George off with his grandma first thing this morning. Daniel was working at the orchard and his mom was already well into her booze.

Abigail was having a terrible time doing nothing and didn't want to be here if Krunk or the local cops stopped by, so she jumped at the chance.

be there soon

When Eli hung up the phone, he was beaming.

"Dr. Carla thinks there's reason to hope," he said, clutching Abigail in a hug. "We're going to, she and I, the extremophiles? Between the jars and the vents, there's hope that some of them might have gone dormant."

"Like hibernating?"

"More or less. But maybe not extinct is the point! Maybe not extinct!" And then he kissed her hard on the lips. "I'm so happy to be home. Just let's get through today and we'll have time to catch up. The rest of our lives, really. That sound good?"

In a way, Abigail was glad he hadn't asked her where she'd been all night, knowing that she'd shatter and say things she'd regret.

In another way, she didn't feel married at all.

He kissed her forehead, then stepped back to check the time.

"Library opens in twenty minutes," he said, sniffing his pits and rattling his curls. "Gotta see Miss Nellie about Sophia's job. Give us a ride?"

"Sure."

"And maybe grab her while I brush my teeth? Don't want to be too gross."

"Eli. Wait."

"Yeah?" he said, spinning.

Abigail considered telling him to cancel the trip to the library, that Miss Nellie likely wouldn't be there, or if she was, she'd be in shock over the murder of her brother. But she stopped herself.

"I'll tell you later."

After all, this might've been the perfect time for Sophia to show up, ready to work the desk while Miss Nellie took some time to grieve.

Abigail found Sophia on her porch in her rocking chair, looking glum, with a Styrofoam coffee cup at her feet and a vintage romance novel in her hands.

"Time?" Sophia said, not looking up from the page, immersed in avoidance.

"Time."

Neither spoke as they looked at the distant lake and the cluster of emergency vehicles parked at the end of Main, flashers on.

"You heard about the attack?" Abigail said. "City Building. Ag Office."

"Not the details," Sophia said. "Cashier at the gas station said it involved you-know-who. Brutal morning."

"Miss Nellie probably isn't going to be at the library," Abigail said, and told Sophia what she'd seen. "Her brother, Hal, was one of the dead guys."

Sophia nodded as she processed the information. "I mean, I've heard worse news. But whoa. That's big. Miss Nellie's gonna be a mess."

"Which means they'll need someone there. To fill the void." Sophia stared at her, wary.

"Meaning you," Abigail added.

"Right!"

"I've got to go watch George," Abigail said, hesitant. "But I was wondering if you could do something for me? After the library." She reached into her bag. "I'm not sure it can wait is the thing. It involves a crime."

Sophia leaned forward. "Stealthy?"

"Very."

"Friend," she whispered, "I am *in*."

Waiting for Eli to meet them in the driveway, Abigail leaned into Medusa's fender, and Sophia leaned into Abigail, fiddling with her rattail.

"If Eli asks anything about me and Krunk," Abigail said, "could you just, I don't know, evade?"

Sophia looked puzzled.

"Nothing happened between us," she added. "Just that Eli and I don't need another complication."

"Of course. It's tragic, though. Krunk was a really good guy."

Abigail turned. "I don't know if I'd call it *tragic*, Sophia. I am married."

Sophia took a step back, biting her thumb. "Oh shit."

"What?"

"Shit. Abigail. You don't know what happened? To Krunk."

"You mean the attack?" she said, pointing downhill, toward the emergency vehicles. "Krunk wasn't there. He's fine. He was off rescuing a deer from the canal. Probably still is."

"He's not fine, Abigail. I thought that's why you were so shaken up. I just assumed you knew. I'm sorry, hon."

Sophia had it on good authority that Krunk's cruiser was found parked along the irrigation road above town this morning, just after sunrise, engine running. His phone, wallet and work boots were sitting on the narrow maintenance bridge that crossed the canal, a metal plank perched a foot or so above the churning water. The assumption was he slipped in while trying to save a deer and was pulled under by the currents.

"Odds of survival are terrible if you fall into that part of the canal," Sophia said. "Like a washing machine. There's just no getting out. Every year it's someone. I really thought you knew."

It took a few seconds for her words to sink in.

"Who told you that?" Abigail snapped, taking a quick step back. "How would you even know something like that?"

"Hey." Sophia gently grabbed her hands and explained that she spoke to the cashier while she was grabbing coffee a little while ago. "That gas station is like the town square, Abigail. The guy knows everyone. The cops are saying the deer probably went wild when Krunk grabbed his antlers and he lost his footing. With everything that's going on downtown they had no backup to send."

"Where is he, though?" she said, as if more questions would reverse their answers.

"His body, you mean? If it doesn't show up downstream by tomorrow, it probably won't surface until they shut off irrigation water in the fall. But even then there's no guarantee. Those canals are made to catch debris, keep it out of the flow, but the currents are so violent that everything basically shreds—"

"Krunk isn't *debris*," Abigail snapped.

"I know that," she said, "but the canals don't. Listen, if he was alive, he'd call in. He was that kind of a cop. Sorry, hon."

As Sophia hugged her, Abigail couldn't help but envision Krunk kicking off his boots and stretching on his belly over the water, timing it to grip the buck's antlers and drag him to the sloped side of the canal.

The buck lashing out. Krunk losing his balance. Rolling into the currents.

"I was just with him," she said with a sinking heart.

Or maybe, face down on the bridge, occupied by the drowning deer, TreeTop pounced.

He's probably watching me right now, Abigail…waiting for the right moment.

Or maybe, she couldn't help but think, there'd been no deer at all. He'd left his cruiser running and planted his belongings on the bridge to create the illusion of an accident. Then rolled into the currents on his own. No note.

I don't need this shit in my life, he'd said on the morning they'd met.

She felt a tiny bubble of hope rise through her as yet a different scenario occurred: last night, when she climbed into Krunk's cruiser at the gas station, she had to move his work boots and cooler out of the way to make room to sit up front. And later, as they were looking out over the lake, Krunk stooped to tighten the laces of his bright blue running shoes.

He hadn't been wearing his work boots, so why were they found on the maintenance bridge with his wallet and phone?

There would be no *debris* because Krunk had finally fled his hometown.

Sophia gave her arm a quick shake as Eli hustled up the driveway, smelling of toothpaste and deodorant. He stared at the two of them for a second, concerned. "Everything okay?"

Neither made a peep.

"Okay, then," he said, squeezing into Medusa's back seat and drumming his thighs. "Let's go fuck up a librarian."

When Abigail showed up at the Calderon house, George was on the porch turning the old flip phone into a ray gun and playing *pew-pew-pew*. Through the screen door she could see his grandmother kneeling in the living room, sponging up a spilled drink with a stuffed animal.

He showed Abigail the phone, metallic blue with a small gray screen.

"Grandma's okay with you having this?"

"It's *old*," he said, hopeful.

She rubbed his hair, scooped the booster seat off the porch and led him to Medusa. She thought about taking him to the lakeshore, but that seemed like a bad idea with all that was happening in town. So they decided to drive to the orchard, to bring Uncle Daniel lunch from Dairy Freeze. Abigail had a lot to tell him.

They found Daniel working alone on the far side of the storage buildings. Abigail parked in the shade and rolled down the windows. She gave George one of the foil-wrapped hot dogs they'd picked up on the way and told him to stay put.

Daniel was stirring a pitchfork through a fire in a metal drum, the air around him tinged with acrid smoke. His skin was sweaty and smudged with ash.

"You're busy," she said, looking toward the smoldering barrel. "I brought lunch. I should've called."

"Just cleaning up. Too hot for a fire anyway."

When he turned toward her she saw a tight shiner growing below his left eye, and his lip was cut. Red welts pocked his cheek and neck.

"Thanks for getting George," he said. "Been kind of avoiding town today."

"I can see why."

He looked across the orchard and sighed, clearly in pain. The way he listed to the right made her wonder if he'd broken a rib or worse.

"What're you burning, Daniel?"

"Old messes."

Daniel was a gentle soul, but he was more than that, too. She recalled the boxing bag chained to the ash tree in front of his house, and the tales of his teenage rage, going savage to protect his little sister. As he stared into the fire, she wondered whose faces he saw glowing behind the smoke.

"You know," she said, "there was something down at the City Building earlier, and—it's been a violent morning." She forced herself to take a breath. "They think Krunk drowned."

Daniel looked up. "*What?* Abe Krunk?"

"In the canal. Helping save a deer."

"Ah, man. Really?"

"Around the same time as the attack. But unrelated."

"I know, Abigail," he said, catching her eye. "That it's un-related."

She studied the webby eaves of the outbuilding, looking in any direction but his.

"I saw you," he said. "Outside the police department this morning. Parking a bike."

"I didn't see you," she said. "Though I did see TreeTop."

"Can I explain, Abigail?"

"I don't know that there's anything to say, Daniel. I was there right after. So I saw. Inside the office. My god."

Her hands were trembling and she kept nodding, as if forc-ing herself to acknowledge the memory she'd been trying to stifle all day.

"I'm sorry you had to see that," he said. "But I need to say a few things, and then I need us to never talk about it again, okay?" Sweat dripped down his face, leaving clean tracks on his smoke-smudged skin. "I stood outside the door to the Agricul-tural Appreciation Office and used a burner phone to call the number you showed me. Same number you called from Pres-ton's kitchen."

Girl, you just committed suicide.

"I dialed it and sat back, watching the phone on the desk ring, and watching that old parade dude pick it up," he continued. "One of the cops on Esme's case was there, too. McDaid. He was back in the storage area and heard us, uh, scuffling. Came running in, still holding a cup of coffee. I caught him by sur-prise. But even then." He clenched his hand. "It was them, Abi-gail. The guys in that office. I don't know who else. Other cops. Townsfolk. But Preston was right. You were right."

"I know," she said.

"And Preston's map, the one in your photos, was in the guy's desk drawer. Ripped and crumpled, just sitting there. Still stained with Preston's blood."

"I saw it on the floor."

"You get close enough to see the feathers stuck to it? From his coat? Just think about that—his map, direct from the scene of his death, sitting in an office across the lobby from the police station. They barely even hid it. Didn't need to. The arrogance, you know? The *power*. Just assuming they could run him down and keep his map and always get a pass. Just like they assumed they could kill my dad, and for what? Trying to unionize the dairy? For that, they dump him on the couch and light our trailer on fire. With us kids sound asleep. *We* didn't matter to them, you know? And then Esme. George's *mom*. My little *sister*—"

Abigail stepped forward and hugged him for a quiet minute, thinking about how right he was, and how easy it was to justify, and the poetic justice of disguising himself as them.

"One more thing," he said, sniffling, taking a deep breath. "I don't know if TreeTop will die with those two men. Or how long before someone else steps forward to control the strings. But that makes no difference. I'm glad those men are dead. I don't know where I'll be in six months or six years. But I'll go after the next ones, too. Someone's got to."

Together they stared at the rising smoke.

Abigail felt a small relief, despite Daniel's words about the continuation of TreeTop. With all that had happened today, TreeTop would be in retreat, reconfiguring—napping in the branches overhead—which meant Eli would likely be safe. At least for now. She was less sure about Daniel.

"Daniel?" she said, after a minute. "Eli just got back and he's got all kinds of work to do in the lab. So maybe you and I could take George to Seattle for a few days. I could show him the octopus at the aquarium while you're talking to the people at UW. A financial aid officer or someone in cinema studies. Just to see. Maybe they can even recommend a health clinic?"

Tears welled at the ledge of his swollen eyelid.

"We need to get the boy somewhere safe," she added. "If this goes bad, he can't see his uncle get dragged away. That can't happen, Daniel."

"Eli's really home? Is he gonna care...?"

"He's so immersed in his microbes, he'll be fine. I'll text him from the road."

"What're you gonna say? *My turn, chump.*"

She smiled. "He and I, we need to... I don't know."

Daniel nodded, but didn't pursue it. "Okay. This'll be good. George does love his cephalopods." He peered into the smoking barrel. "Give me a minute to finish cleaning up."

"We'll take Medusa."

"God help us."

George had crawled out of his booster and now sat in Medusa's front passenger seat with his nose buried in the flip phone.

"What're you playing?" Abigail asked, climbing in.

The tiny screen didn't reveal a pixelated game of *Space Invaders* or *Snake*, but rather a low-res photo of a woman with her head down on a kitchen table, with a mangy ginger cat licking her dinner plate.

"You found pictures?" she said. The woman in the photo was George's grandma, only younger, with slightly darker hair and a newer bathrobe. Definitely not flattering. "You know what? Grandma may not want us looking at these. Here..."

Abigail tugged the phone away from George and made him hop in back, then hit the arrow button. An hourglass appeared as the next photo loaded.

"Hey, Daniel?" she said, leaning out the window. "You know this old phone still has some pictures saved on it?"

"Let's see?" he said, climbing into Medusa and inspecting the phone. "Yeah. This used to be mine before I gave it to Esme. Mom gave it to him to play with, but I had no idea there was anything on it."

The image that popped on-screen was blocky with pixels and its quality was poor, but the subject was clear: a ginger cat in a sunny field.

"That's Blossom. One of mom's strays. Esme definitely took these."

Another photo showed Esme's mom, making dinner at the stove, and the next showed a pimply Daniel, wearing a violet bandana, peering over his Game Boy.

"Cute," she said.

"More like *sad*," he said. "Look at that purple Prince bandana. Tell me I'm not gay."

There were a few photos taken at the Tetanus Playground and a few more at the library. The next showed a chubby blonde baby, maybe a year old, being held from behind by a wide-eyed Esme, around eighth grade, wearing her *Soap Lake PE* T-shirt.

"Whoa," Daniel said.

"Who's the kid?"

"That's Baby Grace. From when Esme was babysitting. The accident?" He glanced in the rearview at George and lowered his voice. "Silas's little half sister. Silas and Esme took these right before the TV thing. They were just messing around, you know. Being obnoxious. Esme was mortified when the cops saw them." He took a deep breath. "I've never actually seen them. I always assumed the police took the memory card for evidence against Silas. Not that they ever pressed charges."

As Daniel clicked from photo to photo, Abigail could see why Esme was embarrassed. One of those bad childhood decisions that had followed Esme her whole life, captured on a crappy phone:

Baby Grace grinning and clutching a knife, blade out, with Esme hamming over her shoulder.

Baby Grace clutching a corkscrew. A pizza cutter. A lighter—

Baby Grace clutching a long, flathead screwdriver, with white paint drizzled along its handle.

CHAPTER 53

ESME

Esme opened her eyes to find the door to the Cutlass open and George kneeling in the dirt with his head in her lap, inches from the screwdriver's paint-drizzled handle. He was holding her hands and sobbing. His SpongeBob blanket covered her legs.

When her eyelids grew heavy George pressed them open with his sticky fingers.

"Find the car keys, George. I can drive if you find the keys."

He crawled away from the car and began crisscrossing the headlight beams, hunting for the keys with his hands clasped behind his back, tears falling down his face.

The night was gray over the eastern hills. The sun would rise before long.

She could send him running toward the canal road.

A tractor would pass. Or a cyclist.

She tried to focus on George but the memory of TreeTop was relentless—

The memory of his sleeve inching up as the screwdriver came

down. Of the bald halo around his wrist where his elastic metal watchband had rubbed the hair from his arm.

When she thought about the days after the shooting, burying herself in bed, his last words to her still stung: *I may be ready to forgive you someday, Esme. Just not today.*

She shouldn't have needed his forgiveness or approval. But his lack of forgiveness, in any other tongue, meant blame.

Pastor Kurt's life had fallen apart after the television fell. And he blamed her.

It wasn't Esme's job to correct his delusions, but it had been her job to make sure that she and George would be safe. Pastor Kurt needed to be okay with her coming back to town.

She thought she was being smart when, on the night before driving away from Bakersfield, she'd dug up his number and called him from the payphone by her apartment.

After the shock settled, Pastor Kurt explained that he was still splitting his time between Soap Lake and Montana, but he was always on the lookout for the kind of job that would help him make the move away from Soap Lake for good. Just not much for him in town anymore.

For a second, she thought she might share all that Krunk had been unearthing in his police department files—that it didn't add up, Silas killing Kevin—but then her senses took hold. Krunk hadn't told her enough just yet, and there'd be time for that when they finally saw each other in person. Maybe together they could even figure out a way to expose the truth. Bring TreeTop down.

"Why are you calling me, Esme?" Pastor Kurt said.

She'd be arriving in Soap Lake in three nights, but hardly anyone knew, not even her family, and it would be her first trip back since—

"Since the police killed Silas," he said.

Yes, and she was seeking to clear the air with those directly involved.

Mr. Polk was okay with her return, and he'd work on Mrs. Polk when the time was right.

Abe Krunk was also okay, and was even going to meet her at the Rock Shack late on Saturday night when she got to town.

"So I guess I'm asking if you're okay, too. If I come visit. Or even decide to stay."

Pastor Kurt didn't say anything, and she hated that she felt as if she were begging for his blessing, when she was just as battered as he was by everything that had happened. It helped to think of George.

"I just want it behind me," he finally said, and sounded like he was scared. "I just want to be free of it all." And then he hung up.

Esme's hands hurt and she realized she was squeezing the SpongeBob blanket in her fists.

Pastor Kurt had blamed her, at least in part, for the wrecked path of his life. But that alone couldn't justify—*this*.

There had to be something else. Something more.

Beyond the windshield, George was crawling now, dirtying his favorite pajamas, looking all over for the keys. It was getting hard to see him—

I just want to be free of it all, Pastor Kurt had said, as if burdened by a very old debt.

CHAPTER 54

ABIGAIL

Abigail drove Medusa along a pitted dirt road, looking for the alfalfa farm where Pastor Kurt was living in a trailer. Sophia had given her directions over the phone, so Daniel sat up front, squinting through the sunny windshield, navigating. In the back seat, George listened to a Magic Tree House audiobook with Abigail's earbuds.

Abigail had wanted to drive straight to the safety of Seattle. But Daniel was adamant about confronting Pastor Kurt and promised to do so peacefully—then dragged a four-lugged tire iron from out of the hatchback, *just in case*.

"You sure this is a good idea?" she said, turning onto yet another dirt road.

"You sure it's the same screwdriver?"

"Same model, same size," she said. "And the paint on the handle. I'm sure."

He looked out the window, at the apple orchards spreading toward the horizon.

"Of all the ways to do it, you know?" he said. "It was so *intentional*, using that. The records showed payphone calls to Montana right before she left Bakersfield. Pastor Kurt spends half his time in Great Falls near his daughter. That had to be Esme reaching out to him, right?"

"Makes sense she would. She called the Polks, who also lost a son that day."

"So she respected him enough to let him know she was coming back to town," Daniel said, "maybe even when and where, probably so he could brace himself, prepare his emotions. And he murdered her." He shook his head. "Seems *off*, though, doesn't it? Holding a grudge for that long. It's like it grew bigger in her absence."

Abigail's hands trembled as Pastor Kurt's camper came into view. It was shaped like a can of ham and skirted by plywood scraps. At one point it had been white, but most of the finish had flaked off, revealing dull aluminum the color of a shark. Next to it was a firepit and a crowded lean-to workshop. Everything was stagnant in the sun.

"We're so close to getting out of here," she whispered. "We shouldn't be here, Daniel. *George* shouldn't."

"I can't let him get away with it, Abigail."

"He won't," she said. "I was thinking. When we get to Seattle, while you and George are getting pancakes, I'll visit the FBI office and tell them what I know about Esme's murder. I'll have the flip-phone photos and the juice box, right? And Pastor Kurt going back and forth to Montana makes it federal, I think. I'll tell them about the corruption in the department. Encourage them to look into Esme's death, Preston's death, maybe others. To look into the payphone records, the murder weapon. I'm just a bored newcomer to town, poking around because I've got nothing better to do. Like those true-crime weirdos in all the podcasts. But right now we need to *leave*."

She pulled Medusa off the road to turn around, but Daniel

jumped out with the tire iron and began walking toward the trailer. A few brown cattle watched him from behind a barbed wire fence.

Abigail shut off the engine and hopped out.

"Daniel, wait!"

He paused in the road, his back to her, the tire iron hanging from his hand like an anchor.

"You're not TreeTop!" she said. "Daniel. You're *not*."

A faint cloud of dust moved through the fields, and she could hear the aggressive whine of a pickup shifting gears, and gradually going quiet as it disappeared beyond the orchards. Daniel's head dropped and he stood in the sunlight for a minute, looking defeated. Then he walked back to Medusa and tossed the tire iron into the hatchback.

Abigail handed George her water bottle and rolled down all the windows.

"Is that a good book?" she asked, but he just grinned between the earbuds, oblivious. She mussed his hair and followed Daniel up the road.

She could hear the squawky chatter of a police scanner coming from the camper, but when Daniel peeked in the door, no one was inside. They circled the weedy perimeter. On a plastic table outside sat a congealing bowl of tomato soup and a half-eaten grilled-cheese sandwich. Flies buzzed around.

"Still warm, if you're hungry," he said, touching the side of the bowl.

"I'll pass."

"With that scanner, Pastor Kurt would've known all hell was breaking loose at the Ag Office. Probably panicked when he heard us coming up the road. Fled to Montana in a hurry would be my guess."

"To see Grace before everything hits the fan?"

"She's all he has left," Daniel said. He glanced toward the camper door. "I'm gonna grab that scanner. It'd be good to know if they're looking for me. Be out in a sec."

He hopped inside and she could hear him rummaging around. Against her better judgment she wandered into the lean-to, its workbench crowded with car parts and bins. She drifted toward the cluttered shelves, thinking it would be useful to find more screwdrivers from the same set as the murder weapon. Further proof, she supposed. A few plastic bins were stacked on the dirt, and when she lifted one, the cool earth beneath scrambled with centipedes and black beetles, and pill bugs curled into balls.

Daniel was taking his time in the camper, clearly hunting for more than the scanner. She pawed through boxes of junk, but found no matching screwdrivers. Maybe the FBI would have better luck. She'd planned to call their Seattle office from the road, but since Daniel was still rummaging, she looked it up on her phone and ended up in a Tipline chat, arranging to meet late this afternoon.

They asked if they could send someone but she declined. They said they'd be expecting her.

The day was bright and hot, and so much was coming to an end. Like Daniel, Abigail suspected that TreeTop would live on, continuing to profit those in power, but she also knew that Tree-Top was only part of the story of this lakeside town: Eli would push forward with his precarious work, seeking to create global change out of microscopic miracles; Mr. and Mrs. Polk would continue to offer a place of healing for the scabbed and the afflicted; Sophia would continue to ignore the abuse of those who dwelled on her past, and focus instead on pressing books into the hands of all the people who needed them. And someday the glow of the World's Largest Lava Lamp would provide a beacon of hope for those willing to place their faith in the future—those who would dare to Believe.

"Daniel?" she said, giving up on the bins and approaching the camper. "We need to go."

When he appeared in the doorway, he was reading through

a small stack of pink papers, covered in handwriting and flowery doodles.

"Love letters," he mumbled, skimming the pages. "To Pastor Kurt. From Trudy. His ex-wife." He sneered. "Lots of fawning. *If only* this. *If only* that."

"Any particular reason you're reading them?"

"Because *fuck him*," he said, looking up intensely for a second, before returning his sight to the page. "Plus he left them out. On the shelf next to his bed. Must've been reading them lately. Most are from when Trudy bailed town, when all that stuff happened with Esme. The TV falling. Silas."

"Can you maybe read them in the car? George is waiting."

Daniel ignored her in a way that seemed more reckless than rude.

"This one," he mumbled, shaking the sheet on top. "Summer 2006. A few months after Trudy left town."

"What's it say?"

"Here. Read it and tell me if...or if it's just me. Because it sounds like..."

Abigail noticed small ripples in the pink paper, remnants of someone's tears.

July 6, 2006

My Darling Kurt,
I'm sorry for hanging up on you tonight but there was nothing more to say. The TV collapse was an accident, yes. But not the bag of bricks. Not the clothesline. You know what he was planning to do to our precious little girl. I wish you would just admit it. At least to me.

I agree you have every right to see Baby Grace, but I will never set foot in that town again and never be in the same room as Silas. You have to protect him, I get that. But I told you how many times if you did *whatever* to keep him out of jail you would lose me in the bargain. You're a good man, Kurt. A father looking out for his son. I believe in forgiveness. But I'm not dumb.

I know you think you did the right thing but when you make a deal with the devil you join forces with the devil. You said so from your pulpit many times. Yet here you are. Silas is free, but you are not.

Maybe once this is behind you we can try again, become the couple we're meant to be.
With love and longing,
Trudy

PS: I will never say a word about this to anyone (obviously!!!) so please don't involve me.

As Abigail reread the letter, Daniel stared out toward the fields.

"How is Silas not in jail?" he mumbled, as if to himself. "It's what we always asked. He took his hurt little sister and hid her in the shed. Got caught before he could drown her. Yet was never charged."

Abigail lifted the letter. "Because Pastor Kurt made a deal?"

"With TreeTop," he said. "He had it in for Esme already, blamed her when his life took a dive. So when she called him before coming back here, it sealed it. Gave him a chance to finally get off the hook."

"No wonder he couldn't move to Montana full-time," she said, speaking as quickly as the pieces came together. "Not until he paid them back."

"With Esme's life."

Daniel wandered to the front of the camper and sat heavily on a rusty propane tank. He seemed so drained, so defeated, she wondered if he'd ever lift his head again.

"What a waste," he said, barely audible. "What a waste."

Abigail walked through the weeds and touched his shoulder. "Daniel? George is in the car. And the FBI is waiting."

He glanced up.

"Not for you," she added. "I think you're in the clear. For everything else. But we should go while we can."

He took a deep breath and wiped his eyes.

"Yeah. Yeah."

When they climbed into the car, George was standing between the front seats with the Magic Tree House still spinning in his ears. His hair was messy and sweaty, and he was staring across the stubbled fields to where the orchards began.

Abigail imagined his mom, playing between these trees as a little girl, and she thought of something Mr. Polk had told her, not long ago, while sitting on the shore:

Sometimes the story has no end. Sometimes it just keeps going.

She wondered if the same could be said of TreeTop.

"Don't worry, buddy, we'll come back," Daniel said, forcing a smile. "Time to get buckled. Long drive to Seattle."

But George only stooped closer to the windshield, squinting through steady brown eyes.

"What're you seeing?" Daniel asked. "Is something there?"

Abigail felt a chill as she followed his gaze beyond the fence line to the leafy wall of apple trees. She clutched her keys and scanned the rows for a man dressed head to toe in white, wearing gloves and a mask, turning a tool into a weapon—

"What is it, George?" she said, a tremor in her voice.

George didn't speak, just bounced and pointed.

It took her a minute to see the deer, a doe with big twitchy ears, watching them from between the trees. Above her head, tall sprinklers ratcheted in circles, spraying mists and beads of water, creating little rainbows in the air.

CHAPTER 55

SOPHIA

Sophia stood in the middle of Preston's basement, stunned by its terrible beauty.

Plucking the first pin out of the wall was the most difficult, but each of the subsequent pins was easier. The strands dropped to the floor, creating wavelengths of color.

As Sophia moved through the room she assembled stacks of data into piles: articles and reports, autopsies and interviews, photos and illustrations. And when the piles grew thick enough, she banded them together with pieces of fallen yarn, like ribboning a gift, and carried them outside to her bike and tow-along trailer.

Night had fallen by the time the trailer was full. No one would see her leave, and no one would see her when she moved Preston's collection into the depths of her cottage.

When that library job came through, she would become master of the scanner.

But first, Sophia had a final task to complete. Crossing Preston's basement one last time, she retrieved a single newspaper article from her back pocket—the one her friend Abigail had given her this morning, the one that chronicled the most recent of TreeTop's victims—and pinned it to the empty wall:

"Local Man Killed in Hit-and-Run."

On her way up the steps, as the lights blinked off, she quietly raised her fist.

EPILOGUE

ESME

Esme presses her hands into George's face. She blinks and the
blood is gone.

They are sitting on the shore. She is rubbing sunscreen on
his cheeks.

They are wading in the lake. She's up to her chest in water.
If you close your eyes you can feel it.

She opens her eyes and George is there, hugging her, and she
is reminded of all the times he has stared at her in the morning,
face-to-face on the pillow, sometimes tracing a finger down the
slope of her nose, or making putty of her lips, the sun slicing
lines through the bedroom blinds.

Time to get up. Waffle time. Tickle time. Cartoon time.

The happiest she's ever been. Thinking Kevin would love this.

But something is wrong.

"You're going to go see Uncle Daniel," she says. "And
Grandma, too. Be nice to her, okay?"

George is hugging her, arms around her neck, chest to chest. The screwdriver is almost out, resting against her thigh.

The Cutlass door is open. The sun is beginning to rise.

"First you need to find someone," she says.

But George won't go.

"You have to go find someone, George. I'll be with you."

She wipes his face.

"I'll be with you, sweetheart. Every step you take, Mommy will be with you."

You'll feel me, okay?

You'll feel me. Walking with you.

You'll feel my love.

now go

find someone

go

go

★ ★ ★ ★ ★

AUTHOR'S NOTE

This novel is pure fiction, an imaginary expression of a place that is real: Soap Lake, Washington. I know it's real because I lived there.

In 2003, right after our first baby was born, my wife, Libby, and I moved from Boston (population: 4 million) to Soap Lake (population: 1,500).

Working as a teacher-bookseller and librarian, we'd managed to cobble together a living in Boston, but affording day care was not an option, and we missed the West. So when I landed a job at a small community college in rural Washington, we jumped.

While house hunting from three thousand miles away, we kept coming across Photoshopped images of a sixty-foot lava lamp in the center of Soap Lake, a small town that hugged the southern shore of a rare mineral lake, twenty miles from the college. We'd soon learn that these mock-ups were part of the dream project of an architect and artist named Brent Blake, an upbeat guy who rode a Harley and wore an easy smile and a gray goatee. He envisioned building the giant lava lamp as a way to lure visitors to town.

Besides being immensely affordable, Soap Lake had its own charm—a new community theater, eye-popping views of the shrub steppe, a small group of energized locals—but like a lot of places in the rural Northwest, it had seen better days. Empty storefronts dotted the downtown, a lot of buildings had fallen into disrepair, and meth and other downward spiral drugs were easy to come by. Travelers drove past on the scenic highway that skirted the town, glancing at the lake on their way to the Grand Coulee Dam, but most didn't stop. In Brent's eyes, they just needed a reason.

Brent was onto something. After all, other Washington towns had turned themselves around. In the nearby Cascades, every building in Leavenworth went full Bavarian—wooden scroll-work and alpine balconies—and soon the village exploded with year-round visitors donning lederhosen and raising beer steins. The small town of Roslyn had become a pilgrimage site for fans of *Northern Exposure*, and Twede's Cafe in North Bend had gained its own cult status after starring as the Double R Diner on *Twin Peaks*. Out on the Olympic Peninsula, the declining logging town of Forks—the setting of *Twilight*—was about to be overrun by vampire lovers from around the world. And all of them had wallets.

Soap Lake could attract people, too. It just needed...a giant lava lamp.

With infant and sheepdog in tow, Libby and I settled in to our new home, up the hill from the old brick police station that Brent had transformed into an art museum (think about *that*). There was no lava lamp, but there were fairly convincing post-ers of it all over the region and an enormous banner draped from the side of his building. Brent had been on a publicity blast, too, broadcasting news of the prospective giant lava lamp all over the world. He'd given over two hundred radio interviews and hosted major newspapers and networks, including the BBC, which re-ported that Soap Lake was "well on its way to becoming a ghost town." For the crop circle crowd, Brent and Tim Ray, a local farmer, mowed a one-thousand-foot-long lava lamp into a nearby hay field.

The idea caught like a cheatgrass fire, but the engineering and financial hurdles were insurmountable. Many of us were thrilled when, after a few years, the Target Corporation, hearing about Brent's dream, donated a fifty-foot lava lamp that had once hung above their Times Square store, and even paid to ship it across the country. They did all they could to help, but when it arrived—something like 48,000 pounds of parts—it came with no platform upon which it could be attached and no instructions for assembly. It all ended up in storage.

For years, the lava lamp continued to act as a beacon in the town, though the excitement came in waves. After the failure of the Target lamp, another iteration arrived: a proposal for a tower, almost like a lighthouse, that would display projected globules on a lava lamp–shaped screen. As of now, there is no giant lava lamp, and there is no base.

When I was writing this novel, it seemed fitting to give Brent's dream yet another nod, this time in fiction.

But, as Eli tells us, "The lake is the real magic."

Much of the lake in the novel is accurate to the lake in reality. People from the Moses-Columbia and other Colville tribes visited the lake for centuries, seeking spiritual and physical sustenance in its waters and environs. European settlers adopted many of the practices of these peoples, and in the first half of the twentieth century, the lake became a destination for masses of visitors seeking recreation, as well as healing for Buerger's disease and ailments such as arthritis and assorted skin disorders. The science was convincing enough that, in 1938, the Veterans Administration opened a small hospital near the lake for treating vets. Today it's a nursing home.

Like the lake of the novel, the lake of reality is meromictic—it doesn't turn over the way most lakes do—and its composition is exceptionally rare. Because of this, it is home to microbes that haven't been discovered anywhere else, including extremophiles...just not the kind that can transform toxins into electricity. One particularly promising microbe found only in Soap Lake could potentially streamline the process of creating hydrogen fuel.

The canning jars of ancient lake water that appear in the library basement are fictional, but they, too, grew from seeds of truth. A limnologist from the University of Washington named Dr. W. Thomas Edmonson began regularly collecting samples of Soap Lake water beginning in 1952, and apparently no one in town knew about them. After he passed away, the bottles were donated and stored—poetically, I think—in the dark basement of the old VA hospital. But rest assured, the samples eventually landed in proper labs. Researchers have used them to help establish a baseline for their work, including the argument that the irrigation canals that are the lifeblood of the region are slowly adding fresh water to the lake and diminishing the very qualities that make it special.

Not long after our second baby was born, we moved six miles down the road to an old house in a different town. We stayed in the area for sixteen years and continued to spend time in Soap Lake, swimming and playing in the mud, hiking the rocky shoreline, visiting local orchards and farms. The town still struggles, but it remains one of the more colorful places in a truly colorful state. A few dedicated small businesses have popped up and stuck around, including an organic kitchen, an eastern European deli, and a wood-fired pizza place called, co-incidentally, La Cucina di Sophia. No relation.

Brent Blake died of leukemia in 2013, but his spirit lives on.

In early 2024, the Washington State Department of Ecology declared the lake an "Outstanding Resource Water," giving it protected status. In their joint application for this protection, the Confederated Tribes of the Colville Reservation and the Soap Lake Conservancy cited the ongoing impact of irrigation water on the lake.

As for TreeTop, he is entirely a figment of my imagination. Really. I swear.

But it never hurts to check the branches above your head...

ACKNOWLEDGMENTS

I'd like to thank my friend and agent, Kirby Kim, who is endlessly affable, professional, and invested in storytelling above all. Still glad you rescued me from the slush pile! It's an honor.

Thank you to Eloy Bleifuss, whose keen eye helped sharpen this story, and to the rest of the remarkable team at Janklow & Nesbit.

I'd like to thank John Glynn, my friend, editor, and fellow writer, whose gifts have only grown since our time working on *Bright Ideas*. It's a joy to be creating with you again.

Thank you to Cat Camacho and Cicely Aspinall for your fabulous feedback and support, to Eden Railsback for juggling so much without breaking a sweat, to Gina Macedo for your shrewd consideration of every word, to Martin Hargreaves and the Harlequin Art Department for your visual interpretation of this world, to Randy Chan, Pam Osti, Laura Gianino, Ciara Loader, Ronny Kutys and Wendy Cebellos for enthusiastically spreading the word, and to the rest of the team at Hanover Square Press, Harlequin, HQ, and HarperCollins...your books lift up our lives.

Thank you to Ali Lefkowitz at Anonymous Content for your imagination and persistence in working to get TreeTop onscreen.

Thank you to my reader friends, Cara Stoddard, Jim Johnson, John Bartell, and The Bullsnake Literary Society (namely, John Peterson, Matt Yawney, and Dave Hammond). Your feedback and support boosted me and this book. Thank you to my Sullivan and Eastman families, for all of your love, and all your love of stories.

In the story, Dr. Carla says, "Community college is where the action is at!" This is something I heard the poet, Marvin Bell, say at a community college conference in Seattle. He was right.

There are ample resources out there to explore the history, culture, and science of Soap Lake. I am especially grateful for the research and information provided by Leo Bodensteiner, Jahn Kallis, and Anthony Gabriel; Roger Sonnichsen and Anita Waller; the Columbia Basin Irrigation District; the Confederated Tribes of the Colville Reservation; Humanities Washington's Speaker's Bureau; the Soap Lake Conservancy; and the State of Washington Department of Ecology. The books *Grand Coulee* by Paul C. Pitzer, *A River Lost* by Blaine Harden, and *Soap Lake* by Kathleen Kiefer were exceptionally helpful, as were Kiefer's documentary, *Dirt Roads*, and her other short films about this colorful town and its people.

To the libraries and bookstores who have invited me to visit, and to the many readers who have astounded me with your generosity: thank you!

To my kids, Rachel and Lulu, out in the world, but always in my heart.

And, as always, my biggest thanks goes to Libby for being my best reader, best friend, best everything.